Praise for *The G...*

"*The God Wave* is a mind-twisting 'what if?' story with some crazy cool science and true-to-life characters you can't help but root for. It feels like those vivid dreams where everything is normal except you can do this one thing other people can't. A fun and disturbingly believable foray into the paranormal. Don't mess with the Zetas!"

—Sylvain Neuvel, author of *Sleeping Giants*

"This is an astoundingly good debut novel. . . . An electrifying story, enhanced greatly by excellent character studies and a serious tone."

—*RT Book Reviews*

"[*The God Wave*] has that cutting-edge realism that many fiction authors have to fake. . . . A fun (and fast) read. . . . The tension ratchets up and I couldn't put it down as the danger to the team begins to climb."

—*Wired*'s "GeekDad"

"If you're interested in what would happen if the full potential of our brains was unlocked, *The God Wave* is definitely the book for you."

—*Sci-Fi Addicts*

"Like *The Martian* before it, it is the science in *The God Wave* that makes for such an engrossing and convincing tale. The story feels utterly believable and meticulously researched, whilst not being overbearing; the novel will please hard- and soft-sci-fi fans alike. . . . The fact that this is Hemstreet's debut it pretty astounding."

—*Fantasy Literature*

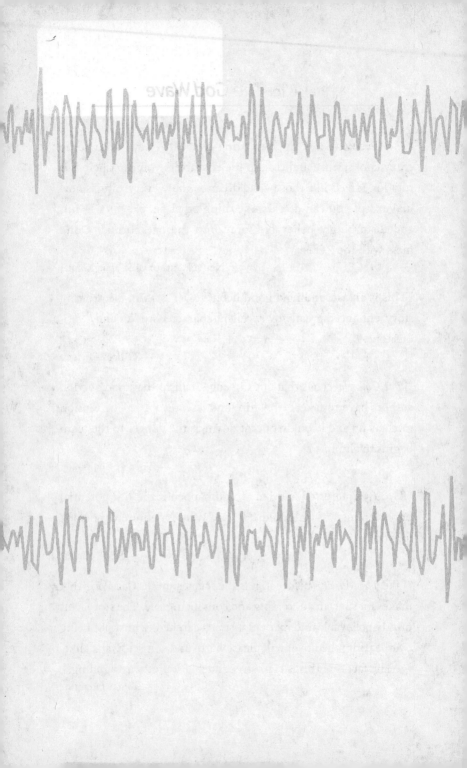

THE
GOD
WAVE

Patrick Hemstreet

HARPER Voyager
An Imprint of HarperCollinsPublishers

Harper Voyager and design is a trademark of HCP LLC.

THE GOD WAVE. Copyright © 2016 by Patrick Hemstreet. Excerpt from *The God
Peak* © 2017 by Patrick Hemstreet. All rights reserved. Printed in the United
States of America. No part of this book may be used or reproduced in any
manner whatsoever without written permission except in the case of brief
quotations embodied in critical articles and reviews. For information address
HarperCollins Publishers, 195 Broadway, New York, NY 10007.

HarperCollins books may be purchased for educational, business, or sales
promotional use. For information please e-mail the Special Markets Department at SPsales@harpercollins.com.

A hardcover edition of this book was published in 2016 by Harper Voyager, an
imprint of HarperCollins Publishers.

FIRST WILLIAM MORROW PAPERBACK EDITION PUBLISHED 2017.

Designed by Shannon Nicole Plunkett

Library of Congress Cataloging-in-Publication Data has been applied for.

ISBN 978-0-06-241952-1

17 18 19 20 21   OV/RRD   10 9 8 7 6 5 4 3 2 1

For Abby, Gideon, and Ezra

Chapter 1

CHUCK

Charles "Chuck" Brenton had a Ph.D. in neuroscience. For this he credited (and sometimes blamed) his philosopher-artist father and musician mother, both of whom had bequeathed to him a fascination with the hidden things that made people tick. He was most interested in what drew people headlong into particular callings, what caused them to choose specific careers, to follow whatever paths their lives took. That fascination had decided his own calling, which now had him seated behind a desk in the Traylor Research Building at Johns Hopkins University as a full professor in the Solomon H. Snyder Department of Neuroscience.

He pulled off his glasses and put his chin down on his crossed arms to study the electroencephalogram rhythm on the computer display before him. While the screen was flat, the image on it was not. Once upon a time, EEG charts had been composed of simple lines, but the scan Chuck was viewing looked more like a topographical map of a mountain range than the seismic pattern of squiggly lines usually associated with an EEG.

This particular mountain range, rendered in jewel-like hues, represented his favorite rhythm and one of the rarest: gamma. It belonged to a cellist he'd had in the studio that morning. She'd been hooked up to his prototype EEG machine as she'd sight-read a complicated and unfamiliar chamber piece. Her lack of familiarity with the composition had ensured she would be multi-tasking, using eyes, ears, and hands as she navigated the music. The result was a literal symphony of brain waves, the so-called gamma rhythms that happened only when a subject blended brain states instead of juggling them.

Gammas were frenetic little rhythms—sharply pointed and closely set but elegant, Chuck thought. They were also hard to maintain. The brain preferred switching rapidly between solo states to performing a concert, but his cellist had produced a steady stream of beta waves before slipping into a gamma pattern she'd maintained for several passages, the longest of which was close to twelve seconds.

He'd worked with this subject before, charting her brain waves while she played pieces she knew well. Her rhythms were different then, and though her body was in motion, she produced a delightful montage of theta and beta waves—rhythms usually associated with meditative and actively focused states, respectively. These states were not supposed to overlap, but the cellist closed her eyes, relaxed into the music, and meditated while active.

That had been interesting enough, but this concert was exhilarating. Chuck reached out to touch the spiky gamma rhythm on the monitor, as if he could feel its ridges and vales beneath his fingertips.

"Remember when we did this with little inked needles and lo-o-ong pieces of gridded paper?"

Chuck looked up from his ruminations into the face of his

senior lab assistant, Eugene Pozniaki, a graduate student in his second year in the Snyder program.

"No," Chuck said, "and neither do you. No one's used paper for a decade."

Eugene gave him a lopsided smile and handed him a small stack of half-sheet forms. "New study subjects who've cleared the initial interviews."

Chuck leafed through them. There was an architect and a specialist in computer-aided design, a classical guitarist, a video game designer, a sculptor, and—he smiled—Mini.

"What?" asked Eugene.

Chuck held up the card. "Minerva Mause. She's a graphic artist. Junior at Maryland Institute. Her dad is a friend of Pop's from their college days. The way Pop describes their relationship, I've always pictured them sitting around smoky coffeehouses after midnight, wearing berets, and chatting about life and art."

"Minerva Mause?" Eugene looked as if he wanted to laugh.

"Yeah, yeah. I know. And she goes by Mini, too. Spelled M-i-n-i. But don't call her . . . you know."

"Minnie Mouse? Aw, c'mon, Doc. You can't avoid it." Eugene was laughing outright now. Catching Chuck's look, he cleared his throat and pushed his glasses up his prodigious nose. "So are you gonna bring her in?"

"Probably, just as a favor to the old man. I've already got data on a couple of graphic artists, although Mini is a unique personality. But I think this CAD/CAM architect looks interesting. Maybe her and the game designer. We've already looked at several musicians. Can you see if there are any folks from more-physical disciplines?"

"Such as?"

Chuck looked back up at the cellist's gamma rhythms and studied them for a moment. "Well, some of our musicians have produced interesting combinations of alpha, beta, and theta waves and given us marvelous gamma patterns. But I'd be interested in seeing the contrast between people who deal entirely with representations of reality and those who interact with reality directly. The architect and game designer are great for one end of the spectrum, but I'm wondering what sort of activity we'd get from a baseball player or an airplane pilot or someone who operates heavy machinery."

Eugene was nodding. "What're the differences between designing a building and actually constructing it, you mean."

Chuck matched his assistant's nodding, up for down.

"You realize," said Eugene as he gathered up the cards Chuck had set to one side, "that just for a moment there, we looked like a couple of academic bobblehead dolls."

"I prefer to think of us as academic action figures. So leap into action. Get me some more lab rats."

With Eugene gone, Chuck once again considered the cellist's varied rhythms. Alpha, beta, theta, and then the elusive gamma. He shook his head. Beta—you'd expect that in a performance situation, but the meditative theta waves and the blending . . .

He used the touch screen to move the wave chart to just below the cellist's face, so he could study her expressions in tandem with the rise and fall of the bright mountain peaks. He watched the graph as she read, concentrated, executed difficult figures, and, on the last refrain of the piece, leaned back, closed her eyes, and played the new passage with emotion and vigor.

How amazing that this level of concentration could move pixels on a screen and, as Eugene had reminded him, had once moved a needlelike pen up and down on a piece of graph paper.

Chuck frowned as an idea tried to push its way into his conscious mind. He sat back in his chair and hit the space bar to pause the playback. The cellist's eyes were half-open; a smile played on her lips. Her right arm was a blur. The graph below showed the tightly packed gamma grouping.

The bow, the arm, her face were all responding to that wave.

Like a needle dancing on paper.

What if . . .

What if these electric impulses could be harnessed to move something other than a pulse of light on a screen or a slender filament of metal? What if they could make other objects dance?

He was on his feet and standing in the doorway of Eugene's office before he realized he'd moved.

"What if the brain waves a person generates to screw in a lightbulb could actually screw in the lightbulb?"

Eugene, sitting at his chaotic desk, looked up and gawped at Chuck. "Is this a lightbulb joke?"

"No. It's a 'what if.' "

Eugene's side chair was covered with papers that had oozed onto it from his desk. Chuck swept them to the floor and sat down.

Eugene pointed at them. "Do you see what you just did?"

"I cleared off a chair and sat down."

"You made a mess. You. Made a mess."

"*You* made a mess. I simply moved it." Chuck held up his hands. "Forget the mess. Forget the lightbulb. Listen. Even with old-style contact probes, a person's brain waves could operate a digital EEG reader or an old analog reader."

Eugene's brow knit. "Well, *operate* isn't really the word, is it? I mean it's more like a trigger—"

"Stop distracting me, Eugene. God, you're disorganized. Listen. If brain waves can move a needle or a digital image, why couldn't they move the actual thing, given an appropriate interface?"

Eugene opened his mouth, closed it, then opened it again. "Actually screw in the lightbulb, you mean?"

Chuck waved his hands. "Bad example. Don't know why

I chose it. Imagine our architect—what's her name? Sara?—imagine Sara sitting at her CAD console, thinking about what it takes to draw elevations. The touches, the mouse clicks, the drags. Whatever. But instead of putting her hands on the keyboard or the drawing pad, the interface is an EEG net with positron transceivers instead of contact electrodes. The net is connected directly to the CAD/CAM."

Eugene blinked. "Connected how? USB? Oh! Or Bluetooth! Bluetooth could be wireless—" He faltered to a stop and rubbed the bridge of his nose. "Um, please continue, Professor."

"Do you get the gist of what I'm saying, Euge?"

"Yeah. Of course I get it. You're talking about telekinesis."

Chuck took a deep breath and counted to ten very quickly. "No. Telekinesis means moving an object directly with your mind. I'm talking about harnessing the electrical power of the human brain using a mechanical interface. Think about it, Euge. How does an EEG work?"

"The electrodes sense electrical impulses in the brain and chart them as pulses of varying degrees of amplitude—as waves."

"Right. Now, what if the energy used to generate the picture of the wave could instead be used to generate something else? Some real activity in the external world? Like Stephen Hawking's typing mechanism, but more."

Eugene sat back in his chair and stared sightlessly over the top of his computer display.

Chuck watched his facial expression. Good. He was engaging. Finally. When Eugene wiggled the temple of his glasses, that meant he was getting ready to verbalize something. God only knew what until it came out of his mouth, but Chuck held out hope this time.

Eugene spoke: "The interface would have to be interpretive, wouldn't it?"

"To a degree, yes. As it is, the human brain is exactly that: an interpretive interface between the mind and the human body—or, more broadly, between the mind and the external world. When you use your mouse there to click or drag something on the computer screen, your brain is interpreting what your mind wants to accomplish, then it does whatever representational translations are necessary to produce on the screen what you preconceive in your mind. When it does that, it generates energy patterns. There's a difference—a measurable difference—between the electrical impulse that puts your hand on the mouse and the one that depresses the mouse button."

"Well, yeah. I suppose there is. But are the transceivers fine-tuned enough to capture the difference?"

Chuck felt like bouncing out of his chair and dancing around the room, which would, he supposed, be undignified for a man of his position.

"I don't know. At this point, no—probably not. But I'd like to find out. Wouldn't you?"

Eugene's expression was wary. "O-o-okay. What do we have to do?"

What indeed?

Chuck had already modified a state-of-the-art Brewster Brain Pattern Monitor to work with his enhanced BPTs—Brenton Positron Transceivers. The transceivers looked like little LEDs in a variety of colors, but they were far more than that. While the lights jigged or foxtrotted or waltzed over the outer contours of the net that held them to the subject's scalp, the emitters fired a stream of positrons into the brain to pick up the most delicate of energy pulses. As a result, the EEG rig that Chuck used was capable of generating three-dimensional images and, he was beginning to hope, much more.

I think we can do this.

THE INTERFACE WAS SIMPLE, REALLY . . . for Chuck and Eugene, that is. They used fiber-optic cabling to bridge the Brewster unit and what they referred to as the "activity platform," or the receiver of the neural impulses from the subject. They used USB to send and receive data, and so naturally the computer interface had been the most readily adapted. It required only a software program to be written, an extended version of the signal detection software that already ran on the Brewster and that allowed an interpreter to read its data.

Chuck had selected a handful of subjects who were conversant with computers and worked with them regularly: CAD/CAM engineer Sara Crowell, game designer Tim Desmond, two gamesters Eugene had recruited from among the underclassmen in his mentoring program (and whom he referred to as Tweedledee and Tweedle*doh!*), a writer named Pierce Flornoy, and Mini Mause.

Chuck had constructed a testing profile that moved from the utterly simplistic (pushing pixels around on a screen and doing field entries) to the specialized and complex. He hoped it would get the subjects to interact with their most familiar software programs and, as Eugene put it, make magic happen.

The problem they encountered immediately was that magic didn't happen. Or at least the expected magic didn't happen.

Because even though Sara Crowell generated a perfect beta wave while imagining she was moving the mouse pointer a hundred pixels to the right, the pointer didn't do what the brain wave predicted; it flew off the screen. At the same time, Tim "Call Me Troll" Desmond was able to perform the same mental mouse move, but the bloody thing would barely wiggle—notwithstanding that his beta waves were every bit as pronounced as Sara's. On top of all that, there was the problem that they were not in the same range. To his 10 Hz waves and 3 microvolts of energy, Sara was generating 15 Hz waves with 6 microvolts of energy—which meant there was nothing Chuck could parse from their attempts.

So Chuck backtracked. He got real computer mice, not connected to anything, and asked the subjects to physically move them as they watched the computer display. The results were the same. Sara's mouse pointer went into hyperspace, and Tim's just did a tiny dance.

The rest of the subjects did the same simple exercise. The results were all over the map. Even when Chuck and Eugene pared the experiment down to the simple act of moving the mouse pointer between two fixed boxes on a black screen, the subjects achieved no repeatable results. And when Chuck and Eugene arrived at the conclusion that different individuals must simply generate stronger impulses than others, they were thrown another curveball.

Mini Mause—who, like Sara, could move her mouse smartly from point A to point B and points beyond—came in one morning sleep deprived after a rock concert. Sitting at her station with the neural net over her pert head, she went through a set of protocols she had previously knocked out of the park.

"Oh, man . . ." Eugene raked his fingers through his riotous hair and pushed his glasses up his nose. "She didn't even make it out of the infield."

Chuck peered over his shoulder at the 3-D EEG graph. "And neither did her brain waves. Look at it. That's one of the most lackluster betas I've ever seen."

"I'm just a little sleepy. If you let me take a five-minute power nap and brew a cup of tea, I'll be fine." Mini peered at the two neurologists through the gap between the Brewster unit's tower of electronics and its side-mounted computer display. Her pale, coppery cap of hair glittered with positron jewels, and her heart-shaped face wore an earnest expression, which—despite being tired—made her look even younger than her nineteen years.

"Sure," Chuck said absently. "Sure. Go ahead. Um, back in fifteen?"

"Fifteen," Mini agreed and turned to walk away. "Kitchen's down on the left, right?"

Eugene, far more alert than either his boss or their subject, leapt after her. "Mini! The rig. The net. We need to disconnect you."

She stopped just short of disaster and put her hands up to her head. "Oh! Oh, yeah. I feel pretty disconnected already." She giggled as Eugene unfastened the net and slipped it off her head. She left the lab still laughing.

Eugene stood in the middle of the room with the net in his hands, staring after her. "She always like that?"

"What?" Chuck looked up sharply from the data on the Brewster's display. "Oh, yeah. I mean no, she . . . I guess you could say she's a woman of many moods. Right now she's just operating on too little sleep." He shook his head, muttering to himself. "So the differential isn't just an individual amplitude setting, with some people being louder than others. It's even more variable than that."

But Eugene heard him, and pulled his gaze from the lab doors, moved back to the brain pattern monitor, and set the neural net on its spherical rest. "You were hoping it was just a matter of adjusting the gain, weren't you?"

"Just," Chuck snorted, shaking his head. "Even if it were just individual amplitude, I have no idea how to adjust for it. I have no idea how far off the charts Sara and Mini might go or how much boost to give Tim—"

"Troll," Euge interrupted, informing Chuck of Tim's preferred moniker.

"—or the others. If there's no standard deviation from a norm, and we haven't even calculated the norm, then I don't know how to make this work."

Eugene considered that for a moment. "Well, maybe someone else does. Maybe if we write up what we've got so far and get it into the community—"

"We'd get laughed at." Chuck grimaced.

"Not gonna happen, Doc," Eugene promised him. "You've already proven something: that brain waves can make magic happen."

Chuck pointed a finger at his assistant's nose. "Don't say that. Don't use that word. It's not magic." For some reason, the very idea made him angry.

"Okay, okay. Then brain waves make *shit* happen. You like that better?"

Chuck didn't. But it mattered little, for neither magic nor shit happened. Mini did come back from her power nap and tea with more verve, but that served only to underscore the problem: there was no baseline for the raw energy that a given subject's brain waves generated and no way to arrive at a differential to which the interface could adjust.

"GIGO," Chuck murmured, looking over their results at the end of Mini's session. "Garbage in, garbage out."

"Except it's not garbage," Eugene argued. "It's data. About which you should write a paper, I'm thinking. Who knows? Maybe it's a matter of focus. Maybe our subjects can be trained to moderate or control their brain waves themselves."

"I don't think it works like that, Euge. When Mini or Sara is interacting with the apparatus, they're both generating beta waves. They're just not generating them in the same energy range, and I'm not sure why, and I'm not sure what I can do about it. We need a . . . a transmission box. Something that ramps the energy output up or down dynamically, so when Sara and Pierce, say, set out to screw in the metaphorical lightbulb, the same amount of energy is fed to the apparatus."

Eugene was laughing.

"What?"

"I was thinking about that NPR *Science Friday* interview you're supposed to give next week. I can just hear Ira Flatow asking you to describe your latest project." He held out an imaginary microphone. "'Dr. Brenton, what fascinating experiments are you doing at Johns Hopkins currently?' 'Why, Ira, we're trying to calculate the amount of mental energy it takes to screw in a lightbulb.'"

As much as he didn't want to, Chuck laughed. He laughed all the way back to his office, where he sat down to compile his notes. He had no intention of mentioning anything about his brain wave experiments on national radio.

He had no intention of ever talking about it with anyone at this point.

Chapter 2

MATT

Matt Streegman glanced up at the clock over his office door and realized it was too dark to see it. Stupid anyway. He was sitting at his computer, his face bathed in the glow of his cinema display. All he needed to do was glance at the menu bar at the top of the screen: 1:10 a.m. On a Wednesday night. Correction: Thursday morning.

A long, depressing holiday weekend was already under way. He wished, not for the first time, that he could crawl into a suspended animation tank that would let him sleep away Thanksgiving without having to move or interact with people or think.

That was the worst thing about most weekends: the thinking. The worst thing about this particular weekend was the people.

Oh, he'd found a myriad of ways to keep working on projects he was supposed to leave in the lab and games he could play that challenged his Mensa-class brain. His favorite weekend pastime was to head over to Dice's house to help him (or, mostly, watch him) build robots. Dice—aka Daisuke Kobayashi—had, alas, gone down to his parents' house in Charlotte for the Thanksgiving weekend. No joy there.

There was a tap at the door of his office. A shadow fell across the bubbled glass along the right-hand side.

"Yeah?" Matt rubbed his eyes and blinked at the code he'd just generated. He caught three syntax errors in the time it took for the night watchman to open the office door.

"Oh, hey, Dr. Streegman. It's, um, it's getting kind of late, sir." The security guard—a twentyish fellow named Zack Truman—regarded him apologetically from the half-open door.

"Yeah. I know. I was . . . just finishing up." *Hell, I was just making a complete mosh of this code.*

"It'd be great if you could do that pretty quick, Professor. The whole campus is shutting down for the rest of the week. We've been asked to lock this building down, in fact."

"And I'm in the way." Matt smiled and held up a hand when Zack started to protest. "No, don't apologize. You're just doing your job. Give me about ten minutes to upload some stuff, and I'll be out of your hair."

Zack glanced at the computer. "You're not going to work over Thanksgiving, are you? You should be, y'know, with your family and friends. Drinking eggnog and eating turkey, not . . ." He gestured at the screen.

Zack, Matt had come to know, was newly married and very happy, and as is the nature of very happy people, he wanted everyone else to be equally ecstatic about life. It would not occur to him that someone might not have close friends or might not want to spend some Hallmark holiday in the bosom of his ersatz family.

Matt was not, however, going to say anything about that. When Zack had wandered off, he uploaded the program he was working on to the cloud, backed it up onto his flash drive for good measure, and snagged his laptop from the corner of his desk. He was out and had locked the office door before Zack reappeared.

At home, the message light on his telephone blinked accusingly. *You have seven unanswered, unlistened-to messages. What are you going to do about it?*

He considered listening to them, his hand poised over the playback button, but the fact was he didn't want to listen to them. He knew that at least three would be from his sister, Chelsea, asking where the hell he was.

Instead, he picked up his iPhone, opened the remote for his entertainment center, and flicked on NPR, hoping there would be something distracting to listen to. There was—a repeat broadcast of *Science Friday* was in progress. He took some General Tso's out of the fridge, removed the metal handle from the container, and popped it in the microwave.

A few minutes later, lulled by the voices of public radio, Matt dove into his reheated dinner and considered taking a hot shower before he turned in. He was half-asleep already, only barely managing to chew his food. He polished it off, put the dish in the sink, and flicked off the kitchen light.

Shower or straight to bed?

" . . . your work," Ira Flatow was saying on the radio. "I read your paper, 'A Musical Mind.' I was especially taken by your description of the gamma waves your cellist friend generated."

Gamma waves?

Matt paused in the middle of his living room. Who was Flatow interviewing?

"I was wondering, Dr. Brenton, if you've come to any new insights since you wrote that piece."

Brenton. Where had he heard that name before? *Had* he heard that name before?

"A few."

"A few," Flatow repeated.

Brenton laughed. "I'm really not trying to be coy. It's just that what I'm working on right now probably sounds more like science fiction than science."

"Try me."

"Well, as Erica was playing, it occurred to me to wonder if the same brain waves that move a pulse on a computer screen or a needle on a graph can move physical objects, given the proper interface."

"Like drones?"

"Not just drones. I mean when the human brain is engaged in an activity—even just going through the mental motions of the activity—it creates rhythms that describe that activity via brain waves. Theoretically it should be possible to harness those brain waves and channel them, so they can perform the activity remotely."

Flatow laughed. "That *does* sound like science fiction. What sort of applications are you considering?"

Matt sank onto the sofa without registering that he'd done so.

"Sky's the limit, isn't it?" Brenton answered. "I mean just imagine what it would mean for disabled people. A thought to perform an act—operating a wheelchair or even a car or a computer. Imagine if, I don't know, a scientist of the caliber of Stephen Hawking could perform any action just by thinking about it. Or people who are completely paralyzed but still have working minds that produce discrete brain waves. Those rhythms could allow them to communicate with the outside world, with their loved ones. Could permit them to manipulate their environment, even create art. Write. Perform. *Live.*"

Matt was stunned by the thought.

Lucy . . .

He remembered Lucy—his wife, his *everything*—lying in a hospital bed, dead to the outside world—dead to him—while her brain, her magnificent brain, continued to pulse out brain rhythms he could read but not understand. Did this man understand them? Matt still had the record of the last weeks of her life as EEG readouts. If this guy could read and translate these brain waves into some sort of coherent message, what would it be? What had Lucy's mind been doing once her body stopped translating its messages?

"Or imagine," Brenton was saying, "being able to perform operations in the vacuum of space without sending astronauts outside. Or even robots. The spacecraft could be built in such a way that between the mind of the technician and the interface, they'd be reparable by remote thought." He laughed again. "I know—science fiction. There would be commercial applications too, of course. Theoretically brain waves could drive some tools with far more nuance than the hands, even hands with robotic extensions."

"So what's stopping you?"

"At this point, you name it," Brenton said with a chuckle. "But the main issue is the interface. Or, more to the point, a translation device."

Matt realized his heart was pounding in his chest. They didn't have a translation device? He listened as Brenton described the problem he'd encountered with the relative amplitude of the brain waves generated by different brains or the same brain under different circumstances, and his mind forgot all about sleep or showers or anything else.

"What we need to develop is a translation interface that will allow us to set a baseline and then compensate for variances in the energy generated by a subject's brain waves."

"How might that be done?" Flatow asked.

"Mathematically," Matt murmured. "It would have to be done mathematically."

He knew that better than anyone. He had done it. Or at least he had described the variance in the oscillations of Lucy's brain waves mathematically. He had worked on the algorithms persistently as he'd sat by her bed, watching her EEG speak to him in a language he couldn't interpret.

He had his laptop out and open in mere moments and then dithered between digging Lucy's files out of a folder with her name on it that he hadn't opened for two years and Googling the *Science Friday* guest. He opted for going to the NPR site and finding out who this guy was, maybe read a transcript of the session.

The name of the scientist was Dr. Charles Brenton, from Johns Hopkins. That covered a lot of territory. There were Johns Hopkins campuses and hospital facilities in as disparate population centers as Baltimore, Maryland, and Nanjing, China. He figured the main campus in Baltimore was the most likely. He e-mailed the transcript of the interview to himself and began an online search for Dr. Charles Brenton.

A few links later, Matthew was looking at a photograph of the good doctor, a fellow at the Solomon H. Snyder Department of Neuroscience.

Surprise. The neuroscientist was younger than Matt had expected—even younger than Matt himself. He had a boyish face, a smile that probably still made his mother want to bake him cookies, hair that was a little too long.

Does your mommy know you're doing science, Professor?

He tracked down the paper Ira Flatow had referenced in his interview: "A Musical Mind." Halfway through it, he felt one of his math fugues coming on. He navigated to the Lucy folder on his laptop and opened a file named LM_alg_001. His eyes filled with the equations based on the output of Lucy's dying brain.

The samples in Charles Brenton's paper were based on the output from several different subjects. If Matt's observations were accurate, if his calculations were on—and he'd bet good money they were—it would be a relatively simple matter of testing the algorithms he'd gotten from Lucy's EEGs against the sample waves. When he was done, he should have a way of calculating a baseline for any subject.

He opened a new document and set to work.

He decided he might have a good holiday after all.

Chapter 3

PARTNERS

"There's this guy in your office," said Eugene.

Chuck looked up from the diagnostics he was running on the latest software upgrade to the Brewster unit. "A guy in my office. Can you be more specific?"

"Says his name is Streegman. Dr. Streegman. From MIT. Something about hearing you on *Science Friday*."

"He drove seven hours to talk to me about *Science Friday*?"

"He says he may have something you need." Eugene shrugged. "Look, I asked already. He's being mysterious."

"Great. Just what I need—another mystery. Here." Chuck slid off the station chair and waved Eugene into it. "Continue the diagnostics on this upgrade. It's checking the transport subroutines right now. When it's done with that, plug in Sara's last session, and see if we're still getting a hiccup on those theta waves."

Chuck slouched down the hall to his office, hands in his jean pockets, wondering what Dr. Streegman of the Massachusetts Institute of Technology could possibly have that he needed. He opened the door and swiftly assessed the man leaning against the window frame, staring out over East Madison as if there were something fascinating happening on a rooftop across town. Streegman was of average height, averagely nerdy-looking, probably in his early forties, wearing standard-issue khakis, blazer, and loafers.

Standing in the doorway in his jeans, sweater vest, and Converse high-tops, Chuck felt indecorously underdressed.

He cleared his throat and held out his hand. "Dr. Streegman? Chuck Brenton. To what do I owe the honor?"

Streegman jerked to attention, turned, and took the proffered hand. His smile was late and superficial. As if he hadn't had to use it in some time. He also looked as if he hadn't slept in a while. He had a nick on his left cheek where he'd cut himself shaving. *Sleep dep, most likely.*

"Dr. Brenton, thank you for seeing me."

Chuck ran through the usual set of niceties—"please sit down, would you like coffee or tea?"—and Streegman asked for coffee with the gratitude of a man who really needed the caffeine.

"Did you really come all the way from Boston just to see me?" Chuck asked as he brought the man a cup.

Sipping his coffee, Streegman sat in the antique wingback chair across from Chuck's desk and nodded at the *Lord of the Rings* action figures on one of the bookshelves.

"Fantasy fan, huh? Funny. I would've expected, I don't know, *Star Wars* or *Star Trek* maybe."

Chuck smiled. "Those are at home. But they all stir the imagination. So what can I do for you?"

"Imagination . . . exactly. It's actually more what I can do for you . . . I hope." The smile turned on itself, becoming self-deprecating. "I heard the *Science Friday* broadcast. It was . . . galvanizing."

Chuck blinked. "Really? I hadn't expected that response from anybody. To be honest, I was expecting derision, which I've definitely received my fair share of in the past few days."

Streegman put his coffee cup down on the edge of the desk. "That's because they're idiots."

"But you're not."

"Definitely not. You said you need some means of establishing a baseline and some sort of standardized adjustment for variation in brain wave output."

"Yes. Yes, I did—I *do* need that."

"I have it."

"You . . ." Chuck shook his head. "What do you do at MIT, Dr. Streegman?"

"Call me Matt. I'm a mathematician, a sometime programmer. I spend a fair amount of my time creating working algorithms for the robotics guys. I'm a locus, Dr. Brenton—"

"Chuck," he said absently.

"Chuck. I am where math meets robotic interfaces."

"So how's that help me?"

"It doesn't, completely. But some years ago, I had the occasion to closely observe, over a period of weeks, the EEG activity of a seriously debilitated and eventually dying brain. I rather instinctively view things through the prism of mathematics, including this experience. I naturally began looking at the brain rhythms being generated as mathematical expressions. I set about describing them, calculating them, quantifying them." He paused, whether for dramatic effect or—as Chuck suspected—because there was a subtext to the story that made it hard to recount. What he said next made any reasons irrelevant.

"When I was done, I had a baseline equation for this individual."

My God . . .

"I believe," Streegman continued, "that if I were to have access to your data, I could provide you with the equations to establish a baseline for each subject and, further, with equations that would adjust for the variations in their output. In fact . . ." He dug a flash drive out of his pocket and placed it on Chuck's desk. "I did some sample calculations using data from your paper on the musical mind."

Chuck reached for the drive, barely conscious of what he was doing. His hand hovered over it. "What software do I—"

"It's just a set of charts and equations in a document file. Your word processor should read it. Though if your application has a programming feature set, it will allow you to parse the equations more clearly."

Chuck realized his hand was shaking. He snatched up the flash drive and plugged it into one of the USB ports on his laptop. In seconds he had opened the file and was looking at twin columns of data. On the left an EEG graph of a subject, on the right a mathematical equation describing the brain wave.

"The first expression in the equation is the baseline," the mathematician told him. "The second is intended to calculate any deviation from that baseline. Or should I say variation?" He shrugged. "The peaks and valleys."

Chuck knew enough math to understand that the second half of the equation would need to be iterative—applied repeatedly to adjust the output of the subject to any interface. He cleared his throat noisily. "You could program this into a software interface?"

"Not by myself. I have a colleague, though—well, a postgrad student, actually—who would do the programming."

"And the mechanical part of the interface?"

Streegman's smile was suddenly broad and genuine. "Dice is a genius when it comes to robotics. He's the whole package—software and hardware. I'd like to bring him in, too."

"Bring him into what, exactly, Dr. Streegman?" Chuck asked, his voice distant and breathless. "What are you proposing?"

"What I'm proposing," Streegman said, still smiling, "is a partnership. And I'll go further. If our collaborative efforts yield the sort of fruit I believe they will, I'd like to propose that we go into business together."

"Business? What sort of business?"

"A research and development firm, Doctor. A business that takes what we learn in the lab and applies it to real-world situations in a wide array of disciplines: art, manufacturing, computer science, agriculture. You name it. I propose that we"—the smile became a grin—"change the world."

Chuck's breath stopped in his throat. *I'm dreaming,* he told himself. *I've fallen asleep at my desk, and I'm dreaming this.* He closed his eyes slowly, squeezed them shut, and opened them again.

Matt Streegman was still there, still waiting for him to respond.

"I don't know. It's all very sudden, no?"

"Bigger decisions happen in a fraction of the time. This is a chance to make your ideas a reality."

"That sounds wonderful, but I'm an academic, Doctor. Matt. Not a businessman. If numbers represent monetary values, my brain goes tilt."

"You don't have to worry about that. Not any of it. I've got the math and the money covered."

"And the mechanics? This guy, Dice, he'll build the interface between my EEG reader and the real-world object?"

"Like I said, he's a genius. If this algorithm works, he can build an interface to apply it."

Chuck licked his lips. "If you build it, he will come?"

Matt laughed. "If he builds it, everything will come."

DICE WAS ASTONISHED BY THE warren of mismatched buildings that made up the Johns Hopkins campus around the Traylor Research Building. It reminded him of a box full of Legos that he was pretty sure still existed in the closet of his room back home in San Francisco—a room his proud parents had turned into a sort of shrine to their only son—that had been upended onto the grounds.

In fact, the Traylor Building was one of the oddest toys in this particular box. A narrow, sand-colored parallelepiped building sandwiched between two larger, taller, more modern-looking ones, it was unimpressive. Or would have been had it not been sporting the words JOHNS HOPKINS in huge, white letters across the top of the façade. There was nothing else to indicate the level of research that went on there. Nothing to indicate that history was being made in a research facility on the third floor.

Dice liked that sense of anonymity. He felt sometimes as if he were putting one over on the world—that he was part of a great geek conspiracy that, when the time was ripe, would announce to all and sundry that they had solved society's problems through the simple application of technology. Ta-da!

"How goes it, Dice?" Matt Streegman had appeared silently out of nowhere, as he was in the annoying habit of doing, to peer over Dice's shoulder at the small robot on which he was working.

Dice put the cover back on the rounded carapace and smoothed out the cabling between it and the Brewster brain wave reader.

"It goes swimmingly. Not that I advocate robots swimming. Especially after a large meal." Dice paused for Matt's laughter, which didn't come. Dice cleared his throat. "I think our little guy is ready for Dr. Brenton's subjects. Who do we have?"

"For this phase we have us. Well, Chuck anyway. He'd like to do the test drive before we bring in his lab rats."

"About that . . ."

"What?"

Dice grimaced. "I've actually done a bit of a test drive, hence my messing with Roboticus here."

"It works?"

Dice rolled his eyes. "Of course it works. I just had a little glitch in one of the connectors—a bent pin. I soldered it. Should be fine now."

"Show me."

"Before Chuck tries it?"

"You did."

"Touché."

"I just want to know how excited to be."

Dice grinned. "You should be very excited."

"And of course I want to be able to maintain my professorial mien in the face of your world-shaking accomplishment."

"Right."

"So show me."

Dice set the robot in the middle of the lab floor. It was basically a glorified Roomba—little more than a drive mechanism in an aluminum and plastic casing—but it was all they needed as a proof of concept. It had a little red joystick mounted on the top of it that would allow an operator to steer it manually. And, if all went right, with his mind.

He allowed himself a moment of glee at that thought.

He moved back to the Brewster unit and took the neural array from its stand. He put that on his head, making sure he had the transceivers pressed as tightly against his skull as possible. A gleaming twist of lightweight fiber-optic cabling ran from the neural net to the brain pattern monitor and thence to the robot.

The important part of the device—the kinetic converter—was

a software module that resided in the BPM and fed commands to the firmware aboard Roboticus.

Dice flipped the EEG monitor on. "Okay, now, Roboticus. Let's see what we can do."

He thought at the ersatz Roomba. He thought it forward. Or, more accurately, he thought of pushing the joystick forward. After a moment of hesitation, the robot went.

"Okay," Dice murmured. "Let's go right."

The joystick toggled right; the robot turned and trundled off in that direction.

"Left."

It went left.

"Let's pop a wheelie."

The little bot executed a slow 360.

"God, it's working." Chuck Brenton's airless whisper issued from the lab doorway.

Technically the last move hadn't worked, but still Dice was pleased. He glanced up. Dr. Brenton and his senior assistant, Eugene, stood staring at the now-motionless robot.

"Oh, hey. Sorry, Doc," said Dice. "I just wanted to make sure it works before we have you try it. I hate it when the machinery flakes during a demonstration." He switched the Brewster to standby and reached up to unfasten the neural array.

"That's a good look for you," said Eugene.

After two weeks of close proximity, his flat, nasal voice was only minimally irritating. His sarcastic attitude . . . well, Dice had to admit, it had sort of grown on him.

"I'm thinking that's a great sideline," Dice came back. "While the good doctors are making millions with their oh-so-helpful and socially redeeming technology, I figure we market the blinky net as the latest in futuristic fashion."

Dice helped Dr. Brenton don the net and position the transceivers. With the BPM on, Brenton turned to face the robot. He rubbed the palms of his hands on his jeans. "Okay. What do I do?"

"See the little red joystick on the top of the carapace?"

"Uh-huh."

"You just think about operating it."

"As if by hand."

"Exactly. The kinetic converter will take a second to establish your baseline, then it should respond to your directions."

Dice watched the neurologist closely. He was half-afraid the guy was going to hyperventilate and pass out. He didn't, though. He faced the robot with a look of intense concentration.

Roboticus responded—tentatively at first, then with more certainty. In about three minutes, the scientist had the little bot running straight lines at flank speed and weaving slowly around obstacles. At this point Chuck was seized by a sudden fit of laughter that left the robot quivering in the middle of the lab.

"Can I try it?" Eugene asked.

IN THE END THEY ALL tried it and then sat down and came up with a game plan. Matt would compose a précis for prospective investors, Dice would begin generating code for a computer interface that would give them access to commercial software controls, and Chuck and Eugene would continue to expand their experiments with Roboticus and a variety of their subjects— experiments they would, of course, record.

"Not," Eugene noted, "that anyone will believe what they see in a video."

Matt shook his head, his fingers already flying over his laptop keyboard. "They won't have to commit funds on the basis of a video. We'll let them try it live."

Chuck frowned. "We're going to bring them here? Matt, that's not going to work. I mean it's not kosher to use Johns Hopkins resources to start up a private business."

"We won't be using Johns Hopkins resources. The first thing I'm going to do is lease this rig." Matt nodded at the brain pattern monitor, his mind racing ahead, making connections, calculating potential. "The next thing you're going to do is figure out how to downsize it, so we can fit it into our own lab."

"Our own lab," Chuck repeated as if Matt had just said "our own space station."

"Of course our own lab. You didn't imagine we were going to continue to work out of Hopkins, did you?" Matt shook his head and dove back into organizing his précis.

I have a lot to teach them, he thought.

Chapter 4

FORWARD KINETICS

Our own lab.

The words had a sort of magic to them, Chuck thought. Their own lab had a name, Forward Kinetics, and it stood at the center of a technology park (emphasis on *park*) in Silver Spring, Maryland. It was a stand-alone facility—something Matt had insisted on—and was contained in a low, eight-thousand-square-foot, split-level building that seemed to be in the process of tumbling down the gentle slope it occupied. It was beautiful as well as functional, a masterpiece of wood, concrete, and glass with some slate accents. Frank Lloyd Wright would have approved.

Chuck had to admit that Matt had a well-developed sense of aesthetics. Rather than the lightbulb-filled, primary-color, plastic script logos that most other high-tech firms used, theirs—a stylized human brain full of gears that meshed with the letters *FK*—appeared in backlit bronze across the façade.

Chuck noticed the building's external features and parklike setting every Monday morning when he pulled his car into the small, tree-bordered lot at the top of the slope. But the internal features captivated him iteratively, on a daily basis, moment by moment. From the tall windows that flooded the two-story foyer with light to the Prairie School roofline with its thick cedar beams, and from the travertine floors to the stylized Craftsman light fixtures, the lab was warm and welcoming.

Today was a special day in the nascent life of Forward Kinetics. Today they would finalize their research plan. They had been brainstorming for weeks, looking into the range of applications on which to begin their initial trials. Today they would nail down the final selection and plan the recruitment process.

Chuck already knew that he and Matt did not see eye to eye on what constituted a worthy discipline, but they had agreed to take input from the entire executive staff, which now included Eugene and Dice. Their formal designations were laboratory director and robotics director, respectively. Those were the titles on their business cards and office doors anyway. Chuck doubted either of them thought of himself as a director of anything.

The junior lab staff—there were only six of them—was savvy and self-directing for the most part, so the lab took on the complexion of a parliamentary democracy instead of a benevolent dictatorship . . . at least as long as Matt Streegman wasn't giving the orders. Matt, Chuck quickly learned, had definite opinions about everything—even things he'd only known about for a matter of seconds—and acted on those opinions unless someone could offer him a damn good reason he should not.

That caused some ripples in the smooth flow of ideas and activities, but the upside of Matt Streegman was that once someone showed him that his opinion was flawed empirically, he didn't hesitate to say, "Oh. Right. Well, then let's do it another way."

The problems arose when no one could prove clearly that his opinion was flawed. Then there were two options: find empirical evidence or roll over and do things Matt's way. And that's what they did . . . kind of. Chuck was an old hand at appearing to roll over. His mother had always said he was passive-aggressive. It took one to know one.

"Morning, Dr. Brenton." This from the receptionist who manned a curving, wood-paneled desk in the sunny foyer and who'd had precious little to do since the initial frenzy of moving in had concluded.

"Morning, Barry." Chuck threw the kid a lopsided grin. "How's that game of Temple Run coming?"

"Uh. Great. I haven't died for fifteen minutes."

Chuck's smile deepened. "To the disappointment of zombie monkeys everywhere. Enjoy the lull, Barry. I have a feeling it's about to get crazy around here."

"Yes, sir."

Chuck trotted down the short flight of stairs to the office level of the building. Matt was already sipping coffee in the small conference room where they gathered every morning for a brief review of activities and goals. So far the meetings had been focused on establishing the lab's basic equipment and processes. That done, they now turned their attention to the primary goal of identifying lucrative and profound uses for kinetic tech.

"Hey," Chuck greeted his partner. "Dice and Euge in?"

Matt glanced up from his iPad and nodded. "They've been here awhile, doing their geek thing in the lab. Want to make a bet?"

Chuck set his laptop bag down on the oblong conference table and moved to the sideboard to get coffee. "I don't gamble. I'm terrible at it."

"This one's easy. I bet you and I don't have any overlap on our short lists."

Chuck snorted. "Are you serious? I'm not taking that bet."

"C'mon. Ten dollars says I'm right."

Chuck crossed back to the conference table, set down his coffee mug, and unpacked his laptop. "I told you I don't gamble. If I did, I sure wouldn't gamble with you, especially not with real money."

"What else is worth gambling with?"

"I think that's the wrong question. I think the question is: what else is trivial enough to gamble with?"

Matt opened his mouth to retort but was interrupted when Dice and Eugene sailed through the door in the throes of one of their frequent yet friendly fights.

"I'm telling you, Euge," Dice was saying, "until we can sever our reliance on firmware, this is all just exploratory. Who the hell is going to want to run a deep-sea exploration at the end of a freaking umbilical cord? One of the first things we've got to do is design a remote interface."

"Be that as it may," Eugene protested, "to focus on that now would be to put the cart before the horse."

"You see?" Dice made an "I give up" gesture at the two men already in the room. "He's a Luddite. Carts and horses."

"Good morning, gentlemen," Matt said. "If you're going to get coffee, please do it now, so we can get down to business."

Eugene saluted and pirouetted toward the coffeemaker. Dice set his laptop down and pulled a can of Coke out of his jacket pocket. Matt called in the senior lab assistant, Ventana Salazar, to take notes.

Matt drove a tight meeting—something Chuck alternately appreciated and regretted. There were times when a little digression was good for the creative juices. It's why emotional quotient had become almost as important a human diagnostic tool as IQ. Matt's mind, however, dealt more readily with numbers and statistics than it did with touchy-feely creativity. And it was Matt's numbers, Chuck reminded himself, that had allowed him to take the field of neurokinetics from theory to reality.

"Chuck?"

Matt was looking at him with an expression that accused him (correctly, as it happened) of woolgathering.

"Sorry. Thinking."

Matt gestured at his laptop. "You want to trot your list out first?"

"Yeah, sure. Um, I've got five: the handicapped, especially people with cerebral palsy, Parkinson's, or MS; medical applications; law enforcement; first responders; and artists, especially computer-based applications in art and music."

"That's six, Chuck."

"Well, okay, just art then."

The big plasma display at the end of the table went live as Ventana typed up Chuck's short list.

"Good thing you didn't take that bet," Matt told him. "Good thing for me, that is. I was wrong. We do actually have some overlap. I've got computer-aided design, manufacturing, private security—not quite law enforcement but close—video game creation, and video game play."

Chuck frowned. "What about medicine? We've at least got to do medicine."

Matt raised a hand. "Lists first, then discussion. Dice, what do you have?"

Dice had firefighting/law enforcement ("bomb squad, I'm thinking," he said), construction, handicapped access, and medical.

Euge offered handicapped mobility, medicine, computer art, deep-sea exploration and salvage, and archaeology.

Chuck nodded at the big screen. "So are the ones where we overlap automatic ins?"

Matt shook his head. "No."

No?

But before Chuck could protest, Matt said, "I think we should discuss the pros and cons of each selection. Let's go for the low-hanging fruit first, though. Take law enforcement or private security. Great market there. Just think of the applications: disarming bombs, using bots to secure—well, whatever needs securing. Physical safety of the remote operator would be a big plus."

"You can already do that with mechanical drones," Chuck argued.

"Not like this, Doctor," said Dice. "It would be as if the guard were there. Combine the kinetics with VR—that'd be an unbeatable combination."

"Not to mention that removing the safety of the officer out of the equation, you can eliminate a lot of fatal error in the heat of the moment," Eugene mused, "and I can see it having a strong social impact."

"*That* law enforcement and private security firms would be willing to pay a significant amount for," concluded Matt. "I think we definitely need to consider security applications relatively soon."

"That'll take some more doing in the robotics department," Dice admitted. "But, yeah, I'd prioritize it."

"Good. That will also give us some ancillary technologies to go with the primary offering. Security robotics."

"Do I hear a yea on security?" asked Tana, looking askance at the four men.

Matt glanced fleetingly at the others and then made a thumbs-up gesture.

I guess so, Chuck thought. *But it is a good use of the tech.*

Tana typed and highlighted the words "security, law enforcement applications."

"Great," Matt said. "Now how about computer-aided design? Benefits are obvious, and we've already got someone in the program."

"We've got two people in the program, actually," said Chuck. "Sara and Mini."

Matt was silent for a moment, his expression opaque. "Mini doesn't do CAD. She does art."

"With a computer."

"Different application, Chuck. There are industrial applications for what Sara does. There's a market for it. Can you really claim that what Mini does, as creative as it might be, is marketable?"

Chuck felt his throat tighten up. He swallowed. "Matt, Mini's been with the program from pretty early on. She has a bright, experimental nature."

"She's helped us hone our approach a lot," Eugene added.

Matt skewered them both with his too-direct gaze. "We need to prove to potential investors that what we're working on can have real-world benefits."

"Real world?" Chuck laughed, pointing at the screen. "Video games?"

"Not only is video gaming a huge market," Matt said calmly—infuriatingly so, if Chuck was being honest about it—"but it provides a great prototype process to show that neurokinetics will allow programmers to code and test that code much more efficiently and effectively. And again, we've already got a programmer in the existing plan who happens to be an artist as well. Troll creates his own creatures, after all, and programs their movements. I'd say he's ideal—as is his discipline—to give us the sort of model that would interest investors and potential customers."

Chuck exhaled noisily. "Fine. Okay. I see that. But what about applications for people with mobility issues?"

"I don't think we need to test using handicapped people at this juncture," said Matt, glancing at Chuck. "Whatever Troll can do in the realm of programming or Sara can do with a CAD/CAM machine, a handicapped programmer or designer could do just as well." He swung his chair toward Chuck, his eyes bright. "Think of it. Our neural interface could allow a handicapped engineer to run a CAD/CAM program and let construction workers safely run dangerous equipment or perform dangerous procedures from a distance. Just think of the benefits to rescue operations or firefighting."

"I *am* thinking of those things."

"Have you thought about how hard they'd be to test, though? Are we going to burn down some buildings to show that a fire truck can put out a blaze without a squadron of firefighters putting their lives on the line? Have you considered how expensive it would be to even attempt to explore that before we've proven the efficacy of the tech for other, smaller disciplines?"

He had a point. "Fine, but computer games?"

Matt leaned toward his partner, his elbows on the table, his face earnest. "Chuck, today computer games, tomorrow medical programs that allow doctors to do delicate manipulations inside the human body without having to use tools that are too large for the job. We need to demonstrate the efficacy of the process in a way that makes the point but without endangering any lives. Say we did test a medical application right out of the box. Who'd sign up for that study?"

"Nobody."

"Exactly. Now, let's get back to work here. We have security, CAD/CAM, and video game creation and testing. What's next?"

What was next was construction. Chuck started to argue against it, but Matt convinced him this was the ideal way to find out if their tech could allow a seasoned construction worker to manipulate large machinery. Surely they could afford one little backhoe.

The final list was tightly focused: CAD/CAM, programming, video game play, construction, and security. Matt's argument—

from which he could not be turned—was that those were gateway applications for all others.

Chuck could not help but note that they were also the most commercial—and were Matt's original list.

CHUCK HAD EXPECTED IT WOULD be hard to tell Mini Mause she wasn't needed for the program anymore. He hadn't expected it would be harder on him than it was on her and that she would end up consoling him for letting her go.

"Hey, it's okay, Doc," she told him, one small, capable hand on his shoulder.

They sat face-to-face in a couple of side chairs in his large, bright office on the lower level of the building. He had been unable to sit across a desk from her like a college professor flunking a student . . . or a boss firing an employee.

"Really. I think I got a little too caught up in it all anyway, you know? I wasn't getting as much artwork done as I was daydreaming about what I would do the next time I was in the lab." She laughed—a light, breezy sound that made Chuck at least want to feel better. "Who knows? Maybe I could come in on a volunteer basis. You know, sort of a proof of concept after you've tried the gear out on the other guys."

Chuck studied her pert face carefully. "You'd do that? Just on your own time?"

"Sure, why not? I love using this lab as an art studio. Where else would I get access to this kind of equipment? Not to mention a fully stocked kitchen? Besides, this is cool stuff, Doc. This is like, you know . . . what the future is made of."

He sat back in his chair and regarded her with narrowed eyes. "I suppose the fact that you're sweet on my lab director doesn't enter into it."

Her cheeks went pink.

"Heck, no. I don't have to be here every day to get to Eugene."
She flashed him a blinding smile and popped out of her chair.
"Now, I'm going to go over to the lab and see what he thinks of
my being let go. Wanna watch?"

He followed Mini as far as the door to the lab where Eugene
was slaving over a computer model for the CAD/CAM interface. She went directly to his workstation and stood silently for a
moment, then moved just enough to make the fabric of her long
skirt rustle.

Eugene glanced up at her, his eyes focusing on something outside his head faster than Chuck had ever seen.

"Mini. Hi. I didn't know you were here."

"I'm just here to say good-bye, Euge. Doc Brenton just told me
he won't be needing me anymore for the program, so . . ." She
shrugged artlessly. "I guess I won't see you."

Euge's eyes were locked on hers with a stunned expression.
He'd known, of course, that her part of the program was going to
be terminated but, in true Eugene Pozniaki fashion, had apparently not considered the ramifications of that.

He glanced from Mini to the clock on the wall above his
lightboard. Almost one. "Look, I'm at a stopping point here.
Can you . . . that is, can we go get some lunch?"

She nodded, smiling. With her hands laced together in front
of her, her head tilted to one side, and her short hair haloing a
heart-shaped face, she managed to look pleasantly surprised by
the whole exchange she had just orchestrated. Chuck almost felt
sorry for Eugene. *Almost.*

Grinning, he turned and went back to his office. Minerva
Mause might be small, but she was clearly a force to be reckoned
with.

Chapter 5

LAB RATS

Matt loved to win. He had definitely won the battle to steer the neurokinetics program toward the commercially viable side. He could only shake his head at Chuck's wish list of disciplines for initial experimentation. Leave it to the academic to come up with impractical, feel-good choices. Of course looking at medical and mobility applications would make sense at some point, but medicine was a low-margin operation given that only well-funded teaching hospitals such as Johns Hopkins had the wherewithal to make substantial financial commitments. People covered by the Americans with Disabilities Act were underwritten by public funds that were at the mercy of the ballot box, which shivered every time the political winds changed. Besides which, the Food and Drug Administration was notorious in delaying approval, and delays were the last thing they needed.

Matt had his eyes on a cadre of investors that would be able to provide almost limitless funding and would enable Forward Kinetics to produce commercially viable applications for Chuck and Dice's co-invention, the Brenton-Kobayashi Kinetic Interface, or BKKI.

The Brenton component was a highly modified Brewster Brain Pattern Monitor—so modified, in fact, that Matt was already pursuing a patent on the unit. The CPU ran a program based on his conversion algorithm. Dice's input, in addition to continual work on the miniaturization of the monitor, was a lightweight transceiver system that linked the monitor to the mechanism it was intended to drive.

It was all coming together.

And now, after months of preparation, they were ready to begin working with their first round of subjects.

They were in the lab, getting ready for some field testing with the devices Dice and his select team of self-described minions had modified to take input from the BKKI, or Becky, as they insisted on calling it. In addition to Sara Crowell and Tim Desmond, there was a raw recruit named Mikhail Yenotov.

They were a study in diversity, Matt reflected as he watched them through the high window of the gallery, which gave their main lab the appearance of a huge operating theater. Sara was a tall, cool brunette in her thirties. No nonsense. Remote. Watchful, with high-intensity gray eyes. Matt understood that she used her privacy like a shield. *Understand? Hell, I practically invented that.* Like him, something in her past had hurt her, had gotten in somehow. Probably a relationship. Possibly a woman—Matt couldn't see her getting worked up over something as stupid as a man.

While Sara kept her private life to herself, the same could not be said for her opinions. Those she spread liberally, almost joyfully, like in those old experiments in which DDT was sprayed over swimming pools full of smiling children. A lot of those opinions were reserved for the male-dominated industry in which she worked. She had bumped up against the glass ceiling so many times it had given her a thicker skull, and she refused to even entertain ideas that she might not be as good as the boys, which she'd been hearing all her life, starting with her father. It was this constant battle that made her hard. But it also made her better.

Tim—or Troll, as he preferred to be called—was in his twenties. The guy was such an archetypal computer-gaming nerd that he made Dice and Eugene both look like high school jocks. He had that pale, damp mushroom complexion one associated with dimly lit computer grottos and game arcades. It went with his riot of thick, unevenly cut hair. His watery, colorless eyes reminded Matt of photos he'd seen in *Nat Geo* of bush babies or whatever those little big-eyed buggers were called. Troll spoke in monosyllables except when describing his latest creations or nattering about computer code with Dice or Eugene—or insulting someone. Even then most of what came out of his mouth was incomprehensible to half the listeners half the time.

And then there was Mike Yenotov. A meat-and-potatoes construction engineer in his early forties, he was straight up, straightforward, blunt, and quietly, mulishly stubborn. What he didn't understand he filed away with a blink of his brown eyes and a shrug that Matt took to mean, "I don't get it. I don't need to get it. If I need to get it, someone will just have to stop and explain it to me . . . and if they condescend to me, I'll leave—after punching them in the mouth." Mike was practical and knowledgeable about his craft—what he didn't know about heavy machinery could probably fit on the head of a very small pin—but seemingly little else.

Then there was Minerva. If Chuck thought he was being clever about sneaking her around like a pet mouse in his pocket to hide her continued involvement from his business partner, he was fooling himself. Matt knew Mini was still coming in after hours (if there really was such a thing in a place like this) and working with the interface. He let it happen as a way of throwing Chuck a bone after blackballing most of his list of applications. What made Chuck happy made Matt's life easier. He also wasn't sure how effectively a no would work on Mini. One, could he bring himself to say it to her face? Two, would she understand what no meant anyway? Naturally she would not get as much time on the equipment as the three official subjects, not by a long shot. But if it was enough time to make Chuck content, that would be all that was necessary.

In the event that Chuck demanded she have greater access (requested, rather, because it was hard to imagine Chuck Brenton demanding anything), Matt was prepared to offer her an official place in the program, but he had no intention of doing that voluntarily . . . and only as a last resort. Time with Becky was at a premium—they had only the one unit until Dice's team could assemble another—and Matt was determined not to waste any time on what he viewed as a frivolous pursuit.

Seeing Chuck enter the lab through the main doors below, Matt left the observation gallery and hurried down the stairs.

Leaving Chuck to steer the sessions alone was a bad idea.

THERE'S AN OLD APHORISM ABOUT being happy as a clam. Chuck had no idea what clams had to be happy about, only that they lacked the neural mechanisms to be unhappy about anything. Nonetheless, he was, he decided, happy as that proverbial clam when he rolled into the lab on the first morning of official experimentation with the new Brenton-Kobayashi Kinetic Interface.

Because up until today, the subjects had been working with Dice's Roboticus, learning to steer it smoothly about the lab. And while that was exciting to see, now they'd begin working within their own disciplines.

One step closer.

There were two arenas of experimentation set up in different sections of the large laboratory. One involved a powerful computer system that was outfitted with both Sara's CAD software and Tim's programming package; the other required a scale model of a backhoe that had been placed in a ten-by-ten-foot container, three feet deep in sand.

Despite his being the rookie, the experiments started with Mike Yenotov, figuring that his discipline was closest in nature to driving Roboticus, which he had proved apt at. Sara was slated for the next day and Tim for the day after that.

Mike's first session went about as well as hoped. The kinetic converter functioned flawlessly, capturing his brain waves as he envisioned himself controlling the model backhoe and translating them into energy and force that Becky could use to manipulate the machine's modified mechanisms.

The backhoe was joystick operated, just like Roboticus, and after about a half hour of getting used to the model's controls, Mike was almost making it dance as it dug a hole in the lab's sandbox.

"I gotta tell you," he said, his voice betraying just a hint of New Jersey, "this is bonehead simple. I'm thinking one guy could operate a team of hoes and watch what each one is doing from the most useful POV. Viewpoint, I mean," he added. "Think of it: if I don't gotta be in the cab, I don't need a spotter tellin' me about depth and dimensions. I can be checkin' that stuff myself."

Chuck did think of it, and the prospect excited him. It hadn't occurred to him until just that moment that the most useful POV, as Mike had put it, wasn't always the first-person one. Dice, meanwhile, was almost dancing at the prospect of combining the Forward Kinetics system with the VR piece—a virtual reality component he intended to meld with the neural net.

"Just think of the possibilities," he enthused at the end of the day as they assessed their work with Mike. "The construction guy or the firefighter or the security guard now has a choice—look at the environment from inside the remote mechanism or look at it from the external viewpoint. All at the speed of thought."

Chuck was thinking of the possibilities, even as he looked ahead to pairing Sara Crowell with her CAD software for the first time. Because although he was optimistic based on Mike's performance, he couldn't help but be cautious, too. There were bound to be differences between operating a purely mechanical device—even one with onboard computer assist, like Mike did—and operating software. One was solid, logical; it was obvious how the parts all moved and fit together. The other was ethereal, abstract. It relied on code to call it into existence. Chuck expected it would be a challenge to operate the intangible.

He'd said as much aloud when he, Dice, and Matt were alone in the conference room at the end of the debriefing session. Matt looked at him in a way that made Chuck feel as if he'd somehow turned plain old English into something untranslatable. "I don't foresee any problems, Chuck. You're such a damn worrywart. Clearly if they've driven the robot, they can run other machinery." He got up, took a last drink of soda, tossed the can into the recycle bin, and left the room.

Dice raised his eyebrows then afforded Chuck a rueful grimace. "Sometimes I wonder what color the sky is in Matt World. He occasionally has trouble understanding that one equation does not fit all."

That's not his only problem, Chuck thought. Chuck sensed this was an ongoing debate between Matt and his engineer—in a series of ongoing debates Matt had with pretty much every person he ever encountered.

And he couldn't help feel that he wasn't sure whether he was looking forward to Sara's session or dreading it now.

CHUCK SEATED SARA WHERE SHE could see the large, flat-screen display of the computer but not reach the mouse, keyboard, or track pad. The kinetic interface was wired to the USB port of the machine, and Sara's familiar software was running.

"What do I do?" she asked. Her excitement was not evident in her voice. Chuck could only see it in glimmers in her eyes.

"Something drop-dead easy," said Matt. "Something you do almost without thinking about it. Only this time think. What would you normally do when you first sit down at the keyboard?"

"I'd open a project file or create a new one."

"Okay, so try that. Think about what moves you make to create a new file."

Grasping the arms of her chair, Sara gazed intently at the machine. There was a long moment of silence in which absolutely nothing happened.

"What are you trying to do?" Chuck asked.

"Move the mouse. I'm imagining my hand moving the mouse to the 'file' menu."

"I don't think that's gonna work," said Dice. "That would require physically touching the mouse. It's the sensors in the mouse themselves that need to be affected."

Sara glanced over at him where he sat on the edge of a work-table. "But I don't understand the mechanics of that."

Chuck chewed the cap of his pen. "Try a different input. The track pad or keyboard maybe."

Sara nodded, took a deep breath, and shifted her gaze back to the computer. Her eyes narrowed, her lips compressed, and a fine dew broke out on her upper lip. On the computer screen, the mouse pointer shifted in a wobbly upward crawl.

The room erupted in cheers and laughter.

"I told you," Matt said.

You'd think we ended world hunger, Chuck thought. But he was laughing, too, with the sheer adrenaline rush of seeing even such meager success. Because he could see a future where they might just do something equal to that.

It was Dice who brought them back to the present. "What did you do?" he asked. "How did you make that work?"

"I imagined I was touching the track pad. Or that I was drawing a line across the contacts. That I understand. Let me see what else I can do."

What she could do, she discovered, was move the pointer up to the menu bar by mentally scraping the same spot on the track pad over and over. Doing that, it took her several minutes to get the pointer to the "file" menu, but she did it.

But once there, she hit a roadblock.

"I'm not sure how to click." Her voice was edgy with impatience.

"How would you do it normally?" Chuck asked.

"I'd tap." She demonstrated on the arm of her chair. "But I'm not sure . . ." She peered at the track pad again, tapping several times on the chair arm.

Nothing happened.

Chuck was about to suggest she take a break when she growled in frustration, grasped the arms of the chair, and blinked.

The "file" menu flew open.

After a moment in which everyone in the room took a deep breath, Sara snaked the pointer down to the "new" command, gritted her teeth, gripped the chair arms, and blinked again. A new file opened.

There was much celebration.

However, it was the last celebrating they did that day. While Sara could shakily use the track pad to move the pointer, open menus, and click buttons—though she could even type using a mental map of where the letters were on the keyboard—she could not use the higher functions of the software. Nor could she draw a damned thing freehand and place it in the workspace.

"The problem is the user interface," she told the team later when they paused in momentary defeat. She ran a weary hand through her dark, collar-length hair, mussing its usually sleek texture. "I have to concentrate so hard on triggering the track pad that I can't focus on what I'm producing. The moment I take my attention off the pad and think about the workspace, I lose control of the mechanics. And, well, frankly I can't think of a way around that."

"We've got to think of a way around it," growled Matt. "There's no reason this device would work for Mike and not work for you—unless it's your lack of computer savvy that's the issue."

Chuck winced at that.

"My computer savvy is just fine, thank you," said Sara coolly. "What I don't know about that software and my work you could stick up your cute little button nose and still have room for the Washington Monument."

"I think we should quit for the day," said Chuck, flipping his laptop shut to underscore the point. "Let the subconscious work on the problem. It never fails that when I hit a wall and sleep on it, I've got some piece of the solution by morning."

Sara nodded.

Matt sighed and rolled his eyes. "You'll have to forgive Chuck," he told the group. "He still believes the science angels visit him in his dreams."

Chuck shook his head. "I didn't say anything about angels," he said quietly.

"And you'll have to forgive Matt—he still believes he knows what a normal interaction between people is," Dice said. Chuck smiled, but Matt wouldn't let it go.

"You do believe in angels, right? Being a religious type and all.

Do you think God will visit you with a vision of how to solve our little interface problem?"

Where's he going with this? He almost seems angry. For a nonreligious person, he sure has his crusades.

"Actually," said Eugene, hoping to defuse the situation, "they're more like science fairies. Or elves of invention maybe."

Sara gave Matt a frosty smile. "I think maybe Chuck's right. Happens to me all the time. A design is intractable, impenetrable, unworkable. I go to bed whacking my head against the wall and wake up and realize there's a gate hidden behind some ivy. Don't mock the elves of invention, Dr. Streegman. They work."

Chapter 6

ELVES OF INVENTION

This time the elves of invention didn't work. Not fairies or angels or elfish intercessors or even Elvis himself visited any member of the Forward Kinetics team overnight, and when they began their day's work with Sara back in the harness and Tim the Troll postponed until the afternoon, little had changed.

Matt's look said it all: *I told you so.*

As if we did this to him on purpose, Chuck thought. Despite that resentment, he couldn't help feeling frustrated, too.

Certainly Sara's skills with the basic maneuvers were slightly smoother, but she still had no clue how to manage the simplest activities within an interface she knew inside and out. She could move the mechanisms. What she could not do was create objects.

They worked at it all morning. Just before lunch she suggested she go back to working with Roboticus for a while. That sabbatical relaxed her and renewed her confidence.

Unfortunately, it did little for her performance with the software she used every day.

By 2:20 P.M., the time Tim Desmond chose to stroll in late, Sara was sagging in her chair, the neural net twinkling like stars in her hair, while the others tried to assess the situation.

"It's clear that the kinetic converter is working," said Matt tersely. "And that the subject's brain waves are generating sufficient triggers to drive it. The problem has to be the warmware."

Sara shot him a sideways glance. "Meaning me, right?" She shook her head. "Maybe it's because I don't understand the computer side of the equation. I only understand the computer *operator's* side. You're asking me to direct the computer's internal processes, but I don't understand them well enough. If that's how your interface is supposed to work, then even someone with my experience and training won't be able to use it. That's not a warmware problem, Dr. Streegman. It's a technology problem. *Your* technology problem."

Matt opened his mouth to reply, but thankfully Tim forestalled whatever he'd been about to say.

"So how've you been doing what you've been doing so far?" the programmer asked. Hands in the pockets of his blazer, he lounged against a nearby worktable.

Sara explained her work with triggering the track pad and keyboard and how she lost it every time she pulled her attention away to consider the workspace.

Tim wandered over to the test machine and wiggled the mouse. The pointer did a wild jig on the screen. "So you've been interacting with the input devices and trying to use them to make stuff happen."

"That's what I just said, isn't it?"

Chuck winced. He hated it when people got short with each other, and there had been a lot of that this day.

"Okay, so that's what you've done," said Tim. "What've you been trying to do?"

Sara made a frustrated gesture at the computer. "Draw a damn cube. A stupid, simple, three-dimensional object. I can't manipulate the input devices the way I normally would to create it."

Tim shrugged. "Then don't manipulate the input devices. Manipulate the input. Use the Force, Luke."

Sara blinked at him, her face going red. "What?"

"Didn't you ever see *Star Wars*? Use the Force. Obi Wan Kenobi says that to Luke Skywalker when he's trying to save the day, and he shuts down his onboard computer interface and just shoots. Bam! One dead Death Star. A little too easy, if you ask me."

Sara glared at him. "You've got to be kidding me. This isn't a movie, Troll Boy. I am not shooting swamp rats or vampire squirrels or whatever it was Luke was taking potshots at on Tatooine."

While Tim congratulated Sara on knowing what Tatooine was, Chuck stared at the wide, flat computer display and had a quiet epiphany . . . or a gift from the elves of invention. "No, Sara, he's right."

"What?" Sara said.

"What?" Matt said.

"Told you," Troll said, although it was clear he didn't know what he was right about.

But Chuck did. "I'm serious. Don't think about manipulating the interface. That's not what you want to do. Just *draw* something. There's a CAD/CAM in your head. Use it."

"What?" Sara said again, and everyone else in the room—except for Tim—stared at him as if he'd spoken in Swahili.

Chuck took a deep breath. "I know it sounds crazy, but trust me. Think of it this way: Before you interact with the physical interface of your CADware, you form a mental model of an object. You instinctively draw the thing in your head a split second before you draw it on the screen. I think what Tim is saying is that you don't want to interact with an input device at all. You want to interact with the software directly." He glanced at the programmer, who shrugged.

"Yeah. I guess that's what I'm saying. Make the thing in your head, and let the software interpret those impulses instead of using the track pad as a go-between."

Sara let out a breath of pent-up air. She thought about it, calculating—if Chuck had to guess—whether or not Tim was trying to pull a fast one on her. But Chuck gave her an encouraging nod, and she nodded back. "A go-between. Sure. Sure, why not?" She straightened in her seat. "Am I up and running, Euge?"

Eugene checked the machinery. "You're online."

She took a deep breath, grasped the arms of her chair, and closed her eyes.

The others all watched her at first—the play of tension and release on her face, the furrowed brows, the subtle twitches of her fingers. They watched her until Tim said, "That's what I'm talking about."

The spell broken, Chuck jerked his head around to look at the large display monitor. A cube was coming into being there, growing in size. When it stopped growing, it rotated slowly on one corner, stopped, and diminished in size.

Sara's eyes opened, the light in them fierce. "How's that for using the Force?"

Tim strolled over and held up a fist. "Good work, Padawan."

She laughed—more emotion than Chuck had ever seen her display—and joined the programmer in a fist bump.

"What do you mean *Padawan*, Troll Boy? I'm a freakin' Jedi!"

IF SARA CROWELL WAS A Jedi, Troll Desmond was a Jedi Master. Attached to Becky, with lights sparkling through his spiky hair, he was ultimately, after several days of work, able to make the CPU jump through hoops. And he discovered a variety of ways to do it.

Matt was particularly interested in the programmer's manipulation of what was under the hood: binary. Numbers. Mathematics. Troll could reach down into the stream of ones and zeroes and pull the strings that made them dance. He drew directly to the computer display, graduating swiftly from smiley faces to words to opening higher-level programming modules and coding.

He was not fast at first, something that frustrated him greatly—and Troll was a sight to behold when frustrated—but he did it. He spent long hours doing it. Then he moved on to manipulating even higher-level programming languages and from there to the graphics software he used to create gaming environments.

At that point, Sara, who insisted on being in the lab whenever Troll was—to keep an eye on him, she said—began to kibitz.

"I know this software package," she said the first time he fired up his 3-D graphics program. "I use it to create settings for some of the architectural work I do."

They compared notes and traded places under the neural net. She taught him to run her CAD system. He taught her how to raise buildings from the virtual ground and play first-person RPGs.

He stopped calling her Padawan; she stopped calling him Troll Boy.

As an aside, Chuck said to Matt, "Look, we've succeeded at something already. Here are two people who seem on the surface to have nothing in common. Two people who had been antagonistic toward each other at the beginning of it all."

Matt agreed with Chuck's assessment but not his understatement. Sara had thought Troll was thick; Troll had thought Sara was a bitch.

"They may never be soul mates, but they're already team-mates," Chuck went on.

Matt tried not to sigh. *Leave it to my "teammate" to focus on the people, not the results.*

Chapter 7

ELVES OF INVESTING

"What we need," Matt said, "is investment money. A lot of it. More than I can marshal." He looked over at Chuck, who sat at the far end of the worktable, tapping away at his laptop, his brow knit in a way that suggested one of his EEG plots had just started to talk to him in a language he didn't understand.

"Did you hear me?"

Chuck flicked a glance his way. "Uh . . . uh-huh. But I thought you said Becky was going to turn a profit by the end of the year."

"It is. The problem is while we can make a marginal profit building one-off units, we can't go into production on them anytime soon. And building them one-off is soaking up all of Dice's time and energy. I need him to get out of the fabrication business and back into the design end, where he belongs. We need the material resources to build a small manufacturing facility."

Chuck sat back from his computer keyboard and considered that. "Yeah. That was what we'd discussed going into the subfloor."

Matt shook his head. "We can't afford it, though. Not the way we're going. It's time to try to stir up some interest. Give some presentations, approach some investors."

"What kind of investors?"

"Ones with money."

Chuck rolled his eyes. "I mean who—"

"Not as important as the *what*," Matt interrupted. "All those other disciplines we targeted that we couldn't take on . . . If we had the right investors, you could expand your research. Bring Mini into the program officially, maybe."

Chuck's eyes kindled. "Well, I'm all for that. I'm glad one of us has a brain for business. I wonder what sort of waves yours generates."

Chuck threw Matt a lopsided grin and went back to whatever it was he was doing, which suited Matt just fine. He hated having to explain things to people. Hated having to account for his actions and thoughts. Hated having to dumb things down.

Not that Chuck was dumb—he wasn't. He was a brilliant neuroscientist, but he really understood nothing at all about economics or business or cash flow. He was an academic. In Chuck's experience, money was something you wrote a grant for, not something you had to earn by offering a return on investment. Matt had some ideas about that and had already set processes in motion to get what Forward Kinetics needed to succeed beyond Dr. Chuck's wildest dreams.

He glanced at his watch. In fact he needed to go check up on one of those processes right now. He got up from the worktable and tucked his iPad under his arm.

"Gotta run. I've got an appointment off campus. See you this afternoon."

"Oh, sure. We've got Tim—Troll in the shop later today. He's going to be trying out Dice's new VR helm."

"I'll be there," Matt promised.

He definitely would. That virtual reality helm, which Dice

had worked hard to integrate with the neural sensor net, would be of paramount importance to the direction in which he was planning to take Forward Kinetics in the next year.

"DR. STREEGMAN? I'M CHEN LANFEN."

The young woman who approached his table in the sunny courtyard of the Café Clatch Bistro could have been Emma Peel in a previous life, if Emma Peel had been Chinese. She was unusually tall for an Asian woman, dressed in black skinny jeans and a black turtleneck sweater. Her shoulder-length hair was black as well, which gave her a vaguely gothy look—except that her skin was an even shade of gold, and she appeared to be wearing little or no makeup. She was striking.

But she wasn't Lucy.

"So," Matt said, standing to take her proffered hand and shaking it, "you're Shifu Chu's star pupil."

She smiled. "Is that what he said?" she asked in barely accented English.

"Well, it's what I asked for when I called him. I said, 'Send me your star. Your best and brightest.'"

The smile deepened, and she sat down at the small, round table and nodded toward the server, who was making his way toward them. "Well, if you're going to flatter me that way, Dr. Streegman, then I really ought to buy you a latte."

"Call me Matt, and I'll have a large cappuccino." This last part he delivered to the waitress, who'd just arrived at the table.

The girl favored him with a nod, then glanced at the woman with him. "And you, miss?"

"Soy latte, please. Triple shot."

The waitress headed into the shop to fetch their order, and Matt seated himself, setting his iPad on the table.

"So," he said, "Chen Lanfen. Which is your surname?"

"Chen. I maintain the traditions of my very proper family, so please call me Lanfen."

"Of course."

"Thanks. Master Chu said you have some sort of technology you want me to test?" She spread her hands questioningly. "I can't even imagine what that might be—or how I'll be of help."

"Robotics. Specifically a line of humanoid robots that might be used for security work."

She shook her head. "Using kung fu?"

"Let me begin at the beginning, and all will be made clear," Matt told her, opening his iPad and starting up the recruitment slide show he'd created. "I'm the COO of a unique technology company called Forward Kinetics . . ."

CHUCK WAS ONLY VAGUELY AWARE of Matt's leaving the small ancillary lab. It had become their favorite place to collate data, and they often inhabited it together in companionable silence as they analyzed their various collections of information. Chuck rather enjoyed that. It made him feel as if they were on the same wavelength, though Matt seemed to deal chiefly with financial numbers these days while Chuck pored over EEG charts.

He was surprised to think that he actually missed Matt.

He didn't dwell on it, though, so focused was he on a new set of charts. The ones he was looking at now were, in a word, baffling. All of the subjects, but especially Sara, had been experiencing more and more frequent spikes of gamma waves. This latest session, in fact, showed not just spikes but several sustained spikes that lasted for roughly thirty seconds each.

Chuck tugged at his lower lip. What did that mean?

Of course biologically it meant she was in several different states at once or juggling states so swiftly it was effectively the same thing. But what did that mean to her mental state?

He knew from postsession interviews how exhausted she and her cohorts were by the end of an experiment. The data he was looking at now, from the session they'd had yesterday, reflected a particularly exhausting set of tests. Sara had commented on it. Mike had also shown a couple of fifteen- and twenty-second gamma peaks and had retreated into an uncharacteristic taciturn state. Tim . . . well, Tim was always aloof and moody. Even with that established, though, at the end of his session yesterday afternoon he had drunk three cans of Pepsi in quick succession rather than the usual two.

Which means . . .

He just didn't know.

"You look unhappy."

Chuck glanced up to find Dice standing in the doorway, regarding him quizzically over the rim of his coffee cup.

"Not unhappy. Not at all. Just . . . puzzled. Concerned, maybe."

"Concerned about what?" Dice wandered farther into the small lab and over to where Chuck pondered what was on his laptop's broad display.

Chuck gestured at the screen. "That's Sara's last session with the CAD/CAM."

"Uh-huh. What concerns you about it?"

"This here. This long gamma pattern."

"That's where the brain is playing a concert, right?"

Chuck smiled. "Good metaphor. Yes."

"So what was she doing during that time?"

Chuck popped up a second window that showed what had been happening in the CAD program during the prolonged gamma burst. She had been doing detail work apparently, creating and placing landscape elements for the exterior of a building.

Dice glanced back and forth between the EEG and the video of Sara's architectural project. "I see. She's doing creative work."

"She's always doing creative work."

"No, I mean she's designing as opposed to simply placing design elements. She's designing the garden area."

Chuck reran the sequence, watching for what Dice meant. He opened a third window that showed what had been happening on the subject's face as she was experiencing the gamma waves.

"Heh. Sara Cam," said Dice. "There, see? Watch her eyes. I know that look. That is the look of someone who is concentrating very hard on a pattern problem."

"A pattern problem," repeated Chuck.

"She's thinking about the shape the garden will take. The same way I might think about the shape a robotic arm would need to take in order to fulfill different uses. Make sense?"

Chuck frowned, knowing Dice was onto something, but he still wasn't sure what.

And then it clicked.

"Yes!"

"Chuck?"

"It makes perfect sense. And it explains the data I was getting from the cellist I had in a while back. She went into gamma when she was beginning to interpret a piece she was still sight reading. What you're telling me suggests we're seeing gamma bursts from our subjects when they're molding original content."

"Yeah. I guess you could put it that way."

"How would you put it?"

"I'd say they're investing themselves in it, I guess."

That is *a good way to put it*. Chuck nodded. "Which might explain why Sara has seemed especially tired after a session in which she's produced a lot of gamma rhythms. But here's what I'm wondering: These gamma fugues are growing in duration. Are they dangerous? Are they harmful to the subject?"

Dice shrugged. "I have to assume a lot of people experience

them. Especially creative people—musicians, writers, painters. Are those people more likely to be, I don't know, unstable than your average bank teller or factory worker?"

Chuck stared at the engineer, his mind filling up with the data from decades of research into mood disorders. Kay Redfield Jamison had written several volumes about it. One of them came to mind now, a historical retrospective on the link between creativity and mood disorders. *Touched with Fire,* she'd titled it.

Chuck Brenton briefly contemplated the possibility that the course of experimentation they were pursuing might be pouring gasoline on neurological flames . . . and it worried him.

MATT, ON THE OTHER HAND, couldn't have been more excited about the direction the company was going in. With his new recruit tentatively on board, Matt moved to the next part of his plan to put Forward Kinetics on the road to real success. He had contacts at MIT who could help him with that—people who could suggest where he and/or Chuck might speak or present to garner attention and backers for their enterprise. A TED conference was a real possibility for Chuck. He could wax poetic about the strides that could be made in medicine. Get an audience to empathize with a quadriplegic who could use the technology to manipulate his or her environment.

Matt, on the other hand, would represent the company to those whose interests were more about commercial applications and ROI and less about warm fuzzies. Both polarities, he knew, could be exploited to take Forward Kinetics from science fiction to science fact—from a small-scale entrepreneurial shop to a large-scale commercial powerhouse.

It's why he hadn't dismissed the warm fuzzies out of hand.

The third stage of his plan was to get Forward Kinetics' tech out in front of an assemblage of potential backers. With that in mind, he registered the company for a major robotics trade show that was months away.

He did this work from his apartment, leery of being overheard. He guarded his business plans as a writer might guard an unfinished manuscript; there were few things more annoying than having someone peeking over his shoulder. Also, if he was being honest with himself, he knew Chuck would object. Better to ask for forgiveness . . . no, screw that. Better to be right, and let others catch up to him when they finally realize it.

By the time he walked into the afternoon meeting at their corporate HQ, he had set in motion a sequence of events that would crescendo at that April trade show. After the meeting he would contact a design house that specialized in fabricating eye-catching booths for such events. He already had a series of sketches he'd made for a two-story megabooth; it would sit in a corner and incorporate three separate stage areas on the ground floor, with two small conference rooms upstairs . . .

"Hello? Earth to Dr. Streegman."

Matt looked up from his booth doodles to find Dice staring at him pointedly.

"Sorry?"

"Chuck just asked if you have anything to bring to the table."

Matt hesitated. He was actually quite full of news, but now, glancing around at the others, he wasn't sure how much he wanted to share. *Well, it can't hurt to float a trial balloon.*

"Actually I've spent the morning putting some plans into action. I've scheduled several presentations of our technology with regional business organizations, submitted a proposal for a TED Talk, and registered us for the Applied Robotics conference in April."

Chuck gaped at him. "You did *what*?"

"Holy mother of pearl," murmured Eugene. "D'you think we'll be ready for that?"

"Why not?" Dice challenged him.

"Exactly," Matt agreed. "Why not? The presentations are easy. The TED Talk, too. We can use video for some of that. Although for the TED conference, if we can present a live demonstration, maybe using Sara or Troll, that would be best. By the time the AR conference rolls around . . . well, we'll just need to make sure we're ready. But there's no reason to think we won't be." He shrugged. "Of course all of this may be academic, since acceptance isn't guaranteed."

A little white lie—it was true they *might* not have been accepted. They didn't need to know that they were *already* accepted for both because Matt had clout in some quarters and knew how to exercise it. As the group continued to voice their concerns, Matt took up his pen and continued his doodle.

Chapter 8

LIGHTNING

"This gamma burst is almost a minute in length!" Matt stood in the doorway of the main lab, his iPad in one hand and a cup of orange juice in the other.

Chuck, Dice, and Mike were in bay three, setting Mike up for a session with Dice's new Wi-Fi system. Chuck was adjusting the neural net over the engineer's head but stopped and looked up, the focused expression on his face clearing like a morning fog.

"That the data from Mike's last session?" Chuck asked. "Interesting, isn't it?"

"Thank you, Mr. Spock. Yes, it is interesting. It's more than interesting. But what does it mean?"

"You know what it means. It means they're—"

"Yeah, yeah. They're double- and triple-tasking. I get that. But the bursts are growing longer. Hell, they're not even bursts any-more, Chuck. They're full-blown states."

"Yes. They are," Mike said, awe mixing with pride.

Chuck made a final adjustment and turned to face his partner, jamming his hands deep into the pockets of the white lab coat he insisted on wearing. "I think what we're seeing is like muscle memory. I think their brains are becoming more effective and efficient at working this way."

Matt stared at him, aware suddenly of the beating of his own heart. "You mean they're building mental muscles?"

"That's what I'm thinking, yes. It's like any other skill. Take skiing or playing tennis, for example. You may be awkward and slow when you start out, you may tire easily, but if you keep doing what you're doing, you get better. You develop the muscles appropriate to the activity, and you learn how to use them most effectively."

"So what we're seeing here is . . . evolution on a micro scale."

Chuck flashed a winsome smile. "Yes! Exciting, isn't it? I mean we know that the human brain is plastic, adaptable. But just how adaptable, we're only now discovering."

Matt came farther into the lab, looking at Mike a little differently now. "To be clear, what we're doing here is creating an evolutionary imperative."

"Well, I wouldn't call it an imperative. More like an evolutionary opportunity."

"An evolutionary opportunity. Can I quote you on that, Doc?"

"Sure. Why not? But if anyone laughs, tell them it was Dice's idea."

Dice snorted and stood up from where he'd been tinkering with Roboticus's Wi-Fi transceiver. "We're ready to give it a try. You all set, Mike?"

"Yeah. Can't you see me flexing my brain muscles?"

Dice smiled and glanced at Matt. "You got a moment to watch the maiden voyage of the Wi-Fi interface?"

"Sorry, no. I have to go write a speech."

"AND THAT, LADIES AND GENTLEMEN, is perhaps the most exciting thing about our research: the subjects we are working with on a frequent basis are rewriting their own internal software. They are, in essence, taking advantage of an evolutionary opportunity afforded them by the Brenton-Kobayashi Kinetic Interface. And as they do, we've discovered one other thing: the possibilities are endless."

Matt wrapped up his talk to thunderous applause, after which he did some Q and A. Mostly the questions were about real-world applications, which he was more than happy to provide. Here Matt was careful to speak his audience's language. He was courting a mixed group of politicians and businessmen, with a handful of medical professionals who worked for a medical equipment manufacturer thrown in. That audience required a broad-based approach that made use of some of Chuck's favorite words: *transcend, surmount,* and *quality of life.*

"Imagine," Matt told one manufacturer of printed circuitry, "that you have an employee—a highly skilled, well-trained employee—whose job is to design PC boards. That employee suffers a broken finger. Your normal course of action in that case might be to put the employee on disability, right?"

The man nodded.

Matt walked to the whiteboard that was set up behind him in the hotel ballroom and wrote "short-term disability."

"Okay, and you'd have to put someone else in the position, meaning you'd have to hire and train another CAD/CAM operator, yes?"

"Yes."

Matt wrote "hire and train" on the board.

"And while that person is coming up to speed, is he or she going to be as productive as the original designer?"

"Hell no."

Matt wrote "lost productivity" beneath the other notations.

"What about the quality of their work? Is that going to be up to par?"

"No."

Now others were shaking their heads.

Matt turned back to the board and wrote "increased quality-assurance hours."

"So all in all, you're looking at a pretty costly situation. What does it cost to hire and train these days?"

"Pretty close to ten grand for that level of employee," said the manufacturer.

"Ten grand," Matt repeated. "Per employee." He capped the marker. "Now let's imagine that the same injury befalls someone trained to work with the CAD/CAM machine through Becky. That employee could return to work almost immediately. Heck, they could even lie down on the job if they needed to. As long as they could see their workspace using our patented kinetic converter, they could continue to output designs or finished product. No need to hire and train anybody to take their place. No need for them to avail themselves of disability insurance, thus cutting their paycheck. No need for their quality to fall off, thus creating more work for your QA teams and more rework for them or another employee."

"I'd like to see this in action," said one older gentleman with a ramrod-straight bearing that spoke of the military.

"Absolutely. We'll be demonstrating our technology at the Applied Robotics show coming up this spring. If you aren't going to be there, or if you would like a preview, let me know, and I'll arrange a visit to the lab."

As it turned out, he did end up scheduling a walk-through for the older guy, who was, he learned, an ex-marine by the name of

Leighton Howard. He did it on a day when Chuck was off doing a gig of his own, and Eugene and Dice were running the lab.

And he did it close to quitting time, too, so that after Howard was impressed by Sara and Mike, he could be equally dazzled by Chen Lanfen.

FOR CHEN LANFEN, KUNG FU was more than a workout routine, more than a means of self-defense, even more than a martial art form. It was a whole body and spirit meditation, for she understood the words *kung fu* as much in their original meaning of "work" or "accomplishment" as she did their later application, which referred to a particular set of martial arts. When she'd first undertaken learning kung fu, she had also sought to master the highly ritualized Fujian tea ceremony, kung fu cha. She used the principles of kung fu in Chinese calligraphy, in cooking, in music. She wrote the odd line of poetry, too, but did not feel she rose to the level of kung fu there. Hard work, maybe, but not much achievement.

Her initial work with the device Matt called Becky had been awkward. Martial arts required a free flow of energies through the body and a free flow of the body through space. That had not been possible wearing a crown of transceivers and twinkly lights, and she had immediately gotten out of the meditative state required for her discipline and into a stormy mental funk.

Then Matt's assistant, Dice, had presented her with a Wi-Fi alternative to the fiber-optic cable and linked her to the funny robot that had become an extension of her will.

She'd started work with Roboticus like everyone else, pushing him hither and yon with her brain waves, making him twist and turn, spin and zigzag. Once she had perfected that, though, Dice had built her a different sort of robot, one that not so subtly reminded her of the battle droids in the Star Wars movies. It was three feet long and vaguely football shaped, with four legs that could pivot a full 360 on their joints. The feet were about the size of a man's hand and curved along the bottoms, which had rubber soles. Because of these feet—and the gyroscopic mechanisms at either end of the football—the bot was incredibly well balanced. If Lanfen could balance herself on one foot, Pigskin—as she started calling it—could do likewise.

She was working through a series of simple exercises with the robot—step, kick; step, tiger-claw strike—when Matt came into her practice area with an older fellow whose thick white hair reminded her of soft-serve ice cream. She hesitated in the middle of a move, and the bot keeled over, its native programming taking control to draw in its appendages and put it into sleep mode.

Matt frowned at it. "Keep practicing, Lanfen. I'd like Mr. Howard to see what you've been doing."

She said nothing about the fact that it was their interruption that had stopped her practice in the first place, and she did as requested, settling back into a horse stance as Matt turned to his companion and began a running narrative. Lanfen tracked them peripherally as she put the bot through a series of moves that echoed her own.

"Ms. Chen is a black-belt-level kung fu practitioner. She's a native of Shanghai. Began learning martial arts there. As you can see, the robot she's manipulating is only marginally humanoid. But it has arms and legs, so she can make it echo her movements through the BKKI."

"Does she have to do all that herself?" the older man asked, gesturing at Lanfen.

"Ideally no." Matt turned to look at her. "Lanfen, can you drill the bot without moving?"

She stopped in midkick and planted both feet firmly on the practice mat. Then she bowed to the bot, which bowed in return, tucking its front limbs up around its elongated middle. She had never done it this way—using just her mind—but she had listened to Dice talk about the others' experiences and felt it wouldn't take much to figure it out.

At first, nothing happened. But as she concentrated, Pigskin began to exercise a series of odd backflips, tipping backward until it could balance on its arms, then flinging its legs and torso over to repeat the movement.

It looked like a clumsy Slinky made of oversize bicycle-chain links, but Lanfen's confidence in the robot's performance—meaning *her* performance—was all she needed. When it reached the far wall of the lab, she had it rise up and execute a sequence of kicks, blocks, and turns, her muscles tightening and loosening in time with the robot though she stayed as still as she could.

When she'd done that, she let the bot revert to its normal pill-bug behavior and turned to the watching men.

White Hair was nodding. "Let me ask you, young lady: does the shape of the robot offer any particular challenges?"

Interesting question, she thought, to which she had an immediate answer. "Yes. I realized how important my head is to the art only when I tried to balance a headless mechanism the first time. Also the fact that its torso is solid and doesn't bend limits the range of movement significantly. Still, I imagine if you had a team of these metal puppies guarding something, they could be quite imposing."

"Guard dogs?" he mused.

"Of course," said Matt. "And guard dogs that can't be bought off for the price of a steak with tranquilizers in it."

"Yes, but could you make them bulletproof?"

"To a great extent," Matt told him. "The materials they might be made of are pretty broad."

"Very interesting, Dr. Streegman. I shall most certainly relate the impressive nature of this demonstration to my associates."

"That's all I ask, Mr. Howard."

The two men left the lab, Matt favoring Lanfen with a wink and a smile on the way out. She felt good. She was an unofficial member of the Forward Kinetics team, but if she could help generate funding, she might become official all the sooner, which meant more time training with the robots.

And what girl wouldn't want to spar with R2-D2?

SARA CROWELL WAS A PRODIGY. Since her "use the Force" breakthrough, she had sailed ahead of the rest of the team in the sheer ease with which she'd learned to work with Becky. In fact, she had expanded beyond the CAD/CAM program to manipulating software programs in general. Tim could do likewise, but Sara's use of the kinetic interface seemed effortless by comparison. She had surpassed the Jedi Master and was now capable of ease and speed that neither Tim nor Mike could demonstrate.

She was also, Chuck noted, able to do simple things like open and close programs and set up her workspace with her attention half on other things: a conversation, note taking, watching another subject work.

Tim, on the other hand, could move mountains (literally, in the case of the software he used to build strange alien worlds for his video games), but he had to concentrate every ounce of himself on the task at hand. Distracting him derailed his train of thought, which brought on a fit of dark sulks.

It's as if Sara is a fine-tuned athlete, used to using multiple muscles in harmony to execute a particular skill, while Tim is a power lifter, only able to handle one—albeit substantial—task at a time.

Chuck realized this was the only time Troll would ever be compared to a power lifter. Either way, it was impressive to watch both of them work.

Sara was in the lab one day, under Eugene's and Chuck's

watchful eyes, as she ran through the demonstration she was prepping for the Applied Robotics conference. It was as impressive as all get-out, Chuck thought. She started with the easy stuff—opening a new file, setting up the workspace, and launching into a whiz-bang, lightning-fast demonstration of design at the speed of thought. Buildings grew up out of the digital ground like time-lapse crystals; trees and shrubs slid into place as bright, wire-frame skeletons and gained texture and color as if sentient paint flowed over them.

It was a potent demonstration, made all the more extraordinary by the fact that Sara was no longer connected to her computer by strands of fiber-optic cable. With the neural net, she was free to stand, pace the room, stare out a window—whatever would aid the creative processes going on in her nimble brain.

Chuck found himself laughing with exhilaration as she put the final touches on her casually constructed masterpiece.

"You know," said Eugene wryly, "some people are going to think they're being hoaxed. They're going to think this stuff is all preprogrammed or that someone is doing this offstage."

Chuck's laughter died in his throat, and he turned to look at his lab director. "That never even occurred to me." He thought about it some more. "This is a huge problem. How can we prove it's real?"

Euge watched Sara fly through rendering and saving her file. "Well, what if we took requests?"

"Requests?"

"Eugene," said Sara, "you're a genius." Chuck noticed that even as she talked, the computer continued to be manipulated. *Impressive.*

"He's right, Doc," she was saying. "If there are any Doubting Thomases in the crowd, we can ask them to propose tests of their own devising. I'm up for it. It doesn't have to be architectural, either. I can do widgets. Same thing for Timmy, I imagine. Someone could hand him a drawing of something, and he could render it for them. Or they could describe it and have him create it on the fly. It'd be fantastic."

Euge's eyes lit up. "Can we try it?"

"Sure." Sara swung back to look at the large plasma screen across the room and opened a new, blank file. "What do you want?"

Eugene glanced at Chuck, who nodded at him to take charge. Eugene's eyes went to the BPM readout charting Sara's brain state.

"Okay," Eugene said. "I'd like a Frank Lloyd Wright–style building with two stories. No, three."

"Material?"

"Brick below and limestone above."

She gave him a funny look. "Limestone?"

"Yeah. Like the pyramids."

"Right. Pyramids. I can build one of those if you'd like."

"No, thanks. A Prairie School abode will be sufficient."

She went to it, Eugene adding bits and pieces as she went: tree-of-life stained glass over and around the front door, a water feature along the front veranda, a slate roof. She kept up, creating what he asked almost as swiftly as the specs came out of his mouth.

Chuck glanced at her brain wave readouts: *She is doing this in one immensely long gamma fugue.*

He had turned back to watch Euge's house take shape on the computer screen when the BPM uttered the shrill bleat of an alarm. Chuck stared at the digital readout: the wave pattern had literally flown off the chart. The vivid trace of light went up and disappeared at the top of the window. It didn't drop back into visible range until Sara broke concentration. Then it settled down into a normal but heightened beta state.

"What the heck was that?" Eugene asked, leaning in to look at the readout.

Chuck grimaced. "I have no idea."

"Maybe there's something wrong with the machine," Sara suggested.

Chuck ran a diagnostic, during which Sara put herself through some simple exercises geared toward generating a series of different states. There seemed to be nothing wrong with the machine.

"The trace flies out of the frame at the top," noted Chuck. "Maybe Sara's producing an effect outside of her normal parameters. I'm going to try increasing the frequency range."

He did, and they tried the experiment again.

Again the alarm sounded when Sara was fully engaged in processing Eugene's verbal instructions. Again Chuck increased the range.

The alarm went off a third time.

He recalibrated yet again.

This time the alarm was silent. And this time the brain state appeared on the monitor screen as a solid bar of brilliant amber.

"Seven megahertz," murmured Chuck, even as Sara continued to design. "That's . . . extraordinary. There's no human brain activity in that range."

"Gotta be static discharge," Eugene replied quietly. "Gotta be." He gave Sara another direction.

"Static discharge?" repeated Chuck. "Why?"

"Because the most common thing I can think of that generates a wave at seven megahertz is lightning."

Chapter 9

MURPHY'S LAW

After Sara was sent home, Dice dismantled the rig and ran diagnostics on each individual component. While the system wasn't supposed to feed back into the neural net, Chuck refused to take a chance that it might.

Everything checked out clean.

Of course it does.

Dice stared in frustration at the disassembled parts of the kinetic converter. It had to be some permutation of Murphy's law: if something can go wrong it will, *and* you will not be able to reproduce the results or determine the cause by running diagnostics. Or it was a codicil to the aphorism that a watched pot never boils—in this case the screwed-up mechanism would refuse to malfunction while you were watching.

"There's nothing wrong with the mechanics," Eugene said wearily. "And there's nothing wrong with the software program."

"There has to be, though," said Chuck. "Somewhere among these pieces of the puzzle, there has to be one that's malfunctioning. Which means we have to find it—we can't ask our subjects to interact with a faulty system. There's no lab on earth in which that should be an acceptable risk, and especially not ours."

Dice rubbed his eyes. "What if we test it on one of us?"

"To what end?" Chuck asked.

"We all know how the rig works. If there's something wrong, it should go wrong no matter who's at the helm, right?"

"Theoretically," Chuck admitted. He was gazing at the neural net, his hazel eyes suddenly vague and unfocused.

Eugene was watching him. "I know that look. What are you thinking?"

"That I might be wrong."

"It's been known to happen."

Chuck gave Eugene a withering look, but the young man just smiled.

"Seriously, I'm thinking it might not be the converter. It might be the subjects. They're building mental muscles—we know that. What if the result is simply that this is a new muscle group? One that's producing a higher voltage of output? One that's producing a new rhythm?" Chuck's eyes went from vague to laser focus so fast, it made Dice's hair stand on end. "Reassemble the rig. I'm going to test it."

"No, you're not," said Eugene. "If something fries your brain, Forward Kinetics comes to a screeching and high-profile halt. It's kaput. *I'll* test it."

"Euge—"

"Time-out, guys." Dice made a T with his hands. "Let me reassemble it first, make sure there's nothing in the connections that's misfiring. Might as well eliminate mechanical reasons so we can confirm Chuck's theory. Then we can draw lots or something."

"Draw lots for what?" Tim had just wandered in for his afternoon session, making Dice realize belatedly that they'd forgotten to call the other participants to cancel their lab times.

"Becky had a bit of a meltdown during Sara's session this morning," Dice told him. "Shot out a burst of static in the seven-megahertz range."

"Seven megahertz? No kidding. That's like lightning, isn't it?"

"Exactly."

"So you were afraid you were going to stir-fry Sara's brains?"

"Something like that." Dice winced, forgoing the idea of Chinese for dinner.

"So you want me to go home?"

"Yes," Dice said, then added, "No, wait. There is something you can do, Timmy Troll. While we're reassembling the mechanics, can you check the software modules again just to make sure I didn't miss something big and incriminating?"

Tim smiled. "Nothing would make me happier. You write beautiful code, man. I love the way you self-document. I wish some of the guys at work could learn to do that."

Dice took a moment to set the programmer up at a workstation and showed him which files to check.

"Wouldn't it be a laugh if it was, like, an odd curly bracket or something?"

Dice grimaced. "I'm almost hoping it is something that mind-blowingly simple."

It wasn't something that mind-blowingly simple.

Troll's perusal of the interface code revealed nothing out of place and only served to make him more of a Daisuke Kobayashi fanboy.

They drew lots, excluding Tim, who pouted and then consoled himself with a can of Pepsi. Dice won the right to test the rig, which was fine with him. He had more online time with it than either Chuck or Eugene, after all.

Under the neural net, he interacted with a block of code he'd been working on to enhance his virtual reality interface. He wanted his test to be as close to the conditions Sara was in as possible. With the code, he was in his element: he knew the ropes, and he knew what he wanted it to do. But while he managed a couple of decent gamma bursts, he was unable to make the BPM shriek like a banshee or generate even a spark of lightning.

"Let me try."

That was Timmy Troll, of course. For being such an archetypal loner, he hated to be left out in matters of archgeekitude. The three scientists argued with him for several minutes, at the end of which he recited the entire fourth clause of the waiver he'd signed, taking care to point out that "acceptable risk" was a vague concept and surely one he could define for himself.

In the end Chuck relented and allowed Dice to hook Tim up to Becky. They'd no more than gotten him suited up when Sara sauntered back into the lab.

"Thought you could have a party without me, did you?" she asked.

"I sent you home," Chuck said.

"Obviously I didn't go home. I took the day off to work in the lab here, so I'm working in the lab. I've been watching from up there." She tilted her chin up toward the wraparound gallery.

Dice had all but forgotten about it. He looked to Chuck and shrugged. "She signed the same waiver Tim did. If she wants to stay . . ."

Dice could interpret the expression on Chuck's face as nothing other than raw anxiety—possibly even fear. But he nodded anyway.

"All right. Stay. But if it does that again . . ."

Tim worked with the rig for half an hour with no recurrence of the Tesla coil effect. By the time he gave up on it, he seemed disappointed.

Typical programmer, Dice thought. *Gets a giggle out of breaking someone else's code but pouts when he can't crack it.*

They were on the verge of giving up for the day, but Sara was having none of it.

"Look," she said, "you've been through the system from front to back, and no one's caused the Tesla thing to happen again. Since I'm the one who broke it in the first place, it makes sense to have me test it just to make sure."

She was perfectly correct, of course. That was the logical thing to do. So, Chuck's visible angst notwithstanding, they did it.

Sara, being Sara, was calmer than any of them—except possibly Tim, who opted for an air of relaxed boredom. Dice could tell, though, that Troll was as anxious to see her do it as he was to see her fail.

Once Chuck had adjusted the BPM back to its original range, Sara donned the neural net and fired up the project she'd been working on when the alarms had gone off. She archived the work she'd done on the garden and had Eugene feed her a fresh set of instructions from which she laid out hardscape areas, built fountains and statuary, and created trees and shrubs. She slid easily into a steady gamma pattern, her eyes on the creation process.

Dice was just beginning to relax when the alarm shrilled, its tone unwavering and continuous. He glanced at Sara's face and was surprised to see no reaction from her—it was as if she didn't even hear the sound the machine was emitting. He looked from her to the big display. The garden was coming into full bloom as if caught by a time-lapse video. Patterns and colors coalesced on the screen. It was like watching a Pixar movie, with digital greenery taking over the entire screen.

Chuck leapt to the BPM's touch screen and adjusted the output to the 7 MHz range. They all saw it: the solid, 3-D bar of activity. *Lightning.*

But where is it coming from—the hardware, the software, or the warmware?

Dice thought he knew—that only one answer possibly made sense at this point—but clearly Chuck wasn't convinced.

"No, no, no," Chuck murmured, staring at the BPM's display before finally shouting, "I'm shutting down!"

In the moments before his hand found the "abort" button on the touch screen, Sara broke her concentration and turned to glare at him. The 7 MHz blast simply stopped, replaced by an agitated beta. Chuck hit the kill switch, and the Brewster-Brenton unit went dark and silent.

"Why did you do that?" Sara asked peevishly. "I was flying, Chuck. I was . . . I was totally in sync."

"Maybe," Chuck said. "Maybe you were in sync. And maybe you were that close to overloading your synapses." He pinched the air with a thumb and a forefinger.

"I feel fine," she told him. "I *am* fine. I want to go again. I want to see if I can make lightning happen again."

"Hell," said Tim, "I want to see if I can make lightning happen at all."

Chuck shook his head. "No. No, Sara. It could be dangerous. We're stopping now."

"Aw, c'mon, Doc," Tim whined. "Things were just getting interesting. And I want a shot at it."

Dice glanced at Chuck again. He could tell how badly the neuroscientist wanted to say no but knew how easily he let himself be railroaded by those with stronger personalities. And for an introvert, Troll could be exceedingly pushy when he wanted something.

"It's four P.M.," Dice observed, and Chuck shot him a grateful look. "Let's call it a day. Eugene and I will go back over the activity logs, so they're ready for the five-thirty meeting, okay?

We're too close to this right now. We need some time to think it through, figure out what to do next."

"Let's try a different project—maybe start a new one from scratch," said Sara. "That's what makes the most sense to me."

"We are *not* taking this any further today," Chuck said.

Dice had never heard him sound so dictatorial. He supposed raw fear would do that even to someone as mellow as Chuck Brenton.

"All right, Doc. Why don't you go get a cup of tea or something? Euge and I will upload the material for the meeting."

Chuck nodded and stepped back from the BPM, looking like a kid who was leaving his pet at an animal shelter.

"Doc," said Dice. "Tea."

"No tea." Chuck turned to Sara. "I'd like to take you over to gamma lab for an MRI."

"If it will make you feel better, sure."

"Making me feel better is not the point. I have to be sure we're not damaging your brain, Sara. I have to be sure."

She shrugged. "Okay. I'll tell you what. I'll go for the MRI right now if you'll let Tim and me sit in on the meeting tonight."

"That's highly irregular," said Eugene.

One corner of Sara's mouth tilted upward. "So are my brain waves."

Chuck and Eugene exchanged glances, and then Chuck acquiesced. He led Sara from the room.

As she slipped through the door, she turned and gave Tim a double thumbs-up.

THERE WAS NOTHING DANGEROUS-LOOKING IN Sara's MRI, though there was an overall marked increase in activity in the frontal lobe on both sides. Even as she lay in the resonance tube, working out a series of problems in her head, her brain showed activity across a larger area than it had during her last MRI two weeks earlier.

What does that mean? Is it an artifact of the way her brain worked? Or is it something we caused by subjecting her to the rigors of the program?

Or is it both?

Chuck went into the meeting not knowing how to interpret the results of either the experiment or Sara's MRI. He'd studied neurology for nearly a decade and could say without hubris that he was one of the ten most knowledgeable people on the planet about the subject. And yet this was something so new, it made him feel like a rank undergrad reading his first MRI plot.

"So what you're saying," Matt said when Chuck and his team had finished their purely factual description of the situation, "is that Sara has started producing a new brain pattern—one we've never seen before. I'm impressed."

"I'm not sure that's what we're saying," argued Chuck. "What we *may* be saying is that the machinery is creating a sort of feed-back loop and exciting Sara's brain to unusual activity."

"There's nothing wrong with the machinery," said Dice quietly.

"We don't know—"

"Yes, we do know," Dice said. "Whatever is happening, it's not happening because of the hardware or the software. The hardware is fine, and the software is only reading what Sara's brain is outputting—a wave in the seven-megahertz range. The wave is a legitimate neurological event that's originating in Sara's brain. Hell, Chuck, you're a neurologist. Why can't you accept this?"

Sara, who was seated next to Chuck at the table, leaned in and tried to capture his gaze. "What he said. It's me, Doc. *I'm* doing it. I can even *feel* it when I get into the state that's producing the pattern."

"You can feel it?" Chuck asked, locking eyes with her. "You

didn't mention that before. In what sense can you feel it? A head-ache—"

"Nothing like that. It's . . . look, have you ever ridden a horse?"

He laughed. "No." It was about as emphatic as he'd ever said anything.

"Fine. But you *know* about riding horses, right? That some people do it?"

Chuck nodded, slightly amused.

"Well, there's a moment when a horse is at a full gallop and hits its stride, and suddenly you can't feel the individual hoof-beats anymore or the movement of the animal under you. It's as if you're riding on the air—smooth, flowing. That's what this felt like. It was that kind of all-encompassing sense. I couldn't hear the sounds of the room. I couldn't see anything but the results of my work. I felt as if I was riding on air. Getting to the gamma was hard work.

"This felt effortless."

Chuck frowned, rubbing the bridge of his nose. "I'm just afraid that if this wave is sustained over a period of time, espe-cially repetitively, it might damage you in some way. Burn you out, even. I have no way of measuring what's happening to your synapses in real time. I can only look at your brain after the fact, which might be too late." He turned to Matt. "You said you were 'impressed.' The word I think we should be using is 'concerned.'"

Matt's gaze bored into him, heavy and unrelenting. Finally the mathematician asked his partner quietly, "What do you sug-gest we do?" Chuck had learned to distrust that voice. Matt used it in conflicting ways. It could mean he was experiencing trepida-tion and was legitimately awed by the potential dangers of this new event. However, it could also mean he thought Chuck was being dense and obstructionist, and he was trying very hard not to show how much that annoyed him.

And usually it's the latter.

Regardless, he offered his honest opinion. "I think we should pull back. Have Sara and the others go through some testing to make sure we're not harming them in any way."

"I thought we agreed we're just bulking up mentally," said Tim. "Y'know, using the muscles and making them stronger and more efficient. Maybe we're just having muscle cramps."

"It's not a cramp, Tim," said Sara. Was there just a hint of smugness in her voice? She was, after all, the only one to have experienced this firsthand. "It's the opposite of a cramp. Everything in my head was running as smooth as glass."

Chuck shook his head. "Even in the case of bodily muscles, you can overwork them and cause injury. I don't—"

Matt cut him off. "I understand your concern, Chuck. I really do," he said in that same übergentle voice. "But we can't afford to pull back. We've got commitments now. People who are waiting to see what this technology will do, banking on it doing something useful."

Chuck continued to shake his head. "Commitments? Banking on it? No, Matt! Dammit, we can't let business imperatives drive our research. Too many people—scientists, politicians, businesspeople, you name it—use business commitments as excuses to take terrible risks. I'm not going to let us go out with a product that is potentially dangerous, let alone risk these people testing—"

"Chuck . . ." Sara leaned forward again and put a hand on his arm. "I promise you if I feel the least bit stressed, if I have the tiniest headache or dizziness or anything like that, I will let you know. Just don't shut us down or ask us to wait to find out what we can do." She glanced sideways at Tim. "Whatever it is I've done, I'm willing to bet that Tim and Mike won't be far behind. Don't stop us before we can find out what this means."

"There," Matt said. "From the horse's mouth." He felt the icy daggers of Sara's side glance at his equestrian comparison but chose to ignore it. "Let's not hesitate on the verge of a potential breakthrough."

A breakthrough. *Is that what we are on the verge of?* Chuck prayed that was so but couldn't shake the idea that they seemed willing to risk everything, including the scientific method, for it. He knew he should say something else, something to convince the others how *wrong* this felt, but as he looked around the table, all he saw was everyone looking at him with varying degrees of anticipation. He shook his head.

"Are you all on board with this?" he asked quietly.

Everyone nodded or answered in the affirmative. Surprisingly the only hesitation came from Dice, but in the end even he gave a yes vote.

"All right. Tomorrow we'll pick up where we left off. Mike is scheduled for first thing in the morning. We'll bring him in on the situation and give him a choice about whether he wants to continue with the program. Is that acceptable?"

Chuck glanced around the table again. They were all sitting back in their chairs, smiling or looking thoughtful.

"He'll stick it out," Tim prophesied. "Guaranteed."

Chapter 10

THE GOD WAVE

"So what is that, then?" Lanfen asked, running her finger along the bar of light that dominated the BPM's touch screen. She glanced up at Matt.

"We haven't actually named it yet," he said. "Although I heard someone refer to it as the Tesla coil effect."

"That's a mouthful. I think you're going to want something catchier for PR purposes."

He smiled. "Yeah. I'll think about it. Right now what I'd like to do is see if you can reproduce it."

She stared at him but couldn't read his face in the semidarkness of the delta lab. "Seriously? But I have no idea what Sara's doing."

Matt crossed the darkened lab to stand at the edge of Lanfen's workout mat. "She said it was like riding a horse at flank speed. I don't suppose you ride?"

"No. Sorry."

"She described a state in which everything she was doing

went from high tension to effortless. Like she was in sync. In the zone. Do you ever experience that while you're doing kung fu?"

"Of course—that's basically a goal of the discipline." Lanfen moved to stand beside Matt, gazing at the practice space and the currently inert robot. "So you're hoping I can get into the zone and direct the robot from there."

"Yes. Willing to try?"

"You bet. Hook me up."

She worked with the robot for over an hour, until she was weary and dripping with sweat. She'd managed to do most of the workout in a steady gamma state, but the elusive lightning refused to strike.

"I'm too aware that I'm moving a foreign object and not my body," she said. Sitting cross-legged at the edge of the mat, sipping water, she considered the problem that had both Matt and her frustrated. "There's a disconnect. The bot is not me. Or it's not enough like me to put me in the zone. Either way, I have to be too conscious of everything I'm doing."

Matt was silent for a long moment, then asked, "What if you were looking at the world from the robot's point of view? What if you were looking *out* from inside the bot?"

She thought about it for a second. "Well, I imagine that might improve my mental mapping. I'd still say the bot is pretty limited in the ways it can move, though."

"I'll work on improving that," Matt told her. "Though I can't do anything about it immediately. The other part—the viewpoint issue—that I can deal with right now."

Lanfen looked at him askance. "Really? How?"

"Dice has integrated a VR helm into the rig in the alpha lab."

Lanfen gestured at the room. "Doesn't do me much good down here."

"No. We're going to have to move you upstairs."

Her heart leapt. "Officially? I can be an official member of the program?"

He shook his head. "Sorry, no. Not yet. I'm thinking spring of next year. In fact, I'd like your debut to be at the Applied Robotics show in April."

"Then we'd better get working on that VR component, Professor."

WHEN CHUCK BRIEFED MIKE ABOUT Sara's new wave the next morning, the construction engineer took the news with characteristic tranquility. His only indication of surprise was a slight raising of one eyebrow.

"New brain wave, huh? What are you gonna call it?"

Chuck clearly hadn't considered that. "I don't know . . . um, a supergamma?"

"Lame, Doc," Tim offered. "We can do better than that."

"We've been sort of calling it the Tesla coil effect," Dice offered.

"Oh, man, that's almost as lame," said the game developer. "Don't the other waves all have Greek alphabet names? What comes after gamma?"

"Delta," said Dice. "But I think that's taken. Epsilon comes after that."

Tim wrinkled his nose and looked at Mike as if to ask what he thought. Mike shrugged, and Tim rolled his eyes.

"Let me ask you this," he said to Chuck. "It's several stops past just the next letter in the alphabet, isn't it?"

"Yes," said Chuck.

"What if we call it a zeta wave, then? That's a three-letter jump, and z is at the tail end of the English alphabet."

"Zeta wave," said Chuck, testing it out. Tim, on the other hand, was already committed.

"Yeah. I like it. It's not lame."

And that's how decisions get made at Forward Kinetics, Chuck thought ruefully.

By not being lame.

Regardless, zeta it was . . . and yet zeta it wasn't. Because although they spent the day trying to coax it into showing itself in Tim and Mike's brain waves, it was always without success. They put Sara back in the harness, and she was able to generate the wave after roughly ten minutes of sustained work. Chuck let her carry on for about two minutes, then broke her concentration and pulled her out of the state.

"Maybe it's something not everyone can do," suggested Eugene.

"Unacceptable," said Tim. "I'm going to keep trying until I can do it. I mean look at it from the usefulness standpoint. What good is the tech if only rare individuals can use it to its full potential? This is proof of concept, man. You gotta have proof of concept. Am I right?" He directed this comment at Matt, who had come into the lab to witness their progress and in whom Tim found a ready ally—at least when it came to taking risks with the subjects.

"Troll's right," Matt said. "We need to know how rare or how common this state is. If it's really as rare as all that, we need to develop a procedure by which our customers can quickly and efficiently identify people who can generate it before they've invested a ton of resources in training."

And that's the other way decisions are made here:

Matt makes them.

SO CHUCK SPLIT THE TEAM up, putting Eugene in charge of working with Tim in bay one while he set Mike up with his current device—a large, mechanical arm he had been using to move weighted boxes from a shipping pallet to a raised platform that stood in for a truck bed. He asked Dice to float between the two teams, monitoring the interface.

That duty suited the engineer just fine. He was legitimately curious to see what would happen with both of these guys but was willing to wager that Tim would be the first of the two to achieve a zeta state.

MATT WANDERED OVER TO WATCH Dice start a preflight check of Mike's rig; the robotic arm used a computerized drive mechanism not unlike the backhoes and cranes Mike was used to piloting in his workaday life.

"I have a favor to ask of you," Matt said quietly.

Dice paused to read the expression on his boss's face. It didn't take a degree in robotics to tell that what he was about to say was for Dice's ears alone.

"Yeah?"

"Karate bot. I need you to do some extracurricular work on it."

Dice turned his attention back to the servounit. "What sort of work?"

"It needs to flex more like a human body. It's too stiff. I know you were experimenting with more-humanoid forms back at MIT."

"I was. I turned it over to my minions. Brenda Tansy is in charge of the robotics program now."

"I remember her. Bright. Postgrad now, right?"

Dice nodded.

"I'd like to get a unit like that here. Money is no object."

Dice took a deep breath, considering. "Are you thinking we buy one off the university or just get the schematics or—"

"If you had the schematics and the materials, how long would it take you to put a prototype together?"

"If I had an experienced team . . . three months maybe."

"Steal undergrads from MIT. They can intern. I'll pay them."

Dice felt his heart rate kick up. He loved his job. "Okay. Sure. But why the sly?"

Matt smiled. "It's . . . sort of a surprise. Something I'm hoping to spring on Chuck at the AR show."

Although Dice didn't really like the secrecy, he couldn't help but think this sounded like a lot of fun. He grinned.

"Professor Streegman, you got yourself a stealth robotics project."

MIKE YENOTOV HAD NEVER GONE to college. He had a high school diploma, which he'd earned by being thoroughly average in every class but two: math and machine shop. He had played football, enjoyed working on cars, and was now married with two kids. Neither that bio nor his blunt manner—not to mention his regular-guy view of the world—hinted at how truly bright he was. Chuck stood in frank admiration of the man. From a fabrication standpoint, he was a gold-plated marvel when it came to figuring out logistical problems.

When Dice had first constructed the scale-model backhoe, it had tipped over when Mike had tried to move some "boulders" with it. Dice had sworn loudly and colorfully. Mike had waited for him to calm down, then explained in simple, competent terms why that was happening despite the fact that the engineer had calculated the weight differential. Dice had then built a counterbalance and a bracing leg for the rig, and it had performed just like its larger cousins.

"I should've known that," he'd told Chuck later. "I freaking build robots for a living, but I've never had to build one to function as a backhoe. I failed basic logistics, and Mike got the gold star."

Mike got a gold star on this day, too. His task was to move a scattering of colored crates from chaos to an orderly stack. He'd been working his hydraulic arm for perhaps half an hour, performing a series of exercises with the rainbow crates, when he'd fallen into a breathtaking gamma state. He was cruising.

Chuck was thrilled. "Okay, let's try this," he told Mike. "I'd like you to stack the crates in a pyramid. The goal is to be careful enough that they won't fall over."

Mike hunkered down and constructed a colorful pyramid that did not fall until he was trying to seat the last crate. He did everything from the second row up in a solid gamma state. He was visibly frustrated by the failure of his last placement.

"I'm gonna do it again," he announced.

Chuck opened his mouth to say that wasn't necessary, but he could see by the mulish look on the other man's face that it was indeed necessary. Mike ran the drill again, this time getting it right.

"So," he said, "Sara got this zeta thing happening when Dice was telling her what to do, yeah?"

"Yeah," Eugene told him. "She was taking instructions, interpreting them, and making them happen in the plotter. It was pretty cool."

"Okay, so you give me instructions, too," Mike said. "Why don't you tell me which blocks to use for the pyramid?"

Chuck was impressed. Mike instinctively caught which elements of Sara's exercise might have contributed to her zeta fugue. Eugene looked to him for a thumbs-up. He gave it unhesitatingly.

Mike used the robotic arm to knock the boxes down, then Eugene called out colors, and the builder constructed a seven-tiered pyramid.

The zeta burst occurred as he was setting up the third course of crates. It lasted for several seconds, until the construct began to become a bit unstable. He then reverted to gamma until he was in the center of the fourth course, when it recurred.

"Huh," Eugene grunted.

Chuck glanced sideways at him. "What?"

"I'll tell you when we're done." Eugene stepped a few paces to the right of the growing pile of blocks, watching as Mike slipped in and out of the zeta state to complete the pyramid.

They sent Mike off to lunch at that point and sat down to debrief.

"What did you see?" Chuck asked Eugene.

"I'm not sure." Eugene shook his head, tugging at an ear. "It seemed to me that every time he went into the zeta state, the robotic arm . . . I don't know, shimmied or hesitated or something."

"Are you thinking the apparatus is causing the phenomenon?"

"No, no, nothing like that. I just wondered if the zeta might be too much for the bot's onboard unit, that's all. Maybe we should have Dice come take a look at it, and it just needs a little tweak."

Just a little tweak—that'd be a nice change.

After lunch they went back to it, putting Mike through the same drill. He fugued out, as Dice put it, as he reached the center point of the three upper courses this time. Dice watched the robotic arm carefully throughout and agreed with Eugene.

"Yeah, I see it," he said after their first trial. "It's definitely bucking a little bit."

"You think Mike might be overdriving the onboard unit?" Chuck asked.

"Possible, I suppose. Let me set up a diagnostic and see what voltage he's generating."

"Is there any way to detect feedback?"

Dice looked down at the floor. "Sure, but I don't see why we'd need to since I can't see how the system could feed back in such a way that it would harm the subject . . . if that's what you're worried about. The zeta is being generated at this end." He pointed at a returning Mike, who sniffed.

Chuck nodded. "Yes, I know that. But if Mike is overdriving the system, any feedback generated might affect the interface or the onboard computer. If it can do that, we'll need to have Matt take a second look at his equations and see if he needs to adjust for this new frequency."

Dice's eyes widened. "Oh, sorry, Doc. That should've occurred to me. Yeah. Let me check this out."

Dice's diagnostics, however, showed no bump in Becky's output.

Oh, joy, Chuck thought. *A mystery. Or, rather, another mystery.* Just what they didn't want with a trade show looming. The good news was that Mike wasn't overdriving the arm's CPU. But that was also the bad news.

Whoever said no news is good news wasn't a scientist.

"Okay," Chuck said. "I think maybe it's time to put Mike in his element. Do we have that John Deere ready to go?"

Dice grinned. "Boy, do we. She's a pearl, that one. State of the art and then some, with Becky on board."

"Great." Chuck turned to Mike. "Tomorrow, class, we're going on a little field trip to the sandy patch out back."

Mike smiled. "Now we're talking."

WHILE THE CORE GROUP WAS working with zeta, Mini was doing her own thing. It wasn't lightning, but it definitely sent off sparks. Mini loved to move. She loved to paint. This experiment that Professor Brenton had made her a part of allowed her to do both. No more keyboards. No more mice. No more GUI. She could just put on her neural net and create things in her art program unencumbered. She did dragons and kelpies and Pegasuses (or was that Pegasi?) at first just because she liked fantasy creatures and fantasy worlds—and, at the moment, felt a little like she was living in one.

Her paintings were heavily influenced by Roger Dean, John Howe, Alan Lee, and her own imaginings. She liked creating landscapes and fanciful buildings, but she loved creating creatures most of all. It puzzled her truly and down to the bottom of her soul that she and Tim could not have a conversation about creature creation without setting each other off. Tim, who also made up creatures out of a fabric of dreams and visions and memories from his childhood, did not love his creations the way Mini loved hers. His relationship with his dragons was one of king and serf or wizard and golem.

Mini was her creatures' mother. Their liberator. Their friend.

"How can you create what you don't love?" she'd asked the programmer once.

"Creating this stuff makes my blood pound and my head spin and my d—" He'd swallowed whatever he'd been going to say and said instead, "It's kind of sexy, if you get my drift."

"Sexy?" she'd repeated, wrinkling her nose. "I guess."

Mini didn't find her creatures sexy. Not in the way she found Eugene sexy. But she did find that creating them filled her with a deep and profound joy. It made her feel buoyant, competent, and complete. And yet, when she was particularly on in the creative sense, she had to admit it *was* exciting.

She was on now, moving beneath her glittering halo of transceivers, making a quartet of colorful dragons come to life on the big display in the beta lab. There was a dragon for each point of the compass: white, black, red, and gold.

The dragon of the north was the white one. She gave it a patterned effect that looked like the pearly layer of ice atop wet snow. The southern dragon had to be black, and she chose an effect from the filter gallery that made it glisten like obsidian. East was golden, and west was red—the colors of sunrise and sunset.

Her arms swept them into curving shapes, and her fingers scattered tiny points of light across their scales, and in the midst of making them pop and glow and appear to come to life, she swept herself into a prolonged gamma state where she seemed to be more dancing than moving. It didn't end until she spun around and caught a glimpse of Eugene, who'd been manning the BPM throughout her session. He was staring at her, his face beet red and his forehead shiny with perspiration. When their eyes met, he blinked several times in quick succession.

Mini frowned, suddenly self-conscious. "What's the matter, Euge? Is there something wrong with the machine? It seemed to be working okay."

"Oh . . . no," Eugene said, sounding breathless, as if he'd been dancing with her. "Everything's . . . everything's fine. It's just. Uh. You . . . uh. Can I . . . ?"

"Can you what?"

"Can I just say that . . . that was about the most erotic thing I've ever seen?"

"Erotic?" Mini stared at him. Tim thought the act of creation was sexy; Eugene apparently found *her* act of creation erotic. How did she feel about that?

On one level she was pleased that Eugene thought she was sexy. On another level she was appalled that Eugene thought she was sexy. At least while she was doing this—creating her beloved creatures. But then sex is creative in a primal, physical way. Why did it feel wrong here?

"Erotic?" she said again.

"Is there something wrong with that? I find you really attractive. You know that. It's no secret."

She carefully removed the neural net. "It's just that for me, this is like . . . like worship. Like prayer. And when you get turned on by it—well, it's sort of like saying watching me *pray* is erotic."

He blinked as if viewing an image of her at prayer. He reddened again and looked away.

"Really?" she said. "*Really?* Oh, that's . . . that's . . . men!" She left the neural net lying on the floor and stalked across the lab.

"Yeah, but it's erotic in a *wholesome* sort of way," he called after her. "And you have to remember—I went to Catholic school."

She stopped. "So if I came back in here wearing a short, plaid skirt?"

"My brain waves wouldn't be the only thing to spike."

She turned back to glare at him, then burst into laughter. She laughed until she started to hiccup. Eugene took matters into his own hands at that point and stopped her hiccups by marching across the lab and kissing her.

"I think I'm in love with you," Eugene said with a breathy whisper when he'd raised his head and brought his eyes back into focus.

"Let me know when you're sure," she told him, then turned and swept out of the lab.

MIKE SEEMED, IF NOT HAPPY, at least contented to be finally taking their trials out into the real world of construction. Their outdoor lab was outfitted with a real, full-scale John Deere 310K backhoe loader with a digging depth of a little more than fourteen feet. Mike had picked the unit. It was a machine he knew inside out.

It was sitting at present in a flat, sandy area just to the northeast of the Forward Kinetics building, flanking the parking lot and kitty-corner to the loading dock onto which they'd rolled the BPM machine and Becky's transmitter. Becky generated its own Wi-Fi hotspot, so Chuck had no doubt the signal would be plenty robust for the real-world trials.

While Matt and Dice argued the pros and cons of staging a full-scale demo of the backhoe for the Applied Robotics show, Mike inspected it. Or maybe he made friends with it, the way one would with a horse.

"Beautiful machine," he said, patting the backhoe's vivid yellow flank. "It's gonna feel weird not sitting in it, doing the work, though."

Chuck looked over in time to catch the flash of wistfulness in the construction engineer's eyes and was momentarily stunned. How in God's name had he overlooked that aspect of the subject's neural activity? Pushing buttons wasn't just about pushing buttons. It was about interacting with the environment, tactile feedback. He made a note to ask the team about their subjective feelings when working in this way. Sure, they were all excited now, but once the newness wore off would they mourn that missing physical interaction? Would it make the work less fulfilling? Less attractive? Less engaging?

He thought about how he'd felt the first time he'd been able to do some simple work wearing the kinetic interface. He'd been manipulating neural plots from MRI sessions—nothing complicated—but he had missed the tactile sense of keys beneath his fingertips and, absurdly, mouse clicks. Sara seemed not to care that she no longer had to finger mouse buttons, but he knew the response was still there by the way she tapped and stroked the arm of her chair during a session.

"Euge." Chuck glanced over the top of the BPM module at his assistant, who was detangling the power cables on the off side. "Could you take over here for a moment? I need to go talk to Mike about something."

"Sure. Where are you on your checklist?"

"I was just getting ready to run a quick diagnostic on the neural net."

"Got it." Euge came around the five-foot-tall bank of machinery to take Chuck's iPad from his hand. "You know we're going to have to reduce the size of this thing by a lot if it's ever going to be commercially viable anywhere but a factory setting."

Chuck looked at the Brewster-Brenton and nodded. "That'll come. Dice already has a team working on miniaturization. Just out of curiosity," he added, "how'd your last session with Mini go?"

To his surprise, Eugene colored all the way to the roots of his hair. "It . . . it went . . . great. I guess."

Chuck read his expression and laughed. "I don't need to know about that part of it. What I'd really like to know is if she misses working with the GUI and other things like the keyboard, drawing pad, mouse, whatever."

Eugene cleared his throat. "She doesn't seem to miss that at all. She moves so freely, she practically dances, you know. When she's being creative . . ." He waved his arms in the air. "It's really . . . interesting."

"I'll bet." Chuck turned away, still snickering, and made his way off the loading dock and across the sandy patch to where Mike was still getting acquainted with the backhoe.

"Have you named her yet?" he asked, shoving his hands into the pockets of his jeans.

"What?" Mike blinked at him, then smiled. "Well, not officially. But she seems sort of like a Darya to me. That's my daughter's name."

"Darya Deere. Lovely name." Chuck patted one fat tire. "Hello, Darya. Pleased to meet you." He nodded up at the cab. "You gonna miss that a lot? Sitting in the cab, hands on the controls?"

"I'd be lying if I said I wouldn't. It helps me concentrate, y'know? That sense of touch. I imagine part of the problem with making this tech work right is getting people to concentrate hard enough. It could be pretty bad if someone, I dunno, sneezed or got a phone call or got distracted in some way while they were doing some kinds of work."

Chuck ran a hand through his hair, only now realizing how long it was getting. "Yes. That's something we're clearly going to have to address."

"You bet. I mean when you're in the cab, driving, and you have a stray thought, worst that happens is you idle for a second or two until you get your hands moving again. If it's all up here"—he tapped his head—"then a stray thought could cause you to drop the ball. Literally. Or throw it somewhere it doesn't belong."

Chuck pulled a little three-ring notebook out of his back pocket and made another note. Mike made a sound Chuck realized was a titter. He looked up from his notes. The other man was pointing at his notebook.

"See what I mean: all this technology, with you right in the thick of it, and you still write notes with a pencil."

Chuck looked down at the pencil in question—a .07 mechanical one—and grimaced. "Tactile feedback's important to me, too, Mike. I'm not sure why that only just occurred to me. In some ways what we're doing to you all is putting you in a self-constructed isolation chamber."

Mike shrugged at that. He then jerked a thumb up at the backhoe's cab. "I'm gonna climb up and check out the controls. Make sure I know where everything is. Wouldn't want to push the wrong button—kinetically speaking."

Chuck nodded and returned to the loading dock. The rest of the team had appeared to watch the trials. Tim and Sara sat on the edge of the dock, while Matt and Dice hovered around the BPM. Eugene handed Chuck his iPad as he hit the top of the loading dock stairs.

"So what was that about?" Eugene asked, nodding toward the backhoe. Mike had started it and was raising and lowering the loader and flexing the digging arm.

"Just following up on my thoughts about tactile feedback. Mike really enjoys the sensations of being in the machine, having his hands on the controls." He glanced down at Sara and Tim. "Do either of you have any thoughts on that? The loss of tactile feedback, I mean."

Tim disappeared inside himself for fewer than two seconds,

then shrugged and shook his head. "Not me, man. I like the new *me* interface."

"Sara?"

She looked pensive. "I suppose . . . yeah, there is a certain enjoyment level that goes with clicking and dragging or holding a stylus in my hand. But it's so much slower to work that way. I think the trade-offs are all on the side of this technology. To be able to create blueprints and elevations as fast as my brain and the computer interface can work? That is priceless. If I miss a mouse, I can always click one while I'm playing Timmy's games." She smiled at the programmer, who bent at the waist in a sitting bow.

"And for people who do need that feedback," Dice said, "we can probably use the VR to at least allow them a mental map of some interfaces—like Mike's backhoe cab, say."

"That's definitely something we'll want to consider in the next phase," Matt said.

"Okay. But there is one other thing we need to discuss now," Chuck said, his gaze going to Matt. "Mike brought up an important point: distractions. When your thought is your reality, marshaling those thoughts is critical. Concentration is critical. We already know that the human mind can only concentrate at high levels for relatively brief periods of time."

Sara was nodding. "He's right. If I can draw plots at the speed of thought, I can screw up at the speed of thought, too. In my work it's no big deal—just undo, redo. But if you're piloting an aircraft or running one of those"—she nodded toward the Deere—"you could seriously hurt people."

"Failsafes," Dice said. "We'll just have to build failsafes into Becky, so when an operator loses concentration and their brain waves lose focus—go from a strong gamma to a beta, say—the interface holds steady rather than returning to a default or starting state. I can work on that."

"Hey, I'm ready to go." Mike was climbing the stairs to the loading dock. "You want me to sit there?" He gestured at the chair Eugene had brought out. The neural net was draped carefully across its back.

Eugene hastened to pick up the net. "Yeah. Have a seat, and we'll get you set up."

Moments later, Mike was suited up, Chuck and Eugene were on the monitors, Dice was looking at a direct feed of Becky's power flow through, and Darya was awaiting her first set of commands.

They had her dig a hole, ferrying each bucket full of sand to a container roughly twenty-five feet away, on the opposite side of the sandy patch. Mike did it all in a pulsing gamma—off for the digging, on for driving the hoe. He didn't enter zeta once.

His next task was to use the front loader to scoop up a stack of railroad ties and move them to a chalked-off area next to the sand container. This was a more delicate task, and Mike was clearly concentrating on getting the ties into the loader without splintering them. He had turned the backhoe and was speeding across the sand to the chalk outline when he went into zeta. He was still in zeta when he carefully spilled the first load of ties onto the ground, still in zeta when he turned and used the bucket to nudge them into order.

"Chuck . . ." Eugene was staring at the clock on the BPM screen. "Chuck, it's been three minutes. He's been in zeta for three minutes. Maybe—"

"Yeah. Pull him out."

"Okay, Mike," Eugene said softly. "You can stop now."

The backhoe continued to move. Mike never took his eyes from it.

"Hey, Mike!" Eugene said more loudly. He put a hand on the man's shoulder. "Let up, okay?"

Mike kept his eyes on the backhoe; Darya kept moving.

Eugene threw Chuck a startled glance and stepped in front of Mike, obstructing his view of the sand patch. It made no difference. Mike stared as if he could see right through Eugene's body.

Tim had clambered up to the loading dock and was calling now, too. "Hey, snap out of it, dude!"

"It's been five minutes," said Dice tersely. "We should shut down the interface."

Chuck nodded and tapped a finger on the BPM's touch screen. The BKKI came down.

Out in the sand, Darya continued to juggle railroad ties.

"Shit. Something's wrong with the rig," Dice said. He stepped over the cabling that was feeding power to both the Brewster-Brenton and Becky and, after a moment of hesitation, yanked the plug out of the back of the rack. The machinery shut down with a mechanical sigh; the screens and meters went dark.

Yet out in the sand, Darya carried her last load of ties to the growing pile and deposited them carefully atop it.

Chuck felt the hair stand up on the back of his neck.

"That's not possible," said Matt softly. "That's just not possible."

Chapter 11

MAKING WIZARDS

The conference room was silent as the team filed in and seated themselves. Door closed, they all sat for several minutes staring at each other—and trying *not* to stare at Mike. For his part, the construction engineer looked puzzled and uncomfortable. He kept his eyes on the knees of his jeans and picked at a callus on his hand.

He was the first one to speak. "So . . . what did I do exactly? What was that?"

Chuck cleared his throat. "You, um, apparently manipulated the backhoe directly. You bypassed the interface."

"But *how*?"

"I don't know."

"Is that what the zeta wave is?" asked Sara. She'd crossed her arms on the table and rested her chin on them. "It's us manipulating things directly? Telekinesis?"

Tim let out a short bark of laughter. "Zeta wave my ass! God wave is more like it. *Z* is for *Zeus!*" He turned his pale eyes on Chuck. "I want to try it, Doc. I want a shot at it."

"You'll get it," said Matt curtly. "Obviously we have to see if this . . . anomaly is reproducible in all of you."

Tim nodded. "Yeah."

"Clearly," Chuck said, "we need to verify that the zeta wave—"

"God wave," prompted Tim.

Chuck shook his head. "I'm not comfortable calling it that."

Tim shrugged and made a rude but quiet noise.

"We need to verify whether it's causal or at least concomitant with the . . . the ability to—" Chuck broke off and looked up at Matt. "Do you realize what we've done here? Do you have any conception of what this means?"

Matt grinned. "I get it. Believe me. If these results are reproducible then we have not just invented a human-machine interface. We've invented a training device capable of turning just about every industry on its head."

"Forget industry," Tim said. "Think of what you're turning *us* into."

"Okay," Chuck said, growing a bit uncomfortable. *Are we making them different?*

Are we making gods? Monsters?

He shook that thought away and went to stand by the whiteboard at the foot of the table. Picking up a marker, Chuck began to write. "Okay, so the first thing we need to do is see if Mike can repeat his results. Then we need to get Tim and Sara into zeta states and see if they can reproduce his results."

He paused to look at his three-item list.

"Then," said Dice, "we need to see if any or all of them can initiate the telekinetic link without first ramping up using the kinetic converter. That's going to be critical."

"How so?" asked Sara.

"Well, if Mike was manipulating Becky instead of the actual drive mechanisms of the backhoe, then that raises the possibility that we'll have to continue to build and market interfaces, so the machine operator is working with something he can understand and therefore manipulate."

Sara nodded. "Of course. That was the problem I had with the computer initially. I didn't know how the optical interface on the mouse worked, so I couldn't operate it. But I understand pixels, I guess."

Chuck added "isolate what's being manipulated" to the list of items.

"And," said Matt, "depending on what we determine, we'll have to rethink our upcoming presentations."

Chuck turned to look at him. "I have a TED Talk in two weeks. What do I tell them? These are open-minded people, Matt, but if I tell them we've induced telekinetic powers—"

Dice pointed a warning finger at the scientist. "Don't use that word—*powers*. Don't *ever* use it. It will totally give the wrong impression and create all sorts of weird images of mad scientists and Frankenstein monsters. We are cultivating abilities."

"Capacities," said Chuck.

"Talents?" That was Sara.

"Mental muscles." Mike looked up and glanced around the table. "Isn't that really what we're doing? Building mental muscles? It's all perfectly natural, right?"

"Yes, yes, it is," said Chuck. But he knew damn well that some people would refuse to see it that way. He looked at Matt. "But we still need to *sell* that. What do I say at the TED conference?"

"Maybe we should cancel," suggested Eugene.

"No, no, and no," said Matt. "We are not going to cancel. Let's stick with the program. We're developing an interface. The interface works. We let the audience see there's something new going on here. We simply say we don't know quite yet what it is. But I think we should plant the idea that our subjects are learning new methods of mental mapping. That they're developing new capac-ities. Then when we hit Applied Robotics in April, that's where we pull the rabbit out of the hat."

"Publicly?" asked Chuck. He fought images of torches and pitchforks and Senate hearings. "Is that wise?"

"We'll play it by ear. If it seems like the right time, we'll go with a public display. If not . . ." Matt shrugged. Then he looked around the table for consensus. "Plan?"

Everyone nodded.

"Great. Now, do we want to take the rest of the day off to design experiments, or do we want to dive back into it?"

Tim raised his hand. "I'm for diving."

Sara echoed the movement. "Me, too."

"Sure," said Dice, and the others nodded.

Mike, Chuck noticed, was the last one to give his silent approval. A nod. "As long as I can go home on time," he added.

"You all right with this?" Chuck asked the engineer later in the lab, as Dice wired him up to work with his robotic arm.

"Why wouldn't I be?"

"Telekinesis has been a fantasy—a dream or night terror for human beings for a very long time. It would be understandable if you were leery of playing with it."

"But I'm not playing, Doc," said Mike, meeting Chuck's eyes. "This is important work. It's important to me, to my kids. They're five and eight. By the time they've grown up and are getting jobs, the world could be really different."

Chuck nodded and then got sucked into a debate with Eugene and Dice over whether they should remove the neural net once zeta had been achieved.

Mike just stared ahead, wondering how different the world would be.

IT TOOK MIKE TEN MINUTES to achieve a zeta state, but once he did, he completed a series of complicated activities while Chuck and his scurrying minions brought down the system one element at a time. The last thing they did was remove the neural net from his head. That made Matt want to shout out loud. Once it was off, there was nothing—*nothing*—in the outboard machine interface that seemed necessary to the kinetic link between Mike and the robot.

That left him with only one puzzle to solve: was Mike manipulating the robotic arm's native mechanisms, or was he manipulating the part of the Brenton-Kobayashi interface that was resident in the machine? He tugged at his lip, watching the arm swing to and fro, stacking colorful milk crates.

"Mike," he asked when the last crate was stacked, and Mike pulled himself out of the zeta state. "Can you articulate—can you tell me what you're doing to move the robot arm?"

"I know what *articulate* means, Dr. Streegman. The robot's got gimbals. I move the gimbals. I move the robot."

Matt turned to Dice. "That's part of the interface, right?"

"Well, yeah, but it's not as simple as 'this is part of the bot, and this is part of Becky.' When my team built Becky's mechanisms into the robot, we really built them in. The signal that Becky interprets for the drive mechanism acts like a thought transmitted by the human brain. The interface acts as a synapse. When Mike was using the Wi-Fi transceivers to execute his commands, the impulses were traveling through the entire physical interface. Now they're jumping the gap somewhere. I'm just not sure where that is. So when Mike says he's moving the gimbals, we won't know until we've offlined all the connections from the servo-mechanisms whether he's moving them directly or through the synapses." Dice grimaced. "Did any of that make sense?"

"Did to me," said Mike, giving Matt a wry look. "Let's see if I can *articulate* it. Are my mental fingers pushing the gimbals, or are they firing impulses through Becky's synapses and moving the gimbals that way?"

Matt smothered the flash of irritation Mike's pointed phrasing sparked and raised his hands in mock surrender. "Hey, don't look at me. I'm just a paper-pushing math geek. I'm out of my element. This is the realm of practical engineering, which I will leave you practical engineers to work out. What we need to know at the end of the day—and I mean that literally—is how direct Mike's manipulation is."

Dice glanced at Chuck, who nodded. "Sure. We can do that."

Matt stifled another surge of annoyance. It took him a moment to recognize the cause. It bothered him, he realized, that Dice—whom he had brought into the business in the first place—had looked to Chuck for guidance, not him.

Stupid, he thought. Jealousy was a stupid reaction to something so small, not to mention a waste of energy. Chuck was the genius behind all of this. Why *shouldn't* Dice look to him for guidance?

Matt decided the best use of his time would be to monitor the progress of Dice's ninja-bot squad and start reworking their R&D and promotional plans. What Mike had done—and what Sara, Tim, and Lanfen might soon do—would change the entire direction of Forward Kinetics. If this turned out to be something they could teach anyone to do, they wouldn't need to build a factory; they'd need to build an academy.

He tried very hard not to think of it as Hogwarts.

TIM ACHIEVED ZETA AFTER TWENTY-TWO minutes; Sara did it in twelve. Cut off from the Brewster-Brenton, they were both able to continue manipulating their respective environments.

Dice wasn't sure whether he should be stoked or bummed out. His inventions had been the beginning, middle, and end of the mechanics involved in the process. Now he'd be lucky if he even got to participate in the endgame.

Dice snapped out of his mental whining. If nothing else he'd be expected to design special mechanisms for the new or modified applications. Ninja bot was just the beginning, but that wasn't the most important consideration by any means. He recognized that, and the knowledge stunned him.

They had set out to create a human-machine interface and had instead obviated the need for it entirely. They had created . . .

He shook himself, trying to keep his attention on the piece of firmware he had just pulled out of Sara's CAD/CAM. What had they created? Wizards? Demigods?

Nightmares?

"What do you think, Dice? Will it work?"

He jumped. Chuck was standing about four feet away, a frown rippling his brow.

"Is there a way to disconnect Becky entirely without disrupting Sara's zeta state?"

Dice brought himself back to the here and now. "Yeah, I think so. It will be a kludge. I'll have to go in and pull this card loose while the computer is running. I can't right offhand think of any reason that should disrupt things—that is if Sara's manipulating the machine directly. If she's using the USB connection to the firmware to trigger the software, then . . ." He shrugged, then replaced the card in the machine, reattached the USB connector, and left the rear panel open.

Sara was put through her paces a second time. She made zeta in nine minutes and forty-five seconds, and they shut down the rig. All of it, starting with the Brewster-Brenton. Then, while Sara was in full swing, making buildings rise up out of the virtual ground as fast as she could visualize them, Dice pulled first the USB connector then the card out of their sockets.

On the CAD screen, buildings continued to grow like crystals.

There was a mass exhalation in the room. Dice only then realized that he, along with everyone else, had been holding his breath. He also realized he had expected her signal to fail. Her system was, in its way, much more straightforward than Mike's. There were no mechanical parts; the entire interface was a matter of driving electrons.

Even as he registered the awe, excitement, and speculation of the rest of the team, he found himself wondering about the way Sara and Mike used their new kinetic capacities: were they the same or fundamentally different? There was a chance Mike was manipulating matter while Sara was manipulating energy. If that was the case . . .

His thoughts were interrupted by a debate that had broken out among the experimenters. Timmy Troll was loudly arguing that he didn't care how late in the day it was. He wanted his shot at the brass ring, wanted to know if he could replicate the hands-on stuff Mike and Sara were doing.

Chuck was arguing just as vehemently—if not as loudly—that they at least needed to take a dinner break. "Really, wouldn't you rather come at this fresh?"

"Hell, no!" objected Tim. "I do my best work between one and three A.M. on a liter of Dr Pepper and a bowl of Froot Loops. I'm ready now, dammit!"

"Uh . . ." said Eugene.

"Can't we call it a day?" asked Sara. "I'm shot."

"I could eat an elephant," said Mike in a deadpan. "Doubt Helen's cooked me one, though. Have to settle for a cow or two."

"Well, fine," said Tim. He looked as if he might be ready to descend into a fit of sulks. "I think there's a zoo about four blocks from here. Go find an elephant to chew on. You and Sara already got your fifteen minutes of fame, big guy. I want mine now, okay? You guys can just go home and rest if you're too tired to stick around and watch."

Sara shook her head, setting her dark hair swinging. "No way, Tim. I'm not missing any of this. Not one moment. We're either all here, or we're all gone."

"And you acting like a spoiled brat is making me want to be gone," Eugene said.

"I'm not just doing this for my own glory," Tim protested. "We're on the edge of something big here. We either take a break or make a breakthrough."

They all stood and glared at each other for several seconds—except for Chuck, who didn't glare so much as he looked deeply concerned. Then Mike shrugged and said, "Okay, I'm up for some overtime, I guess. I'll call Helen and tell her not to hold dinner up for me. But let's eat first, okay? We can send out for pizza," he added when Tim opened his mouth to protest. "Or hey, Froot Loops and Dr Pepper if you want."

Tim grinned.

Chuck looked over and saw Dice standing by the CAD/CAM, with the unnecessary piece of firmware in his hands. "You up for a late session, Dice?"

He nodded. "Sure. Pizza sounds great." As if to offer an opinion of its own, his stomach chose that moment to utter a deep growl. He figured that was approximately the noise Matt was going to make when he had to cancel his after-hours session with Chen Lanfen.

"Um, someone should probably tell Matt," he said. "In fact, I'll go do that now." He set the PC card down and headed for the door.

"Any particular specs for the pizza?" Eugene called after him.

"Nah. Oh, except sausage, not pepperoni; bacon, not anchovies; and tomato sauce, not pesto. I hate pesto."

"Engineers," Eugene said, shaking his head. "Working on how to build the perfect pizza."

THEY ATE DINNER IN THE small conference room. Matt was in an unpleasant mood. Dice was pensive. Mike and Sara were comparing notes while Eugene asked questions and Tim looked on and sulked. That did not keep him from putting away more than half a pizza all by himself before leaving to hit the head—information that, unlike the pepperoni slices, he graciously shared with the others.

Chuck was too distracted to taste the pizza he ate. His mind darted in a thousand directions at once: to the next experiment, to his TED Talk, to the trade show that was only a few months away, to the papers that would need to be written, to the magazines that would offer peer reviews. That was going to be difficult. There was bound to be much Sturm und Drang when the essence of what they were claiming they'd done hit the journals. A part of him dreaded that, and a part of him relished it.

"How do we make this palatable to the scientific community?" Chuck realized he'd said the words aloud only when everyone else stopped and stared at him.

"What?" asked Matt.

"How do we frame this so we don't get dismissed summarily?"

Matt didn't look surprised or even thoughtful. "Don't worry about it."

"Don't worry about it? You realize, don't you, that people will say we're hoaxing them."

"Sure, I do. But they'll investigate, and they'll find that we're on the level. We've documented what we've done. We can reproduce our results. We can even invite any naysayers to bring in their own subjects."

"What if we can't reproduce our results?"

"That's absurd!"

"You're kidding me!"

Sara and Mike objected in eerie harmony.

"What I mean is," explained Chuck, "what if you two are just exceptional individuals? What if this isn't something anyone can do? What if only certain people can do it? If it's not something anyone can do, even in part, then we're going to have a heck of a time proving ourselves. Our first failure could be our last failure."

Matt dropped a crust onto the pile of crusts on his paper plate and wiped his hands on a napkin. "Chuck, sometimes you can be such a pansy ass. You're like a bluebird of doom. Cheerful as all get-out one minute and certain everything will end in abysmal failure the next."

"Did you just call me a 'pansy ass'? Where the hell do you get off? And where did you get your third-grade insults?"

"In third grade." Matt shrugged, as if that was all the explanation he owed. Chuck half rose from the table, when he felt Eugene's hand on his arm.

"You're just cautious, Doc. Matt is being a putz."

"I didn't mean anything by it," he said.

"It sure as hell sounded like you meant something by it," Chuck said, but sat down.

Matt seemed to ignore that. "You're wrong about something, Eugene. I'm not being a putz. I'm being *confident*."

"A confident putz," Eugene muttered, and Chuck smiled slightly.

Whether Matt heard it or not, he ignored that comment as well, saying, "We aren't hoaxing anyone. Therefore, though some people may suspect us of a hoax, we will ultimately be vindicated."

He put his elbows on the table and leaned in. "Don't you guys get this? We are taking a hand in the evolution of our species."

"*Homo kineticus*," murmured Eugene.

A loud cry from beyond the half-open door of the conference room cut off all further discussion. There was the inevitable moment in which everyone's eyes locked over the last open pizza box at the center of the table, and then they were on their feet and out into the hall.

The cry was repeated, which allowed them to pinpoint the source—the main lab. Dice was first to the door, with Eugene and Chuck practically on top of him as he pushed through into the room.

Tim was standing in the center of the chamber, fists clenched, a fierce grin on his face. His overbright eyes were on the plasma display of the computer dedicated to his work. On-screen, a couple of CG characters were slashing at each other with large swords, which—as the others watched—transmuted into Klingon bat'leths.

"What did you do?" asked Chuck. "Running this equipment without Dice or someone here—"

Tim turned to look at Chuck, grin still intact. He pointed at the display, where the two warriors had frozen. "I'll show you what I did, Doc. I'll show you what I did. And I did it without even touching your precious equipment. Observe."

He waved a hand, and the screen went dark. He turned to look at the empty digital canvas and said, "New file."

The software opened in a new window.

"Human wire frame, large."

A wire frame appeared on the screen.

"Walking."

It began to walk. Then it acquired muscles, flesh, clothing. The clothing changed style, then color. The warrior's hair went from blue-black to red. A sword hung at his hip. It grew—became a broadsword. He drew it, took it in both hands, turned, and faced his gaping audience.

Tim had adopted the same stance: feet apart, hands together on an imaginary sword hilt. He threw back his head and uttered the same cry that had brought the others to him.

Chuck stared at the dormant BPM, the neural net lying limply over its rest. Tim had done it. He had made the leap from the converter's assist to fully independent manipulation of the application.

As if he could read their understanding of this singular feat in their faces, he smiled and bowed deeply from the waist.

"Thank you, my adoring fans." He straightened, his gaze going past Chuck to Sara and Mike. "I told you I meant to have my fifteen minutes. Beat that, bitches."

Chapter 12

FIFTEEN MINUTES OF FAME

Mini's reaction to the newest developments was the last one Chuck might have imagined: "Oh, I'm sure I can't."

He had always known her as a confident, spirited, creative individual. He hadn't thought the word *can't* was even in her vocabulary, so her sudden diffidence was unexpected, to say the least. He and Eugene had met her for a session on the weekend after the big breakthrough and had brought her directly to the main lab, where they had debriefed her and shown her the video record of the other subjects' sessions.

"But you've done so well with the interface—"

"Right. *With* the interface. The interface is what lets me manipulate the images. There's just no way I could . . ." She made a rolling gesture at the computer.

"Why not?" Eugene asked. "The others have done it. Why should you be any different?"

"Because I *am* different," she said, pressing her hands over her heart. "They're engineers and programmers. I'm just an artist."

The two men exchanged glances and then Eugene said, "There is no *just,* Min. You're an artist. You've learned to use the kinetic interface to make art. That's no different than Tim using it to make CG game characters and environments."

"Yes, Euge, it is. Timmy is a programmer. I'm not. I don't get all that technical stuff. I'm just going on instinct and adrenaline."

"And," Chuck argued, "a solid grasp of your tools. You understand your software no less completely than Sara understands hers."

She shook her head, looking resigned. "It won't work with me, Dr. Brenton. It just won't."

And it didn't. They got her into a gamma state, although it was harder than usual, and she began working with her constructs. Dragons, angels, people, scenery. When she went into a full zeta, Eugene pulled the firmware, and her creationary celebration shut down.

"As if the cops arrived to break up the party," Euge murmured when he and Chuck went off in a corner to consult about what to try next.

"What if we don't let her know that the connection is broken?" said Chuck.

"You think she's psyching herself out?"

"Don't you?"

"Maybe. Or maybe this isn't something just anyone can do with the right training. Or maybe someone really does have to understand the raw mechanics of the software."

"No. That can't be it. Of any of our subjects, I would have pegged Mini as the one most likely to transcend the machinery. She produces very strong signals in zeta, Euge."

He turned Eugene toward the screen where Mini was working, through the kinetic interface, with a set of drawings. "Look at her work, Euge. Look at the subtle shading on that horse's flank. Look at the detail in the mane and tail. As brilliant a game designer as Tim is, none of his work has that kind of subtlety. She's got the skills. I think she just doesn't believe she's got them."

"But how do we do it without her noticing?"

"Leave the firmware alone—she'll see you disable it—and just focus on the machinery on her periphery. Let's prove to her she can do this."

"Okay. She's in a strong gamma right now. Let's see if we can turn her up to eleven."

Chuck did just that by asking her to create a landscape with one of her favorite creatures in it. They wanted baselines, he explained—brain waves they could compare to the others. She immersed herself in the exercise, painting her electronic canvas with light and color and life: in a forest of immense redwoods, a wolf with silver-flecked fur tipped its head back to gaze up into a tree where a peregrine falcon looked back in unruffled splendor.

She went into zeta as she was filling her sketch with solid color and form. They let her virtually disappear into her created world before cutting her free of the machinery. Eugene had stationed himself just behind the Brewster-Brenton, but that was not the piece he shut down. The BPM monitor's fans were relatively noisy. Mini had said she could even sense the charge the electronic components gave off. Instead he simply flipped the switch on Becky's transmitter; the BPM continued to chart Mini's brain waves, but the transmitter was no longer feeding them to the kinetic actualizer at the other end. The firmware was no longer getting a signal from the neural net.

And yet Mini's forest scene continued to unfold. Chuck caught Eugene's eye over the top of the BPM and grinned.

DICE'S NEW NINJA BOT WAS beautiful in its own crazy way. It was about five feet tall when standing, and it had a head—a roughly human-head-size egg of plastic and aluminum that was equipped with a gyroscope and cameras. The body was segmented much like a centipede's; each smoothly rounded segment was about three inches tall, four inches deep, and six inches across. Each one was connected to the ones above and below with a spinal column of wire, fiber-optic cabling, and braces that behaved like the stays in a corset. The limbs were roughly humanoid in form and function with the exception that, unlike human limbs, these could rotate a complete 360 degrees at the shoulder or hip.

"It's like a ball-jointed doll but made of Slinkys," Lanfen said, then smiled at Matt Streegman. "I don't suppose you'd let me take it home and dress it up."

Dr. Streegman didn't get it. "Dress it up how?"

"I was thinking it might look cool as a member of Qin Shi Huang's imperial guard—you know, the Terra-Cotta Army?"

"That would impede its movement. Do you really think it needs clothes?"

Lanfen laughed. "Sorry, I realize this is way more expensive than my whole doll collection put together. But seriously, I guess whether you dressed it up or not would depend on what its job was. I mean what if you wanted someone to think it was human? Imagine how surprised a robber would be if he tried to knock over a bodega only to discover that the night watchman was a robot."

Dr. Streegman was suddenly staring at her in that disconcerting way he had that proclaimed eloquently that the rest of the world had just disappeared as far as he was concerned. "That's . . . that's a very interesting idea," he said at last.

"Your crown, your majesty."

Lanfen glanced over to find Dice holding the neural net out to her. She put it on, then stood quietly as he adjusted it to her head.

"So everyone else has made the leap, huh?" she asked. "They've all got spooky mind powers."

"They're not—" Dice began, but Lanfen waved him down.

"Just kidding," she said. "I'm just taking it all in. It's hard to believe, you know. And I'm . . . well, I'm not sure what to expect."

"Don't expect too much," Streegman told her. "The bot is new, after all. It may take some getting used to."

"It's not only new," said Dice. "It's not really complete. We've still got work to do. Right now it's made up of six distinct modules. It was the only way we could get it done in the time frame Matt set."

He didn't look at Streegman when he said that—something that Lanfen marked. *A little tension there. Not really my concern, though.* She wandered away from the two men.

She studied the bot, trying to get a sense of how it would balance and move. It was really a pretty cool design. Standing up on its legs, it really did have a human look to it. If it had clothing on it and a hat or helmet, she could almost believe it was a small adult. The segmented backbone gave the thing a very natural stance. Lanfen found it easy to put herself inside the frame even without the VR connections.

"You're online." Dice's voice called her out of her study.

She took a moment to reorient herself, then began working the bot. It was just as she'd suspected it would be: the robot's weight distribution was much more natural than its predecessor's. Its thick spine flexed (though not as ably as her own), and the legs and arms moved with more humanlike grace. Its feet had the same rounded, padded bottoms as the last bot (in fact she suspected they were the same feet). She wondered how hard it would be to make a foot that flexed like the backbone.

She put the bot through a series of simple kung fu postures, starting with the basic eight: horse, bow and arrow, low tiger, lotus, empty, rooster, tai chi, unicorn.

"This is great, Dice," she enthused as she moved the golem. "It feels as if I'm moving a human body. The balance is really nice. The lotus positions are kind of stiff. You might want to work on some sort of flexible pelvis. Just a thought. And I was wondering if you couldn't design some flexible feet . . ."

"Concentrate, Grasshopper," said Dr. Streegman quietly.

"I am concentrating." She kept the bot moving through a series of kicks and punches while maintaining her horse stance. "I should be in gamma now, right?"

She peripherally saw Streegman turn his head toward the BPM's display.

He chuckled. "Yes, you're in gamma."

"Know thyself," she shot back and tried to get the bot to execute a leg sweep. It fell over gracelessly. She saved it by tucking it into a roll and managed to get the thing back up on its feet.

"Yeah," said Dice. "I see what you mean about the pelvis. We'll work on that."

"Same deal with the shoulder area," Lanfen told him as she righted the ninja and began again with the basic poses. "I also think he needs a name. I'm going to call him . . ." She took the bot from a low lotus to lotus to high lotus. "Bilbo."

"Cool," said Dice. "He's about the right size."

Lanfen was silent for a moment, thinking about shoulders and hips and the widths they should be. The bot's shoulders and hips were narrow and ball-jointed directly into the first and last spinal segments. She tried to imagine that her own were narrower than they actually were—tried to adjust her imagined movements to that paradigm.

Ah, that's better.

She slid into sync with the little metal hobbit, trying to tailor her mental moves to its slightly off-kilter conformation. In a moment she was immersed in the movement, simply trusting that the bot was echoing her thoughts. She closed her eyes, imagining she was the robot.

This is so easy, she thought. *So natural.*

"I can hardly wait for you guys to get that VR piece in place. That'll be cool."

Lanfen became bolder in her mental movements. Without the real weight of her body, without its limitations, she felt freer and even attempted a flying roundhouse kick, laughing when she heard Dice gasp and Streegman murmur, "Atta girl."

She swung the bot into a shoulder roll, bounced it upright, and made it do a cartwheel then a series of three backflips, which took it to the edge of the mat.

"It's intermittent," she heard Dice say.

"Wait for it to go solid," said Streegman.

But their voices were background noise now. She ignored them, feeling like an Olympic gymnast about to do a final tumbling pass.

She started the bot into a run.

"That's it," Streegman said.

Backflip.

Somersault.

Up.

Roundhouse kick . . .

Then something went wrong. She could feel her mental grasp on the bot slip. She grabbed hold of it with her whole mind and forced it into a tuck and roll. There was a clatter of sound, then a loud popping noise, followed by a shouted curse from Dr. Streegman.

Lanfen's eyes flew open in time to see Bilbo the ninja hobbit break apart, its upper half crashing to the mat while its lower half flipped through the air and into the equipment rack, sending Matt and Dice scrambling. It struck the BPM dead-on, smashing the console and the display as if they were made of tin and calling forth a cascade of sparks. The equipment rack wobbled, then toppled in slow motion, falling against a workbench before skidding along it and crashing to the floor. The sound was deafening. The silence after more so.

Lanfen pulled the neural net from her head and ran across the mat to the fallen machine.

"Oh my God, I'm so sorry." She was winded; the words barely made it past her lips. She glanced from Dice to Streegman. "Are you all right?"

Dice, who had fallen, picked himself off the floor. "I'm fine. That wasn't your fault."

Streegman was already kneeling over the broken equipment. "What happened? Was it her intermittent signal?"

Dice shook his head, sinking to his haunches beside his boss. "No. How could it have been? The bot came apart because it wasn't ready for this level of trial yet. The spine is a weak point. I think it needs an exoskeleton as well as a backbone. Or at least a musculature to hold the frame together. Look. It broke apart right at the fourth vertebra."

Lanfen moved to stand behind the two men. She could feel Dice's anger, could see Streegman's determination to ignore it in his icy-blue eyes.

"My signal was intermittent?" she asked.

Streegman glanced up at her. "You weren't producing a solid zeta, just spikes in a strong gamma."

"Then why did you—"

"You gave us a sustained burst. I figured it would stabilize, so I had Dice turn the back end of the interface off. The monitor was still tracking your brain waves, but the kinetic converter in the Brewster was dormant. Only Becky's actualizer was still live."

"Well, it's dead now," said Dice. He held up the bot's onboard computer. It had been crushed.

Lanfen wrapped her arms around herself and watched as the two men pried the broken machinery apart, laid the robot out on the mat in pieces, and stood the machine rack back up on its casters. Intermittent. What did that mean? That she didn't have what it took to do this? She'd spent years learning the meditative state necessary to master kung fu and couldn't focus well enough to create a decent zeta state? That was too ironic for words.

Matt stood. "I'm going to take the hard drive out of the Brewster and see if I can get the data off it. Is there someone on your team who's especially handy with that?"

Dice gave him a sidewise glance. "You're forgetting what time it is, boss. They've probably all gone home."

"Fine, then I'll see what I can do. Lanfen, why don't you go on home?" He didn't wait for an answer but moved to the BPM and unfastened the brain wave monitor's casing from the machine rack. Then he tucked it under one arm and left without a backward glance.

Lanfen watched him go, then turned back to Dice, who was inspecting the bits of bot. "Do you need help?"

He shook his head. "You can go home."

"Let me rephrase. May I help? I feel like I ought to do something to . . ." To what? Make up for destroying thousands of dollars' worth of specialized equipment?

Dice raised his gaze to her face. "Lanfen, you didn't cause this. Maybe the intermittent zeta caused the bot to hesitate, and maybe that sudden hesitation torqued the thing's spine, but if it's going to do kung fu and smash through barriers or chase bad guys, it's got to be able to take some rough-and-tumble. It wasn't ready."

And she realized what he was saying. "Which isn't your fault, either."

Dice sighed and looked at the severed vertebrae in his hands. "I suppose I could have said no more forcefully."

Lanfen settled beside him, cross-legged. "Does he hear no? Does he even know what the word means? I get the feeling not."

"Definitely not. Here, see this?" He tilted the robotic joints so she could see the spinal column—or what was left of it. A bouquet of particolored wires and transparent fiber-optic strands exploded from the piece he held. "We had to jury-rig the big connectors to the pelvic bus. Solder and pins. The solder parted, and the pins pulled apart. These long pieces . . ." He flicked several dangling ends, some of which still had flat, gold connecting pins attached. "Pulled out of the bus altogether, which means the fiber optics must have parted first. And they did that because they're too fine. Part of my team was working on that angle of the problem. They'd recommended braiding the fiber-optic cabling to give it additional strength, but . . ."

"Dr. Streegman didn't give you time for that."

"Dammit!" Dice threw the broken piece to the mat. It hit with a heavy thunk. "If he'd been willing to wait one more day—two at best—we'd have been able to strengthen the core enough to have avoided this. But he just . . ." He shook his head and made a frustrated gesture with both hands.

"What will you do now?"

"Go back to the drawing board and design . . ." He frowned and picked up the broken piece of bot again. "A coax," he murmured. "That's what it needs—a coaxial core structure."

"A what?"

"A coax is a cable that's essentially got three layers. The interior core, which would be our core power and data cables, then a sheath composed of shielding and an outer mantle of some sort of fabric or coating."

Lanfen raised an eyebrow. "Kevlar maybe?"

Dice laughed. "Not Kevlar, but it's going to have to be something strong, flexible, and resilient."

"What if he doesn't give you time?"

"Oh, he will now. I know Matt. When his hubris blows up in his face, he disappears for a while, I think in the hope that by the time you see him again, you won't want to wring his neck. Or at least won't feel compelled to remind him of his mistake. My team can probably count on at least a week of blissful solitude before we have him in our faces again. I hope to have this flaw fixed by then—at least on paper. Besides, Chuck's got that TED Talk coming up next week. I expect Matt will be too busy pestering him to think about Bilbo's last stand."

Lanfen nodded, turning her gaze back to the disassembled robot. "Poor Bilbo. I feel like I hardly got a chance to know him."

Dice stood. "Lanfen, I promise you that Bilbo Mark II will be better, faster, and more flexible." He grinned. "We can rebuild him. We have the technology."

"I DID THAT," MINI ASKED, "without the machinery?"

She was still not ready to believe it, Chuck could tell, and he had to wonder what or who had convinced her that her artistic talent should be described with such adjectives as *just* or *only*.

"Why shouldn't you have?" he asked her. "In fact, if I'd known this sort of thing was possible, I would have said you were the *most* likely candidate to do it. You're so passionate about your art."

Mini gazed at the equipment, a slight frown between her brows. "Is that what this is really about? Passion? Is that what the zeta wave represents?"

Chuck had to think about that one for a moment. "I can't prove it—it's hard to really quantify passion—but I also can't help but think it is an integral part in all this."

She looked at him, her eyes squinting slightly, her lips pursing. "You're a passionate person. Have you experienced the zeta state?"

"Me? No. I've gone into gamma a little bit, and I can manipulate a slave unit through the interface, but I've never experienced zeta." He shook his head. "I'm not sure I could."

She laughed at him. "Charles Brenton! Really? You're lecturing me about self-doubt?"

He smiled ruefully. "Guilty as charged. But a large part of my self-doubt, as you put it, is just an extreme lack of time to experiment on myself. I'm pretty busy tracking everyone else's progress."

"And working on your TED Talk, I'll bet."

He felt his stomach tighten. "That, too."

"You're nervous, Doc? You?" She was laughing at him again.

"I am. Public speaking has never been one of my core skills."

"What are you using for show-and-tell?"

In answer he ran the playback of her session and watched her watching herself make a stunning piece of art using her talent alone.

"I'd like to use that, if I may. That wolf is extraordinary. And the detail in the forest scene . . ."

She blushed. "I don't know. You won't give my name, will you?"

"No—unless you want me to."

"God, no!"

Chuck laughed. "Pretty shy yourself. But I'll say one thing: people *are* going to know your name one day. You're too talented—regardless of this experiment—to go unnoticed for much longer."

She blushed harder.

Eugene came through the lab doors just then, shrugging into his jacket. Mini's trench coat was draped over one arm. He looked at both of them with curiosity . . . and possibly a touch of jealousy.

"Everything okay?"

"Yes!" Mini said. "Chuck is just being silly about my art."

"Not silly," he said. "I'm sure Euge here would agree your art is amazing."

There was no hesitation in Eugene's vigorous nod. Chuck smiled broadly.

"Ready to go?" Eugene asked. "Or should I ask Chuck if he's ready to let you go?"

Chuck just waved them toward the door. "You go. Have fun. I'll lock up."

"Thanks, Doc." Eugene helped Mini into her coat. "Oh, by the way, did you know that Matt is still here? I just saw him come up from the delta lab with what looked like a damaged BPM processor. What's he doing over there?"

"I'm not sure," said Chuck, "but I suspect the same thing we're doing here—experimenting. I don't know who they've got in the lab, but I'd bet it involves the robots Dice's team has been working on."

"You didn't ask?"

"No, on the theory that if I didn't poke into his extracurricular activities, he wouldn't poke into ours."

Mini wrinkled her nose. "You guys have a weird relationship, you know that?"

That was true enough. Chuck turned to Eugene. "Did you talk to him?"

"No. I don't think he saw me, and I was kind of in a hurry, so I didn't want to stop and schmooze." He winked and tilted his head toward Mini.

Chuck smiled. "Have fun."

Eugene hooked his arm through Mini's and started to lead her to the door. She glanced back over her shoulder. "Get some dinner, Doc. You know you could come with us."

"No, he couldn't," said Euge quickly.

"No, I couldn't," echoed Chuck and pointed at the door. "Out."

When they were gone, he sat for some time, looking at the equipment and wondering why he hadn't experimented with it himself more than he had. Was it fear?

God, he hoped not. He could admit to nerves. He was nervous about working with the rig. What he couldn't identify was *why* he was nervous about it. Was he concerned about losing his scientific objectivity? Or was he afraid of losing something else? Did he have some vestigial fear that what his subjects were experiencing now was changing them irrevocably?

He stood slowly, a chill creeping up from the pit of his stomach. What did that say about him if he was willing to subject others to something he was afraid of?

He had turned the system off. Now he turned it back on and picked up the neural net.

"Heavy is the head that wears the crown."

Chapter 13

PATIENCE

Matt watched Dice and his techs work on the new, improved ninja bot for several minutes before he let them know he was in the workshop. Dice noticed him first and gave him only a swift, goggled glance and a nod before returning to his inspection of the bot's vertebrae. His two assistants afforded Matt smiles and brief greetings before reengaging with their fearless leader.

They were quickly immersed in a discussion of the gear in a language Matt only half understood. Words like *coax* and *impedance* and *tensile strength* were sprinkled liberally throughout. Matt knew the meaning of the individual terms; still it was difficult to assign connotation in the fast-paced patter of tech talk.

Rather than interrupt, for he sensed the discussion was important, he circumambulated the workbench the three tech heads were gathered around and observed the object of their attention: the ninja's spinal column. It was disconnected from the rest of the components at the moment, and Matt couldn't help but notice that where before he had been able to see the wires and cabling that connected the vertebrae within the spinal cord, they were now covered with a flexible coating of gunmetal gray; only the ends of the connecting wires and their terminal pins were visible. The pins were significantly more robust than the ones the prototype had used. Instead of the long, flattened connectors, they sported thicker, barrel-shaped pins that would, he supposed, be less inclined to bend or break.

He waited for a lull in the conversation before asking, "How's it coming?"

Dice glanced up again through his safety goggles, his brown eyes wary. "It's coming. We've made a number of improvements."

"So I noticed—heftier hardware and a sheath over the components. Isn't that going to make them harder to get to if something goes wrong?"

"Nope. Because the cabling is pulled through from the top of the spine. If we need to get to something, we just detach the lower torso, pull the core out, open up the sheath, and fix whatever needs fixing. Then we apply a new sheath, shrink it, pull it back through the vertebrae, and wire it up."

Matt frowned. "There's more holding it together than just wires and pin connectors, though, right?"

Dice's mouth twitched. Before he could respond, one of his minions said, "Of course. There's a physical locking mechanism in the pelvis."

The minion was a pretty, young thing—slender, athletic-looking, and blond, her long hair braided and dangling over one shoulder. Matt tried to remember her name. Brenda something. He tried not to take offense at the fact that her "of course" sounded an awful lot like "well, duh."

It wasn't any easier as she continued.

"The spine anchors there," she explained as if she were speaking to a small, dim-witted child, "and then the pelvic structure clamps shut over the connection."

"We're working on an external sheath for the whole megillah," added Dice. "A tough one. Not Kevlar, but tough. We're still working on the specs for that."

Matt stifled a smile. It was weird to hear his Japanese-American cohort spouting Yiddish. He wondered if Eugene had picked up as much slang from Dice as the robotics engineer had picked up from him. "Not an exoskeleton?"

Dice shook his head. "We think having a brittle exterior would be a bad idea."

"Okay. But what if someone shoots at your robocop? Then what?"

"Fit it with a Kevlar vest or body armor. It'd be cheaper and more flexible in a number of ways." He paused and gave Matt a speculative look. "You need something?"

"Actually I just finished analyzing the data from that train wreck we had last week. Got a minute?"

Dice glanced at his techs, then nodded and removed his goggles. "Bren, why don't you connect Bilbo up and get him ready for a systems trial?"

The young woman smiled. "Sure thing, boss."

She was huddled over the bot before Matt and Dice were halfway to the door.

"So what did you find?" Dice asked once they'd reached the privacy of Matt's office.

"You tell me." Matt went to his desk and turned his laptop so that Dice could see the display. It showed a jagged bar of brilliance that, if it were an audio waveform, would indicate a loud, continuous noise with spikes of explosive percussion.

"What the hell?" Dice glanced up at Matt. "What is this?"

"This is Lanfen's state just before she swept old Bilbo off his feet."

"She swept him off his feet?"

Matt shrugged. "Or so it appears. Her zeta is . . . rambunctious, to say the least. So rambunctious it blew my formula right out of the water."

Dice straightened. "It overloaded the input?"

"Basically. My formula assumes an input that falls within a certain range. When the others have gone into zeta, just raising the threshold on the input filter has done the trick. But Lanfen's topmost output—"

"Is outside the range."

"Way outside the range, which may or may not mean she's more powerful. It may just mean she's got a chaotic profile."

Dice raised a sleek eyebrow. "A martial arts master who's got a chaotic energy profile? That's counterintuitive."

"I suppose it is. At any rate I set up a new unit in the lab and adjusted my equations to broaden the range significantly."

"But that means she's not bypassing Becky, doesn't it?"

"I'm not sure *what* it means. I'm not sure it will solve the problem even if she isn't bypassing Becky. There's only one way to find out if it will."

Dice shoved his hands into his pockets and met Matt's gaze. "The bot's not ready," he said slowly, emphasizing each word.

Matt bit back his impatience and took a deep breath. "Okay. When?"

"Not until the beginning of next week at least."

"What?" Matt's attempt at patience failed catastrophically. He pointed in the direction of the team working on Bilbo. "I saw the bot, Dice. All the components are there—"

"And need to be thoroughly tested, so we don't have to start from scratch . . . *again*. If you want this to be the centerpiece of our stealth Applied Robotics presentation, we have to be double damn sure it's not going to fly apart on us during a demo."

Matt swallowed his frustration. "Yeah. Sure. I see that. Okay, look, however long it takes, okay? In the meantime I'll have Lanfen work with Roboticus to try to get her zeta waves calmed down."

"About that," Dice said. "Is it just that she's erratic, or is she überpowerful?"

"Her baseline is different, and her range is longer. Maybe the chaos isn't anomalous, or maybe it's not really chaos. Maybe it's because she meditates regularly. I've heard there are studies showing that people who meditate generate significantly different brain patterns than those who don't."

"Chuck might be able to tell us that."

Matt lowered his gaze and turned his laptop back around. "I'm not ready to have Chuck know what we're doing."

Dice was silent for a moment, then said, "Well, if we're going to make this work with Lanfen, he may have to know." He turned and left Matt's office without further comment.

When Dice was gone, Matt sat back down at his desk and studied Lanfen's zeta signature. Letting Chuck in on his work with the martial artist wouldn't be his first choice. There was just something about the doctor that was too cautious. He thought back to the time in the conference room, when Chuck had gotten angry at Matt. He couldn't remember the exact reason—it had seemed so trivial at the time, and even more so now—but if Chuck could get so upset then, he wasn't sure how the man would react to this news. And yet Dice was right—it was something he might just have to do.

Might.

"SO YOU'RE NOT GOING WITH Dr. Brenton to the TED conference?" Mini was clearly pleased by that prospect. In the pool of flickering light from the single candle that sat in the middle of the restaurant table, her smile was brilliant, her green eyes sparkled, and her skin took on a golden glow.

Eugene was inclined to tell her that he wouldn't go to that show even if Chuck ordered him to if it meant being away from her for an entire week. What he said was, "No. He thought about it but decided we couldn't afford to slack off on the program for a week. So I'm staying here to keep things moving."

"Are you disappointed?"

"No." He hesitated, then added, "Frankly I'd rather be with you than with Chuck at a conference."

"That's sweet," she said, then her smile slipped a bit. "You're not just saying that, are you?"

"Just saying it? I just said . . . what do you mean just saying it?"

"You know. Are you just saying it because you're trying to impress me?"

"Of course I'm trying to impress you. Obviously I want you to be impressed with me, but I'm saying it because I mean it. I like being with you."

"Why?"

Minerva Mause could be the most disconcerting person when she half tried. Eugene glanced toward the ritzy, wrought-iron servers' elevator, hoping their two orders of linguine Pomodoro would come sailing out and forestall this conversation. He was all thumbs when it came to dating and was beginning to think there was no way this could end well.

Two paths diverged in the snowy wood of his brain. One led to some simplistic "how to talk to women" lines he'd read in *Esquire* magazine, the other to something entirely other and alien: dissecting his actual feelings and trying to articulate them. A glance into Mini's eyes blew all his *Esquire* training right out of his head.

"I'm not good at this," he warned her. "I'm really not. I don't know how to talk to women."

"I'm not women," she said. "I'm me."

He blinked. "There. That's why I like to be with you. You're you. You're quintessentially Mini. You're alive and fresh and creative, and you've got all these things going on inside you that I really want to know about. And okay, you're also very beautiful, and you're . . . you're . . ."

"Erotic in a wholesome way?" she asked teasingly.

"Yeah."

She was still smiling but pulled her eyes away to look down at her hands. "Here's the thing, Euge. I don't always feel beautiful. I mostly feel like a gawky tween. And I sometimes think my creativity is all in my head." She was silent for a moment while he tried to formulate a response. Then she looked up at him and said, "Guys are always telling me I'm cute. Like a kitten or some other small animal no one takes seriously. They want to pet me or put me on a leash. They think my art is *cute*, too. Do you understand what I'm saying?"

Impulsively Eugene reached across the table and took her hand. "Yeah, I think I do. And I don't. I mean I don't think you're cute—at least not like a kitten or a pet. I think your art is amazing and powerful. I think *you're* amazing. When I first met you, I thought you were a little . . . odd. But you're just so creative and smart. Heck, the last thing I'd want to do is put you on a leash, Mini. It's that sense of freedom and impulsiveness you have that's so intriguing."

She was smiling at him full tilt now—a thousand-candlepower smile. She squeezed his hand. He'd somehow managed to get it right, to speak the right words. He was breathless with the sheer unexpectedness of it.

He smiled back. The candle on the table suddenly flared, making both of them sit up straight and let go of each other's hands.

"Whoa," Eugene said. "What was that?"

"I'm so sorry. Let me replace that for you." The server, who'd arrived at the table unobserved, set their entrées down in front of them, picked up the candle in its cup, and blew it out. "I'll just bring another one. They sometimes do that when they burn all the way down."

He went away then, frowning into the candleholder.

Looking after him, Mini laughed, and Eugene reflected that he understood exactly how that candle flame felt. Something was flaring in him at the moment, too. It prompted him to ask, "So are you happy I'm not going to Long Beach with Chuck?"

She paused in the act of coiling linguine around her fork and gave him a look that questioned his intelligence. "Of course. Shouldn't I be?"

"Oh, I think you definitely should be. No, sorry, that came out wrong. I mean I hope you are. I mean if I had my way, you'd be head over heels in love with me already."

"Head over heels," she repeated, and wrinkled her perfect nose. "Have you ever thought about that saying? Our heads are always over our heels. It should be the other way around, shouldn't it? Shouldn't love upset the natural order of things?"

He met her eyes and couldn't look away. Something was certainly upsetting his natural order.

"I told my mom about you," he said, surprising both of them.

"Really?" She was looking at him as if he'd said the most fascinating thing she'd ever heard. "What did she say?"

"She said I should be patient but not stupid patient."

Again the nose wrinkle. "That sounds like great advice . . . for a fisherman."

"I am sort of fishing," Eugene said, twirling up some linguine and popping it into his mouth.

"Have you been stupid patient before?"

He nodded. "Mom thinks so. She thinks I've blown my chances with women before by not speaking my mind. But honestly, this is the first time I've had a strong mind to speak."

She set down her fork and gave him her entire attention. "What's your mind saying?"

He set his fork down, too, glancing around to make sure there was no one within earshot. Their table was up on a low balcony overlooking the noisier lower room of the restaurant. He took a deep breath and hoped he wasn't screwing this up.

"Well, that's the problem. Sometimes I can't hear my mind because my body's talking too loudly. I think you're incredibly sexy, and it's hard to separate that from the other stuff."

Her expression was suddenly very serious. "Try."

He nodded. "Okay, I will. But you may have to be patient, too. I don't want to mess this up."

She smiled suddenly, brilliantly. "Well, that's something right there, isn't it?"

He supposed it was. "What about you?" he had the temerity to ask. "What's your mind saying?"

She picked up her fork again and went back to her linguine. "Oh, it's pretty much in agreement with my heart and all my other parts on this one.

"I've been in love with you from the moment we met."

Chapter 14

QUESTIONS

"So is what you're saying," asked the guy in the third row, "that these people have developed a form of telekinesis?"

Chuck glanced back at the screen behind him on the large stage. It was frozen on Sara's "use the Force" moment as she high-fived Tim. He had covered the genesis of the project from inspiration to fruition, had shown each subject during different phases of development (to increasing murmurs and bursts of applause that never seemed to sweep the whole audience), and had stopped with the videos of the team in their pre-zeta gamma states.

Yet the first question was about telekinesis.

He had thought that describing each component of the rig and what it did would have inoculated him against this question. He was momentarily stumped because the truth was something he had agreed he would not tell, and the truth was that, yes, these people had developed a form of telekinesis—a form that relied on their maneuvering the mechanics of whatever it was they were trying to control. Chuck, who knew himself to be a terrible liar, had to find a way to say less than the truth without telling a lie.

"What I'm saying," he said finally, "is that these people are . . . flexing mental muscles we didn't know they had. They are manipulating these components using the electrical impulses of their brains thanks to a formula created by Dr. Matt Streegman of MIT that modulates the impulses—or conditions them—so they can be interpreted by the interface."

"So you have a wireless transmitter and a transceiver that remotely controls machinery." The guy shrugged. "What additional value do you get over just manipulating the machinery remotely in any other way?"

Chuck smiled. This part he knew cold.

"Well, just imagine you've got a highly skilled programmer who loses the use of his hands. With the Forward Kinetics system, you would not have to lose the knowledge and skill of that programmer, and he wouldn't have to lose his job or go on long-term disability. With our system he could learn to manipulate his software without having to use his hands. Or consider the plight of someone who's had an advanced stroke. He's still in there, thinking, feeling. He just can't communicate. With the Forward Kinetics system, we have hope he will be able to communicate—and more."

Another man took the microphone. "Have you been approached by the military? Because the military implications of this are stunning."

Chuck blinked. "The military? No, we haven't been approached by them."

"Don't you think that's kind of weird? You'd think they'd be all over something like this."

"They probably think we're just an uptown version of the loony geeks who wear tinfoil hats and build robots in their parents' basements." Chuck got an appreciative laugh from the other geeks in the room (roughly the entire audience) and smiled. But the question did bother him. The military must have noticed him and his partners in some way. The thought gave him a chill.

"Given the state of drone technology," said someone else, "what are the advantages of a system like this? I mean what might the military gain if they had operatives outfitted with this sort of tech instead of the immersive VR systems they're beginning to use now?"

As uncomfortable as he was discussing military applications, Chuck warmed to contrasting the Forward Kinetics tech with state-of-the-art VR guidance systems.

"Simply put," he said, "the technology will be smaller, more portable, and ultimately far less expensive. Right now the military spends millions—billions perhaps—on physical VR system interfaces. They'd have none of that with the Forward Kinetics technology."

"What would someone need to avail themselves of your technology?" was the next question.

Another minefield to peck through. If what Chuck thought was happening to his subjects really was happening, the customer wouldn't need any of the equipment except for training purposes. Their operatives could train at Forward Kinetics, then leave to pursue their missions. He couldn't say that, though, so he answered at the highest level—what they needed to train a zeta operator.

"Well, there's the brain pattern monitor, the neural net, and the kinetic interface, which is made up of the Streegman converter software and the Brenton-Kobayashi Kinetic Interface, which includes an actualizer unit. We're working to miniaturize all of that. Theoretically they wouldn't even need a huge facility for their operatives. Anyplace they had access to a power supply would do. We're working on that, too, of course—enabling the use of a variety of power sources."

"What is the mechanism, though, Doctor?" asked a young woman with an earnest expression. "What exactly is it that the subjects are manipulating? I mean the diversity in your group is . . ." She broke off, looking at the screen. "Manipulating hardware and manipulating software would seem to be two completely different modalities."

Back on terra firma, Chuck relaxed. "Well, not really. Even the robotic arm you saw Mike working with before and the John Deere backhoe on which he took his," he paused, thinking of how to put it before settling on, "midterm exams, I guess you'd say, have a software component that requires a command set. Even a mechanical device has a command set. It's just that the command set for Tim's or Sara's software-hardware combination is written in ones and zeroes, and the command set on a mechanical device is written in ergs, in units of applied energy. It's still binary—on/off, forward/backward, left/right—and all of these things can be accomplished using the electrical impulses of the brain. That's the difference between what we're doing and direct telekinesis. Our subjects aren't moving things; they're manipulating the mechanisms to cause things to move."

The thought hit him just as the last word left his mouth. He'd flirted with the idea before, but now it came back to roost: if what he'd said about impulses and ergs was true, then *could* his subjects one day manipulate any material object directly?

The implications of that were swept away on a tide of questions: If the gamma wave showed a variety of brain modalities working in concert, what did he theorize the zeta wave represented? Did he think anyone could generate zetas? What was the next step in the Forward Kinetics process? Were they accepting job applications?

He was sitting in the hotel restaurant enjoying a late-night dinner when his mind wandered back to the question of the zeta wave's implications. Clearly the fact that they'd been able to spur the state in all three of their primary subjects and Mini meant something. It suggested that this new brain state was very near the surface in some individuals. Which, in turn, suggested that they were evolutionarily close to its emerging on its own.

How close? If they sped up the process artificially, would humanity be ready for it? In a world where power-hungry men still used any tools at their disposal to arrogate control, resources, and territory, was even the most enlightened society ready for the God wave?

He was shaking himself and trying to put the idea out of his head when two of his talk attendees sidled up to the table and asked if they could chat for a moment. He smiled, was pleasant, and said he welcomed their questions.

They were far more welcome than his own.

MATT, TRUE TO HIS WORD, had not pressured Dice to make his bot ready any earlier than he'd promised. It took close to two weeks of intense work, but Bilbo the Second was finally ready for a workout. Chuck was in transit from the TED conference in Long Beach and not expected back in the office until the next morning, so they brought the video rig down from the main lab to record their activities.

Bilbo was beautiful in his own way, Dice thought. His head was humanoid, of clear, molded, high-impact plastic and steel. It had LEDs that marked where his cameras were set—not strictly necessary, but as Brenda said, "very cool-looking." The front set was blue, the rear set red, the side set green. The cameras had infrared lenses that could be deployed, presumably, at a thought. The VR rig would allow the operator a 360-degree view in day or night. Dice and his team had built small headlamps into the forward video apparatus as well.

The head swiveled on a pair of shoulders that were roughly as wide as Lanfen's. The hips were of equal width. The whole body was covered with a shiny, silver, titanium aluminum alloy skin that was tough as nails and flexible and hid the vulnerable spine. The arms and legs were jointed more or less like a human body's, but the joints could be flipped so the bot could reverse course by simply swiveling its head 180 degrees and repurposing its joints. That was supposed to happen pretty much automatically when the operator reoriented the head and began backward momentum.

In theory.

It was features like these, Dice thought, that spoke to the recurring question of what a zeta operator could do that a manual VR operator could not. An operator wearing a standard VR rig could not spin his head around 360 degrees—or even 180—or reverse direction fully without turning around. Even with a normal human operator in a full VR suit that transferred kinetic information directly to a humanoid bot, the bot would be limited to what the human body could do.

He'd seen the models the Japanese were experimenting with. In his opinion their approach was all wrong. They were thinking C-3PO and Data when they should have been thinking Slinky. If the real estate mantra was "location, location, location," the robotics mantra was "application, application, application." This application clearly required flexibility and balance above all else, so trying to make the robot more humanoid in the ways the Japanese had made little sense. It was the flexibility of the human spine—the shock-absorber qualities of its joints and muscles—that he wanted to emulate more than its upright stance or proportions or even the precise way in which it was jointed.

When Lanfen came in at nine that night, she gratified him by agreeing that Bilbo II was indeed a work of art.

"Wow," she said, shivering and rubbing her hands together as she warmed up next to a heater vent. "He's beautiful, Dice. I love the way his spine flexes." She grinned. "Hey, Papa, can I have the keys to the robot?"

Dice returned the grin. "Only if you promise not to wreck him again."

Lanfen's face fell. "I . . . I'm sorry . . ."

"No," he said, mortified at his mistake. "I'm sorry. I didn't mean it the way it came out. I promise. Look, Matt put on a fresh pot of coffee. Why don't you have some? Warm up before you take a test drive."

She nodded and shrugged out of her coat. She was sipping her coffee when Matt came in, humming. That was unusual in and of itself—Matt hummed only when he was on a high from having pulled off a major coup or germinating a really good mathematical theorem. Dice knew better than to ask outright, but he probed just in case Matt was in a mood to share.

"You sound chipper, Dr. Streegman. I take it something miraculous has occurred?"

Matt stopped and looked at Dice as if he'd only just realized he was there. "Miraculous? No. Just positive." He rubbed his hands together. "Are we ready to rock?"

"Just a moment," said Lanfen, setting down her coffee cup. She took off her shoes, walked onto the exercise mat, and went through a series of stretches and breathing exercises. With that done she pronounced herself ready to rock, and Dice wired her up.

He checked all the inputs, had Matt double-check his algorithm to make sure they had the latest rev of the software running, and fired up the rig. Lanfen had created a sort of routine for herself—a set of exercises she always used to get in the zone, as she put it. Dice was fascinated by the process not just because she was awfully attractive but because of the surreal grace, control, and balance she showed. She looked sometimes as if she were floating above the mat rather than standing on it, and the way she moved from one kung fu pose to another reminded him of Olympic gymnasts on a balance beam—only about ten times more elegant.

"You're staring," Matt murmured. "Not that I blame you. She's something special. You should ask her out."

Dice shook himself. "Uh . . . I'm seeing Brenda."

Matt's eyebrows rose. "Doesn't she work under you?"

"This isn't the military, Matt," Dice said more sharply than he meant to.

Matt just shrugged and turned away to watch Lanfen put Bilbo through his paces. She was doing the moves herself at that point, getting used to the balance of the bot and the new VR component that allowed her to see the world from Bilbo's point of view.

"What do you think?" Dice asked her. "Ready to go mental?"

She laughed. "Funny you should put it that way. I feel like I'm mental whenever anyone asks me what I do in my free time."

Matt's head jerked up. "You signed a nondisclosure contract, Ms. Chen. What are you telling people you do in your free time?"

Lanfen shot him an unreadable glance. "I tell them I do the same thing I do during my workday—kung fu." She and the robot pivoted toward Matt and performed a most proper bow. Then she settled into a lotus posture and sent Bilbo into a series of moves without as much as a twitch on her part.

Dice was impressed.

She'd gone through the sequence of basic postures twice when she began to throw in more difficult moves that she might use in a sparring match.

"You know," she said as the bot bobbed and weaved and kicked, "it would be much more realistic if Bilbo had someone or something to spar with. Maybe you need to get another martial artist on staff."

"We don't officially have one on staff now," Matt reminded her.

"True."

The bot executed a roundhouse kick and rolled into a somersault. It came up on the far side of the mat, then Lanfen flipped the head around and had the bot execute a series of kicks and rolls in the opposite direction.

"Oh, this is sweet," she said enthusiastically. "This is really a nice feature!"

"Why does she have to chatter like that?" Matt murmured.

"I heard that," she said. "I'm multitasking. Gets me to gamma faster. I'm in solid gamma right now, right?"

Dice nodded and glanced wryly at Matt. "Yes, you are."

"Okay. I've been watching from the outside up to now. I'm going to switch to bot cam." There was a pause and then she said, "Oh, wow. This is weird. Bilbo is shorter than I am."

The bot blocked an imaginary assailant then kicked, came down in a crouch, and flipped backward several times. Then it ran, executed a flying kick, and tucked into a forward roll.

Dice's jaw clenched. This was approximately what Lanfen had been doing when the catastrophe had occurred. This time, though, the bot popped up at the edge of the mat, reversed its orientation, and did a similar set of kicks and rolls back again. Dice glanced at the monitor; Lanfen was in a solid but spiky zeta. A moment later, as Bilbo touched down after a terrifying and spectacular twisting leap, Dice silently shut the kinetic interface down. There was a tiny hesitation in the metal man's next move, but it was small enough that Dice doubted anyone watching would have noticed it.

He glanced at Matt. The professor's expression was unchanging. Dice almost smiled. The boss hadn't noticed the difference, and Lanfen . . .

Whoa. Hold the phone.

"Hey, Lanfen," Dice said casually, "you getting used to the view?"

"You mean vertically challenged Bilbo cam? Uh-huh."

And that's what was so crazy: she was still seeing from the bot's point of view. The mechanical interface was shut down, and she was somehow using the robot's camera eye. Dice was about to speak to Matt when he was distracted by something beyond the lab window. Over in the main wing, lights had come on in Chuck's office.

"Uh-oh."

Matt looked at him and followed his gaze. "Dammit. He would have to come in his first night back. I should've known." He made a frustrated noise then nodded toward Lanfen. "See if you can't wean her off the interface. I'll go over and make sure you're not interrupted."

"She's been on her own for the last three and a half minutes, and, Matt, she—"

"Good work. Fantastic!" Matt clapped a hand on his shoulder and breezed out of the lab. Out on the mat, Bilbo continued to dance.

"Tell her, not me. I just work here," Dice murmured at his boss's back.

"SO IT IS YOU." MATT leaned in the door of Chuck's office.

Chuck blinked up at him past his desk lamp. "Uh, yeah. It's . . . who else would it be? The cleaning crew comes in over the weekend, doesn't it?"

Matt sauntered in and sat down in the chair on the opposite

side of the desk then rolled it toward the door a foot or two to draw Chuck's eyes away from the window. The horizontal blinds were down, but they were half-open; if Chuck looked, he'd be able to see there were lights on in the delta lab in the lower wing. He might have noticed already.

"So how was the conference?"

Chuck took a deep breath and let it out before answering. "Interesting."

"A Mr. Spock sort of interesting or actually interesting?"

"A bit of both, actually." Chuck closed the lid of his laptop and propped his elbows on it, running his long, slender fingers through his hair. "I had the most mixed bag of reactions you could imagine. People who thought it was a hoax and said they were going to complain to the organizing committee, people who were so excited they wanted to apply for work or internships here, people who were fascinated by the machinery, others who were intrigued by the neurological implications, and those who asked if we thought it was the next-best thing to telekinesis." He shook his head. "In fact, the very first question was 'Is this telekinesis?'"

"And you said . . . ?"

"I tiptoed carefully around the subject and simply reiterated that this is merely an interface between the brain's naturally occurring electrical impulses and output devices. No interface, no go. It wasn't that big a deal." He was silent for a moment, then asked, "Matt, have we been approached by the military?"

Matt's internal warning bells went off. "You mean has the Pentagon come knocking on our door, asking us what the hell we think we're doing?"

Chuck looked at him. "Something like that."

Matt had a moment of hesitation, which was not something he was used to. Chuck—however geeky, however inconvenient—was the closest thing he had to a friend. Hell, in a moment of weakness he'd even told him about Lucy and given him a copy of her read-outs. Inscrutable as it was to him, that was the only sacred text Matt had ever known. Now, with his partner's trusting hazel eyes fixed on him, he felt as if he were plotting to kick a puppy. And yet he couldn't help himself.

"Why do you ask?"

"It came up. A few times, actually."

Chuck had clasped his hands together and was wringing them—a gesture that betrayed the depth of his concern.

"Ah. Well, no. The Pentagon has not asked us out on a date. Nor have we heard a peep out of the men in black."

"Don't you think that's odd?"

Matt blinked. That was unexpected. "Do you?"

"Yeah. What we're doing has obvious military applications—you even brought it up when we were considering what disciplines to include in our primary study. If they haven't made an overture, I have to wonder why."

Matt relaxed farther back into the chair, striving for nonchalance. "You have any theories?"

"One. They think we're a box of wing nuts, and our technology is one step away from dowsing or Kirlian photography."

Relieved that Chuck hadn't tumbled to the real reason he hadn't heard a peep out of the military, Matt laughed. *"The Men Who Stare at Goats:* Next Gen?"

Chuck smiled wanly. "Yeah. That. Do you think that's it?"

Matt heaved himself out of the chair and shoved his hands into the pockets of his jacket. "Probably. Don't let it get to you, though. We're going to knock their socks off at Applied Robotics."

Chuck unplugged his laptop and started rolling up his power cable. "I'm not sure I want to knock their socks off. I like that they think we're wing nuts."

"You really don't like the military, do you?"

"Five sides," Chuck murmured. He set his power supply down atop the computer and stood stock-still.

"What?" God, but Chuck could be unnerving sometimes.

"The Pentagon. Why five sides? Pentacle. Pentangle."

Oh, good grief. "Five branches of the military? Army, navy, air force, marines, coast guard?"

Chuck laughed and ran his fingers through his hair again. "Yeah, that was weird, wasn't it? I'm tired. Jet-lagged probably. My brain makes random connections when my mind is too tired to supervise."

"What?" Matt said again, hoping it hadn't come out sounding like a guffaw.

Chuck's dark gaze fastened on his face. "Brain and mind aren't the same thing," he said deliberately. "You know that, right? The brain generates the electrical impulses that run our bodies. The mind is what steers them, oversees them."

"Okay, that at least sounds scientific. You had me going there for a moment. I thought you'd been smoking religion or something."

Deep down in Chuck's eyes, something flashed a warning. "Why can't a scientific idea also be a religious idea? 'Greater than the senses is the mind. Greater than the mind is Buddhi, reason; and greater than reason is He—the Spirit in man and in all.' Bhagavad Gita, chapter three, verse forty-two."

"Forty-two, huh? Answer to life, the universe, and everything?"

"I think so."

Matt held up his hands in surrender. He was not going to get into a religious argument with St. Chuck, the true believer. "You on your way out?"

Chuck took a deep breath and glanced around. "Yeah. I just came in to get some notes Euge left me."

"I guess I'll see you in the morning, then."

Chuck nodded, then scooped up his computer bag and slid the laptop into it. Matt turned and walked toward the door.

"So what are you doing here this late?"

Matt stopped and scratched behind one ear. "Oh, Dice and I are working the kinks out of a robot his team's been developing. A security bot. He's been using it to alpha-test the VR unit."

"How's that supposed to work with the zetas? The VR works fine when you've got a hard interface, but how can it work when Becky goes offline?"

Matt stared at him as if he'd begun to recite "Jabberwocky" backward in Yiddish. Had the VR interface continued to work when Dice offlined the hardware? The question sent his heart and brain (mind, whatever) into hyperdrive.

"That's a damn good question, Dr. Brenton. I'll go ask the expert."

He escaped before Chuck asked him something else he should have asked himself.

MATT FOUND HIMSELF IN THE peculiar position of holding information that could be critical to the course of Forward Kinetics. He was unable to discuss it with anyone but Dice, because he was the only other person who knew that of all the zetas, only Chen Lanfen was able to use the VR interface without Becky's physical connection. Why that should be so while her control of the bot was still problematic was a mystery.

Matt didn't know what that anomaly meant—whether it had to do with Lanfen's discipline as a master of kung fu or her meditation techniques or the unique functioning of her brain. He only knew that while the other subjects had the ability to control their various mechanisms, they could not transfer kinetically to VR on their own. When Becky's connection was cut, Mike could still motivate his machinery, but he could not see the world from its

viewpoint. Tim, whose coded characters were not physical enti-
ties and therefore possessed no VR capabilities, could not view
the world from his creatures' eyes at all.

It was annoying enough to have the anomaly surface, but to
have it surface in a subject who was not an official part of the program was doubly so. The fact that Matt's co-conspirator felt they
should come clean was triply annoying for the simple reason that
Matt knew Dice was right. Keeping Chuck and company in the
dark about Lanfen was keeping Matt and Dice in the dark about
what Lanfen's peculiar strengths and weaknesses augured.

And he needed the neurological expertise of Chuck and
Eugene to examine the problem.

Yet he said nothing and forbade Dice to say anything as well.
"All in due time," he told his lab director. "All in due time."

"The time," Dice had said during their last encounter, "is due."

He'd made it his walk-off line—something Matt thought was
cheap and unprofessional. It had caused him to chase Dice down
and ensure that regardless of his strong feeling they should let
everyone else in on their progress with the ninja bots; he would
keep their secret. Matt had an arsenal of arguments up his sleeve.
That he had taken him under his wing when he was still just Daisuke, a no-name, and fast-tracked him professionally. That he had
brought him into Forward Kinetics in the first place. That he'd
have Brenda and the rest of the lab assistants fired if he breathed
one word to Chuck. Or that they'd all work together on this and
every following development after the show.

But none of that was necessary.

Dice had turned around and said just one sentence to him:
"I'll do it for you out of loyalty—but I'll do it just this once, and
then we're even."

Fair enough, Matt thought, though he didn't see himself and
any of the other members of FK as "even." He would always have

an advantage, always put himself first. After all, he was a numbers guy.

Now Matt leaned back on his apartment sofa and took a sip of the merlot he'd poured half an hour before and forgotten about. His eyes were still on the screen of the laptop that sat on his coffee table. The image was of Chuck's face, frozen in a moment of crusader zeal as he described his vision for the Forward Kinetics technology at the TED conference.

His last words still echoed in Matt's head: "Consider the plight of someone who's had an advanced stroke. He's still in there, thinking, feeling. He just can't communicate. With the Forward Kinetics system, we have hope he will be able to communicate—and more."

Still in there, thinking, feeling.

God.

No.

Matt Streegman did not believe in God—not a God who had imprisoned Lucy's soul or spirit or mind in a body that had ceased to work. Caged her in a brain that was slowly being eaten away by anonymous entropy.

He knocked back the last of the wine, barely tasting it, and tipped his head back and stared at the wood-paneled ceiling. Had Lucy still been locked in her slowly malfunctioning brain somewhere, like Rapunzel in her great stone tower? If she were alive today, would the Forward Kinetics technology serve as her hair rope?

He remembered a walk he'd taken through a shopping mall in the days before Lucy had died. *Howl's Moving Castle* had been playing on a high-def TV screen in a video store window, and he had stood, mesmerized—stricken—by a sequence in which the sentient castle, relieved of its animating spirit, staggered through the hills, losing pieces of itself with every step. The analogue to Lucy's deteriorating condition had been more than he could bear.

Something had broken inside Matt that night. Something had changed. He couldn't say he had believed in God then—he hadn't—but he had not regarded God as his enemy. He had since. If there were a God worth worshipping, surely Matt would have met Chuck Brenton before Lucy's illness had set about destroying her.

His mind whispered the obvious: if he'd met Chuck then, they would have had nothing in common, for Chuck had not yet begun his experiments with brain waves, and Matt had had no reason to spend endless hours calculating their range and power and pondering their meaning.

The pragmatism of that thought frustrated him even more.

He pulled himself back from that abyss. He was not one of those pathetic characters who used the death of a loved one to become an activist in some cause related to their death. He was a polymath. A pragmatist. Sure, Forward Kinetics could devote itself to medical advancements, but if medicine couldn't save Lucy, why did anyone else deserve the chance? To him, the company was a means of reaping scientific credibility and professional standing from a most arduous and painful period of his life. A way of grasping profit from pain, to gain something tangible from his suffering. A way to even the score.

It was also his way of kicking God in the teeth. If God wasn't there to save Lucy, then screw Him. And screw Chuck—a scientist, someone who's supposed to know better—for believing in Him.

Matt reached out and flipped the laptop shut. Forget telling Chuck about his experiments with Lanfen and VR. He knew they were experimenting after hours; Matt knew the same of him and Mini, wasting their time with more imaginary creatures like angels and unicorns.

While the whole team could help work out the VR angle, it wasn't critical to their success, and right now that was all that mattered. Let Chuck be as surprised as everyone else when Lanfen came out onstage at Applied Robotics. Let the physicality of her demonstration kick his angels' asses. Let them all stand in awe of what Matt could do without anyone there to help him.

The way it's always been.

Chapter 15

SHOW AND TELL

They'd hired a moving van to truck the kinetic interface components to San Antonio, Texas, for the Applied Robotics convention. The setup crew, which included Dice and Eugene, flew out early to supervise the hired hands. Everyone else would follow later in the week, leaving time to rehearse the show and work the kinks out of anything that needed working out.

Bilbo and his nearly identical backup unit, Frodo, had gone by air in the belly of the chartered jet that carried the Forward Kinetics setup crew. Dice felt as if he were involved in some sort of dastardly conspiracy. He hated secrecy, even when—as Matt kept assuring him—it was a *temporary* secret and that, after the show, they'd all work on this together.

"Trust me," his boss had repeatedly assured him. "Chuck will be thrilled."

Dice wasn't so sure about either of those things; plus, the matter of Lanfen's unique ability to work with the VR telekinetically intrigued and puzzled him. Was it something as bonehead simple as the fact that the robot looked relatively human and therefore invited her to identify with it—to literally get inside its empty head?

Ghost in the machine.

Dice shook himself, watching the wisps of cloud that glided past the airplane's fuselage as it descended toward San Antonio International Airport. He was neither a believer nor a disbeliever when it came to the squishy topic of the supernatural (or perhaps hypernatural). Who knew? He was firmly in the camp of agnosticism—as oxymoronic as that probably was—but he had to ask himself: what phenomenon was Forward Kinetics exploring and exploiting? If the zetas were manipulating machinery with their minds, what part of that mind was the actor, and by what agency was it acting?

A more disconcerting question was this: when Chen Lanfen was looking out at the world from inside Bilbo, what part of her was doing the seeing? Even a master puppeteer, though he might throw his voice into the puppet's mouth, couldn't see out through its eyes. While Lanfen was seeing from Bilbo's point of view, what was happening with her body? Were her physical eyes still seeing something? They'd asked her that. She'd suggested they were, though she'd said things looked "different." She couldn't articulate what she meant, though, and that had only led to more questions.

Were her muscles offline? They'd asked that, too. She couldn't say. She hadn't tried moving her body while going mental. That was the whole point, after all—not to need to move the body while driving the bot. Clearly her autonomic functions were fine. She still breathed; her eyes still blinked; external input didn't seem to distract her.

Recalling how she liked to talk her way into gamma, he realized that she handled multitasking, as she put it, exceptionally well, which might have been the secret of her success with the VR. Chen Lanfen was one of those rare individuals who could walk, chew gum, pat their head, and rub their tummy all at the same time. The questions were: Was that a learned ability or a native one? Was it in whole or in part responsible for her inconsistency in handling the bot?

On the ground in San Antonio, Dice and Eugene settled in at the hotel, then went over to the venue to begin moving the largest pieces of equipment into the exhibitor's booth. Dice had the two ninja bots brought over from the airport and stowed in the company's storage cubicle beneath the main auditorium. It was just bad, dumb luck that Eugene followed a pallet of empty crates down to their unit and saw the two large Anvil cases that contained the bots shoved up against the front wall.

"What are those two big silver cases in the storage area?" he asked as he strolled back to the booth. "I don't remember anything like that on the manifest."

Moment of truth. Dice was surprised to realize his overwhelming emotion was relief. "It's a surprise. For Chuck. Something Matt and I have been working on."

"A surprise? That you're going to pop in public? That sounds a little dangerous."

"You know Matt. He's Mr. Risk Taker. Plus he assures me that Chuck will love it. I dunno . . . d'you think Chuck likes surprises?"

"I'd say that depends entirely on what the surprise is," said Euge cautiously. "What is it?"

"Just a piece of tech we've been working on."

"Oh. Oh, yeah. The security bot. Matt mentioned that to Chuck already, though."

"Well, there's a bit more to it than that . . ."

Euge raised his hands. "Say no more. Far be it from me to rain on another man's *khidesh*." He lowered his eyes and glanced off down the red-carpeted aisle. "Chuck has a surprise, too."

"Really?" Dice was gratified to hear it.

"Really."

Message received. "Ooookay. Well, I guess the surprise will be mutual."

"When's Matt planning on springing his?"

"Day two."

Euge looked relieved. "Good. Chuck was going to wait until day three."

Dice laughed. "Can you believe these guys? All this revolutionary stuff, and they're acting like it's a surprise birthday party."

Euge grinned back. "Well, let me know if you need help with yours. I promise I will not leak a word of it to Chuck."

Dice regarded him solemnly for a moment, then took a deep breath, glanced around, lowered his voice, and said, "Okay, here's what we've got . . ."

MATT AND CHUCK ARRIVED LATE the next day, bringing with them the various videos of the work they'd done in the lab. Chuck also brought an edited-down version of his TED Talk to explain the technology after the formal presentations. In addition to those, Sara or Tim would be available to provide a live demonstration of their software, followed by a show-and-tell on how the results had been achieved, followed by Mike performing a drill with Roboticus III. A key component to the demonstration was audience participation. They'd experimented enough with their own interns to know it was possible for a rank novice to drive Roboticus in mere minutes with Becky's aid. They'd practiced the show repeatedly at home and did so again here at the convention center behind a concealing set of curtains that ran on a track down both flanks of the booth.

The secrecy was crucial. Anyone who wanted to know about Forward Kinetics needed to attend the show, and so everything currently available to the public was designed to suck them in.

Brochures were distributed throughout the conference hall, and yet were singularly uninformative: long on background and goals and descriptions of the components of the FK system and short on information about what the technology actually did. Each rack of brochures was accompanied by a computer set into a niche along the outer wall of the booth that would show videos of the TED Talk . . . and beyond, but only if the visitor had seen the stage presentation and received a key code.

Control of information would build anticipation. At least that was Matt's idea.

Anything having to do with control usually was.

CHUCK WAS MORE NERVOUS THAN he'd ever been in his entire adult life. The Applied Robotics show was either a dream come true or his worst nightmare. He suspected he would not really know which until it was all over. Possibly not even then.

At nine the doors of the convention center opened, and the Forward Kinetics booth immediately attracted a lot of attention. It was what Eugene had called "stupid big"; it was done up in a silvery gray offset by electric blue and gold graphical elements and chairs, and it sat on the trade show equivalent of a Miracle Mile.

The paid interns and lab assistants dealt with most of that attention. All were dressed in "nice casual"—black jeans and attractive, logo-bearing T-shirts, and electric blue Converse sneakers. Not that they needed them to stand out.

Chuck spent most of the first hour of the show behind the stage, going over the presentation in his mind. From his hiding place (and he was honest enough to recognize it as such), he could hear the booth staff trying to deflect questions about what sort of technology they were going to be showing. This early in the morning, with the time for the first show fast approaching, the grumbles were mild.

It was far too soon when Matt entered the backstage area from a side door and said the inevitable:

"Showtime, team."

Sara, who was perched on an Anvil crate, reading from her iPad, glanced up and nodded. She looked businesslike, poised. Almost grim. Apparently that was how she showed nerves.

Chuck smiled crookedly at Matt. "Are you sure you don't want to run the circus?"

"You're the word guy. I'm the numbers guy. I'll be stage right if you need me to step in and answer technical questions . . . or catch tomatoes and whip you up a salad."

"Technical questions like, 'Are you freaking kidding?'"

"Chuck, we know we're not kidding. It's weird, it's unexpected, but it's real. You know it. I know it. It's time for the world to know it."

Chuck nodded, flipped on his nearly invisible headset microphone, took a deep breath, sent up a prayer for calm, and nodded at Sara. Together they stepped out onstage.

He had heard the murmured voices of the audience and so knew there was one. It was smaller than he'd hoped, though. Of the forty-two chairs they'd set up, only about twenty-five were filled, though there were a few noncommittal souls hanging out on the periphery. In a way, it was a relief.

Fewer people to laugh us off the floor.

He leapt into his introductory comments as the big-screen TV behind and to his left switched from the company logo to a computer desktop. Sara, meanwhile, moved to sit in a chair at extreme stage left, facing the computer screen at an oblique angle. Chuck introduced her as Sara Crowell, CAD/CAM engineer, and then introduced himself, giving his full credentials and affiliations. He saw at least one member of the audience checking her smartphone, ostensibly looking him up online.

He described the company's work as being an exploration of

the interface between man (or woman) and machine. All during this Sara was opening her CAD program and creating an elevation of one of Frank Lloyd Wright's houses—something she had virtually memorized. She kept her eyes on the huge monitor, her hands on the arms of her chair.

"For the last minute or so, you've been watching a demonstration on the screen to my left."

He glanced at it. In the time it had taken him to rattle off their creds, Sara had erected the two-story frame of the home and sketched in the main areas for landscaping.

"I'd like you to watch a moment longer," he said, "then answer a question for me."

Sara, a smile ghosting across her lips, completed the building's frame and clad it in finishing materials. Then she laid out pathways and started on the plantings—all at a pace hampered only by the speed of the software itself.

Chuck turned back to the audience and was gratified to see that several of those standing at the periphery had found seats. "So here's the question: what do you think we're demonstrating here today?"

There was a puzzled silence before a man in the front row said, "Well, it's not the software. I recognize that app. We use it for architectural drafting, too."

As frequently happened in classroom situations, the bold first commenter opened a small floodgate of guesses.

"It's not the monitor. I think we're all familiar with Samsung."

"The chair?" someone guessed, and everyone laughed.

Chuck laughed with them. "No, not the software or the monitor or the chair."

"No-brainer," said a middle-aged woman in a bright red blazer about three rows back. "Your company is Forward Kinetics. You create interfaces. She's using some sort of new controller."

"Bingo. What sort of new controller?" Chuck asked.

All eyes went to Sara, who was putting a glittering, cream-colored exterior material on the Wright house.

"Palm glove?" the woman asked.

"Sara?" Chuck found he was actually enjoying playing game-show host.

She paused momentarily to show the audience her empty hands, holding them palms out in plain sight.

"Retinal?" someone asked.

"She'd be triggering the menus," said the woman. "She's doing this with finger macros—in a manner of speaking."

"It's in her mouth," called a man in a pale gray sharkskin suit who was standing at the fringes of the group. "Some sort of oral manipulation."

"Oooh, baby," said someone else to more laughter.

Chuck was shaking his head. "No and definitely no."

"Wait, wait, wait," said the woman in red. "You're a neurologist, right? Oh, I heard you on Ira Flatow's show ages ago."

"I am a neurologist," Chuck said, "and when I did *Science Friday*, I had a wild idea about brain waves and nothing to show for it. Today, I do have something. First of all I'm going to show you what's driving the demonstration."

He left the podium and moved upstage, where he drew back the curtain behind it.

"I am Oz," someone in the front row murmured, "great and powerful."

"Pay no attention to the man behind the curtain," said someone else.

Of course there was no man behind the curtain. But there was Becky, now far more portable on a sleek stand with casters. Chuck rolled it to the front of the stage, lifted the neural net from its stand, and moved to place it on Sara's head. Then he touched a button on his iPad, and the image on the giant display split—one half showing the ever-growing Frank Lloyd Wright house, the other showing the peripatetic roil of Sara's brain waves.

"What you're seeing on the big display is the EEG output from Sara's brain. Specifically those are zeta waves."

There was a general burst of static from the audience. Of the comments, Chuck heard: "They're what?" "I've never heard of zeta waves." "What sort of readout is that?" "You've got to be kidding." "Oh, wow!"

He let them stare at the screen for a moment or two while Sara made magic happen on the screen, and her brain waves danced like a sea in a storm. Then he said, "This is a Brewster-Brenton Brain Pattern Monitor. What you're seeing displayed is the three-dimensional representation of an EEG. I'm sure you're familiar with those—at least with the two-dimensional version. The neural net Sara is wearing is a literal net of positron transceivers that read the brain waves she's generating. The positrons are able to penetrate the brain to pick up electrical impulses deep inside, thereby making the resolution much finer."

He turned back to the podium, where he'd set the iPad from which he was controlling the show. A touch, and the half of the big display showing the BPM output switched to a series of standard, two-dimensional tables showing different types of brain waves.

"I heard someone say they'd never heard of zeta waves. Here you can see the standard set of brain waves the human brain generates. From lowest to highest frequency: Delta, which runs up to four hertz. Theta. Alpha. Beta, which is the dominant active rhythm. Gamma, which is a veritable brain symphony and tops out around one hundred hertz. Then there's the overlapping mu wave, which, like alpha, is a resting wave. By comparison the zeta wave has a frequency of seven megahertz."

He paused to let that sink in for a moment, glancing again at Sara's progress with the drawing. She was adding shrub roses to the garden.

"YOU'VE NEVER HEARD OF ZETA waves? Well, neither had we," Chuck admitted, "until we started tracking the changing brain waves through a variety of activities and started wondering why, if a brain wave could make a needle jump on a chart, it couldn't also make other things happen."

Sara continued her design, and Chuck continued to answer questions while going deeper into the science he and Matt had developed. Eventually, though, *the question* came from the floor.

"Wait a minute," said Sharkskin. "When she started her demo, she wasn't wearing the neural net. What exactly was she doing? What is it you're selling?"

Okay . . . moment of truth.

At the periphery of his vision, Chuck could see Dice and Eugene standing together near one of the booth's clear Plexiglas support pillars, attention fixed on the stage as if it might suddenly explode. He was aware that it might do just that, at least metaphorically.

"When we started our exploration," Chuck said carefully, "we were trying to see what sort of activity the brain's normal range of waves could accomplish through the Brenton-Kobayashi interface, aka Becky."

That got a chuckle.

Chuck tried not to notice how dry his mouth was. He licked his lips. "The first experiments were exceptionally straightforward—the simplest instruction set we could contrive. Mike, are you ready?"

Mike waved at him from the rear of the audience.

"This is Mike Yenotov. He's a construction engineer who's

been working with our robotics team. He and Roboticus are going to demo what is probably the simplest set of activities."

Mike lifted Roboticus 3.0 over his head. The little bot now looked like a gleaming, silver version of a ghost from the old Pac-Man video game. Mike set the bot down and began moving it in a large circle around the audience and out into the aisles, around the booth, and finally up a ramp onto the stage.

Once there he moved the robot back and forth, around in circles. Finally he parked it beneath Sara's chair.

"That was about what you could do with the normal range of brain waves if you were wearing the neural net and were connected to the slave unit via the kinetic interface," said Chuck.

"But he wasn't using the interface," said a guy sitting in the front row. His face was red, as if he wanted to yell something.

"As I said, we had no idea that something beyond these waves existed until Sara and Mike here spiked into the seven-megahertz range. It scared the stuffing out of us," he admitted. "We thought the machinery had malfunctioned. Then we realized Dr. Streegman's brain wave conversion algorithm just didn't cover a broad enough range. He adjusted it, and then . . ." He glanced at Mike and scratched his forehead. "Well, then we discovered that the zeta waves were interacting directly with the slave unit—either through its native mechanisms or through the actualizer. Which depended on the subject, but all three of our initial subjects were finally able to control their slave mechanisms without the kinetic interface."

He stopped talking and let that idea settle.

"You're talking about psychokinesis," said Red Blazer. "That's nuts."

"This is ridiculous," said Sharkskin, gathering his stuff. "What could you possibly be selling besides snake oil?"

Chuck's throat went completely dry, but this was what they'd prepared for. "We don't know if everyone can learn to generate zeta waves," he admitted, "or manipulate machinery without the kinetic interface. For some applications we may be selling a training program, for others an actual mechanism—hardware and software."

"You can train people to do that?" asked someone in the fourth row—a woman in an Astros jersey.

"It's a hoax," said Sharkskin. "The concom didn't vet them thoroughly enough." He stood and straightened his suit. "I may lodge a formal complaint."

Chuck was vaguely aware of sudden movement at one side of the stage. A moment later Dice was standing next to him.

"Would you like to try it yourself?" the robotics expert asked.

Sharkskin snorted. "Pushing pixels with my mind?" He gestured at Sara. "She's not even really manipulating that CAD software. It's preprogrammed."

On the screen the program stopped in the middle of a shrubbery. Sara turned her head to spear the guy with steely gray eyes. "No, it's not, and I can prove it. Pick any element in the rendering and tell me how to change it. As you can see, I can rock this stuff way faster than anyone could do it with a mouse or a track pad."

The guy made a face.

"Aw, c'mon," the Astros fan told him. "Don't be a wuss."

"All right. The building material—red sandstone."

Sara swung back to the screen. A split second later, a red sandstone façade melted over the front of the building.

"An oak grove where the swimming pool is."

She did it.

"Red maple by the front door."

She grew the tree out of the soil.

"In a container."

"Material?"

"Brass."

"Brass it is," Sara said and made the pot happen.

The guy made an exasperated sound. "It's a trick! It has to be a trick. There's someone backstage—"

"Who can translate your verbal command into an image as fast as you give it?" asked Dice. "Why? Why does it have to be a trick? I've been working on this project for over a year, and I can tell you it's just science—though I admit it sometimes seems like magic."

"And who would you be?" Sharkskin wanted to know.

The young woman in the jersey was grinning from ear to ear. "He's Daisuke Kobayashi, the robotics wiz from MIT. I've seen your work."

Dice actually blushed. "Right. Thanks. I ask again, who wants to come up and try this?"

Sara took off the neural net and held it out. There was a long moment of silence before the woman in the Astros jersey rose.

"Oh, right," said Sharkskin. "A fangirl. You planted her."

"Then you come up," Dice said, taking the helm from Sara. "You can push the bot around, or you can push pixels on a screen. Which do you prefer?"

Chuck was sure the guy was going to refuse, but he didn't. He put his conference bag down and went to the stage with an arrogant swagger.

"I'll try the bot."

It took only a moment to hook the guy—Greg was his name—to Roboticus's kinetic interface. Dice explained the mechanism in the bot: a dead-simple four-way joystick.

"You think about pressing the joystick forward; it will go forward. Right to go right. Left to go left. Back to go back. If you get crazy confident, you can push it diagonally left or right to make a shallower turn."

"I think . . ."

"You think about the joystick," Dice repeated. He glanced at Chuck, who turned to the rest of the audience, which had grown considerably, and explained how the Becky interface translated the subject's brain waves into kinetic motion.

Chuck tried not to read the expressions of distrust on many faces, instead concentrating on the Astros "fangirl" and others who looked merely curious or actively interested.

Greg's first efforts were shaky, but they produced results. Roboticus moved tentatively at first, then with more confidence, and Greg's brain waves played across the big display behind him. The expression on his face went from skeptical to intent as the bot moved shakily around the stage. He completed his dance with Roboticus by turning the gleaming little bot into a tight left-hand spin and generated a fitful gamma wave on the display.

Dice shut down the interface and lifted the net from Greg's head. "Questions?"

The expression on the man's face was priceless. The open mockery was gone, replaced by a look of bewilderment. "It worked. Or at least it seemed to work. *How* did it work?"

"Well, sure it worked," said a man in jeans and a sweatshirt, standing on the sidelines. "You obviously work for them."

"No, I don't."

"No, he doesn't," said another guy in an immaculate suit. "He works for Minolta. In the same department I do." He flashed his convention badge. It matched Greg the sharkskin skeptic's.

"You could be in on it, too."

"In on what?" asked Chuck, suddenly fascinated by the phenomenon of knee-jerk disbelief. "What is it about this you find so hard to accept or even consider?"

Sweatshirt Man made a broad gesture. "Well, it's . . . it's fantastic."

Chuck mirrored the gesture—arms out, palms up. "As fantastic as robotics itself? As fantastic as brain surgery? Or having a space station orbiting the planet that can support human life? As fantastic as discovering new subatomic particles by building massive underground racetracks on which they collide?

"As fantastic as having a machine that tracks brain waves through their direct manipulation . . . like an EEG?

"What is it, exactly, that you find so much more fantastic about this?"

When he got no answer, he came out from behind the podium and gestured at the screen behind him, still showing the last brain waves recorded from Greg the skeptic's session with Roboticus.

"That is just a three-D EEG. It's not magic. It's not supernatural." He paused and considered that. "Well, it's not magic anyway. I'd argue that what the human mind does is supernatural by definition, but that's a different discussion. If human brain waves can push a pin up and down on a piece of paper, why can't they move other things, like Dice's robot here?

"Sara can do it. Mike can do it. This man," he said, pointing to Greg, "can do it. Why can't anyone?"

There was a lot of nodding at that. Murmurs of agreement. People slid into empty seats, wanting to see more. Chuck summoned Tim to the stage and gave them more.

CHUCK, MATT, AND EVERYONE ELSE on the team were run ragged for the rest of the day. Their presentations were standing room only from then on; their interns were slammed, each one having his or her own bevy of curious, eager, skeptical, and sometimes combative conventiongoers to take through the TED Talk or the various components of the Forward Kinetics system or the significance of brain waves. They gave out a ton of literature, answered several complaints that sent Matt to Con Ops to present the same credentials they'd had to show to apply for a presentation booth, and required the security guards to come and shoo off patrons who couldn't tear themselves away.

They ate dinner off campus, toasting each other, Roboticus, and each link in the Forward Kinetics chain. They began the meal with a high degree of energy and a lot of chatter and finished it almost falling asleep over their plates.

It was a short walk back to the hotel, and Matt and Chuck ended up strolling side by side at the rear of the group. Matt scuffed along with his hands thrust deep into the pockets of his jeans. The evening was balmy but cool, normal for April in San Antonio.

"So," said Chuck, "you were fielding the business cards. Any serious bites?"

"A couple I'd call serious. A major teaching hospital is interested in the machines for retraining people with disabilities. They asked about the cost of the FK systems and hiring trained personnel to run an installation."

Chuck's eyes lit up. "Really? That's . . . that's just what I was hoping—"

"I know." Matt looked off down the curve of the river as they turned to climb up to street level. "Not sure they're going to be able to come through with the bucks, though. You've worked in a medical school with public outreach. You know what it's like."

"Which hospital?" Chuck wanted to know.

Matt chuckled. "Johns Hopkins, as a matter of fact."

Chuck grinned. "Anybody else?"

"New York State."

"New York State what?"

"New York. The state. You know, where the Statue of Liberty is?"

"The state government is interested in the kinetic system?"

"Well, the attorney general's office anyway . . . so law enforcement."

"That's all?"

Matt glanced over at his partner. Good God, he was actually disappointed. "Chuck, it's the first day of the con. We just unleashed a brand-new, squeaky-clean science fictional idea on people—"

"A lot of people. Hundreds."

"Maybe even a thousand. But this is revolutionary stuff. We need to be realistic about how people are going to react and how long it's going to take them to go home and look around and see practical applications. But, hey, we've got two more days of the convention to go. And tomorrow is going to be the biggest day. We'll get a bigger bite then, I promise."

He *could* promise it, too, because tomorrow the U.S. military would come to see the show.

Chapter 16

SURPRISE PARTY

Matt was excited . . . and nervous. Nervous enough that he had to force himself to eat breakfast. Nervous enough that he kept glancing at his watch, though he knew Howard and his cronies wouldn't be arriving at the show until the lunch slowdown. During this traditionally thin period on the convention floor, crowds tended to dwindle, and most booths sent their excess staff off to nearby eateries.

It was this lull into which Matt planned to drop Chen Lanfen and Bilbo. The martial artist was awaiting her cue in the comfort of one of the upstairs conference rooms. The bot was backstage, under what looked like a pile of pallet pads. Dice was the key to making it work. During the half-hour break the core team would take for lunch, he would stage everything. Then it depended upon Matt to offer Mike a breather so Lanfen and Bilbo could do their routine.

None of his nerves were showing, Matt assured himself as he

watched Chuck's team go through their initial presentation. Tim was the first trick pony of the day and cheerfully (cheerful for Tim anyway) showed off his code fu and creativity to a standing-room-only crowd. Word of Forward Kinetics' kick-ass show had obviously spread. In fact he recognized a number of the folks who appeared for the Saturday morning session; he'd seen them the day before, some repeatedly. All of this was good news.

When eleven thirty rolled around, and booth staff began trickling off to get lunch, Matt insisted that Chuck and Eugene do the sandwich run since they'd just done two shows back to back.

"Stretch your legs and take some deep breaths," Matt told Chuck. He watched him all the way to the exhibition hall doors, then went to retrieve Lanfen while Dice got the robot out from under wraps.

Let the shock and awe begin, he thought, knowing that was one doctrine the military couldn't resist.

CHUCK STARTED THE TWELVE-THIRTY SHOW with a larger crowd than Matt had expected. Howard and his guests—four of them—were seated in the front row. Even in suits, Matt thought, they exuded military, something about the set of the shoulders and the pike-up-the-spine posture that gave high-ranking military men that peculiar aura of detached wariness.

In addition to rigid posture, Matt reminded himself, the military had deep, deep pockets. Even Chuck wouldn't be able to say no to the level of resources Howard's agency could command. If there were a God, Matt decided, he would pray for Lanfen and Bilbo to knock Howard's dress socks off.

Matt watched Chuck go through his opening spiel, watched as Sara built her house (she could probably do it in her sleep by then), watched as the audience displayed various shades of disbelief (or amusement at the disbelief of others). When Chuck asked Mike to come forward with Roboticus, Matt took that as his cue to walk out onstage.

"I gave Mike the session off," he said, smiling first at Chuck, then out at the audience, "because I have a bit of a surprise for everyone. Ms. Chen, if you would bring your little friend out onstage."

Lanfen entered gracefully from backstage, trailing Bilbo, who effectively aped her movements, right down to the sway of her hips. Granted it looked a bit comic on the robot, but even so, its motions were far more elegant than they had any right to be.

"THIS," MATT SAID WITH A sweep of his arm, "is Chen Lanfen, an expert in the martial art of kung fu. Her companion robot is Bilbo." There was some laughter at the sight of the little bot, but Dice's beaming face put Matt at ease. "Bilbo was designed by Daisuke Kobayashi and the robotics team at Forward Kinetics. The robot has been fitted with sophisticated gyro mechanisms for balance, and, as you can see, he is extremely flexible—in some ways more than a human being. Lanfen is going to put Bilbo through her paces for you, so you can get an idea of the potential for kinetic technology in the areas of security and law enforcement. Imagine, if you will, a SWAT team charged with infiltrating a place where hostages are being kept. Imagine the potential for disarming bombs or doing rescue work in situations that would put a human operative in dire jeopardy but require one's delicacy and intelligence."

He turned to Lanfen and bowed. "Ms. Chen, if you would."

He drew the gaping Chuck off to the side of the stage, lifting the slender podium and carrying it off with them. Lanfen now had the entire platform on which to display her kin(etic) fu—and display it she did. She started by having Bilbo face the audience and bow in a mirror image of her own motions. The two of them executed a series of kung fu postures in eerie unison. Matt knew that the robot lagged a split second behind Lanfen's body, but to the human eye the difference was imperceptible.

At the end of the routine, Lanfen moved to stage left, leaving Bilbo at center, frozen in a middle lotus position. Then she wheeled, settled into a horse stance, and proceeded to put the robot through a series of astonishing kicks, rolls, and tumbles calculated to show, in quick succession, how well the little bot could copy human movement and how well it could do things no human could do. Matt noticed that the audience reacted particularly strongly when Bilbo reversed direction by simply swiveling his head and flipping his back and front, and again when he dropped into a pill-bug curl and rolled across the stage.

Matt glanced at Howard. The man sat stone-faced, showing little more reaction than a slight widening or narrowing of his eyes or the occasional blink. The men who flanked him were only marginally more transparent.

Time, Matt thought, *to up the ante.*

When Bilbo had completed a tumbling pass that brought him to the lip of the stage, balanced on his hands, Matt stepped back up onto the platform.

"Now, as you might expect, the key in many of the duties a robot like Bilbo might be assigned is the operator's ability to see what Bilbo sees. Of course many of you are no doubt thinking we can do that already with VR systems. I see a number of repeat offenders out there. You've already been filled in on the advantages of kinetic training over VR. For the rest of you, we're now going to offer a demonstration. Dice, if you'd be so kind as to bring up the main screen."

Dice, stationed by the Brewster-Brenton monitor, brought it online. The big, flat-screen TV lit up and gave the audience a view of themselves, which was what Bilbo's forward cameras were focused on.

"What you're seeing," Matt told them, "is the signal that Bilbo's optic unit is sending back to the Brewster-Brenton's CPU. It's no different in its basic technology from standard VR. But let's imagine for a moment that Bilbo is on a critical mission. Let's say he's been sent down a mine shaft to see if the miners trapped at the bottom are dead or alive."

The robot dropped to its hands and knees and began to slink along while the audience was treated to a camera-eye view of the carpeted stage and its environs.

"Then just before he reaches his goal, you lose your mechanical connection."

The screen went blank. Lanfen smiled. Matt faced the audience and shrugged.

"Oops. Connection lost. Now what? With standard VR tech, unless the problem is at the operator's end and could be fixed with mechanical intervention, the mission would likely have to be scrubbed. If it's the result of intervening material that is blocking your signal, you're basically screwed. However, with kinetic technology, the loss of signal need never occur. Ms. Chen, if you please."

Lanfen closed her eyes. A moment later the picture returned to the screen, and the audience was treated to a high-definition view of the carpet and Lanfen's red Converse high-tops.

"You're now seeing what Lanfen is seeing through the robot's optics. The connection to the robot is managed not by outboard tech but by the operator herself. The only way for the signal from the mechanism to be lost, insofar as we can determine, is if the cameras are physically damaged or the operator is disabled or severely distracted. The ideal operator, obviously, is someone like Ms. Chen, who is trained not only in martial arts but in meditation and who is a master of multitasking. As long as the robot's servomechanisms are intact, the kinetic agent can operate them."

Matt allowed the show to continue a few minutes more and ended it with Bilbo cartwheeling down the central aisle of the audience and all the way down the length of the booth to the stairs. There he went to a four-footed stance and galloped up and into the conference room at the top. All the while the onstage display faithfully recorded what Lanfen saw through Bilbo's optics.

"You can come back to us now, Ms. Chen," Matt told Lanfen.

She opened her eyes, and for a moment the audience—at least those who were not still staring at the staircase—saw the world as the martial arts expert saw it. Then the screen went black.

The questions were fast and furious. Matt had to defer to Dice and Lanfen for many of them. There were questions about the range of the effect, how it felt to operate the bot in that way, the weight and possible materials of which the robot could be constructed. Conspicuously, none of those questions came from Mr. Howard or his companions. At the conclusion of the show, those gentlemen simply rose from their seats and disappeared, leaving Matt with a lump the size of a softball in the pit of his stomach.

Did we fail? How could that happen to me?

Lanfen and Bilbo had been brilliant. Dice's work was brilliant. Chuck's process was sheer genius. The possible applications were legion. Howard would have to be a blind man not to see the potential.

Christ, even a robot could see it.

Matt was so busy sweating Howard's precipitous departure, he was blindsided by Chuck's response to his surprise. When he caught up with his partner after the show, he found him deeply engaged in an intense discussion with Chen Lanfen about her experiences with the kinetic technology. When Chuck caught sight of Matt, the conversation had arrived at the one point that gave Matt pause: Lanfen's so-far unique ability to ride the robot in VR mode even after the physical connection had been severed.

Matt steeled himself for—well, just about anything but what he actually got. Chuck came at him with a face beaming with scientific zeal.

"Matt, this . . . this is amazing. I mean I knew you were working on something after hours—so was I—but this? I'm speechless."

Matt slid a side glance at Lanfen. "You weren't speechless a moment ago."

"I have so many questions."

"Well, Lanfen is the one to answer them. I'd hang around to watch the fun, but I've got to go make a phone call."

Pleased that he had at least dodged the Chuck bullet, Matt was about to head upstairs to call the number Howard had given him.

"Wait, before you go . . ."

To Matt the sound was like cats clawing a chalkboard. And man, he hated cats. He froze, silently counting to ten to control his temper as Chuck walked over to him.

"I really appreciate the work you put into this. This whole thing. And I have a sort of surprise for you, too—"

"Listen, Chuck, if it involves Mini, I already figured something was up. I've seen her coming in—"

"No, not Mini. That's for tomorrow." He held out a manila folder and said another name: "Lucy."

Matt froze for real this time—not just his strides but his insides. His mind went blank. White. Like a glacier.

"I . . . took the liberty. I remembered what you told me—about wishing you could interpret . . . about why you'd thought of finding me in the first place," Chuck stammered uncomfortably.

Matt didn't move. He was torn between hugging his partner and breaking into tears. Internally he was doing both.

Externally he took the folder and lightly shook Chuck's now-empty, outstretched hand. "I . . . Thank you."

The two men were barely able to meet each other's eyes. But the brief moment they did said everything they couldn't.

Matt turned on his heels and headed upstairs, forcing the emotions down. Chuck had just handed him a message from the past. Matt wasn't sure he wanted to know.

What he needed to do now was make a phone call for his future. He wouldn't let himself wonder about what was in the folder. He wondered instead about how he was going to tell Howard that the kinetic tech he'd just seen came with a small caveat: he wasn't sure if just anyone could do all that Chen Lanfen could. For whatever reason, it already seemed as if the government agent had not been as impressed as he should have been.

Matt's cell phone buzzed just as he started to dial Howard's number shakily. He did not say the first thing that came to his mind, which was, "I was just going to call you." He didn't want to sound overeager. He wanted to sound confident.

"May I assume you enjoyed the show?"

He wasn't sure he succeeded at confident. But he was happy to have gotten the words out.

"It was most enlightening. However, I need further verification that the technology is what you claim it to be."

Matt quashed his irritation at Howard's skepticism and his anxiety over revealing the possible limitations of the tech. "Sure," he said. "Perfectly understandable. What do you have in mind?"

"I need you to bring your operative and the robot to a location controlled by my agency, so I can verify that you're not using covert carrier signals or other mechanical means of achieving kinesis."

"What loca—"

"The show closes at six on Sunday. A car will pick you, Ms.

Chen, and the robot up at the rear of the conference center at seven. Is that acceptable?"

"Uh. Yeah. Quite acceptable."

"Very good. Thank you, Professor Streegman."

"Oh, and Dice. I'll need Dice Kobayashi, too. In case there's a problem with the robot."

There was a moment of hesitation. "Very well. If there are any specialized tools Dr. Kobayashi needs, he should bring them."

Matt exhaled gustily, feeling the tension leave his body in a rush. He had hitched his wagon to Howard's stars and stripes. There would be no looking back.

Chapter 17

GENERALLY SPEAKING

Mini's demonstration the next day was an anticlimax in many ways, but Chuck, still reeling from Matt's surprise, was gratified to have a standing-room-only crowd for which Mini could perform. And perform she did. She created computer-generated images as free as her ability to imagine them, rendered them in three dimensions, and animated them, sending them dancing and flying across the screen.

The three-dimensional quality of the images was stunning. Chuck was almost willing to believe that Mini was driving the high-def TV screen to do things it had not been engineered to do. The creatures seemed to break the plane of the screen as if emerging from a still pool. The landscapes seemed alive, seemed to beckon the viewer through a window into a world at once real and super-real. The audience was amazed.

They were more amazed when Lanfen repeated her performance of the day before. Matt had asked that she be allowed to do so; Chuck had conceded without argument and stood in the wings, grinning until his cheeks hurt. Once that particular genie was out of the bottle, attempting to put it back was futile. Then there was the fact that he really wanted to see the demonstration again himself. The other members of the team were somewhat less eager. Mike was losing time with his family. Sara felt cheated at a chance of using the VR. And Tim just plain hated to be upstaged. Still, mixed with the jealousy and resentment was unmistakable awe.

By the end of the day on Sunday, Chuck was exhausted and vaguely anxious. The audience reaction had been mixed and marked, but they'd had a gratifying number of requests for tours of their facilities from various institutions. The one that most excited him was NASA. He had never considered what full kinetic control might mean in outer space. Now he did. The ramifications were revolutionary. What astronauts had previously done in dangerous and costly EVAs might be possible to do from within a space station or space transport, either via robot or servos or—dare he hope?—by direct control of the vehicle's mechanisms.

He'd been toying with the idea of direct control a lot, and as the show closed down on Sunday evening, he zeroed in on Chen Lanfen, hoping to engage her further about her experience with the ninja bot. He offered to buy her a chai latte, for which she admitted a particular weakness. The two of them strolled down the red-carpeted aisle between swiftly disintegrating booths to one of the ubiquitous coffee carts.

"So when you're working with the bot," he asked as they meandered back to the booth, "are you aware of your interface with it? I mean are you aware of how you're interfacing with it?"

"Wow," she said, sipping carefully at her chai. "That's a question no one's asked me before."

He blinked. "Really?"

"Really."

"That surprises me. I would've thought Matt might've asked you."

"He's only ever asked about the amount of control I have. We had problems with that early on. It was hard for me to . . . to make that final connection. Not sure why. Dice thinks it's because of my training and my tendency to multitask. His particular theory is that my mind isn't solidly concentrating on one thing but is flitting around, trying to cover multiple points on a grid."

"Now that you think of it, though," Chuck persisted, "do you have a sense of what it is, exactly, that you're connecting with? I suppose I mean: what's your sense of the robot?"

She stopped in a red-carpeted intersection. "Well, the closest I can come to describing it is to say I inhabit the robot. I extend myself into it—imagine that its body is my body." She shrugged artlessly. "It's hard to articulate."

"Would you be willing to come into the lab to do some tests? I'd like to take a close look at your brain wave profile while you're engaged with the robot. I don't suppose Matt and Dice . . ."

She laughed. "Them? I assure you they were less interested in my brain waves than what I could make Bilbo and his little friends do. They were quite focused on impressing Mr. Howard."

"Mr. Howard?"

"You saw him. He was front and center at my show yesterday, surrounded by a group of his close associates."

Frowning, Chuck glanced down the aisle, toward the Forward Kinetics booth, which the take-down crew was efficiently dismantling. "Who is he?"

Unease flashed in the young woman's dark, almond-shaped eyes. "I'm not sure, to be honest. But I'm pretty sure he's military or ex-military. I know his interest is in security applications."

Chuck felt as if the carpet had shrugged beneath his feet. Had Matt lied to him? He'd let him believe they'd had no interest from the military when all along . . .

"How long?" he asked through numb lips. "How long has Howard been involved?"

"Months." She hesitated, then added, "Like I said, I'm not sure he's military, but he's asked for a private audience."

"A private . . . ?" Chuck looked toward the booth again. Matt had appeared in the aisle. His partner—his possibly treacherous partner—was waving at them to hurry up.

"When?" he asked Lanfen. "Where?"

"Tonight. I don't know where. He's sending a car to pick us up in about"—she glanced at her watch—"twenty minutes."

Chuck turned and strode down the aisle toward Matt, driven by a completely alien surge of anger.

Lanfen murmured a breathy "damn" and hurried along in his wake.

"When were you going to tell me?" Chuck demanded, bearing down on Matt. "When were you going to let me know about this *private audience*?"

Matt's eyes widened. Then he nonchalantly shoved his hands into his pockets and smiled wryly. "Well, *now,* I suppose. Mr. Howard and his associates are vitally interested in what we're doing, but they need proof absolute that we're not hoaxing them—using electronics or offstage operators."

Chuck glanced at Lanfen and back at Matt. "Who is Howard? Is he military?"

Matt opened his mouth, probably to lie, and closed it again. He nodded. "Some government agency. He called it Deep Shield."

"Deep Shield? Seriously?"

"Yeah, seriously. Very Marvel Comics. I think they're part of Homeland Security."

"HOMELAND SECURITY? AND YOU HAVE a meeting with them tonight?"

"Yes," Matt said, checking his watch. "The car should be here in about fifteen minutes. You can come along if you like. I might be able to get you on the guest list."

"Who's on it now?"

"Me, Dice, Lanfen . . . and Bilbo, of course."

"Yes," Chuck said tightly. "Yes, I'd like to go along for the ride."

In the end, though, Howard's men didn't let him go along for the ride. The driver—a young corporal rigged out in a uniform Chuck didn't recognize—had explicit orders about who was going on the junket. Chuck was not on his manifest.

"But I'm the co-owner of Forward Kinetics," he insisted, a pronouncement that impressed the young soldier not at all.

"I'm sorry, sir," the man said firmly. "I can only transport the persons I'm authorized to transport."

"Then none of them are going."

"Now hold on," Matt said, Dice and Lanfen standing uncomfortably behind him.

"Why can't he just call and have me added to the list?" Chuck said to his partner. "Don't you see this doesn't make any sense?"

"What do you think is going to happen? This is our own military."

"Oh, really? And what branch of the military are you?" Chuck asked the corporal.

"I'm not allowed to speak to that, sir. You'd have to ask General Howard."

"*General* Howard?"

The corporal ignored that and started loading the cargo.

"Matt—"

"It's okay, Chuck. They just want proof of concept. We haven't signed away anything. And we won't . . . yet. Not without you.

But if you're so worried, it's better that we *don't* go together." Without waiting for a response, he helped Lanfen into the truck and followed in after her.

"I'm sorry, Chuck," Dice said. "I didn't realize—"

"Go with them," Chuck said, no anger in his voice. "Just . . . make sure Matt is careful."

Dice nodded and got in the Humvee. The corporal closed the doors and moved into the driver's seat.

Chuck watched with a trembling dread taking root in his stomach as the Humvee pulled away from the curb. He went back into the convention center, where he found Eugene and Mini waiting for him in the lobby. Eugene looked particularly hangdog and seemed suddenly to have trouble meeting Chuck's eyes.

"Please tell me," Chuck said, "that you weren't in on this." He waved a hand at the covered turnaround in front of the center.

"Not in on it, no. Although I did have sort of a heads-up. Dice told me Matt had a surprise planned while we were setting up. I told him we had one, too. We sort of swore each other to secrecy. It didn't . . . I mean I had no idea it'd be something like this. I knew about the ninja bot and Lanfen and all but not about the scary guys in suits and the evil black stretch Humvee."

Chuck stared out at the spot where the aforementioned Humvee had been sitting moments before. "Matt says these guys are Homeland Security. But I don't believe that for a moment. Do you?"

"You're asking me?" Eugene said. "I see conspiracies in my breakfast cereal."

"Is that really the question you want an answer to?"

Both men turned to look at Minerva. She stood with her arms wrapped around herself, as if she were cold, and returned their gazes with a gravity that Chuck found unsettling.

"Don't you really want to know whether *Dr. Streegman* believes it?"

"Matt," Chuck spat out, "only believes in Matt."

LANFEN HAD ALWAYS TRADED ON her ability to look icy calm on the outside while her insides were doing anything from Snoopy dancing to trembling in abject terror. True control, she had come to appreciate, was like a holographic garment one wore. She could generate it from within but relied on a willing audience to keep it in place.

Right now she was more nervous than she could remember being, even when walking Baltimore's less safe streets at night. Self-defense against those with clear and evil intent was straightforward. She knew what to expect; they didn't. Now, though, she was the one who didn't know what to expect. She wondered if Matt did. He also had mastered the art of cool under pressure, so it was hard to tell.

Dice, on the other hand, was the antithesis of cool. During the ride to wherever they were going, he gave up trying to see out through the deeply tinted windows and stared straight ahead at the equally opaque glass between them and the now-invisible driver. His fists were clenched on his knees; his mouth was set in a grim line.

"Where are they taking us, Matt?" he asked once.

"What makes you think I know?" Matt returned. "I'm as out of my element here as you are." He smiled. "Kind of exciting in a cloak-and-dagger way, don't you think?"

"No, I don't," Dice said and subsided into silence.

Eventually, of course, the vehicle stopped, and the driver came around to open the door. They stepped out into a huge shell of a building, with a ceiling and walls that seemed to be miles away. An aircraft hangar maybe.

Howard came out to meet them himself and had the robot carried away and out of sight. Lanfen was separated from the men and taken to a sterile room, where she was searched with embarrassing thoroughness before being issued a formfitting, one-piece uniform of pale gray and canvas boat shoes. She bore it all with silent calm, knowing that no amount of martial arts knowledge, strategy, or skill would do her an ounce of good there. The woman who had been assigned to her was business-like and nonthreatening. She even managed a smile when Lanfen asked her for a cup of water.

Lanfen was reunited with her companions in a lab that was no less pristine than every other part of the installation she had seen, which wasn't much. They were dressed just as she was. Matt looked unruffled, though his earlier nonchalance was gone. Dice looked freaked out; he kept wiping his palms on his grays. Lanfen couldn't help but wonder how long he'd last in prison.

"We checked the bot over thoroughly," General Howard told them. "We're satisfied that it contains nothing that was not included in the specs you gave us." He turned to Dice. "You may begin your demonstration. I assume there won't be a problem if we give your martial arts expert a set of instructions?"

"Why don't you ask her?"

Lanfen stepped forward. "There shouldn't be any problem at all. What would you like me to do?"

"First, bring the robot out to the hangar. We'll do the demonstration there."

She did as asked and found they had prepared an arena for Bilbo to operate in. It was surrounded by screening devices that looked like curved, silver solar panels on short stands. She guessed they were meant to intercept and perhaps screen out any attempt to control the robot electronically from outside the circle of screens. A moment later Howard confirmed it.

"These panels will eliminate any electronically generated signals. Is there a problem with Ms. Chen guiding the robot from outside the screens?"

After a moment of silence, Dice realized he was the one being addressed. "I don't know. I mean, her brain waves *are* technically electric signals. All we can do is see what happens."

Lanfen took her cue, cutting short Dice's nervous stammering. She guided Bilbo onto the mat at the center of the screens, visually measuring the area. About thirty by twenty, she figured—a good-size area to work in.

She had the robot do a cartwheel, a handstand, and a somersault. Even with the screens, it was easy, like Mike moving the backhoe without seeing it. She turned to Howard expectantly. "What would you like us to do, General?"

"Let's start with some simple calisthenics, Ms. Chen. Have him drop and give me twenty."

Lanfen could swear that was a smile creasing his face. She relaxed a bit, then turned and looked at the robot. There was a moment in which she thought the entire hangar held its breath, then the bot flopped forward and did a series of twenty push-ups.

They followed with kung fu postures, which one of Howard's men—a martial arts expert named Reynolds—called out at random. Bilbo executed every one. After a series of these, Howard turned to Reynolds and nodded.

"Let's try some defensive moves now, shall we?"

"Yes, sir," Reynolds said and stepped onto the mat.

"What's he doing?" asked Matt.

"I want to see how this thing would operate in a real-world situation, Doctor. Ms. Chen, prepare to defend."

Lanfen let go of the robot and turned to stare at the general. He couldn't possibly mean . . .

Dice objected then, loudly. "Your guy is flesh and blood. Bilbo's made of steel. Sausage-wrapped in latex but steel nonetheless. It could kill him."

"Agent Reynolds can take care of himself, Mr. Kobayashi. He's skilled and well padded. Proceed."

Lanfen thought for a moment that she would just let Howard's guy whale on the bot but then wondered what that would achieve. Nothing. General Howard wanted a demonstration of the kinetic arts; Dr. Streegman wanted him to have it.

Fine. *Come and get it.*

Reynolds came at the bot head-on. She dodged it out of his way and into a pill-bug roll from which it sprang like a jack-in-the-box, its metal spine clicking. Then she put it into a defensive posture that made it look for all the world like a stainless-steel Bruce Lee or Jackie Chan. Except, of course, that it had no hands—only its odd little rocker feet. Lanfen wondered if Dice could create a specialized device that would be as good a hand as it was a foot. Perhaps even an articulated hand.

Time to think about that later . . .

Reynolds came at the bot again, this time feinting left before swinging around to deliver a roundhouse kick to the bot's head. Lanfen spun out of the way; the agent's boot caught the bot with a glancing blow. It went down but lashed out with a leg that caught Reynolds's pivot foot and swept it out from under him. He landed with a grunt that the hangar's dimensions amplified and echoed.

Inflamed, Reynolds rolled back to his feet and came at the bot again, this time with anger in his eyes.

Bilbo had never taken on a live opponent who was making anything like a sincere effort to do harm. They'd sparred with a couple of the interns and even with Frodo, a model of bot similar to Bilbo, while he was under Dice's somewhat tentative control through Becky and the VR interface. Dice had yet to learn to generate a zeta wave, which made his movements less than authoritative, notwithstanding his hours of computer game play. He could not inhabit the robot as a zeta could. He also hadn't studied kung fu.

Agent Reynolds had no such disadvantages. He was obviously confident in his ability to thrash the little bot within an inch of its battery life.

He'll find out how wrong he is soon enough.

Lanfen feinted Bilbo but not nearly in time. The bot took a blow to its shoulder and toppled. She whipped it into a tight somersault and away from the oncoming attacker. Even as she brought the bot fully upright again, she knew that she couldn't fight this way, at such a remove. It was too weird, watching her adversary from a distance and angle that meant she couldn't see his eyes. How could she predict his moves if she couldn't see his eyes?

She took a deep breath, focused her senses, and threw herself into Bilbo's head. There was no disorientation—she'd done this too often for that—but Agent Reynolds was already coming at her again, and she had no time to strategize. She fell back on instinct and simply reacted, taking advantage of Reynolds's key disadvantage: Bilbo had no eyes to read.

One with the bot, looking out at the world from his optics, Lanfen let her instincts and training take over. As Reynolds came at her, his gaze flicked to Bilbo's transparent cranium. Before he'd even set his foot to aim another booted kick at the bot's head, Bilbo dropped backward to the floor, away from the blow, and brought both robotic feet up to catch his attacker in the butt. Reynolds flipped end over end but managed to regain control of his body before he hit the mat.

Lanfen, meanwhile, turned Bilbo into a pill bug again and rolled directly at her opponent. Reynolds tried to leap up and over the bot. He might have made it, too, if Bilbo hadn't straightened, caught him full in the torso, and flipped him seven feet in the air.

He did not recover so gracefully this time. He landed awkwardly and sprawled on the mat for a moment before he regained his feet and his composure. He was breathing heavily now, and Lanfen half-expected him to growl at her. He didn't. Instead he folded his hands and bowed deeply. Lanfen/Bilbo returned the gesture.

"As you can see," Matt told Howard, "the robot is not only as quick as a human adept but is many times stronger. I assure you, too, that Ms. Chen was not fighting full out."

"So I see," said the general. "You may stand down, Mr. Reynolds."

The man nodded and made his way off the mat and between the screens, to where the observers stood. Lanfen turned Bilbo's head to follow him, not trusting that he wouldn't try a surprise attack. He passed by the bot without as much as a glance.

Lanfen let out the breath she'd been holding and followed that with a bleat of surprise as Reynolds took two long strides and swept her from the floor of the hangar, roping a muscular arm around her neck. It was a strange sensation to be looking at herself from across the room yet feeling . . .

Slammed back into her own point of view, Lanfen sucked in a breath and struck with both heels, going for the man's knees, but Reynolds only lifted her higher, so the blows fell on his rocklike thighs. She went for his ribs with her elbows then. They were padded, but she got him hard enough to make him grunt.

Hardly realizing what she was doing, Lanfen reached out for Bilbo and connected. The bot came hurtling toward them like a giant's bowling ball. Reynolds spun but not nearly fast enough. Bilbo clipped him in the back of the legs and sent him tumbling forward. He loosed his hold on Lanfen, who planted her feet firmly and upended him over her shoulder. He hit the bare concrete with the wind knocked out of him.

Lanfen and Bilbo straightened in eerie unison. She severed her connection with the bot and turned to face her audience.

Howard's face, as always, was inscrutable. Dice looked simultaneously shell-shocked and stoked. Matt looked smug.

She marched into Howard's personal space and peered up into his face. "Did you order him to do that, sir?" she asked. "Did you order him to attack me?"

"I ordered him to do what was necessary to test the system. We had to be sure the system would work. We also needed to know what might happen if the operator was compromised."

"If I may say so, or even if I may not, that was a stupid thing to do. I could have killed him. Or at least broken his legs. The robot is—well, it's a robot. Like Dice said, it's metal with a little silver spandex over the top. I've never used it in a real combat situation before. *Never.* I had no way to gauge its real strength."

The general's graying eyebrows rose. "Really. Then I'm even more impressed." He turned to face Matt. "We're interested, Dr. Streegman. If you can teach a civilian to this level, I'm eager to see what trained operatives can do."

"I *am* a trained operative," said Lanfen, ire rising.

General Howard smiled. It was the first time she'd seen him do that fully. Lanfen found she didn't much care for the expression.

"Ms. Chen, you are a civilian martial arts practitioner. I assure you the advantage you had over Lieutenant Reynolds was largely one of surprise."

Lanfen straightened her spine. "Really? Surprise? How so? He knew he was going to attack Bilbo. I didn't. He also knew he was going to attack me. I didn't know that, either. I'd say I was the one who got surprised. I was also pulling my punches, General. If I hadn't, as I said, I might have killed him. As my *shifu* repeatedly warned me, one should never throw oneself into a fight against an adversary one does not know."

Howard simply chose to ignore her, and it took all her training to calm herself at the slight. He gestured for Matt to follow him and left the hangar, calling back over his shoulder to Reynolds. "Take our friends to the canteen and get them some refreshment. Dr. Streegman and I have matters to discuss."

Reynolds escorted Lanfen and Dice to a surprisingly pleasant cafeteria with an actual kitchen and machines that dispensed various beverages. She chose tea; Dice chose coffee. Reynolds sat down with a glass of Coke.

They sat in silence until Reynolds asked, "Were you really pulling your punches?"

"Mine, no. Bilbo's, yes."

"You really thought that was necessary?"

"Lieutenant," said Dice, "Bilbo has a lifting capacity of close to one thousand pounds. I've seen him dent lab tables and rip tiles out of the floor by just landing hard. You do the math."

Reynolds blinked and absently rubbed his right arm. "Well, thanks then, I guess," he told Lanfen and concentrated on his Coke for a moment before observing, "I couldn't read its intentions."

"There was nothing to read. The intentions were mine."

He nodded. "That was weird. Disorienting. Human adversaries telegraph their moves. These things don't. That would give any force using them a distinct advantage."

She leaned forward, her eyes on the man's face. "But what force? Who is going to be using them? Who do you guys work for?"

"I work for General Howard."

"You know what I mean. Your agency—what branch of the military is it part of?"

He gave her an apologetic smile. "I'm sorry. You know I can't tell you that. We're a special group involved in homeland security. That's all I can say."

"Is all this secrecy really necessary?" Dice asked.

Reynolds turned sober eyes on him. "Our country has enemies all over the world, sir. Some we are only dimly aware of at this juncture. We need whatever advantages we can get. Secrecy is one such advantage."

Hard to argue that, Lanfen supposed, but she had to wonder how General Howard's penchant for secrecy dovetailed with Matt Streegman's desire for publicity. She had a feeling a government contract wasn't something they'd be able to promote on their company website.

And she wasn't sure what she thought about getting into bed with an organization that had no compunction about preemptive attacks. That didn't sound like "security" at all.

Chapter 18

INTELLECTUAL PROPERTY

Matt stood outside Forward Kinetics' main conference room for several minutes, listening to the muted hubbub within. He had stalled for several days over the Deep Shield contract, carefully crafting his presentation of it to the people waiting on the other side of the door. He was ready, though. All he would say when asked—all he had said since walking out of his closed session with General Howard—was that the government deal was everything they had worked for.

He'd used words like *unprecedented, spectacular,* and *amazing.* He had framed it as ensuring not just their continued existence but their ability to expand and hire new staff, take on new subjects, begin manufacturing system components in earnest, and open new, larger training labs.

Of the details of who and how and how much, he had said

nothing . . . until now. Now the contracts had to be signed along with individual nondisclosure and intellectual property agreements. That would precipitate a flurry of activity within Deep Shield as they ran a thorough background check on every member of the Forward Kinetics staff.

Matt took a last deep breath, plastered a wide smile on his face (why not? Wasn't this their dream come true?), and strode into the room with his iPad tucked under his arm.

"Good morning, sports fans!" he greeted them, taking his seat at the head of the oval table.

"I hate sports," mumbled Tim, and Eugene murmured, "Hear, hear."

"Okay. Good morning, tech fans and fellow geeks." He glanced at Tim. "Better?"

Tim gave him a silent thumbs-up.

"You've got a firm offer?" Chuck asked from his seat on the flank of the oval.

Matt looked over at him, vaguely and unaccountably bothered by the fact that he refused to sit at the opposite end of the table. "Yes."

"Is it everything you've been hinting at for the last three days?"

"And more." He put his elbows on the table and folded his hands beneath his chin. "Chuck, I've been over this thing front to back and back to front. I've looked at it upside down and backward. I'm here to tell you, it is everything we could have dreamed: an almost bottomless pool of financial resources, state-of-the-art facilities, the ability to hire whomever we please—"

"You mean whoever passes their background checks," said Tim.

Matt turned a piercing gaze on the programmer. "Yes. You got something you need to tell us?"

Tim reddened but shook his head. "What? Like that I drink a six-pack of Coke a day? That I dream of CGI bimbos? That in my head, I'm a big white unicorn with armored hooves and a titanium horn?"

"I was thinking more along the lines of political activism, drugs, or porn. Stuff like that."

Tim chortled. "Drugs. Do you have any idea what drugs— aside from Dr Pepper and other caffeine-delivery systems— would do to a programmer's little gray cells? No, thanks. And I don't do politics. That stuff is even worse than drugs."

"Porn?"

"My porn is strictly legal."

Matt smiled at that. He turned his attention to the rest of those gathered: Chuck, Eugene, Dice, Brenda, Tim, Sara, Mike, Lanfen, Minerva, and their admin, Tana.

"They will be running a background check on everyone here. Most thoroughly on those of us who will interface directly with their people and who will have access to their facility."

Dice snorted. "We don't even know where their facility is."

"They're careful," said Matt. "Can you blame them?"

"I don't know," said Tim. "You tell us."

Matt had expected this level of skepticism from Tim. Dice's dark expression surprised him a little, but he foresaw no real pushback from that quarter.

"I'm going to go over the main contract that Chuck and I, as owners of FK, will have to approve. There are also the standard NDAs and intellectual property agreements that each of us will have to sign. Tana has sent you those via e-mail, so you can look them over after I lay out the key points. But it's all pretty simple, really. Deep Shield wants us to train their agents to generate zeta waves and to use them for a variety of purposes. What this means, first of all, is that our subjects—all of them—will become full-time staffers at Forward Kinetics at a substantially increased salary than has been attached to their part-time work here as lab rats."

"Full-time?" asked Sara. "I have contracts—"

"That you will be able to fulfill." Matt was careful not to use the word *allowed*. He knew only too well that Sara Crowell did not take well to the idea of being allowed to do things by a second party. "They only ask that you not take on any more outside work for the duration of the contract, which is based on deliverables. The amount of money they're offering each of you is stated plainly in your individual contracts. If for some reason you don't wish to become a full-time employee of Forward Kinetics, you will be asked to train up a replacement in your discipline."

"Even me?" asked Mini, surprise evident in her voice.

"Even you. The DHS is interested in your ability as a nonprogrammer to manipulate pixels."

She frowned, then brightened, favoring the entire room with a brilliant smile. "So I'll still be teaching art—art of the mind. How cool is that?"

"Yeah," said Tim wryly. "Maybe you and I can dress our critters in camouflage gear."

"The other major change," Matt continued, ignoring the sarcasm, "is that we will be able to staff up and build robotics assembly teams. Dice will head that project."

Dice's head came up sharply. "We're going into manufacturing?"

"We're going to build prototypes and train manufacturing teams, so the government can ramp up their own production. I gather that some of the training will take place in their bailiwick. Lanfen and Mike are going to be visiting their facility a lot, I imagine, training their folks. We'll do the initial work here—

getting them to produce viable zeta waves—then send them home for fine-tuning. They have machinery there that we don't here. Naturally we'll also be building them kinetic converters for their specialized machinery."

"Like what?" asked Dice. "What am I going to be translating for?"

"Not sure yet entirely, but General Howard did mention bomb-disposal bots, reconnaissance units, that sort of thing."

"What about our other clients?" asked Chuck. "We've got a serious offer on the table to negotiate with Johns Hopkins for medical applications, and NASA is interested in the potential for using this in outer space."

Well, there it was—the elephant in the room. Matt picked up his iPad and punched it on.

"You will be able to do all the medically related research you want," he told Chuck, his eyes on the screen of his tablet. "You will, however, have to get General Howard's permission for and oversight of any projects that benefit other organizations."

"Meaning they want us to work exclusively for them."

Matt became aware that the other members of the team were now reacting like spectators at a tennis match, watching the ball shoot back and forth between the two execs.

"They did. I managed to wriggle around it by giving them some oversight."

"*Some* oversight? How much?"

"They don't want us to be exclusive to them in perpetuity," Matt explained. "Only until they feel they've trained up enough zetas of their own. Look, the contracts are in your e-mail by now. Read them over. If you see something you don't like, we can negotiate further."

Dice looked up from his iPad, his expression opaque. "The

intellectual property clause says they own any 'defense-related' technologies or processes we invent. That can't stand, Matt. That's way too vague. It's vague as to what is considered a 'defense-related' technology and what 'invent' means in this context."

"Not to mention 'technologies' and 'processes,'" added Chuck. "At the end of the day, they could own our thoughts, our ideas. I've seen those sorts of contracts before. I had a writer friend who had the income from her fiction sales garnished because she had the ideas for the stories while working as a programmer for a defense contractor."

"I'm sure—" Matt started to say, but the truth was he wasn't sure. In his exultation at landing this momentous contract, he hadn't considered the implications of the intellectual property clause for his own contributions to FK—the mathematical formulae that drove the programming modules for everything from the Brewster-Brenton to the individual robots. And while the near-term money was staggering, it was the patents that would truly make or break the financial success of FK.

"Yes. Okay. I see that. Look over the rest of it. I'll talk to the agency brains about these clauses and get them tightened up. Tana, will you put that on the list of subjects to bring up with Howard?"

She nodded, her fingers already tapping the keys.

"And the med tech?" Chuck persisted.

"And the med tech," Matt promised.

He left the conference room flogging himself for not paying more attention to the intellectual property document. If he'd been more on the ball, he might have been able to start sewing up the business end of this today. As it was, he suspected, he had a long week ahead of him.

"Matt."

He turned to find Chuck dogging his tracks.

"Matt, in this contract, do they spell out what sort of applications they want to use kinetics for?"

Oh, for the love of . . . "That will come later. But they'll be defense applications, Chuck. Shielding U.S. interests from harm. Surveillance. Espionage. Undertaking dangerous missions on which the American people would be horrified to send live operatives. One of the applications, I know for a fact, is deep-sea rescue and exploration."

The speed with which the worried frown left Chuck's face was remarkable. "Deep-sea rescue?"

"They've already broached the idea of having Dice's team design bots that can function at extreme depths. There are a myriad applications for that—exploration, planting sensors of various types. From my discussions with General Howard, though, I imagine he's most interested in the potential to rescue people from dire situations without endangering more lives than necessary. Think of the problems we've had with oil rigs historically. Shipwrecks. Downed submarines."

He could almost hear the little wheels turning in Chuck's head, see the thoughts flitting behind his transparent eyes.

"Look, Chuck," he said quietly, aware of others passing by them in the hall. "I'm not going to pretend to you that these guys are as idealistic as you are. Hell, they're probably not even as idealistic as I am. But they're our guys, for God's sake. They're part of our government's defense mechanism, not the enemy."

His partner glanced away, nodded, sighed deeply.

"All right. Yes, you're right about all of that. But we've got to get those intellectual property rights issues straightened out, and we've got to be certain we can do business with other organizations for civilian purposes. I especially want us to be free to work with agencies like FEMA and NASA. And medical applications absolutely must be allowed. That's a deal breaker for me."

"I understand," Matt told him. *I just hope I can make General Howard understand.*

"YOU'RE KIDDING." MATT DROPPED HIS stylus to the tabletop and leaned back in his chair, flipping his iPad closed.

Across the desk from him, General Howard did not look as if he were kidding. The man did not look as if he ever kidded.

"I assure you, Dr. Streegman, our experts have put a great deal of thought into what may or may not constitute defense capacities. I assume your partner is looking at the possibility of using kinetics to do EVAs in space. That is, at least, a sister technology to our deep-sea tech."

Your deep-sea tech? Matt thought. *Without us you've got no deep-sea tech.*

Aloud he said, "What if we put your experts to work defining what we may or may not do for different agencies? Take the deep-sea and space applications, for example. Yes, there are some similarities, but there are some important differences as well. While you want your deep-sea bots to be relatively heavy and dense and to have the capacity to increase and decrease weight situationally, the space bots will need to be as light as possible so as not to increase payload extravagantly."

Howard considered that. He considered it long enough that Matt's patience evaporated.

"Look, General, I can tell you straight up that if you preclude his working with the medical establishment, Dr. Brenton will never—and I do mean never—sign this contract. If you trample his heartfelt desire to use this technology to help other people, to further scientific research and extreme exploration, he may also be persuaded that you are not the sort of organization he wants FK to be in bed with."

The general's face reddened. It was the most emotion Matt had ever seen him show. "We represent the best interests of the American people, Dr. Streegman. I can assure you we will require . . . we will ask nothing of you or Dr. Brenton that does not further those interests."

"I have tried to impress that on Chuck. Trust me. But I think what he's looking for here, General, is a show of goodwill."

The general quirked a graying eyebrow. "Peace on earth and goodwill toward men?"

"That is my partner in a nutshell."

Howard rose. "I'll see what we can do. What you can do is try to keep your partner's attention focused where it will do all of us the most good: on his lab."

IT TOOK SOME DOING, BUT Deep Shield finally came up with a contract that Chuck was willing to sign. The intellectual property and secrecy issues were spelled out in exhaustive detail such that no one found them onerous. Everyone but a single lab tech checked out; he was restricted to the civilian projects. Security clearances were issued, agreements were signed, and Dice's team—supplemented with newly hired (and vetted) staff and engineers from Deep Shield—was set to design and build prototypical robots of different types.

There was a part of Daisuke—a part he tried to keep under wraps—that was almost disappointed that Chuck had been won over. Yeah, sure, there was an eight-year-old, robot-loving kid jumping up and down deep inside him, thrilled to have his playground suddenly expanded almost infinitely. But while he understood the tight-lipped protectiveness and competitiveness of academia, the level of secrecy Howard and his cohort required was unnerving.

Dice had been relieved not to have been faced with his own decision, which, once the owners of Forward Kinetics had signed the contract, was to either sign on or leave FK behind. He had given no more than a second's thought to that option.

The changes wrought by their new partnership were immediate. Some were marked—their hired security company was replaced by men and women from Howard's group. They wore suits, not military uniforms, but the suits, coupled with their military bearing, led to the inevitable comparisons to iconic movies. Within the week everyone was referring to them as the Smiths.

Other changes were more subtle. The inclusion of military robotics engineers changed the dynamic in Dice's lab. The new recruits were not inclined to blend in with existing staff. Most seemed perplexed by the give-and-take, consultative atmosphere that was the norm in Dice's domain. That had a chilling effect on his team, gradually making them quieter and less inclined to levity. It wasn't anything the government recruits did exactly, but they were so watchful and so damned serious. Even the eight-year-old inside Dice had trouble keeping up his giddy good cheer in the face of that.

His staff responded at first by trying to include the Deeps, as they called them, in their conversations, their meals, their moments of relaxation. But the recruits refused to mingle. They took their breaks and meals together and kept talk to a minimum. They spoke to the civilian techs only to ask questions, gain clarification, or make observations. Dice couldn't fault their behavior. They followed his orders respectfully and expediently, but with the exception of one young female officer named Megan Phillips, who seemed to bubble over with ideas, they rarely offered anything to the creative process.

The FK lab techs reacted by circling their wagons more tightly. Within weeks of the start of the new regime, Dice felt as if he were the chief of two separate tribes. He knew from the muted conversations he had with Eugene that the folks on the kinetics teams were having similar experiences. Still, he—no less than his colleagues—threw himself into training the neos he'd been given and thanked God they learned quickly. Dice was used to working with robots.

Working with these androids was something else entirely.

Chapter 19

TRUST

It took roughly two months to train the first class of robotics engineers, neurology techs, and kinetics subjects sent by Deep Shield. They were assigned eight to a zeta class, with a lieutenant in each group as ranking officer. They were quick studies, focused, dedicated. They performed with military proficiency every day and disappeared every night into buses sent to return them, Chuck supposed, to their base. The kinetics trainees came in five flavors: security/combat, machine operators, programmers and VR technicians, architects/construction engineers, and holographic specialists.

They were sharp, every last one of them, and asked a lot of questions about brain waves and the Brewster-Brenton technology. Especially Lieutenant Reynolds—whose first name, Chuck discovered after much prodding, was Brian. Reynolds was the leader of the pack. Everyone else in the first class deferred to him.

Chuck was surprised to find that the biggest hurdle Howard's recruits had to overcome was getting to the gamma state in which the brain used several different modalities in concert. Roughly half the candidates had mild difficulty achieving gamma; the remainder had moderate to great difficulty and had to work harder at it. Chuck was, of course, curious to know why. He sought—and got—General Howard's permission to put all the candidates through a series of neurological tests and to do a full profile of each one to see if any patterns emerged. None did that he could see, with the possible exception of the military training they had all received.

"Is that enough?" Eugene asked him as they pored over the results of their work in Chuck's office early one morning, before the Deeps arrived for their training. "I mean is the fact that they all had the same style of training and indoctrination enough to account for their difficulty . . . I don't know . . . letting go?"

Chuck pulled up a different view of the data, looking at the recruits' answers to a series of questions about their experiences with family, school, and the military.

"Lanfen's recruits have all had martial arts training," he noted. "I thought that was one of the things that made her a good candidate—the mental discipline. Now I don't know. Maybe I'm looking in the wrong place. Maybe it's not the training. Or at least maybe the training isn't their first common denominator."

"Their family and schooling factoids are all over the place." Eugene tapped his laptop's screen with a pen. "This one's from a fully functional family—middle kid. This one's an only child. Lost his father in his junior year of high school. This one's the youngest of six, the only girl in a family of boys." He glanced at Chuck. "What? You're thinking something. I can see it."

Chuck *was* thinking something. The data on his screen had gone into soft focus. "I think we need to back up a step. Maybe the question isn't what they do in the service but *why* they went into the service in the first place."

"Did we ask them that?"

Chuck ran a quick search of the survey. "Number twenty-four."

The question had produced some interesting results. Every one of the responses was a variation on a perceived need for order, certainty, a place to belong. Additionally there were refinements that had to do with wanting to be part of a team, wanting to be part of something bigger than oneself, wanting to be of service to the country. But when all had been asked and answered, Chuck Brenton was looking at a group of people who, for various reasons, felt at a loss to define their own futures. Except for the two who had been determined to go into the military at a young age—both from military families—none had a deep-seated calling, secret talent, or sense of purpose that had to be expressed in a particular way.

Certainly they had passions. Reynolds loved martial arts and had learned a variety of different styles. Seneca Hughes liked to paint but thought of it as a hobby ("who pays for art anyway?" she'd asked). Steve Flores collected baseball memorabilia, which he shipped home to his dad in California. But none had risen to the level of a calling that the individual felt he or she must pursue. Each of them had, instead, handed many major life decisions over to the military.

Trust.

Chuck sat back in his desk chair. Every member of his zeta team trusted his or her own perceptions, his or her own inner voice, his or her own intuitions. In order to work for an agency of government such as Deep Shield, these operatives had to put their trust in their government, their command structure, the officers giving them their orders.

Was that it? Was it a matter of whether trust resided inwardly or in an external power? Surely the martial arts training, which called upon a practitioner to learn to trust his or her own reflexes and judgment, was a balancing factor.

Brian Reynolds had achieved gamma late the previous afternoon. Chuck got up from his desk and went to see if the lieutenant had arrived yet. He found him in the company café (dubbed Steampunk Alley because of the glorious, copper-clad espresso machine that was its centerpiece) making himself an espresso.

"I need your help," Chuck told him. "I need a breakthrough to get the bulk of your team to the next level."

"Of course, sir. What can I do?"

"I want you to think about your own breakthrough yesterday. How it felt. What caused it. What its genesis was. Then I need you to get your team and see if they can't take that same . . . leap of faith."

"Leap of faith," Reynolds repeated. "Sounds sort of religious."

"Yeah. Yeah, it does. And maybe that's not a bad thing. I'm not sure it matters what you have faith in, just that you have it."

Reynolds nodded and looked down at his hands. "For me it was just coming to the realization that if I could master kung fu and tae kwon do, I could master this. Then I just got into it."

"Any imagery associated with that?"

"Imagery?"

"Did you use some sort of image or sound or other element to *get into it*?"

"Yes, sir. Swimming. I imagined I was swimming. Backstroking across a pool."

Chuck smiled. "Backstroking. That's great. Blind, trusting the water to keep you afloat, moving all your limbs. Yes. That's a great environment. Let's see if that or something like it will work for your team."

BY THE TIME LANFEN GOT her first class of recruits, they had all achieved trustworthy zeta states. Chuck had shared with her how hard-won the gamma state had been and that they'd resorted to guided imagery to get everyone up to speed. Reynolds's trick of imagining himself floating and swimming in water had sparked the others in the class to come up with things they could use in the same way, to pry the fingers of focus off their thought processes so they could glide into gamma.

That made sense to the martial artist. Lanfen had used guided imagery her entire life for everything from quelling childhood night frights to avoiding panic attacks when she made a foray into new social territory. The few times she had been required to speak publicly in college, she had used a purely mental version of her kung fu warm-up routine as a nerve-calming device.

The questions the neos in her first class asked her had mostly to do with technique and how she so easily maintained the VR connection when in direct contact with the bot—what they had come to call "ventrilokinesis." Matt had laughed at that characterization of it, and Lanfen had admitted, ruefully, that it was her doing. She had repeatedly referred to her technique as "throwing her self," and Steve Flores had said, "You mean like a ventriloquist?"

"Personally," she'd told Matt, "I'd prefer something more elegant—*kinetoquism* maybe. *Ventrilokinesis* is too long and makes me think of creepy dummies."

Whatever one called it, it proved to be hard for even the dedicated Lieutenant Reynolds to master. Lanfen found this interesting; the trainees found it frustrating.

So did Matt Streegman.

"Why aren't they picking it up?" he asked her at the end of almost every session in which she tried to teach the "throwing" method she used.

"I honestly don't know," she'd told him at the end of her most recent session, in which Reynolds and one of the female recruits had managed a few seconds of connectivity after Becky's hard interface was deactivated. "They're certainly dedicated enough. They're disciplined. They're . . ." She lost the thread of the sentence in a minor epiphany.

"What?" He was reading her face, which, she figured, must have been doing something peculiar.

They were standing in Steampunk Alley, fixing hot beverages. Lanfen turned to face Matt, her lapsang souchong momentarily forgotten.

"They're monotaskers."

"You mean unitaskers?"

She laughed. "No. A unitasker is someone or something that can do only one thing. I mean they can do a variety of things, but they've been trained to do them sequentially. Step by step. They don't juggle or multitask well, or at least that talent hasn't been cultivated."

"Can you help them cultivate it?"

"To be honest, I don't know."

His face said clearly that was not the answer he'd wanted to hear. "Lanfen, this is of critical importance. They must be able to master the VR connectivity. They must be able to learn to see through the robot's eyes without the hard interface. Hear with its ears. Otherwise—"

"Latency issues. I get it."

"I'm not sure you do get it," Matt said tersely. "I'm not sure you understand what those latency issues mean to these people. The seconds of lag between the operator's perception of the bot's position and his translation of what he's seeing into action may make the difference between success and failure, life and death."

"Trust me, Matt—I get it," she said, thinking of her fight with Reynolds. "I'm just not sure I know how to teach multitasking."

"How did your master teach you?"

"He didn't. I come by it naturally. In fact, he claims I taught him."

Matt stared at her a moment, then burst out laughing. "Stop apologizing for being a prodigy, Lanfen. Just see if you can teach them what you taught your shifu."

"It's hard to teach something you do naturally. You do understand that, don't you?"

"Honestly," he said, "I never really thought much about it." He raised his espresso in a toast then and left her standing at the beverage bar.

Always enlightening talking to you, Matt.

She went into her afternoon training session with a box full of beanbags and hacky sacks, determined to teach her recruits how to juggle.

INVOLVEMENT WITH THE MILITARY BRED a certain level of order in the affairs at Forward Kinetics. Chuck reflected that while he had always appreciated order, the sort of regularity General Howard's people brought with them was anathema to the creative dynamic he thrived on, and as Dice and Eugene had seen with their teams, it was changing the dynamic of the company. The crew that had been ever eager to throw ideas at the wall to see which ones would stick was becoming careful—timid even—in its approach to the work. He understood that any organization went through stages, but he knew without a doubt that Forward Kinetics' research and development teams were not even halfway to the norming stage for any of their processes. The military presence was forcing changes that Chuck feared would have an adverse impact on the very processes an enterprise like theirs needed to drive development.

Which was why he was both surprised and pleased to enter the martial arts classroom to find Chen Lanfen and her team playing something he could only describe as beanbag Jeopardy.

Standing in two facing rows, eight recruits tossed beanbags

back and forth, moving them up and down the rows. There was a catch, of course: the recruits were expected to snag a bag with one hand while tossing one with the other, shift the bag to the opposite hand, and toss it to the person standing kitty-corner to them even as they caught the next beanbag from their upstream neighbor. All of this while Lanfen fired questions at them.

"Reynolds! Choose a category: firearms or movies?"

Catch. "Firearms!" Shift. Toss.

"What's the difference between a single-action and a double-action firearm?"

Catch. "Double action requires cocking the gun before pulling the trigger." Shift. "Single action does not." Toss.

"Flores! Category: television series or music?"

"Television!"

"Who played the title role in *The Man from U.N.C.L.E.*?"

"Uh . . ." said Flores, catching a beanbag with his left hand while tossing one to his opposing neighbor with his right. "Solo something." He shifted the new beanbag to his right hand.

"Wrong. That was the name of the character."

"Oh, ah—" Toss, catch. "Uh, um, Robert-Robert-Robert . . . Vaughn! Robert Vaughn!" He shifted the incoming bag and missed it with his right hand. It plopped between his feet. "Dammit!"

His upstream partner smiled, and the whole line of Deeps relaxed. Lanfen clapped her hands sharply. "Keep it going, guys! No stopping! Keep the bags moving until everyone gets back into the swing of things. Don't drop the ball, okay?"

She glanced over at the door and saw Chuck standing there watching (and, he thought, probably looking goofy).

He straightened. "How's it going?"

She glanced back at her group and nodded. "It's going well. In fact, why don't you guys take a break?"

Lieutenant Reynolds frowned. "I think we'll keep going, if

you don't mind. Practice the catch-throw sequence without the trivia questions."

Lanfen looked like a proud parent glancing back at her prodigies as she left the room.

"I didn't mean to interrupt," Chuck told her as she joined him in the hallway.

"No, it's fine. I wanted to go grab a cup of tea anyway." She nodded back toward the lab. "They've been at that for a couple of hours in one form or another."

"Did you think that exercise up yourself?" Chuck asked her as they fell into step.

"Yes."

"I'm impressed. How are they doing really?"

"They're doing well. Really. Some more than others, of course. Mr. Flores has a bit of a problem, as does his lieutenant."

"Reynolds? That bothers him a great deal, I imagine."

"I don't judge. We just keep running the drills until everyone is either locked in or ready to collapse. If they're ready to collapse, I have a backup exercise that's not quite as hard, so they can succeed at something."

They turned in to Steampunk Alley. "You're good at this," Chuck told her. "And you just made my day."

She shot him a sidewise glance. "How so?"

"I was moping around the halls, feeling like our organizational creativity is just seeping away, and here you are inventing a program to teach multitasking."

Lanfen laughed. "Necessity is a mother, I guess. Dr. Streegman made it pretty clear that if we couldn't teach them how to interface directly with the bot's VR unit, it could blow up the whole deal. Or someone could get themselves blown up."

"Latency," Chuck murmured. "The slip betwixt the cup and the lip, the thought and the action."

"In a word, yes."

Chuck watched Lanfen pour herself a cup of hot water and deposit a tea bag in it. "Do you think teaching them to multitask will facilitate their learning to throw themselves?"

"You know, Matt asked me the same thing. You two are a lot alike."

"True," he said. "Except in every way."

Lanfen laughed. "I know what you mean on the surface. But you're both equally driven, just by different things. Two true believers. You'd see it if you were standing outside yourself. Maybe through Bilbo's eyes."

Chuck smiled but tried not to think too much about the comparison—or its implications. "You didn't answer my question."

"The new recruits? They're certainly disciplined enough to throw themselves. A couple of them even meditate."

He pounced on that. "Are the ones who practice meditation doing better than the ones who don't?"

"Yes. To different degrees, though. I'm starting to think the real essential element is self-awareness. Meditation isn't just about emptying your mind. It's about connecting with your self, becoming aware of all the processes happening in your body, mind, and spirit. Your breathing, your heartbeat, your senses, your inner climate and thoughts. It's like . . . you can't throw a ball unless you can feel the ball in your hands. You can't throw your voice unless you have an awareness of where it comes from and what shapes it—diaphragm, throat, vocal cords, everything. If you're uncertain that there's anything to sense, you might be less than effective in doing much more than achieving a resting state. Do you understand?"

"You can't throw your point of view—your *self*—unless you have some grasp on what that is or at least a belief that there's something there to throw."

"Exactly. And my recruits are each coming at that from a different set of experiences and beliefs. I think Sergeant Masterson has the best grasp on it. She's done yoga and meditation, and she has a sort of . . . well, a spiritual foundation."

She was blushing, which suffused her golden skin with subtle shades of rose.

"What?" he said. "Does that make you uncomfortable?"

"Not at all. I was afraid . . . well, you're a scientist. You probably find all that spirituality talk silly. Or at least irrelevant. I know Dr. Streegman does."

"That's Matt. And that's where we're not actually alike. He's a mathematician. I'm a neurologist. The human processes—the processes that make us human—are my whole focus. I'm not at all uncomfortable with the idea of a spiritual reality. In fact I accept it as a given."

"Oh. Then maybe it's you and me that are alike."

Chuck grinned. "Has Matt given you any milestones for teaching your students to know themselves well enough to throw their selves?"

She groaned at the play on words—something he found immensely satisfying. He was not known for his sense of humor.

"I need to show results in ten days, and I don't think Matt's going to accept a fast and furious game of Trivial Pursuit: Beanbag Edition as results." Her brow furrowed. "What do you think will happen if I can't do it?"

He opened his mouth to say, "I don't know," but what came out was, "You'll do it. I have no doubt." He was surprised to realize that was the absolute truth.

MATT WAS A FUNNY GUY. He seemed to be the most laid-back and casual when he was really the most nervous or ill at ease. When he strolled into the robotics lab with his hands shoved deep into the pockets of his khakis and a smile on his face, every alarm bell in Dice's head went off.

"Hey, Dice, how're things going?"

Dice glanced sidewise at Brenda, who was helping him test a new appendage design for the ninja bots. The rest of the crew had gone to lunch. "Uh, things are going really well. We'll have two units ready for testing tomorrow morning."

Matt stopped in the middle of the lab, looked off into the middle distance, and scratched behind one ear. "Yeah, about that. You're pushing the limits of our facility here to get two of these done in a week's time, aren't you?"

That wasn't a question.

"Pretty much. But we really don't have the resources to do more than that."

"We could get more manpower . . ."

Dice shook his head. "That won't do it. Even if I had twice as many people, we don't have the workspace. We could retool our space to create an assembly line, but these things aren't cookie-cutter constructs. The other option is to move, which would take time away from—" He gestured at the bot.

"Yeah, I can see that." Matt looked around the lab as if he were seeing it for the first time. "Well, looks like there's only one solution, then. We'll send a couple of the bots over to Deep Shield with schematics for them to assess. Then you and some of your trainees can go over there and teach more of their folks to assemble them."

"O-okay. When—"

"I don't know. Tomorrow maybe. That'll give them the rest of the week to look the units over and have some idea of who's going to be taking your class. You can go over next Monday. They'll be—well, they ought to be ready by then." He smiled.

"Great. I'll tell General Howard." He sketched a salute and sauntered back out of the lab.

Beside Dice, Brenda made a noise that sounded suspiciously like a snort. "What was that?"

"That," said Dice, "was me being thoroughly manipulated. He came in here to tell me that Deep Shield was demanding access to the bots in their own labs. He ended up asking if they could take some of the work off my hands."

"Wow," said Bren. "He's good."

"Yeah. Yeah, he is. Scary, isn't it?"

Chapter 20

DEEP

Two days after Lanfen was able to get all but one of her first class to throw with some level of success, she arrived at Forward Kinetics to find her classroom lab empty. None of her charges were in evidence; there was no message explaining their absence; there was nothing on the organizational calendar to clarify it.

Puzzled, she headed for Matt's office to see if he knew what was up. She was reaching out to tap on his door when someone called to her.

"Ms. Chen?"

She turned to see Brian Reynolds standing up the hall, toward the foyer. As always he was wearing an unadorned, navy blue uniform.

"Hi, Brian. Where is everybody?"

"They're waiting for us at the facility. We'll be working from there from now on."

Lanfen was an even-tempered soul, but the cavalier attitude this last-minute change suggested raised her usually slumbering ire. She took a deep breath and exhaled, wondering if she should just fling open Matt's office door and find out what this was about.

"Ma'am?" Reynolds was watching her with that air of well-tested patience she'd begun to suspect was taught—no, mandated—by the military.

Fine. She'd take this up with Matt when she got back. She nodded and followed Brian out to the government-issued car that waited for them in the parking lot.

The Deep Shield kinetics facility was impressive, or at least the part of it that Lanfen saw. The working space was large, well laid out, and fitted with everything a kung fu workout required and then some. The main floor area was taken up by a huge, blue mat; around its perimeter stood the members of her class, each accompanied by a gleaming new robot.

It took a moment for Lanfen to realize there was a lone robot standing sentry to one side of the large double doors: Bilbo.

The anger she'd felt earlier rekindled. That they had simply swept her away without warning was bad enough, but that they had come into her domain and taken Bilbo without so much as a word to her . . .

She wasn't sure where to direct the anger—at Howard and his team for absconding with her, her class, and her robot or at Matt and Chuck for letting Howard do it in the first place.

Except, of course, that Bilbo wasn't really her robot.

She gently reined the anger in again. It would do her no good here and would only hamper her training efforts and her personal progress. Nor was it fair to her students to hold them accountable for their masters' behavior. For not the first time today, she promised herself she would have a serious discussion with Matt Streegman when she got back to FK. She took a deep, cleansing breath, let it out, and inspected her class and their metal counterparts.

"I had no idea that Dice's team had built so many of these little guys," she said, realizing only as she said it that these "little guys" were bigger than Bilbo by about a third. There were other differences as well—slightly different dimensions, thicker limbs, a different material on the torso shielding.

"Actually," said Reynolds, "we brought over a few prototypes and built the rest of them here."

She turned to look at him. "Does Dice know?"

Was there just the slightest reddening along his cheekbones?

"Dr. Kobayashi helped set up our operation."

Lanfen relaxed a bit. "Fine, then. Well, let's get going, shall we? We need to put these new bots through a shakedown process, and we're running late."

"Yes, ma'am." Reynolds moved to his bot.

"Let me work with one of yours first, so I can see if they feel any different. That might help me if and when we shift into problem-solving mode."

Every one of the recruits turned to look at Reynolds.

"You can use mine," he told her.

She inspected the robot visually first, asking Reynolds questions about height and weight, noting that the hands and feet were now more like humans'. That was good. There was also a small, brass plate on the bot's right shoulder. Something was etched on it: "#DSRS04 Thorin."

She smiled at Reynolds. "You named them?"

He smiled back. "Of course."

"Okay. What are the essential differences?"

"They're about thirty pounds heavier and eight inches taller and have a different setup with their appendages, as you can see."

"Their heads are larger, too," Lanfen noted. "Any particular reason?"

"GPS system. Infrared camera. Heat sensors."

"Heat sensors?"

"Imagine you're searching a pitch-black mine for survivors. In situations where even infrared tech won't work, heat sensors will pick up the presence of a warm body. May be the only way to find a survivor in a situation like that."

"Cool," she chirped. "Let's see how they work."

Lanfen used the same method to get into Thorin's mechanism as she did with Bilbo. That part worked seamlessly. The additional weight, height, and length of the limbs took a little exercise to get accustomed to, but ultimately she adapted. The new appendages took a bit more getting used to; both hands and feet could adaptively use one of their digits as an opposable thumb. She worked at opening and closing the hands for several moments before she was happy with the result.

She put the new bot through his paces remotely, watching the way he moved from her own point of view. Finally she went into kinetoquist mode and threw herself into the bot. The world looked pretty much the same as it did from Bilbo's POV. She drove Thorin through some rolls, kicks, and postures before returning him to Reynolds, who was watching her with almost exaggerated care.

"What?"

He shook his head. "Nothing. Just wanted to be sure we got it right. Thorin seemed okay to you? No hiccups?"

"None," she told him. "I am a little jealous of your new gadgets, though."

Reynolds turned his head and tossed his classmates a look. She followed his gaze and saw that Seneca Hughes was hiding a smile . . . and looking at Bilbo.

Lanfen turned to look at her bot, only then realizing that he, too, had been outfitted with the new handy feet.

"Very nice," she said enthusiastically. "Do I get GPS, too?"

"Sorry," said Reynolds. "The lab didn't think he needed that. But the manipulators are Dr. Kobayashi's design."

"Well, let's put them to use. No more lollygagging, ladies and gentlemen. Let's get moving. Have you done any practice work with them at all?"

"A little," said Reynolds. "Just proof of concept. We haven't tried ventrilokinetics yet."

"Kinetoquism," she corrected him. "We don't want the bots to think we view them as dummies."

That actually netted her a round of laughter.

Maybe this day would be all right after all.

MINI'S EXPERIENCE WITH THE DEEP Shield people was, in her opinion, both bizarre and uncomfortable—probably as much for them as for her. She did not understand them; they did not understand her; and at first she fled each session to the grounds of the business park, where she would relax in the company of Jorge Delgado, a friend she had made among the gardeners who kept the parkland groomed.

Jorge was a man of many words, with opinions about anything that grew from the ground. She found his botanical wisdom soothing and used the opportunity to study the construction of the plants he tended. She didn't tell him everything she was working on, of course—only that she was an artist and wanted to paint the most realistic flowers possible.

"I want them to leap off the canvas," she told him, which prompted him to supply her with small pots containing clippings from his most-vivid blooms, along with lengthy discourse on the care and feeding of green pets.

"You want them to leap," he said, "then you must feed them energy food."

Mini wasn't certain that Jorge's wisdom would help her with

the Deeps. In fact, at the beginning of their sojourn together, she hadn't been sure she could teach them anything useful for a military application. Why did they care about manipulating art software or even pixels and photons on a screen?

So finally she asked.

"Our goal," the group's lieutenant, Rachel Cohen, had told her, "is to be able to manipulate pixels directly, the way you do it. It obviates the need for specialized software."

"Well, yes, but to what purpose?"

"Just imagine the time saved if we can prototype skins for our robots, create rescue scenarios, and demonstrate them without having to work them out painstakingly, using standard wire frames and animation software. The applications are practically endless."

So she had taught them the art of pixel manipulation, first using the software, then moving beyond that to simply create images on the screen. It did not escape them that there was a different quality to her images and animations.

"Yours look three-dimensional," said Rachel. "How are you doing that?"

The question was a gratifying reward for all of Mini's hard work. She had spent hours working alone in the lab and even at home, pulling and pushing the pixels, extending herself into the medium to draw them out and imbue them with three dimensions.

Using the flowering plants that Jorge had been kind enough to surprise her with, Mini walked her class through 3-D, drilled them on it, and was eventually satisfied with their work, though in her heart of hearts she knew it was not equal to what she could do. She felt a small thrill of satisfaction at that but quashed it, knowing that in the end she was being asked to make them her equals.

Even as she moved her students along, Mini knew she was close to moving beyond what she was teaching them. The prospect excited her . . . as did daydreaming about a fitting way to reveal her new trick.

She'd show Eugene first.

"IS IT MY IMAGINATION, OR are there more Smiths roaming our halls today than there were yesterday?" Sara Crowell set her cup of hot coffee down on the café table between Tim and Mike and pulled up a chair.

"Why do you call them that?" asked Mike, sipping at his own cup. Hot chocolate, Sara could tell by the aroma. The man was addicted to it.

Tim answered. "It's from the *Matrix* movies. I thought you knew that." At Mike's head shake, he added, "Agent Smith is this sort of generic man in black who's, like, everywhere."

"I swear they've multiplied," said Sara. "There are three in the main lobby, and God knows how many wandering the halls."

"Two by the espresso machine," murmured Tim, flicking a glance in that direction. "Maybe they're clones."

Mike laughed. "Naw, the one on the left is shorter than the one on the right. See?"

"What are they doing here?" asked Tim.

"According to Matt," said Sara, "they're supposed to be making sure no one crashes the party or tries to remove classified items from the lab. Presumably the enemies of the US of A would be very interested in what we're doing here. This zeta wave stuff is off the charts as far as human-machine interface tech goes. I'd be willing to bet no one has anything like it."

"I wouldn't be too sure," said Tim. "Stuff like this seems to be in the ether. I've talked to editors who say the same story idea has come to them from multiple writers in a short time period, and scientific discoveries seem to happen in clumps, too. Do you know how many Nobel laureates share the prize with people who were working on the same concept halfway around the world?"

"I don't think so this time, Timmy. It took a serendipitous confluence of two completely opposite minds to get us to this. I mean think of all the threads that have to come together: creativity, openness to seemingly outrageous ideas, a knowledge of the human brain, a deep interest—no, an obsession with the workings of the human mind—and the mathematical and mechanical chops to pull it off. I think we're it, boys. So I guess it makes sense that Uncle Sam would want to guard us like the national treasures we are."

Tim made a face. "So we're just pieces of tech to them. Is that what you're saying?"

"Not necessarily. We're human resources."

"Personnel?" Mike offered.

"Wetware," Tim countered.

"Just be glad they didn't give you a jarhead haircut." Turning to Mike, Sara asked, "How're your troops doing, Mikey?"

"Pretty good. They're operating servos like they were born to it. But . . ." He hesitated.

"What?"

"It's just . . . I've been wondering why we even need the servos."

Tim's eyes lit up. "Sara and I don't use servos."

"What do you mean? You can make *anything* move with your minds?"

"Hardly, or Kate Upton would be sitting here right now."

Sara's eye roll was almost audible.

"I'm not sure I can put words on what it is we do, but it doesn't require a mechanical interface. We're just able to manipulate unmodified pieces of machinery."

"Wow, Timmy, you make it sound as easy as shooting a layup," Mike said.

"Still can't do that." Tim frowned.

"It has to be machinery that we have some idea how to operate," Sara added. "But for you that's pretty much everything. Have you tried it?"

Mike looked over at the espresso machine, with its gleaming copper and brass fittings. The two Smiths were still standing next to it, exchanging notes about something.

Sara followed his gaze. As she watched, one of the taps on the side rotated its nozzle, and a jet of steam shot out of it, forcing the two agents to retreat several steps. The tap closed again just as quickly as it had opened.

She looked back at Mike. His expression was noncommittal and completely innocent.

Tim was chortling. "Dude, you better not let them know you can use the Force like that. They'll classify your ass."

Would they? Sara had wondered that many times since they'd embarked on this partnership with Deep Shield. What if the military came to view the zetas as little more than classified warmware? What happened to people whose brains and the thoughts in them were considered classified?

"We're already top secret, aren't we?" she asked.

Tim cast another glance at the Smiths. "Yeah, well, apparently so are some of the projects our trainees are working on."

"What do you mean?"

"I went up to my lab to snag my coffee cup before I came down here, and one of my students—the lieutenant, what's his name . . . Pierce—was sitting at his computer. I don't think I imagined how fast he shut that puppy down and put up the piece we were working on yesterday."

Sara leaned in. "Did you get a sense of what he was really working on?"

"Something using the same software. He was designing something. Armor, looked like to me."

Mike chuckled. "You caught him playing games, Tim. He's probably designing a video game in his spare time."

Tim seemed to think about that for a moment and grinned. "A man after my own heart."

Sara glanced back at the two agents, who were now sitting at a nearby table, looking anything but relaxed over their cups of whatever. "I wouldn't be so sure."

"What if I told him I noticed he was working on a personal project and suggested I'd be happy to help him with it? Then he'd show me, right?"

"At your own risk, Timmy." She stood and picked up her coffee. "Almost time for class. I'm heading down to my lab. Be careful poking your nose in their business, okay?"

"You're paranoid," Tim said.

"So are you, usually," she reminded him. "Why not now?"

She left Tim with that thought and went off to teach her class.

SOMETHING WOODSY AND FLORAL INVADED Chuck's olfactory senses. Something that made him imagine he heard running water and felt grass under his feet. He knew that fragrance. Smiling, he glanced at the door of his office and found Lanfen standing in it.

The expression on her face put a damper on his smile. "What's the matter?"

She made a closing gesture at the door. "Can we talk?"

Ah. The three most feared words in the English language. "Sure. Come on in."

She carefully closed the door, making sure the latch bolt clicked in the strike plate.

She sat in the chair across from his desk, her arms crossed over her chest. She frowned at the Camden Yards snow globe on his desk as if it had done something rude.

"Where were you today?" he asked when she didn't say anything.

That apparently startled her. She lowered her arms and looked up at him. "You don't know? You really don't?"

"No. What happened? What's wrong?"

"I got hijacked this morning. Bilbo, too. By the Deeps. They carted both of us off to their facility, where we spent the day with our team of recruits and their shiny, new and improved robots."

"They . . . they did?"

She nodded.

He'd known about the new bots but not that the Deeps had planned on changing the venue for their training.

"No one told you this was going to happen?" she asked.

"No. I had no idea. Have you talked to Matt about it?"

"Matt is strangely absent from his office. And his lab. And everywhere else I've looked for him this evening." She leaned forward and put her clasped hands on the edge of his desk. "Chuck, I don't mind working with them at their facility. I don't mind that they gave Bilbo cool new appendages. I *do* mind that they didn't tell me they were planning on doing either. Can you . . . will you talk to General Howard about this? Can you make him understand that we're not used to being hauled around like . . . like ordnance? I'm not government property. Neither is Bilbo. It's not right for them to just take us like that."

"No. No, it's not." Chuck fought the momentary sensation of swimming in a very deep pool, the bottom of which he could not see. There were currents here he didn't understand, much less trust. "I'll talk to Matt. We'll get this straightened out."

"Thanks."

"You said they made changes to Bilbo?"

Her expression brightened a little. "They installed these handy new feet with situationally opposable thumbs." She waggled her thumbs up and down. "Based on Dice's design, they said. In addition to that, their bots have built-in GPS and infrared units. For rescue work." She frowned again. "Am I being ridiculous? I mean we're all on the same team, right? Why should it bother me if they change the drill?"

"You're not being ridiculous. Being a military agency or being our chief client doesn't give them the right to just change everything on a whim. I'll talk to Matt."

"Thanks," she said again and shrugged. It was as if, having divested herself of this problem, she was simply slipping it off the way one slides out of a too-warm coat. Her posture straightened, her face lost its pensive expression, and her eyes brightened.

"It's six o'clock," she announced. "Have you eaten?"

He shook his head, still pondering unseen currents.

"I know a great Szechuan place about a mile from here. You like Szechuan?"

"Love it," he said, though he was pretty sure he couldn't tell Szechuan cuisine from Cantonese or Mandarin. He really didn't care. He decided that if it meant having dinner with Lanfen, he would have said he loved lima beans.

EUGENE LOOKED UP FROM HIS laptop screen at the pinecone that had just tumbled to the middle of his office floor. He turned his gaze to the door to find Mini standing there watching him, smiling enigmatically.

He practically leapt out of his chair. "Wow, is it that late already? I'm sorry. I said I was going to come down to your classroom and rescue you, didn't I?"

She didn't say anything, only crooked her finger at him and backed out of the doorway.

Okay. She was in one of her playful moods. He liked those well enough, though he was sometimes afraid they were a coping mechanism she'd adopted because she was often perceived as young and cute and harmless. *Two out of three of those are true.* But she had a strong will and some cutting insights. The girl could do some damage if she wanted to. Luckily she rarely wanted to.

Eugene rolled his eyes at his own concern. Who was he to worry over someone else's coping mechanisms? He had about three dozen of them himself, from the geektastic use of Yiddish to flaunt his native nerdiness to the clothing choices he made to hide it.

Right now he decided to embrace his inner geek because Minerva liked it. He got up from his desk and moved to the doorway, dragging one foot and hunching one shoulder, so his right arm dangled crookedly.

"Yeth, mithtress," he lisped. "Igor hearth, and Igor obeyth."

He reached his office doorway to find Mini beckoning him from the middle of the A lab.

"Here, Igor," she called.

There was an odd quality to her voice that he couldn't quite put a finger on. Before he could, she stopped beckoning, smiled brilliantly, and held out a hand to him. He reached out his dangling hand to take hers and shivered as their fingers met. It felt wrong—cold, soft . . . like liquid. His mind had barely processed that bit of weirdness when she disappeared. Literally and completely. Vanished. As if she'd never been there in the first place.

Eugene, still hunched over in Igor mode, stared at the spot where she'd been standing, his mind scrambling to make sense of the situation. *I'm asleep,* he told himself. *I've fallen asleep at my desk, and I'm dreaming. I need to wake up.*

He said the words aloud. "Eugene Pozniaki, you need to wake up."

A trill of laughter answered the observation.

He raised his head. Mini was peering at him from around one of the lab's outer doors.

"Did you like it?" she asked pertly.

"Did I like . . . ?"

"My doppelgänger. My apparition. My projection." She came fully into the room on a wave of laughter. "You should see the look on your face."

"No, I'm sure I shouldn't. What . . . what did you do?"

"I projected! I made another me. I fooled you, didn't I? You really thought it was me, didn't you?"

"I . . . I did." He took a couple of steps toward her, then reached out and touched her, just to make sure. She was solid, warm, real.

She beamed at him.

"That was amazing. Does Chuck know you can do this?"

"Not yet. I wanted you to be the first to see it." Her smile faltered. "I haven't shown the Deeps yet. Is that bad of me? I wanted you and Chuck to know first."

Eugene was staring at the spot the doppelgänger had occupied a moment before. "It—she looked so real. So solid. Not at all like a projection, but . . ." He rubbed his fingertips together, vaguely remembering the creeps he'd gotten when he'd tried to touch the ersatz Mini. How could a projection feel like anything at all?

"Yeah. I've worked hard on that," Mini said.

Eugene shook off his heebie-jeebies and grinned at her. "I'll bet you have. Let's go show Chuck. Maybe then I can take you and your twin out for some—"

Before he could finish, he felt an all-too-solid and sharp elbow in his rib cage.

Chapter 21

SHIELD

Dice stared at his reflection in the opaque window of the government Humvee and sighed. Working with Deep Shield was like trying to see through that darkened glass. They'd told him they were having a problem with a mechanism but wouldn't tell him which one. He'd asked which tools to bring. They said none—they would provide the tools. He had to assume, therefore, that this was one of the units they'd developed themselves, which brought up the question:

Why am I being asked to troubleshoot and repair it?

He became aware that he was arriving at the Deep Shield facility by a subtle shift in the road noise—as if the Humvee were driving down a narrow alley or possibly a tunnel. He ended up, as always, inside the big hangar. He was escorted to the workshop he always used when working with the Deeps and was presented with a robot brain case that might have come from one of his bots . . . except for the fact that it was twice the size and oddly shaped. The Forward Kinetics robot brain cases were nearly spherical; this one was roughly football shaped.

Well, there was that, and the CPU was missing. He could tell that without even opening the case. All the weight was in one end.

"What's this from?" he asked the tech who'd been assigned to him—a sergeant named Cherise Kelly.

Sergeant Kelly didn't even blink. "It's from one of our new units."

"Based on the Hob-bot, Bilbo designs?"

"Yes, sir."

"I'm flying blind here, Cherise. What else can you tell me about the unit?"

She looked momentarily uncomfortable. "Sorry, Dr. Kobayashi, but I'm not authorized to tell you any more than that."

"Well, you're going to have to tell me more, because I need to know what the heck you expect me to do with this."

"We were hoping you could fix it."

"Fix it. What's it doing? Or not doing, as the case may be."

"It's not working. The unit loses its balance."

"Where's the CPU?"

"In our lab."

"I'll need to see it."

"Sorry, sir. You can't. It's classified."

He thought about that for a moment, then said, "Okay. You realize I might not be able to do anything without seeing the CPU."

She said nothing.

He balanced the brain case on the palm of one hand. It tilted to the side the gyro was in. "If I have no idea how the casing balances with the CPU in it, I might not be able to troubleshoot this."

"Yes, sir."

"Right." He sighed. *Science without communication rarely ends in progress,* he thought. *How can these guys not get that?* Dice put the case down on the workbench and assessed the tools they'd supplied. They were like the ones he had back at FK but reengineered to fit the closures of the larger unit. Weird. He didn't see any reason the standard sizes wouldn't have worked. No wonder military-issued tools cost as much as a fleet of Teslas.

Dice snagged a tool, slipped the locking pins out of the brain case, and laid it out, open, on the bench. Inside, opposite the empty recess where the bot's not-so-little brain should have been, was a closed housing for the gyro mechanism. Looking at it, Dice realized he had a pretty good idea of what the problem was without even popping off the housing.

Should he let his handler know? He almost groaned aloud at even having the thought. Secrecy was the closest thing to a Newman engine he'd ever encountered—it fed on itself. He'd always worked in an open environment in which everyone shared information. Pooling information was the fuel that drove the engine of creativity and invention. Yet despite that, when confronted with Deep Shield clamminess, he felt less like sharing than he ever had in his life.

He took a deep breath, shook off the momentary lapse of reason, and unseated the gyro cover. Yep, suspicions confirmed.

"So the bot can't maintain its balance, you said."

"Yes, sir. It can't remain upright during the simplest maneuvers. In fact, it's unstable even when standing still."

"That's about what I'd expect. The brain case sits at the vertical, right?"

"Yes, sir."

"Then I suspect you've got two problems. One is that the gyro mechanism is too small; the other is its placement. Either you need a larger gyro that rests on top of the CPU, or you need two gyros a hair bigger than this one—one to each side of the CPU.

That's especially true if you ever plan on having the brain case balance horizontally, which I assume you do."

"I couldn't say, sir."

"Of course not."

The tech was regarding the brain case thoughtfully. "If I may ask, Doctor, why do your bots not require a double gyro?"

"Your engineers changed too many variables at once, Sergeant. They altered the size, shape, and orientation of the brain case, changed the placement of the gyro within it, and—unless I'm mistaken, and I don't think I am—they also increased the size and weight of the CPU. And they did all of that without modifying the gyro or supplementing it to compensate. That'd be my educated guess anyway."

A smile tugged at the corner of the tech's mouth. "Megan said you're a smart cookie, Dr. Kobayashi. She was right. You could tell all that just by looking at a nearly empty brain case?"

"Sergeant Kelly, I live, breathe, and dream robots. Well, I used to dream about them . . . until I got a girlfriend." That didn't get the laugh he was looking for. "Anyway . . ." He gestured at the mechanism lying on the worktable. "That was never gonna work."

"No, sir. I can see that."

"You know this would get fixed a lot faster if you'd just let me into your lab to work on it."

"I'm sorry, sir. We can't do that. It's—"

"Yeah, yeah. I know. It's classified. Why, though? What've you got in there that I haven't already seen?"

She didn't answer.

He ran a hand through his hair in frustration. "Look, Cherise, I just want to see the robot this came from. I don't want access to anything else."

She just looked at him for long moment, then said, "You can't see the robot, sir."

"What the hell are you talking about? I designed the damned things!"

"I'm sorry, sir. You can't see the robots. Except for the improved Hob-bot and the Thorin series, all of our robots are classified." This was delivered in a cool voice that brooked no argument.

"Let me talk to Megan."

"I'm sorry, sir. Lieutenant Phillips isn't available right now. She's engaged in field testing."

Dice didn't even bother to ask what Megan Phillips was field testing. He wasn't sure he wanted to know.

He made some recommendations for a redesign of the robot skull based on the sketchy information he'd surmised and then climbed into the big Humvee for the return trip to Forward Kinetics. He was surprised to find Lanfen already ensconced in the backseat, apparently on her way back to home base from her training class.

He said very little to her on the ride, but as soon as they disembarked at their facility and the Humvee had driven away, he said, "I need to talk to you."

She gave him a sideways glance. "Sure. Your office?"

"Yeah. No, wait." He stopped and peered at the building. What if his office was bugged? For some reason, the idea didn't seem as crazy as it would have a year ago. "Let's just take a stroll around the park, okay?"

"Ooookay," she said and followed him out along the garden path.

He headed away from the building, carefully avoiding the gardeners who were bent over their plantings. He was pretty sure he'd spooked Lanfen but kept walking without speaking until he felt sort of safe.

Finally he stopped. "I have no idea how to start this conversation, so I'm just going to dive in," he said. "Have you noticed anything really spooky out in the Deeps?"

She didn't seem that surprised by the question. "Define *spooky*."

"Do I really need to?"

That got him a wry smile. "Not really. What's the matter?"

"I got called out to troubleshoot a part—a gyro they thought was malfunctioning. It was in a brain case created from one of my designs, but they'd changed the size, shape, everything. They wouldn't show me anything but the malfunctioning bit. They wouldn't even let me see the bot's CPU, never mind let me in the lab with the bots. I had to do everything in the hangar."

"Yes. I know they're making changes. Their fu-bots are bigger, heavier. Is that what it was—a fu-bot skull?"

"No. I helped with the fu-bots. This brain case was several times larger than even their fu-bots, and it was a different shape." He pantomimed an oblate spheroid. "Whatever it was, it was falling over."

"So . . . secret government designs. That was to be expected, right?"

"Was it?"

She chewed her lip. "I don't know. The secrecy does seem a bit excessive. Unless . . ."

"Unless they're doing something that's not in the contract," Dice said, finishing her thought.

"How could we find out? I mean they're not going to let one of us—"

She stopped walking and stared at him. He felt a shot of something tingly go down his spine. He was pretty sure they'd had the thought in unison or at least in close harmony.

She smiled. "*I* can get into their lab. That's what you're thinking, isn't it?"

"It had occurred to me."

"Okay. Tomorrow. I won't be able to stay long."

"You don't need to. You just need to see what's back there."

"I'll try."

"That's all I can ask."

They swung around as if by mutual agreement and strolled back to the building as nonchalantly as possible for two people who had just decided to spy on their own government.

BEEN THERE, DONE THAT, BOUGHT *a T-shirt and already shredded it.*

That was the way Mini had started to think of her involvement with Deep Shield's crew. She was over the first flush of exhilaration at having something to teach these übercompetent people. They were a singularly focused lot who looked at her strangely when she enthused about the art she was teaching them. To them, she realized, this painting with pixels and photons served a purpose external to the art itself or the joy of creation. They concentrated on that external purpose absolutely and drilled obsessively at constructing seamless pictures generated entirely by their thoughts. They were good at it, too, but in Mini's opinion they lacked real passion. To them it was an exercise in control, not creation. And control kind of bored her.

By the end of that Friday's session, she was ready to climb the walls. Several times she had almost lost her temper with the group leader, Rachel Cohen. If it weren't for the puppy in the group—a corporal named Morris Baxter, who seemed to appreciate the sheer joy of creation—she would have snapped. She didn't like to snap. It wasn't a good look on her. Something like the mouse that roared.

When the last of the Deeps had left her lab at the end of the day, she saluted the empty doorway sarcastically and thought about throwing up a middle finger or two, then felt an immediate wave of guilt. They were to be pitied, not scorned. Except for Corporal "Call Me Bax" Baxter, they had no idea what they were missing by focusing so entirely on the product that they failed to derive happiness from the process.

"I need a fix," Mini told herself aloud and headed for the gardens to look for Jorge. A quick talk with the gardener—someone who was passionate about something, even if most people would say they were just plants—would make her forget all about her frustration with her class.

Usually at that time on a Friday, Jorge was cleaning up the tool barn and prepping for the next week's work, but when Mini reached the barn, he was nowhere to be seen. She poked around, looking for him, then gave up and decided a walk along the garden paths would have to suffice to detangle her snarled mood. She'd gotten almost all the way back to the Forward Kinetics building when she saw him working in the shade of a small cluster of maples. But as she drew closer, she realized it wasn't Jorge. She figured it must be another member of his crew, though, who would surely know where his boss was. It was only when she got practically on top of the man that she realized he was a complete stranger.

He turned to look at her as she reached the little grove of trees and smiled. "Hello, miss," he said. He was nothing like Jorge. He was much younger, his black hair cropped rather than slicked back.

"Hi," she said. "Um, have you seen Jorge?"

"Who?"

"Jorge Delgado, the head groundskeeper. He's not sick or something, is he?"

"I'm sorry, miss. Jorge doesn't work here anymore. His company's contract was terminated."

"Why?"

"I don't know, miss."

"So you're with the new groundskeeping company?"

"Yes, miss."

"Who hired you?"

"I don't know, miss. I was just assigned here effective Wednesday."

"I see," she said. "Well, thanks."

She made her way back toward the building, with her mind in a worse tangle than before. Jorge hadn't known his company was going to be terminated the last time she'd spoken to him, which had been—good God—Wednesday morning. It wasn't her imagination that this new guy sounded just like the guys in her art class. "Effective Wednesday"—that was almost formal, as were the "miss" this and "miss" that.

Military speak—that's what it was.

Nor was it her imagination that he'd had a walkie-talkie peeking out of his pocket. She paused to pick a bloom from a shrub rose and watched him out of the corner of her eye. He was speaking into the walkie-talkie. Reporting on his conversation with her?

She set her jaw, tucked Jorge's rose behind her ear, and marched into the building. The effect was half flamenco dancer, half toreador on her way to find the source of this bullshit.

EUGENE WAS CREEPED OUT. THERE was no other phrase that described it. He'd gone off campus to get what Mini called "candy coffee" at a local bistro—so heavy on the whipped cream and extra mocha that he couldn't be sure there was any actual coffee in it at all—and had decided to stop at a drugstore to grab a handful of PayDay bars and some red Twizzlers to restock his desk drawer.

He'd thought nothing of it when a young man in an Orioles T-shirt and mirrored shades had lined up with him at the coffee shop, but when he saw the same guy in one of those angled overhead mirrors at the drugstore, it sent a chill all the way from the top of his geek-chic hair to the soles of his high-tops.

He somehow managed to look nonchalant as he walked back to his car and climbed in. He pretended to mess with the radio and the cell phone charger for a minute or two. It allowed him to see the guy out of the corner of his eye when he exited the store and stood on the sidewalk.

Eugene couldn't tell if the guy glanced at him, thanks to the mirrored shades, but he wasn't surprised when he fished out a cell phone and started talking into it as he paced back and forth in front of the store.

Fine. Play that game.

Euge started his car and backed out of the parking place. He drove across the lot to the exit, his eyes flicking to the rearview mirror. Somewhere between one glance and the next, the Orioles fan had disappeared. By the time Eugene had made it across the parking lot to the street, a silver-gray Honda was pulling out.

He drove back to Forward Kinetics via an alternate route that included the drive-through window at a Dairy Queen, where he forced an Oreo blizzard down on top of the macchiato. He last saw the silver Honda as he turned in at the business park's main entrance. It drove straight past.

Eugene headed directly for Chuck's office, the queasy feeling in his stomach caused by something other than a sugar overload.

ALL WEEK LANFEN HAD LOOKED for an opportunity to get behind the scenes at Deep Shield. The problem was, of course, that she was rarely alone. She was escorted everywhere and spent the bulk of her time with her class.

The opportunity finally came when her class broke up on Friday afternoon. They'd quit a bit early to attend a debriefing, and the limo and driver usually assigned to her were otherwise engaged.

"Do you mind waiting for your driver here?" Brian asked her, gesturing around their practice room. His classmates had already marched their bots out of the room, but Thorin was standing at attention next to him. "It should only be about twenty minutes."

Lanfen shrugged and dropped to the mat cross-legged. "I'm fine with that. I'll just sit here and wind down. A little extra meditation never hurts."

He smiled at her then turned, taking a mental hold of Thorin.

Lanfen closed her eyes to slits and focused on the big robot. In a moment she was looking out at the world through its optics. She'd wondered if she'd collide with Lieutenant Reynolds's consciousness when she finally accomplished this, but she didn't. Then again, she didn't try. She just went along for the ride as the bot and his rider left the practice chamber and entered a part of Deep Shield that Lanfen and her associates had not been allowed access to.

The corridors—gray on blue—looked no different from the ones in the more public areas except that there was an armed guard on either side of the doors. Reynolds gave them each a nod and kept Thorin moving down the hall. They passed by several sets of closed doors, and Lanfen was beginning to despair of seeing anything of interest when the bot turned and pushed through a door on the right side of the broad corridor.

The room they entered was long and lined with what reminded Lanfen of the sort of charging stations the Borg used on *Star Trek*. There were dozens of them. The ones closest to the door belonged to her class members, but beyond them . . .

Back in the practice room, Lanfen sucked in a breath.

Beyond the now-familiar larger Hob-bots were rows of machines that dwarfed them. They were more massive, heavier, and seemed somehow misshapen. Their legs were as thick as tree trunks and ended in constructions that were definitely not feet. They looked more like smallish tank treads.

"What the hell?" Lanfen murmured.

Thorin swung to the left and mounted a low pedestal before turning about to face the room. Lanfen watched through the dwarfed fu-bot's optics as Lieutenant Reynolds left the room. She waited for the door to close before she took charge of the bot and swung its head about to give her a sweeping view of the entire chamber. She wished desperately she could take a picture, but all she had were her powers of observation and memory.

She tried focusing on the treads, the strangely thickened lower arms. But she couldn't quite make out some of the details.

She needed to get a closer look.

She had started to move Thorin back down to the floor when a door at the rear of the room swung open, and a pair of uniformed men entered, engaged in conversation. She froze the bot, one leg half-raised to step down, its head turned toward the newcomers.

Lanfen felt sweat trickle down her back but refused to be distracted by it. Slowly she lowered the bot's leg and swiveled its head back to true.

"Jesus," one of the men swore, staring at her (or rather at Thorin). "Did you see that?"

"See what?" The other guy turned to follow his gaze.

"I'd swear that bot moved."

"Stop that. This room is creepy enough without you saying that sort of shit. Let's get some dinner before I'm so spooked I can't eat."

They left.

Lanfen took a deep breath and began to turn Thorin's head again.

"Ms. Chen?"

A hand came down on her shoulder, making her yip audibly.

She opened her eyes and stared up into the face of her perennial escort and driver.

"I'm sorry," he said, looking abashed. "I didn't mean to startle you. We can leave whenever you're ready."

Lanfen made herself breathe again. "Good. Fine. I'm ready now." She rose and followed the escort from the room, giving Bilbo a parting glance. A part of her wished she could take him back with her, get him out of that place. It was an irrational response; Bilbo wasn't sentient and didn't really care where he was housed. Any personality he had was hers.

She hung on those thoughts for a moment—on the idea that Bilbo was, in some sense, a home for her consciousness, a familiar landing pad in this unfamiliar place.

"Are you okay, Ms. Chen?" the driver asked as he held open the Humvee's rear passenger door for her. "You look kind of pale."

"I think I might be coming down with something." She sniffled for good measure. "Long day."

"Yes, ma'am," he said agreeably and ferried her back to Forward Kinetics, where she knew the first order of business would be a walk in the park with Dice.

Chapter 22

LORSTAD

Chuck had, once upon a time, enjoyed working late. There was a special sort of contentment that came with the peace and quiet of the Forward Kinetics building at night, when most people—excepting often Eugene, Dice, and Brenda—had gone home for the day. There were few if any interruptions, and those were usually caused by Eugene or Dice popping in with a question, an idea, or an epiphany that Chuck also found engaging. Sometimes the four of them would gather to brainstorm ideas and chug coffee.

Now Chuck found that, increasingly, staying after hours left him feeling as if he were doing something subversive and annoying to the Deep Shield people charged with keeping the labs secure. He felt like a stranger in his own lab and found himself going home on time far more often these days.

Tonight was an exception. He had some data he wanted to collate and study, so he stayed. Gone were the days when he could take his work home. General Howard had made it clear that any data related to his agency's work was not to leave the premises. Chuck had a government-issued external hard drive for Deep Shield work.

As the sun dipped behind the trees, and the light filtering into his office turned a lurid red, Chuck gave up trying to concentrate on the data sets, leaned back in his chair, and wondered what the hell they'd gotten themselves into with this government contract: armed men and women wearing suits and earpieces prowled their halls. Their work was no longer their own. He wondered sometimes if their labs and offices were bugged.

He shook that paranoid thought from his head and tried to focus his tired eyes and his mind on the test data from Sara's class of recruits. The sound of a man delicately clearing his throat caused him to glance up at his office door. The man who stood there was a complete stranger. He was tall, thin, and angular, with a long face and thick, wavy hair that was just going to silver at the temples. He wore a frock coat and a string tie that made him look as if he'd just stepped out of a Mark Twain novel or a time machine.

"Dr. Brenton?" The stranger's delicately accented voice was soft but every bit as penetrating as his dark gaze.

"Yes, I'm Charles Brenton. May I help you?" He must surely be one of Howard's people, or he'd have been stopped at the reception desk and turned back.

"I was actually hoping I could help you." The man came into the office and closed the door behind him. He took a device the size and shape of a pitch pipe out of his coat pocket and held it up in the palm of his hand. It made no sound, but a light atop it went from red to yellow to green.

"Ah," he said. "There." He pocketed the device and turned his attention to Chuck. "My name is Kristian Lorstad. I represent a venerable academic and cultural institution that is very inter-

ested in your technological breakthrough. We see it as a potential benefit to humanity."

"Wait . . . you're not part of Deep Shield?"

"No."

"Then how did you get in?"

Lorstad smiled. "I simply showed my credentials to the gentleman at the front desk."

"Then you're with the government."

"No, we are most definitely not with the government. Our
aims are not political, and a great many of the movers and shak-
ers in government, at this juncture, are slaves to political dogma.
That is a poor atmosphere in which to grow programs that will
benefit humankind."

Chuck wondered what sort of credentials would get a nongov-
ernment or nonmilitary player admitted to Forward Kinetics,
but he didn't ask aloud.

Lorstad seated himself in one of Chuck's side chairs and
regarded the neuroscientist soberly. "You wish to benefit humanity, do you not, Dr. Brenton?"

"Yes. Yes, of course I do."

"Do you feel that your current arrangement with Deep Shield
furthers that aim?"

"What do you know about our current arrangement with
Deep Shield? In fact, how do you even know about Deep Shield
at all?"

"The institution I represent is composed of very powerful
people, Dr. Brenton. We know what we need to know."

Powerful people. Chuck was up to his eyebrows in powerful
people. He was leery of them, weary of them. He wanted no
more. He rose. "I'm sorry, Mr. Lorstad. I've about had my fill of
powerful people and organizations. From where I sit, they seem
to be running my life. All our lives."

Lorstad remained seated. "You'd like that to change, would you?"

Chuck blinked. "Yes."

The other man spread his hands as if that change were the easiest thing in the world to accomplish. "Then I can help you after all."

"No. I don't think you can. I think you might be able to help me exchange a devil I know for a devil I don't know. I'm not up for that, thank you. I'm tired of mysteries. Tired of secrets. Tired of overseers and spot checkers and security cameras and probably bugs as well. This conversation is most likely being recorded."

"Oh, yes," said Lorstad, glancing around the office. "Most definitely bugs. But, no, this conversation is not being recorded. It's not even being heard. The bugs are inoperative and will be until they reinstate them."

"What—you expect me to believe you just took them out with that device?" Chuck nodded at Lorstad's coat pocket.

"Believe what you will. This conversation, as far as the surveillance equipment at Deep Shield is concerned, never occurred." Now he stood. "Dr. Brenton, I'm offering you freedom. Don't you want that? Don't you want to be free to run your labs the way you feel they should be run? Free to help all of mankind instead of just this elite arm of the military?"

"Actually, I just want to be left alone by powerful people. No," he added when Lorstad opened his mouth again. "I'm not interested."

"Very well. I'll leave you with this then." He produced a plain white business card and laid it carefully on Chuck's desk. "And a question: has it occurred to you to wonder what department of government Deep Shield answers to?"

It had, actually, and Chuck found that Lorstad's choice of words prompted discomfort. Because the more he thought about General Howard, the more he had a sense that the man was answerable to no one. That couldn't be true, of course. But *who* were his superiors? Matt thought it was the DoD, but it could just as easily be the CIA, FBI, or NSA or an obscure black-ops branch of any arm of the military.

Hell—who's to say anyone in the government even knew about this at all?

Now there was a warm, cozy thought.

Lorstad watched these things parade through Chuck's head for a moment, then turned and left his office, striding through the outer lab. Chuck crossed his arms, listening with half an ear to the progress of the other man's footsteps. They paused. A moment later Chuck heard the door to the gallery open.

He sighed. Chuck almost felt sorry for the guy. To make that grand exit with its oh-so-mysterious question only to take the wrong door and end up in a second-floor gallery with no way to leave gracefully. He rounded his desk and listened for the man's footsteps again. Had they stopped at the top of the gallery stairs?

He went to the bottom of the gallery stairs and called up. "Mr. Lorstad? The exit is on the other side of the room."

There was no answer. Chuck went through the open door and climbed the stairs to the gallery. There was no one on the staircase, and the gallery was empty. The guy must have been snooping. He probably opened the door to the gallery and left via the main hallway.

Chuck went back down to the lab and out into the corridor. He looked both ways but saw no one except a roving guard. The man was a stranger, which made Chuck wonder how many such security people were actually on duty these days.

"Is something wrong, Doctor?" the guard asked.

"No, I was just wondering . . ." He balked at mentioning his visitor, though he couldn't have said why. "I was just wondering if Dr. Pozniaki is still around."

"No, sir. Dr. Pozniaki left approximately forty minutes ago."

"Ah. I see. I guess I'll go home, too. I can talk to him in the morning."

"Yes, sir." The guard swung around and continued on his rounds.

Chuck returned to the lab and made a quick search of any place a grown man might hide, but he found nothing. Feeling suddenly exhausted, he packed up his laptop, locked the Deep Shield–mandated external hard drive in his safe, and turned off the lights. A small splash of white atop his desk caught his eye: Lorstad's card . . . and with it something he hadn't noticed—the little device the man had told him jammed surveillance. He picked both up, stuck them into the pocket of his backpack, and went home.

If he had expected things there to be any less weird or more relaxing, he was doomed to disappointment. He arrived at his house in the early dusk and dropped his laptop bag on the sofa before heading for the kitchen. He was contemplating a beer when there was a tap at the back slider. He only just avoided uttering a startled yelp and turned to find Euge and Mini gesturing at him to unlock the door and let them in.

"Thanks, Doc," Eugene said. "We need to talk—"

There was a knock at the front door.

Eugene blinked. "Oh, man," he said.

Chuck gestured for them to wait and went to the front of the house. Two shadowy figures were on his darkened doorstep. Through the side panel, he recognized them as Dice and Lanfen. He started to turn on the porch light but hesitated. Instead he pulled open the door and let them into the dimly lit front hall.

"Go on into the kitchen," he told them, then retrieved his backpack before joining them. Feeling a bit silly, he got out Lorstad's jamming device, flipped the switch on its side, and watched the light atop it go immediately to green.

"What's that?" Eugene asked.

"I think . . . I think it means my kitchen isn't bugged."

Dice's face went pale. "Bugs? In our houses?"

"Maybe not. In my office it went red first."

"Where did you get it?" Dice wanted to know.

"Not important," said Chuck. "Why are you all here? This looks like an intervention."

"Of a sort," said Lanfen. She glanced around at the others. "I have a feeling we all have something important to say. Who goes first?"

No one said anything. Chuck ran his fingers through his hair. "Okay, can I get a brief preview first? Mini?"

"The entire gardening staff has been replaced by Deeps." That was worth a chill. And the way she blurted it, like something out of *Invasion of the Body Snatchers*.

"Euge?"

"I was followed this afternoon. A guy in a silver Honda. He followed me into two stores then all the way back to HQ."

Chuck looked at Dice. "I'm almost afraid to ask."

The robotics expert glanced at Lanfen then said, "It came to my attention that there are things and locations in the Deeps that are strictly off-limits. Stuff they won't let us see even if a robot's in need of repair. I got curious, so I asked Lanfen to take a look behind the scenes if she could."

"She could," said Lanfen. "I piggybacked a ride on Lieutenant Reynolds's bot and got a look at their storage area. Chuck, there are robots in there that . . . well, let's just say it's hard to imagine them having any humanitarian applications."

All eyes were on the martial arts master now. "Can you describe them?"

"They had treads instead of feet. They were huge. Bigger than even the Dwarf series. They seemed to be armed—in the truest sense of the word. I think their arms may have contained weaponry."

Chuck sat down hard on one of his kitchen bar stools. His lips felt stiff, frozen. "Weaponry?"

"I'm not one hundred percent certain. I'd need a better look. The thing is: what then? We can't exactly confront them."

"Why not?" Mini asked. "Our contract specifies that our tech is not to be used for offensive weaponry, doesn't it?"

"Yes, but they could easily just claim it's *defensive*," said Eugene.

"Or even that it isn't weaponry at all," said Lanfen. "Those big arm rigs might be for grapples for all I know."

"If they are grapples," Dice said reasonably, "why would they hide them from us?"

"So we won't use their designs?" asked Mini.

"That's not the way it's supposed to work, though," said Chuck. "It's just not . . . I'm going to call Matt."

They all stared at him.

"What?"

Dice was the first to speak. "Are you sure that's wise, Doc? He's pretty tight with Howard. If we let Matt know we're wigging out over this, he may say something to the general. If they're following us now, what'll they do if they think we're getting ready to bolt?"

"Are we?" asked Mini quietly. "Are you thinking of bolting? I know I am. Those men in the garden aren't gardeners anymore, Chuck. They're government agents, and more and more I think they're there to guard us from going out as much as to keep people from coming in."

"I know what you mean. And I still can't get over the fact that we really don't even know who they *are*. I kind of doubt they have the kind of oversight most branches of the military do."

"I'm not even sure I know what that means," said Dice.

"I'm thinking black ops," Chuck said.

Dice ran his hands over his face. "I thought that was only in the movies."

Chuck was on the verge of telling them about Lorstad, but he didn't. If they thought black ops was just for films, what would they make of Lord Lorstad the vampire? "I think we should sound Matt out," he said carefully. "But very gently. Very obliquely. And we should probably talk to other members of the team. Find out if there's anything more going on than we know about. Then . . . I don't know."

"Then is then. But right now," said Eugene, "I think we should order pizza." He answered the others' looks quickly. "It'll make this seem like a party to anyone who figures out that we're all here."

Dice paled. "Do you think you were followed?"

"If we were, we lost him. We drove through a parking structure and out again . . . twice."

Lanfen nodded. "Dice and I took separate cars and separate routes. I went home, parked my car, and took my motorbike."

"Wow, you guys certainly weren't taking any chances," Chuck said, slightly impressed.

"We've taken enough chances with these people," Mini stated.

So they ordered pizza. They stayed in the kitchen because Lorstad's gadget (and Chuck prayed to God he was using it right) seemed to say they were bug-free there. Feeling very special ops himself, Chuck started an action movie on the TV in his living room, just in case. It would drown out their conversation and really make it seem like they were all there just hanging out. They talked for two hours, comparing notes and wondering what, if anything, they could do. They decided Dice would be the best person to talk to Matt since he'd worked with him lon-gest and knew him best. Dice was demonstrably unhappy about that, but he had to admit it made sense.

It was pretty much the only thing that did.

THEY MADE UP A SCRIPT of safe questions and put the call on speakerphone, using Dice's cell. Dice sat at the end of the penin-sula in Chuck's gourmet kitchen and sweated even though the fall evening was balmy. Everyone else held their breath.

"Hey, Matt," Dice said. "You still in the office?"

"No, I'm home. What's up?"

"I want to talk to you about something that I . . . I'm not sure should bother me."

"You aren't sure it should bother you? What are you talking about?"

"At Deep Shield the other day, they had me in to fix a gyro component from one of their new bots. They wouldn't let me see the bot. They wouldn't let me see the whole brain case. They took out the CPU before they let me get into the gyro."

"And you want to know if that level of secrecy should bother you?"

"Something like that."

"They're the government, Dice. They're professional paranoids."

"Yeah, about that—which branch of the government are they exactly?"

"Does it matter?"

"That depends on why they are hiding things from us."

"Were you able to fix the problem?"

Dice considered how honest he should be. "I'm not really sure," he said carefully. "I suggested what might be causing the problem, but I have no way of knowing if I'm right. I have no way of testing my hypothesis."

He could almost hear Matt's shrug. "So let them test it. That's what they signed up for—to take our designs and fine-tune them for different applications."

"Someone told me they've built bots with tank treads."

"Who told you that?"

Was he imagining a sudden sharpness to Matt's tone? He glanced up at the four others sitting around the table. They wore almost identical expressions of concern.

"One of the tech aides. I don't know his name."

"Then I guess it's not such a big secret after all if a tech aide knows about it."

"Yeah. Yeah, I guess you're right. Hey, um, just out of curiosity, why did you fire the gardening service?"

"I what? The . . . I didn't fire the gardening service. Why would I do that?"

"That's kind of what we—I was wondering." Dice rolled his eyes, but the slip had been made.

"We? We who?"

Dice glanced up; his sweating increased threefold. Mini caught his eye and pointed to herself.

"Um, Mini, actually. She—uh, she came into the lab this evening to ask Chuck if he'd fired the garden guys. She'd developed a friendship with Jorge Delgado, the guy who ran the crew. Chuck didn't know anything about it."

There was a significant silence on Matt's end of the line. When he spoke again, his voice was distant, tentative. "Neither do I. I suppose the owners of the business park might have hired a new service."

Mini was shaking her head vigorously, making her short, coppery curls dance.

"Yeah," Dice said. "You're probably right. It was probably the park association. It's sort of odd they didn't tell us, though, isn't it?"

"Yeah," said Matt. "It is sort of odd at that. Has Chuck said anything to you about any of this?"

"Chuck? Not really. He's mentioned that the increased security is taking some getting used to."

"Well, I'm afraid he's just going to have to get used to it."

"Yeah. I guess so. Um, one more thing. Are we—this is going to sound really stupid and paranoid—but are we under surveillance?"

"What's Chuck been telling you?"

Startled, Dice glanced across the table at Chuck and felt a swift surge of anger. "Chuck? Chuck hasn't been telling me a damned thing—which is about par for the course, I guess. You sure as hell don't tell me anything about anything. Are you really unaware of the kind of crap that's been going on at the shop, or are you just stonewalling?"

Chuck had gone pale, and Eugene was making a "calm down" gesture with both hands. Mini looked vaguely stunned; Lanfen looked grim but determined, as if willing Dice on.

"Why would I do that? What's gotten into you, Dice?"

"What's gotten into *me*? What about *you*, Matt? It's like you have tunnel vision, solely focused on keeping your sweet deal going. Nothing's gotten into *me*. Nothing but the perfectly normal, rational desire to do the work I love in an atmosphere that isn't toxic."

There was a long pause before Matt asked, "Is it really that bad?"

Dice blew out a gust of air. "Well, maybe I'm exaggerating a little. But dammit, Matt, the level of secrecy and security they've got in place—"

"Is necessary, Dice. We're dealing with Second Amendment stuff here—the security of a free state."

Dice felt the absurd desire to laugh. "Trust you to come up with a new take on the Second Amendment."

"It's not a new take. In great part that's what the Second Amendment is about—keeping the state free from the predations of its enemies. That's also what General Howard is about. Protecting the United States from whatever threatens it."

"What about the Fourth Amendment? Due process?"

"You're starting to sound like Chuck now. Are you sure you haven't talked to him about any of this?"

Dice glanced up at the neuroscientist and grimaced. He was a dreadful liar and knew it. "A little. I was there—you know—when Mini told him about the gardeners." That much was true.

"DON'T TALK TO HIM ABOUT it anymore, okay? It just gets him all worked up. I need to keep him calm and out of the way. You understand."

"Oh, yeah. I do. I guess I'll see you Monday then."

"See you Monday," Matt echoed and rang off.

Dice sat and stared at his cell phone blankly for a moment.

"Keep me calm and out of the way?" repeated Chuck.

Eugene shook his head. "Definitely don't like the sound of that. I mean, it sounds like you're a threat to Howard or something."

Unexpectedly, Chuck laughed. "More likely I'm just an irritant."

"No," Dice said, very serious. "Don't trivialize it. Everything we've seen from them indicates they have unimaginably deep pockets and a lot of leeway where the law is concerned. I don't think putting your contractors under surveillance and bugging their offices and replacing their gardening crew with agents is strictly legal, but who you gonna call?"

Chuck frowned and raised a hand to his shirt pocket, where Lorstad's card was tucked away, but shook his head and said, "I have no idea who to call."

"Maybe we should find out," said Lanfen. "Maybe we should

try to find out what General Howard's chain of command is. Just in case things get really uncomfortable."

"As opposed to now," asked Eugene, "when we're meeting secretly—we hope—and suspect we've been followed and bugged?"

"They're isolating us," said Mini softly. "Replacing our security team, our gardeners, our maintenance people with people they can trust."

"Which sort of makes sense," said Dice, "when you consider how groundbreaking what we're doing is and how important they think it is."

Mini glared at him. "You're defending them?"

"No. Just trying to see things from their point of view. They're focused. Really, really focused on the kinetics program. I think organizations like that tend to lose track of anything outside that focus. It's something we all do as individuals. It's something all of us in this room do. I've seen it. But when an organization with a lot of money and power does it . . ."

"So what can we do?" asked Eugene. He looked at Chuck as if he expected the Ph.D. in neuroscience to go all Nick Fury and call in the superhero brigade.

Chuck leaned back in his chair and closed his eyes. When he opened them again, his face held a look Dice had rarely seen on it—a resolve that maybe wasn't up to steely, but it was pretty solid-looking all the same. "All right, look. I'm going to try to find out if there isn't a higher power that Howard answers to. Someone who might rein him in a bit."

"We could keep asking our Deeps," said Mini. "Maybe one of them will slip up and tell us something useful. There's this young corporal in my group who seems more open than the others."

"No." Chuck shook his head. "I don't want any of you to get yourselves or any of their folks in trouble with Howard. I have a feeling anyone who slips up and tells us something we aren't supposed to know will be reprimanded pretty severely—at best. I'll take that on." He turned to Lanfen. "Can you get inside again, do you think? Get a better idea of what they're doing?"

She looked scared for a moment but quickly composed herself. She and Chuck were like bookends—purpose personified. Dice might have laughed if the situation were not so serious.

"I'll do it. I've been thinking . . . Well, I have an idea."

She didn't want to expand on that at the moment, so they parted company, everyone carrying foil-wrapped pizza and acting as if they'd just left a party. If any of them were followed home, they didn't see the tail.

Dice wondered, if Deep Shield was so good, if they would ever *see* a tail again.

Chapter 23

HIGHER POWERS

General Howard called Matt early Saturday morning, waking him out of a sound sleep. "We need to talk, Dr. Streegman."

Despite his irritation at being awakened by business on a week-end, Matt chuckled. "Are you breaking up with me, General?"

"Please take this seriously, Doctor."

"Take what seriously, Leighton? Why are you calling at this ungodly hour?"

"Are you aware that a group of your colleagues got together yesterday evening at Dr. Brenton's house?"

What the hell? "What? They threw a party without me? How dare they?"

"I'm going to ignore your inappropriate humor, Doctor. It may have been a party. It may have been something else."

Matt sat up, pushing aside his covers. He vaguely noticed that his pajama bottoms had a hole at the knee. He poked at it with a fingernail. "What else could it have been? My colleagues socialize all the time. Hell, Eugene and Mini are practically in each other's pockets, and I'm pretty sure Chuck is sweet on a woman who could kick his butt six ways from Sunday."

"That was pretty much the attendance at the party. The only one you missed was Dr. Kobayashi."

"So?" Matt asked. A moment later the full implications of what Howard was saying hit him like a giant water balloon. He stopped worrying about the hole in his pajamas. "Wait a minute . . . how do you know who was there? You have them under surveillance? And me? You have me under surveillance?"

"For your own protection, Matt. Consider how valuable you might be to foreign interests who discover our involvement with you. You would go from a possibly crackpot bunch of entrepreneurs to a military asset overnight."

A military asset. Is that what we are now? "Our own protection? If you're so concerned about our protection, why are you asking me about an after-hours party some friends had?"

"I am asking you precisely because you were not on the guest list. I find that odd, don't you?"

Matt opened his mouth to make a snarky comeback but changed his mind. "As it happens, I was on the guest list. I was just so exhausted last night and had some work to do on a paper I'm writing for the American Mathematical Society. I begged off. Besides, you can only watch *The Princess Bride* so many times before you start reciting the dialogue in your sleep."

There was a brief hesitation on the other end of the line. "Then you knew about the gathering?"

"Yeah, I knew. General, you need to get out more. You're beginning to sound a bit paranoid."

The general ignored that observation. "Your partner is an idealist, Dr. Streegman. As nice as that is in concept, it can be extremely dangerous in practice. The next time Charles Brenton has a party at his house, I strongly recommend you attend. He bears watching."

"Chuck? He's harmless."

"No one's harmless once you let your guard down."

After the general had hung up, Matt sat back against the headboard and reviewed the conversation. The *party* at Chuck's didn't bother him in and of itself. What bothered him a great deal was the certain knowledge that Dice had called him from there with his concerns about Deep Shield surveillance, probably with the other members of the group listening in.

Matt swore. He'd thought at the time that the connection sounded a bit hollow. He'd chalked it up to a bad signal. Now he realized he must have been on speakerphone, so everyone could hear both sides of the conversation.

He catapulted out of bed and scrambled for a quick shower. He needed to get to Chuck before his partner could throw another "party." If General Howard thought there was some sort of subversive undercurrent at Forward Kinetics, who knew what he'd do to stomp it out?

CHUCK WAS WELL AND TRULY worried now—as much by his own state of mind as by the situation they were in. He'd called in a few favors from Johns Hopkins alums and gotten phone numbers for the CIA and an office at the Pentagon. Those got him at least a bit behind the public curtain of the two organizations. He had his own high-level clearance in at the FBI, having done some neurological studies for them and having participated in training two teams of profilers, and he would exploit that, too.

He had called the Pentagon contact first and said he was an associate of General Leighton Howard at Deep Shield, and he needed to speak to someone about the robotics program. He drew a complete blank at that office but did get shunted to someone in a loftier position, an assistant director of technology. There he took a different tack. He was a defense contractor considering working with General Howard's outfit. He wanted to make sure Deep Shield was legitimate. That had the virtue of being at least partially true.

More blanks. The assistant director bumped him to his director, to whom he repeated his story, and the director put him on hold for fifteen minutes before coming back and requesting his name and a number where he could be reached. He gave it reluctantly, though he didn't actually expect they'd try to contact him.

He had just gone through the same exercise with the contact at the CIA when Matt rang his front doorbell. To say he was surprised to see his business partner standing on his doorstep at nine thirty on a Saturday morning was an understatement. In the time they'd been working together, Matt had not once come to his house. They were business partners and colleagues—collaborators, not friends.

Chuck's surprise was followed swiftly by chagrin then wariness when he saw the look in Matt's eyes. "What's up?"

"That's what I was about to ask you, Doctor." Matt glanced back out at the street, wriggled his shoulders, and stepped into Chuck's spacious foyer. "Nice," he said, glancing around. "Tudor, huh? You alone?"

"Yes. What's wrong?"

Matt uttered a bark of laughter. "Who said anything was wrong? Coffee?" He nodded toward the kitchen, from which the aroma of a freshly brewed pot wafted.

"Sure. Come on into the kitchen."

Chuck led the way, moving to the counter to pour Matt a cup of coffee. Matt, meanwhile, stood staring through the French doors that opened out onto the patio, ostensibly admiring the wisteria-draped pergola. He was frowning and fidgeting with his pocketed car keys.

Chuck put a mug of coffee on the kitchen table and sat down with his own half-full mug. "Care to tell me what's got you so unnerved?"

"That obvious, is it?"

"Yes."

Matt sat down and picked up his coffee. He took a sip before speaking again. "General Howard called me this morning. Early. Something about a party you threw at your house last night."

Chuck tried to hide his sudden unease but knew he failed abysmally. He had one of those faces that give up their secrets before a person even has a chance to remember what they are. "Is that what he called it—a party?"

"Yes, but he also called it a meeting. I called it a party. I told him I'd been invited but had work to do. I told him we socialize all the time."

Chuck turned that over in his head for a moment, then said, "He at least suspects that isn't true, I'm sure. He's been watching us, after all."

Matt's gaze jerked to Chuck's face. "You knew?"

"That's sort of what the meeting was about. Dice, Euge, Lanfen, and Mini have all had . . . experiences with Deep Shield surveillance."

"Jesus Lord, Chuck! Weren't you afraid Howard's guys might be listening in?"

"No."

"How can you be sure?"

"Let's just say I can be sure and let it go at that."

"Let me guess—Dice noodled some high-tech jamming device for you."

Chuck said nothing. He was frankly (and dismally) afraid that if he showed Matt the jammer his mysterious visitor had given him, he'd insist on turning it over to the general.

"Howard is suspicious of you, my friend," Matt told him. "He thinks you might be plotting behind closed doors."

"He's worried about what *I'm* doing behind closed doors?"

"If you're plotting something, yes."

"We're not 'plotting.' Our staff came to me because they are understandably concerned about the fact that they're being spied on and that Deep Shield has started to . . . to manipulate our environment. Without our permission."

"They need to protect us, Chuck."

Matt had lowered his voice and leaned in across the table, though Chuck was now certain there was no one listening. Lorstad's gizmo had apparently worked as advertised. That was something, at least.

"Do you understand why?" Matt asked. "We've become a very important asset to them. They want to make sure that some foreign organization doesn't swoop in and offer us a deal we can't refuse. We would be a tremendously potent military asset to another country or to a terrorist organization."

Chuck made a wry face. "Is that what Howard told you?"

"Yes. Don't you think he's right?"

"Probably. But doesn't it bother you to go from being a person to being a *military asset*? It bothers the hell out of our staff."

"Is that what this is all about? Well, set their minds at ease, okay? Howard is just trying to protect important human resources from becoming prey."

Chuck did not miss the rhetorical shift. "If you say so."

"I do say so."

Chuck opened his mouth to tell Matt what Lanfen had seen at Deep Shield but checked himself.

Matt caught his hesitation. "What?"

"I called a contact at the Pentagon to ask about Deep Shield. I must've talked to half a dozen people, two at the director level. They've never heard of it."

Matt sat back in his chair. "Well, of course they haven't. Or at least they wouldn't tell you if they have. It's top secret."

"The director of technology was asking *me* questions about them, Matt. The CIA said they had no idea who these guys were and—"

Matt stood, setting his coffee mug down with a sharp thump. Coffee sloshed onto the table. "Good grief, Chuck. You're as paranoid as the general. Get a grip. They do classified work. Would you tell some cold caller all your secrets?"

"Paranoid? I'm paranoid?" Chuck forgot his reservations about full disclosure. "Matt, Lanfen discovered they're hiding a small army of robots they've been making on their own. Robots they've been taking pains to conceal even from Dice."

"So? They're experimenting with different forms. We expected that, didn't we?"

Chuck took a deep breath. This was going nowhere good. He let the breath out and shook his head, feigning chagrin. "Yeah. Yeah, we did expect that. You're right. Of course you're right. The team is just being . . . hypersensitive. I'll try to talk them down."

"Will you?" Matt's eyes shone with relief. "Good, because they'll listen to you. Even Dice thinks I'm too cozy with Howard."

"There's an image," murmured Chuck. "Yeah, sure. I'll talk to them. First thing Monday."

"Good," said Matt. "Good. Maybe even before then if you can. Maybe you should throw another party this weekend." He seemed to pull himself together then and left Chuck sitting at the table with his cell phone poised to call the FBI.

THE ALPHA ZETAS, AS THEY jokingly called themselves, had formed a tight clique within the ranks at Forward Kinetics. The better to protect themselves, Sara thought. They watched their watchers intently and compared notes on a daily basis. They were not afraid of surveillance; Tim had found ways to defeat the cameras at the software level while Mike could make listening devices go belly-up mechanically and make cameras simply look the wrong way. Sara was learning to employ both forms of manipulation on her own but had nowhere near their facility with it.

Mike was especially ruthless when it came to the Deeps' surveillance equipment. He'd found bugs at his house and was so riled by having his family's private space invaded, he'd caused several of their devices to die of "natural" causes.

"Watching me is one thing," he'd told her. "Watching my wife and kids is something else. They're not part of this classified crap, and they're not gonna be."

If the Deeps had any idea that their occasional equipment failures and communication snafus were anything more than random glitches, they didn't say as much, and the zetas were careful not to tip their hands. They stuck slavishly to the program, teaching only what they were contracted to teach: basic, bonehead manipulation of Dice's patented servos and software engines with a high-level Kobayashi module that facilitated their work. It was perhaps no surprise then that none of the Deeps—not one—could work directly with the hardware or software.

The alpha zetas communicated with the other members of the team—the beta zetas, as Sara had come to think of them—often enough to know they were also working directly with their devices, and they were no more sanguine than the alphas about the Smiths or the Deep Shield Humvee with its blacked-

274 / PATRICK HEMSTREET

out windows or the government facility none of them had ever seen the outside of.

"It could be under the freaking White House," Tim had commented one day. "Or the Washington Monument. Wouldn't it be crazy if it's under the Washington Monument?"

The chilling news that Eugene had found himself being tailed was enough to send Sara into Chuck's office on a Wednesday afternoon to see if she could get some sense of his reaction to all this. Once she got there, she was at a loss for what to say.

They stared at each other like a pair of startled owls for a moment before Sara said, "So do you have any idea how many more teams of trainees we're going to see before the contract is complete?"

Brenton blinked at her, pulling off his wire-rimmed glasses. "Actually, I'm not one hundred percent sure, but I'd imagine at least two more."

She nodded, scrambling mentally for a way to ask what she really wanted to know. "I still haven't gotten used to the idea that they're probably listening to everything we say." She met his eyes as forcefully as she knew how and reached up to tap her ear, raising her eyebrows questioningly.

He held her gaze for a moment and then glanced at the office door, which she'd closed behind her. "They certainly try. My office, however, is an island of silence and sanity."

"You sure? How?"

"I have my ways."

"Won't they think it's odd that your office is so quiet?"

"Oh, I let them in on things several times a day. Business-as-usual things. They're blocked right now, though."

Sara's knees felt suddenly weaker than they had a moment before. She sat down in the chair across from Chuck. The alpha zetas had been able to compare notes with the betas only infrequently for the simple reason that the general and his minions

(God, she was starting to think like Tim) seemed to go out of their way to keep the two groups apart. She had thought of calling Chuck a hundred times to ask if there were someplace they might meet where they wouldn't be overheard. Each time before today, she'd hesitated.

How much time have we lost with me wavering like that?

"I don't like what's happening here, Doctor," she told him. "None of my team does. The Deeps, the Smiths—I mean the security guys—"

Brenton smiled. "Yeah, we call them that, too."

"It's like we're skating on very thin ice over a bottomless lake. There are things going on underneath that are scary." She cocked her head and gave the scientist an assessing look. "Of course you might tell me I'm imagining things or exaggerating . . ."

"I'm not going to tell you anything of the sort, Sara. They've replaced our grounds crew with their people. They're having us followed—"

She drew in a swift breath through her teeth at the confirmation. "Damn."

"Nor has it escaped my notice that the general's people have worked very hard at keeping the two teams of zetas apart."

"So I'm not the only one."

He smiled again. Really the man seemed to find humor in every situation.

"No," he said, "you're not paranoid. They really are watching us. I think it's just that they don't trust me, and they think of your team as the senior practitioners. You and Mike and Tim are the systems wizards, and that is apparently of primary importance to them. Lanfen's discipline is at a more detailed level than yours, and Mini's craft is simply window dressing to them."

Something about the way he said that. "Are you hinting that maybe Mini isn't just window dressing?"

Brenton got an almost wicked look on his face. "We haven't exactly been forthcoming with the full extent of our . . . accomplishments."

Now Sara smiled, too. "Neither have we."

She told him in broad strokes what Mike and Tim were capable of when it came to the direct manipulation of mechanisms. He was impressed beyond words. Then the flood of questions came.

"All that notwithstanding," Sara said when she'd wrapped up her quick recital, "we can't keep meeting like this. Mike can create dead zones for us and even muck with the cameras pretty effectively, but that will be suspicious after a while. And having me coming to your office repeatedly is bound to draw attention."

Chuck chewed the inside of his lip ruminatively. "Likewise if we were to suddenly start socializing."

"Dice works with us fairly often. I think I might have a way I can pass information to him. Once he catches on, he might very well be able to figure out a way to respond. He's a smart guy."

"He is that," Chuck agreed. "See what you can do."

She realized what she could do the next afternoon as she was rendering an elevation to test her abilities with a new piece of software. On a "whim," she inserted some signage and artful elements into her output.

"Like my work, Dice?" she'd asked when she'd finished the building.

He glanced up at it. Did a double take. She saw puzzlement in his eyes before the light of dawning comprehension produced a slow smile.

"I like it a lot," he said. "Can I keep a rendering of it? I know it's just a practice plot, but . . ."

"Sure thing."

"In fact," he said, "could you maybe do some renderings of my robots?"

So it went. He passed information to her in his instructions for the robots; she passed information back through the renderings. The information mostly came in the form of brief progress reports on their private work with their abilities and any new observations of Deeps' behavior. Anything more complex would be communicated in a series of brief meetings, usually between Mike and Dice.

It was ironic really, Sara thought as she watched her class of Deeps go through their drills with the design software they were manipulating. The zetas had begun this relationship trying to impart their practical knowledge to their clients and now were working to keep it from them. The poor Deeps didn't know what they didn't know . . . or so she thought.

She didn't realize the scenario was changing until lunch one Tuesday. It was her turn to drive to the restaurant the alpha zetas had begun to frequent, and she and Mike waited in the parking lot for several minutes until Tim appeared. Sara could see he was upset when he climbed into the car. His face was red, his eyes glittering, his brows pulled down into an aggressive scowl.

"What's up, guy?" Mike asked, peering around his headrest at the younger man. "You look like a storm cloud."

"Is it secret? Is it safe?" Tim asked in return.

Mike rolled his eyes, then closed them for a second before nodding. "Yeah. What's up?"

"The imperialist monkey boys are asking questions," Tim said darkly.

"Oh, for God's sake," said Sara, laughing. "What kind of questions?"

"One of the guys asked me if there's a way for them to manipulate the hardware directly— bypass the Kobayashi servomodule and act directly on the hardware and firmware. Then he started talking about literally rerouting signals through the traces on a circuit board to make the commands do things they weren't intended to do."

Sara faced front, put the car in gear, and pulled away from the curb, her mind suddenly racing. "For purposes of sabotage?"

"That's the only thing I could think of," said Tim. "But it's out of my area of expertise. I don't do hardware or firmware. I'm a programmer. Machine language, yeah, that I can manipulate. Ones and zeroes are my first language. But these guys . . ." He stared out of the window for a moment, then snapped back into sharp focus. "Y'know, something the little commandant said—"

"Who?" Mike asked.

"The ranking officer—what's his name? Ortiz. He's a lieutenant commander and won't let me forget it. Treats me like—" He caught Sara's look in the rearview mirror. "Anyway, he made this comment about needing to *go underground* to . . . how did he put it? To consolidate their learning. He said he thought we'd be getting our last class of recruits in a couple of weeks."

"The last recruits?" echoed Mike. "Isn't that good news? We'll be done with them. Then we can go back to—"

"Do you think they're going to let us go back to the way things were?" snarled Tim. "We're a freaking security risk."

"Cool it, Tim. If we're getting another bunch of recruits, that means these guys think they're ready to graduate." Sara frowned at the road. "So it wasn't Oritz who asked about psyching the firmware?"

"No, it was one of his minions—Pierce."

"Did you get the feeling Pierce was asking in an official capacity?"

"Well, now that you mention it, no. Ortiz and the rest of his team seem to be dedicated code jockeys. Pierce is a different bag of cats. Maybe a too-curious bag of cats."

"Yeah, but Ortiz is the man, right? And it sounds like he's

thinking they've got all the training they need. Since none of them has shown any ability to manipulate the hardware without the interface . . ." Mike shrugged. "So there you have it."

"I guess."

"Even better, though: all that stuff you said about them not letting us go? We're American citizens. We have families and friends outside of this place." He bobbed his head back toward the receding Forward Kinetics campus. "They can't just disappear us. At worst they could make us sign double-deluxe, mega-strength NDAs that we'd be stupid to break."

Tim's lip curled. "Yeah? You think? And what does *at best* look like in your sunny little snow globe, Mikey?"

"It looks like they pay us, they go away with a reminder to honor the NDA we've already signed, and we go about our business in the private sector. I'm glad they're bugging out after this next class of recruits. Then things can get back to normal."

"Maybe," said Sara. "Maybe not. I've kind of forgotten what normal looks like."

THEY HATCHED THE PLAN IN a noodle shop in the Harborplace Mall. Eugene had been hoping for stupid simple, but the complexities of Deep HQ ruled that out. Their schedules were structured so they worked the end of the week while the alpha zetas worked the beginning. Sara, Mike, and Tim went in for six hours on Mondays and Tuesdays and until noon on Wednesdays; Lanfen and Mini came in on Wednesday afternoons and worked their twelve hours on Thursdays and Fridays. Dice's schedule varied, though he was in most days for a while.

Knowing that, Team Chuck (the nickname was Eugene's doing) conceived of a means of employing available talent to accomplish their goals. At least Lanfen and Mini had devised it; Eugene and Chuck had merely sat back, eating noodles and watching them hatch a plot that relegated the two men to the roles of support personnel, diversionary operatives, and plucky comic relief.

"I can drive any bot," Lanfen had said during their off-campus double date. "That's not the issue. The issue is I can't be in two places at once. Well, I mean I can be, but the me who's left behind is in a state of deep concentration. It won't do to have me camped out doing breathing exercises for the time I'll need to be inside. It only worked last time because my ride was delayed. I need some sort of cover."

There had been a profound moment of frustrated silence until Mini had said, "There's a maintenance closet in the ladies' room on D level, between the canteen and their interior labs. If we could get you into that closet, say on Wednesday evening, you could activate the bot overnight, right?"

"Sure, but the driver will wonder where I went, won't he?"

In answer, Mini had grinned from ear to ear, then glanced up at the hallway that led to the restaurant restrooms. "Look who's here."

They all did look and saw Lanfen step from a rear hallway into the restaurant. She paused a moment, waved at them, then turned on her heel and walked back up the corridor to the ladies' room. In fact she walked right up to the door and vanished.

"That," said the Lanfen seated at the table, "was amazing."

"Thanks." Mini beamed.

"So," said Chuck, "you're proposing that the Lanfen who leaves with you on Wednesday evening is a mirage?"

Mini nodded.

"We'll need to get me into the ladies' room," said Lanfen. "Well, getting me in there isn't such a big deal. It's getting me in without security seeing that I don't leave. I suppose we could use the jammer . . ."

Chuck inhaled sharply. "That jammer is the only thing that grants us a clean place to confer on campus."

"You can use Mike for that temporarily," suggested Mini.

Chuck nodded. "Okay. Good. That could work. I'll need to come up with a valid reason to pull him into my office, but I'll just have to deal with it."

"Great," said Lanfen. "Once the place has shuttered for the night, I should be able to activate Brian's robot, Thorin, and go on a walkabout."

"And in the morning," Mini continued, "I come back into the ladies' with virtual you and a fresh change of clothes, and we walk out together. We should only need to jam any surveillance for a moment or two."

"My God, you're awesome," said Eugene. "And scary. Scary awesome."

"Question," said Lanfen, first glancing at Eugene then raising a hand. "We need the bot to be feeding video directly to Chuck and Euge. How do we do that?"

Dice had the answer to that later. During Lanfen's Wednesday afternoon drills with her class, Thorin developed a mysterious problem with his balance that required Daisuke Kobayashi's expertise touch. When the bot returned to the exercise room, his video feed had been tweaked. Lanfen, who had personally arranged the bot's vertigo, now felt for the firmware switch Dice had installed as he pretended to calibrate the gyro mechanism. She would trip that switch when she was ready to take Thorin out of his alcove. His feed would go live but would send its output to Chuck's personal laptop.

Matt Streegman had ridden with them to the Deep that afternoon—a thing that seemed to make Dice Kobayashi just about crawl out of his skin. Lanfen threw him a look, though, and the engineer calmed down. Once at Deep Shield, Matt had disappeared into the public office area, escorted to a meeting with General Howard and his advisory staff. Dice, Mini, and Lanfen had each gone to their classes of trainees.

Lanfen was curious about what Matt and Howard discussed these days. It occurred to her to wonder if there weren't some way to bug Matt without his knowing it. She felt guilty even having that thought, but then reminded herself about what she was preparing to do and why. She punted the guilt away. Howard had bugged them first. Turnabout was fair play.

Lanfen had to resort to breathing exercises and mental trickery to keep her brain from fixating on her upcoming spy mission. She wanted to avoid anticipation—it was too easy for that feeling to morph into dread. She was especially watchful of her inner landscape because she had such observant recruits. A ripple of seemingly hidden anxiety in an unguarded moment might ping someone's subterfuge radar.

She became aware that Brian Reynolds was watching her about halfway through their afternoon session. Afterward he approached her.

"Something the matter, Lanfen?"

She forced herself to relax. "I'm fine. Why?"

"You seem jumpy. Jumpy for you anyway." He smiled. "Of course your jumpy looks like most people's cool, calm, and collected."

Mental gears spun. What sort of thing might get her adrenaline up? "It's my shifu, Master Chu. The man who taught him everything he knows is visiting his *kwoon*—his school—and he's asked me to give a demonstration of some of the more advanced *shaolinquan* and white crane techniques he taught me." That was actually true. That she felt nerves about it was not. "Performing for Shifu Chu is intimidating enough, though I'm used to it. Performing for his master is terrifying."

"Yeah. I can see that. It's like performing in front of my dad. That routine I did for General Howard on your first day here was merely purgatory. Strutting my stuff in front of my dad is pure hell."

He turned away then and marched off to the bot barn. They were careful, these Deep Shield people, about never leaving their robots alone with anyone from Lanfen's team. She reached out with her imagination and touched the video switch again, noticing that Brian didn't so much as twitch mentally. He seemed oblivious to her presence.

She withdrew, took a deep breath, and went to join Mini and Dice in the canteen. Mini looked like Mini always looked. Dice was shredding a napkin.

"Hey," Lanfen said casually as she strolled up to them. "I need to use the facilities before we take off."

"Oh," said Mini, jumping up from her chair, "me, too."

They headed for the women's restroom.

Once there Lanfen actually did avail herself of the facilities. It amazed her how one's bladder responded to stress. Then she and Mini went to the exit and opened the door. Lanfen stepped halfway through and activated Chuck's mysterious little jammer. Mini kept on walking with Lanfen apparently by her side. Lanfen, trying not to let the glimpse of her retreating back unnerve her, slipped back into the restroom and went straight to the maintenance closet in the corner nearest the door. It was locked. She took only seconds to get into her zeta state. Her imagination was quite literal: she envisioned diving into the lock, tunneling into its mechanism to feel the tumblers with heightened senses. Feel them and manipulate them. It took but a moment of concentration—and some recollection of that YouTube video on lockpicking that she'd watched once after locking herself out—to shift them and let herself in.

The closet was full of the usual sorts of things one would expect to find in a maintenance closet: vacuum cleaner, mops, shelves full of toilet paper, and the like. It smelled of cleaning products and paper.

Grimacing, Lanfen shut the steel door and settled herself on the floor behind a large, rolling cart equipped with two trash containers. She checked her iPhone. It was approaching 6:30 P.M. She slipped an earbud into one ear in case Chuck called, and she wondered how long it would be before the place would be battened down for the night. It occurred to her to wonder how she'd even know in the first place.

The answer was swift and laced with wry self-deprecation. Pulling her senses together, Lanfen closed her eyes and pictured Thorin standing in his little bay. Then she reached for him . . .

He wasn't there.

Damn! Brian must still have had him off somewhere. A sick churning began in her stomach. She worked on calming it, going through several of her rituals before she banished the queasiness. Then she tried again to reach the robot, sympathizing with him being stuck in his little space just as she was squeezed into this claustrophobic closet. This time she was successful. He was there in his niche. She peered out at the workshop through his optics. Four technicians were working at the tables in the center of the large lab. Brian Reynolds was standing just inside the door, chatting with another one of her trainees. As she watched, the two men turned and left the room.

Great, Lanfen thought. *Two down and four to go.*

Chapter 24

MOVIE NIGHT

Chuck decided that Eugene had a twisted sense of humor. It would require one to choose *Transformers* as the movie they were allegedly watching to cover their clandestine activities. Eugene and Dice arrived at Chuck's house first to set up the movie. Dice, being Dice, had added an audio track to the video stream that featured indistinct conversation, laughter, and other sounds in appropriate places. It was the sort of thing only an archgeek would do.

"By the way," Eugene told Chuck as they watched Dice set up the riff-tracked movie, "your exterminator left one of those doorknob ads on your front door. I put it on the hall table."

Chuck glanced into his foyer. "I don't have an exterminator."

Eugene's eyebrows disappeared under his curly fringe of dark hair. "Well, you do now."

Chuck went into the front hall, finding the envelope right where Euge had said he'd left it. It was from a known local pest control business, but one that Chuck had never contracted to do any work. There was even a statement in the envelope charging no fee for a free estimate of monthly service. He had to admire how the Deep Shield crew covered their bases. If he'd called the number on the envelope, he'd get a legit service that would be happy to enroll him for the monthly rate of forty dollars.

Mini arrived late with the Lanfen bogey in tow. That had required a pantomime of epic proportions—Mini driving to Lanfen's townhouse for the pickup, fabricating her at the door, and driving to Chuck's house. Anyone watching would have to suspect that they were looking at a doppelgänger in order to spot the illusion, and Chuck was willing to bet that most of the very levelheaded agents assigned to them would be disinclined to suspect anything of the sort.

Eugene had invited Mike to their movie night—rather publicly—and he came bearing soft drinks and beer. They ordered out for pizza. They made popcorn. They talked shop until Mike had a chance to locate and reorient the surveillance devices Deep Shield had installed in Chuck's study—the room they had singled out as their lair (another Eugene-ism). Mike tweaked the firmware, so the feed presented a static image of an empty study and cut off audio completely.

Chuck beckoned Mike into the freshly shielded room and wrote a note about the exterminators. That sent the alpha zeta on a sweep of the entire house, during which he found two bugs in the kitchen that Chuck knew hadn't been there earlier. They had no doubt been installed in response to the spotty performance of the original ones. They left those devices alone, but it bothered Chuck that his home security system was no deterrent to the Deep Shield agents.

With the surveillance accounted for and the doctored movie playing loudly in the living room, the team gathered in the study. Chuck had chosen the room for their subversive activities because it was precisely in the center of the first floor, had no windows, and was buffered on all sides by other rooms. He'd had it specially built for the study of neurological X-rays.

He set up his laptop on his desk and waited for Thorin's feed to start. In the meantime they tried, in all ways, to behave like a group of friends enjoying a movie night: wandering in and out of the kitchen, eating pizza and popcorn, and ostensibly watching a movie about sentient robots.

AT 8:04 P.M. LANFEN WAS roused from meditation by the sound of the restroom door opening and closing. The footsteps moved more deeply into the main area at first, and she caught the sound of metal on metal. Someone was checking the stalls for toilet paper, which meant . . .

Her heart picked up its tempo; she worked to calm it. If a maintenance worker had to reload those dispensers, he was going to have to get into that closet to do it, and she had to stop him. Unlike Mini she couldn't make herself appear to be a vacuum cleaner. She turned her attention to the locking mechanism in the door, slipped into her zeta state, and attacked the tumblers, holding them fiercely static. On a wild whim, she tripped one of them into a new position.

She had no more than done that when the maintenance worker shoved his key into the lock—or, rather, tried to shove his key into the lock. With the tumblers rearranged and the lock in Lanfen's mental grip, it was impossible. The key simply no longer fit and would not turn.

Through the door Lanfen heard sounds of the man's frustration. He WTF'd; he tried a second and then a third time to get the key to go; he swore extravagantly and vividly; and he pounded the door with his fist. Finally he got out a cell phone or walkie-talkie and called his supervisor.

Lanfen pulled one earbud out of her ear and listened intently.

"Sergeant, I got a problem down here in the D-level ladies' latrine. The damn lock on the damn maintenance closet is hosed . . . No, dammit, I mean really hosed. I can't even get the key in the lock. Damn tumblers must be screwed."

There was a momentary pause as he listened to his sergeant on the other end, then said, "Yeah, yeah. You're right. Nothing I can do about it tonight. Give facilities a call, would you, and get us on their radar? In the meantime I'll get supplies from the men's latrine . . . Yeah, thanks, Sarge."

He left but not before giving the door a good, solid kick. He was back later, apparently with supplies he'd cadged from the men's room across the hall. Lanfen could hear his vacuuming and mopping the floors, filling dispensers, flushing toilets, emptying trash bins. He left a little after nine, and the room fell eerily silent.

Time.

Lanfen made herself comfortable, took a deep breath, and dove back into zeta, reaching for Thorin. When she accessed his optics, she found herself in a darkened room. Silence prevailed there. She waited, using the bot's audio sensors to listen to the adjoining room and the outer hallway.

Both quiet.

Lanfen turned on the video feed and stepped Thorin down from his station. It was 9:05 P.M. She'd have sworn she felt the sudden cessation of power that flowed up from his charging station through the pads in his feet. Another of the Deep's improvements—Bilbo still had to charge through a cable plugged into his thorax.

It took Lanfen several steps to adjust to the differences between Thorin's dimensions and Bilbo's. She imagined herself expanding to fill the larger, heavier skin. She flexed the joints, rotated the head, adapted to the new weight and stature. Concentrating mightily on that adaptation, she turned her attention to the heavier tank bots at the end of the row of charging stations. Each station, like Thorin's, possessed a single, softly glowing LED lamp that bathed the occupant in pale radiance.

She moved to stand directly in front of one of those occupants and gave it a slow once-over from the top of its egg-shaped head to the soles of its treads. She paused on the forearms, crouched to get a better view of the hands and fingers. That was when she spotted an odd construct in the center of the thorax that reminded her of the deflector dishes all the Starfleet vessels had in the *Star Trek* episodes. *What is it?* she wondered, and prayed that Chuck and the others were seeing what she was seeing.

"WHAT IS THAT?" ASKED EUGENE, leaning toward the flat-screen monitor that hung on Chuck's study wall. "A radar dish maybe?"

"Could be." Dice chewed thoughtfully on the inside of his lip. "I've talked with them about implementing various scanning devices, but . . ."

"But what?" asked Chuck, glancing over at Dice from his perch on the edge of his desk.

Dice approached the screen and pointed. "Well, first of all a radar dish that's hard-fixed like that into the torso would require the bot to physically turn around to scan in a three sixty. And see these little depressions in the bot's head? And this bubble on the crown?"

Chuck nodded.

"I think those might be the tracking system. In fact their engineers asked me about the advisability of having a retractable transceiver in the head. They were concerned about messing up the gyro. I think that might be where the radar or sonar—or whatever tech they're using—is housed."

"Then what's the deflector dish for?" asked Eugene.

"At a guess—maybe an EMP transmitter?"

Eugene's eyes bugged out. "As in electromagnetic pulse? That could wreak havoc with an enemy's . . . everything. But that's not possible, right? At least not at that size. That's—"

"Science fiction," said Mini softly. She sat in an overstuffed chair next to Mike and behind the three men who hovered nervously around the TV screen.

Thorin was moving on now, turning toward the set of double doors at the far end of the workspace. In three long strides, he gained the doors to the adjoining lab and opened one a crack. The next room was empty of humans, the dim glow of the light switches offering the only illumination. Thorin lingered in the shadows for a moment, then, without warning, the others at Chuck's house were seeing the place in infrared.

LANFEN SORTED THROUGH THE BARRAGE of visual information and pushed through the doors, deeper into the lab complex. This lab was entirely given to workbenches and computers— diagnostic equipment, she guessed. There were a couple of charging stations there, but only one of them was inhabited. It was one of the dwarf bots, like Thorin, but its forearms were both off. She turned and found the missing parts on one of the workbenches.

She moved toward it to give her remote companions a look at what the engineers were doing to the arms. She couldn't be sure, but it looked as if they were being refitted with an assembly she didn't recognize.

She gave the bot a long look, then moved to the next set of doors. The labs, she realized, were arranged in a daisy chain, though each also had a door that opened onto a central courtyard or corridor. She thought of taking a look out there but decided her time would be better spent going through the labs one by one.

A blinking red light high up in the corner where wall met ceiling alerted her to the fact that someone was potentially watching her—or, rather, Thorin, making his way through the labs. The thought made her heart race and her skin go cold. She moved the bot swiftly to the doors, appreciating how quiet it was. With her in direct control, even the servos were silent. The only sound Thorin made was the soft tread of his padded, articulated feet.

The third lab was huge, easily three times the size of the two she'd just passed through to reach it. There were two long rows of charging stations, and now she had more than enough light to see by using Thorin's normal optics. She shut down infrared—and froze. Along both walls of the long chamber, the charging niches held a small army of squat, beefy robots. Their heads were aerodynamically shaped, like eggs wearing bicycle helmets. *Sinister* bicycle helmets—sleek, with long, tilted optics ports, as if someone were paying homage to the archetypal alien Grays. The armature was gleaming, anodized steel and studded with implements: a grapple, a laser cutter, and what looked like small rocket launchers.

Her phone buzzed. She answered, squeezing the switch on her earbuds. Dice's terse whisper flowed into her left ear: "Get closer."

She turned Thorin to the closest bot and scanned it visually from head to tread. Her heart rate was rising again. These were definitely not deep-sea rescue robots. They were mechanical supersoldiers.

Back in her closet, Lanfen wrapped her arms around her chilled body; out in the lab, Thorin echoed the movement, his arms clanking against his sides. Whispering a curse, Lanfen sorted herself out and divorced herself from her fear. She tentatively reached out one of Thorin's hands and raised one of the other bot's arms, so the overhead niche light illuminated the weaponized hand.

Dice gasped in her ear.

CHUCK SHOT TO HIS FEET, pulse pounding. "What the hell is that?"

Dice moved to stand next to him, leaving his iPhone on the desk, its speaker activated. "There's no magazine, but there's that feed tube. Flamethrower maybe? Plasma weapon?" He turned back toward the phone. "Lanfen, is the other hand the same? Can you show us?"

Thorin returned the first hand to rest and brought the other one into the light. Above the two middle fingers was some sort of nozzle. As with the weapon on the opposite side, this had a tube running back up into the arm.

"That's a nozzle," said Dice. "Can you get closer to the torso? There's an odd bulge toward the back. I can just barely . . ."

The camera angle changed, drawing in on what looked to Chuck like a tank of some sort.

"A fire bot?" murmured Eugene from behind Chuck. "We talked about those, remember? That would explain the laser cutter and the tank, wouldn't it? Maybe it sprays carbon dioxide."

Dice looked skeptical. "Maybe, but—"

From the iPhone, Lanfen asked, "But what, Dice? How can we be absolutely sure this isn't just a harmless rescue bot?"

"I don't know how we can be sure, Lanfen. Can you see if there's anything that indicates what they mean to put in those tanks?"

"Such as?"

Dice didn't want to say it. "Chemical weapons."

"No, no, no." Chuck shook his head emphatically. The surge of adrenaline he'd felt at the first sight of the bot had become an icy sludge solidifying in his veins. "I think it's time for you to get out, Lanfen. Withdraw."

"Chuck, they might have already seen Thorin wandering around down there. We're only going to get this one shot, and I want to make sure of this. We *need* to be sure of this."

"Not enough to endanger you," he argued.

"Endanger me how? That's not me down there in the lab. That's a robot. They'll have no way of knowing who's in control or where that person is."

"But they can make an educated guess, Lanfen."

"But Thorin isn't 'my' robot—it's Reynolds's. Wouldn't the suspicion land on him? Listen—we're wasting time. I'm going deeper into the complex. Maybe there's a chem lab somewhere or something that will at least tell me what they're experimenting with."

"Lanfen, please . . ."

"Let her do it."

Chuck turned. Mike had risen from his chair and was staring at the screen.

"She's right, Doc. If these bastards are doing what it looks like they're doing, we gotta know."

Chuck swung his gaze back to the screen. The view there danced crazily for a moment before focusing on the next set of double doors. Thorin moved through them into the next chamber. This, too, held rows of bots. They were similar to the ones in the room before, though not identical. Thorin moved swiftly to the first one and, as earlier, gave it a thorough visual once-over, but there wasn't really anything that jumped out at the group.

What did capture their interest was in the next room. It was a strange collection of items, to say the least. In addition to four charging stands, two of which were occupied, there were racks that held a variety of robot appendages, each outfitted with different types of armaments or tools. Some of the weapons were recognizable as assault rifles by the ammo magazines built into the upper arms. Another set of racks held ordnance: tiny missiles, egg-shaped pellets, objects that looked like short harpoons.

"Makes sense," murmured Dice. "That's the way I'd do it. Build a bot chassis that can be adapted to different uses just by swapping out parts."

"I hear someone," Lanfen said, and the view slewed crazily again.

"Get out," said Chuck.

Behind him, Mini said softly, "She *is* out, Chuck."

"But the bot . . ."

"Wait," said Lanfen.

She moved the bot to the far side of the lab, its optics trained on a thick, steel-plated door of the sort that might be found on a deep freeze or a vault. There was a round window in the door made up of two thick pieces of glass set about four inches apart. The window grew until it filled the TV screen from top to bottom.

Chuck realized they were looking into a smaller chamber that contained rows of shelved canisters. He moved closer to the screen.

"Lanfen, can you adjust his optics to focus in on the labels?"

But she was already doing it. The image adjusted so sharply, it made Chuck dizzy. When he was able to focus, the lettering on the nearest canister became suddenly readable.

"Oh," said Eugene weakly. "That's not C-O-two, is it?"

"No," Chuck answered, "it's methylphosphonofluoridate."

"What's that?" Mini asked.

"It's used to make sarin gas."

THORIN'S AURAL SENSORS WERE NOW picking up definite sounds of movement in the next lab. Had the bot been detected, or was it just a security patrol on regular rounds? No alarms had sounded, though that might be a measure to catch the rogue robot—or his handler—unaware.

The sounds of approach were coming from the lab Lanfen and her metal counterpart had visited previously. Accordingly, she turned and moved as swiftly and quietly as possible to one of the two unoccupied charging stations. She stepped Thorin up into it. Even partially disassembled, his two neighbors dwarfed him. Lanfen allowed a corner of her mind to be amused that she had once found Thorin formidable-looking and overlarge.

She'd barely gotten the bot frozen in place when the doors at the entrance of the lab swung open, and a single security guard entered and flipped on the light. He swept the lab with an alert gaze once, his eyes landing on Thorin. He stepped over to the bot with a quizzical look on his face, seeming to find its presence bemusing. He leaned closer, eyes focused on the bot's right shoulder.

Adrenaline hit Lanfen like an electrical charge. She needed to shift his attention off of Thorin, and quick.

At the speed of thought, Lanfen leapt mind-first into the battle droid she'd scanned in the previous chamber, powered it up, and sent it careening into the workbenches at the center of the room. They were heavily enough built that the collision caused no damage, but the noise was thunderous.

She leapt back to Thorin in time to see the guard hurry back toward the doors, talking rapidly into his headset, his weapon drawn. He disappeared into the neighboring lab.

Brilliant—now I'm cut off.

That left her three options: continue on through the interconnected labs and hope the guards made a full circuit, venture out into the corridors, or leave Thorin where he was. She opted for the corridors, moving to the chem lab's outer door to take a cautious peek beyond.

Her caution was warranted. A glance into the corridors proved them to be a bit busier than she might have hoped. A team of security guards was already entering the lab in which she'd crashed the battle bot.

She took stock of the situation. If she continued around the ring of labs, she would eventually come to the one opposite

Thorin's barracks. Thorin ducked back into the labs and made haste through one after another, recording everything in his path. That included a stunning variety of robot forms. Forms that tantalized, disturbed, terrified. There were even-bigger battle bots being outfitted with more-powerful weapons. There were sleek, reptilian robots with segmented bodies like Bilbo's and magnetic clamps on their appendages. There were others of the same type but covered with wet suits.

No time to give them a thorough examination. I can only hope Dice and Chuck can figure out what they mean from the footage I'm sending back.

Time was definitely a factor, and she paused only every now and again to create a new disturbance along her back trail—for all the good it did. Alarms were sounding now, and the sensors were picking up a lot of human feet pelting along the corridors. Between the added stimuli and reckless passage through the facility, she had lost track of where she was and was reluctant to poke her robotic head out into the corridor again. Sending up prayers to her ancestors to grant her wisdom, Chen Lanfen at last spied an empty charging station in what appeared to be a repair bay. She put Thorin into it, shut him down, and escaped to her maintenance closet.

Drenched in a cold sweat, she huddled in the corner behind the trash bins and shivered, waiting for morning.

IT WAS PAST MIDNIGHT WHEN everyone left Chuck's house. They had turned on a late-night movie to cover their continued discussions. Anxiety ran high, with anger and fear boiling underneath.

Chuck had never felt so powerless in his entire life. He was out of his element. Trapped in a box, the dimensions of which he couldn't see. He didn't think he could sleep. Lanfen was safe enough for the moment, but just knowing that she was huddled on the floor of a storage closet in a secret military installation and wouldn't be able to get out until morning made him crazy.

What had they been thinking? That they were spies? Super-spies, even, with psychic powers? For God's sake, he was just a neurologist. A scientist who now knew too much about an organization that did not seem to exist on any chart his contacts knew about.

His conversation with his colleague at the FBI had been the most chilling. Chuck had fairly high security clearance there himself, and his friend, Wallace Freely, had stratospheric clearance. Confronted with the names Deep Shield and General Leighton Howard and the blanks Chuck had drawn at the Pentagon and the CIA, Wallace had said simply, "I need to look into this, Chuck. Please don't take this anywhere else."

His imagination went into overdrive. What if the Deeps shut the place down after the incident with the rogue robot? What if they canceled Forward Kinetics' classes? What if Lanfen ended up stranded in the facility with no way to get out?

What if . . . ?

He called her cell phone finally, at around 4 A.M., just to be sure she was all right. He had gone back into his study, where the bugs were still dormant thanks to Mike's tinkering.

"Were you sleeping?" he asked when she answered.

She laughed softly. "What do you think? Were you?"

"No. I'm . . . kind of nervous about tomorrow. If they cancel our classes, if we can't get in to get you out—"

"I have PowerBars and a water bottle," she said. "And there's a bathroom on the other side of the door."

"Are you okay otherwise?"

"Yes. No. I mean . . . the things in those labs . . ."

"Yeah."

"What did your guy at the FBI say?"

"That he needs to look into it. That I shouldn't talk to anyone else about it. Of course I already have. I called the Pentagon and the CIA. I told him that, though. He seemed okay with it." He was jabbering. He stopped.

"How well do you know him, Chuck? Could he be . . . What if he's an insider? What if he goes to Howard? Did you get the feeling he might?"

"N-no," Chuck said. Then he added more decisively, "No. I've worked with Wallace. He sounded . . . spooked. I'm not sure General Howard is anything he claims to be. The fact is, we don't really know anything other than what Howard has told us . . . and Matt has assumed."

"So what do we do? It sounds as if we're trapped. We can't just break our contract on some pretext, can we?"

"No, but there may be another way. Matt might be able to negotiate something. He's good at that. I'm not."

"I hope so." She yawned. "Thanks for calling, Chuck. I think maybe I can sleep for a little bit now."

"Yeah, me, too."

They said good night and hung up. Not for the first time that night, Chuck picked up the business card he'd set in the middle of his desk. It had two words on it—Kristian Lorstad—and, beneath the name, a telephone number. He thought about dialing it but couldn't bring himself to do it. It felt too much like jumping out of a boat into deep water with no idea of what might be living in it.

He had a choice: throw himself to the sharks or talk to Matt.

He'd have to weigh it seriously.

Chapter 25

MATTERS OF SECURITY

Lanfen's iPhone woke her with a soft vibration at quarter to eight in the morning. She was groggy from a lack of sleep and stiff from being still for so long. She checked the jammer reflexively. It was off. There were no security cameras in the maintenance closet.

She'd checked back in with Thorin several times during the night. The labs had been crawling with MPs every time, and they had found Thorin during their sweep of the facilities. Brian had been summoned to return him to his own lab, where he was examined minutely. Lieutenant Reynolds had looked grim and nervous, which made Lanfen cringe with discomfort. She knew what she had done was necessary, but it felt somehow dishonorable.

At 7:55 she heard the door of the women's restroom open and Mini's voice say, "Well, I love those boots, Lanfen. I'm going to have to go to Macy's and see if they've got some in my size."

That was Lanfen's signal to make sure the jammer was off.

They needed the surveillance cameras to pick up Mini and her Lanfen wraith (Lanfen couldn't help but think of Mini's creations that way) entering the room. Lanfen rose from her corner, stretched, and moved to the closet door, listening intently. If this was going to work, Mini had to get herself and the wraith into the two stalls closest to the maintenance closet. Lanfen heard Mini's steps go past her hiding place and heard one of the stall doors creak open.

"Shoot," Mini said. "I forgot my hairbrush. Can I borrow yours?"

There was a moment of near silence, then the sound of a stall door opening. Lanfen switched the jammer back on, slipped out of the closet as quickly as she could, and sprinted the three strides across the room into the last stall. She shut the door and flipped the jammer off. A cold tide of adrenaline surged through her.

Okay, Chen, breathe.

Sweating a little, she reached down to pick up the jeans, sweater, and boots Mini had pushed under the stall dividers. Then she perched on the edge of the toilet seat and sent up a prayer of relief and gratitude.

"So how was your night?" Mini asked. "I had all kinds of weird dreams because of that stupid movie. I dreamed the espresso machine in our lunchroom turned into a big, shiny robot."

"I didn't sleep well either," Lanfen said, pulling off her clothes. "I know what you mean about the robots. Stuff of nightmares."

"I want to pick the movie next time," Mini said.

Lanfen pulled on her jeans and sweater. "Good luck. They're going to want to see the next five Transformers movies now."

"There are five?"

Lanfen laughed as she pulled on her boots. "I don't know. I may be exaggerating. At least I hope I am. I vote we watch a romantic comedy next time."

"You like those?" Mini asked incredulously.

"No. But I'm willing to subject myself to one just to see the boys suffer."

Lanfen shoved her discarded clothing and shoes under the stall divider. Mini bundled them into her voluminous purse. Then Lanfen took a deep breath, stood up, and got her small bag down from the hook where she'd hung it. After a moment of thought, she flushed the toilet. Mini's toilet flushed a moment later, and the two women moved to the sink in harmony, washed their hands, and left the restroom, sidestepping the "wet floor" cone that declared the bathroom closed for cleaning.

By the time they'd made their way to the canteen to meet up with Dice, Lanfen's stomach had settled enough for her to eat a bagel and drink a big mug of black tea before they parted to go to their respective classes.

Up until the time she entered her practice room, Lanfen had seen no sign that the deeper recesses of Deep Shield had had any nocturnal excitement. But her whole class was there with one very important exception: Reynolds.

"Where's Brian?" she asked the other lieutenant in her class, Cathy Letson.

"I can't say, ma'am," Letson answered. "All I know is he's got meetings this morning."

Meetings. No doubt he did. Lanfen felt a stab of guilt. If Brian was in trouble with his superiors, it was her fault. She reminded herself it was for a good cause, though, smiled at the lieutenant, and said, "Well, his loss then."

She began her class drills, praying that no one would connect Thorin's walkabout with anyone at Forward Kinetics.

DICE HAD ALMOST RELAXED WHEN he was called away from the lab to a meeting with General Howard. He told himself he was only anxious about it because he knew all sorts of things Howard didn't. It was probably nothing. The general just wanted an update.

But when he wasn't escorted to Howard's office, he tensed once again. He was led to a far more lived-in sanctuary in the hidden part of Deep Shield—the part that Lanfen had used Thorin to infiltrate. His suspicions were further aroused when he saw Chuck sitting in a side chair before the general's large desk. Chuck came to Deep Shield only on rare occasions, when his expertise with the interface was required. Dice tried to compose himself, getting his brain into some semblance of order. He had a very real fear that if someone asked the right question, he'd blab everything. He wasn't trained for this, dammit. He was a robotics engineer, not a spy.

More Q, less James Bond.

The general was not behind his desk when the polite corporal delivered Dice into the office. He sat in the chair beside Chuck. The corporal offered Dice a cup of coffee, which he accepted just so he'd have something to do with his hands.

When the corporal was gone, he turned to Chuck. "Do you have any idea—"

Chuck shook his head. "None."

Dice opened his mouth to ask another question but quickly closed it. The less said, the better. Chances were good the office was bugged. So he and Chuck sipped coffee and waited. In ten minutes on the nose, General Howard appeared, Lieutenant Reynolds in his wake. Dice knew Lanfen had been fretting over her pet student all morning; she'd be happy to know he wasn't shuffling around in chains.

I hope the same can be said about us after this meeting.

Howard slid into the chair behind his desk. Reynolds stood at ease just to his right.

The general didn't waste time. "We had an incident last night

with a couple of the robots. Lieutenant Reynolds's unit apparently got loose in the labs somehow. Did some damage, including to several other robots. Thankfully it wasn't as much damage
as it could have done. We found it in a repair bay some distance
from its assigned station."

Dice and Chuck exchanged looks that Dice was sure were
suitably startled.

"Wow," he said, barely needing to feign shock. "You think it
was deliberate sabotage?"

Howard glanced aside at Reynolds. "We're not altogether sure
what to think. If it was deliberate sabotage, it was of a most peculiar kind. The perpetrator had the opportunity to do substantial
damage but didn't. I mentioned there were other bots involved—
all were new models that haven't been outside the lab since they
were built. They rolled off of their charging stations in a couple
of cases, doing minor damage to other equipment. But that was
the extent of it. If this was deliberate sabotage, I'd have expected
much more than that. Or at least theft. But nothing is missing."
He hesitated, then asked, "Doctors, have you ever had one of
your bots go rogue?"

Dice and Chuck both shook their heads.

"Never," Dice said. "Ours are controllable only through
energy manipulation of the kinetic interface. They are robots,
not sentient beings. I don't know what's possible with your models, though. You've made modifications to the design, many of
which I don't have firsthand knowledge of."

"So there had to be a human operator," Howard surmised.

"Not necessarily," said Chuck. He set his coffee on the edge
of Howard's desk and leaned forward in his chair. "Depending
on what modifications you've made, you may have introduced
a sensitivity to the kinetic converter that interprets nondirective
energy as instructions. For example, with an enhanced sensitiv-

ity level, the interface might misinterpret output from another source as an instruction set—Wi-Fi, for example, or cellular activity. A radiation leak, perhaps? That might explain the randomness of the bot's activity. Or . . ."

"Or?"

"Or maybe you've got someone on your staff who unwittingly manipulated the bot. Someone who's a latent talent, perhaps, and was in the labs last night. Or maybe one of your regular bot drivers somehow fed the bot instructions unconsciously. Do your human operators ever sleep anywhere near the labs?"

"Wait. That would mean I did it," interrupted Reynolds, then to General Howard, "Beg pardon, sir, but he's suggesting I did this."

"Not consciously," Chuck clarified. "And not you specifically. Regardless, I'm also not saying you did it with intent. Frankly we don't know how the subconscious mind of the operator would affect the robot. We've never tested that. But it stands to reason it would work once a mind was trained to exert itself in that way. Were you anywhere in the area last night?"

Reynolds nodded slowly. "I was in the barracks two floors down. Is that . . . would that be close enough?"

"Again, I don't know. As I said, we never experimented with that. And our operators sleep off campus, miles away. At that distance, I don't think it ever occurred to us something like this was possible. Two floors down, though . . ." He left the thought hanging.

"But why would I take Thorin out into the labs? If I was dreaming, why wouldn't I remember it?"

"It may be the same neurological state as sleepwalking, which the subject rarely, if ever, remembers."

"But why would it affect *me*? I wasn't the only operator in the barracks last night. There were at least three others."

"Again, we're not saying it was you. But, if I had to make a guess, you'd be at the top of my list," Dice said.

"Why?"

"Because you're somewhat of a prodigy, Brian. You're ahead of the curve when it comes to throwing yourself into the bot. Plus you've been working with the bots longer than just about anyone outside of our teams, and you have a special affinity with Thorin."

General Howard looked like a man with a deeply perplexing problem—which Dice supposed he was. "This poses a whole new set of possibilities we hadn't anticipated. Not only might our own operators unexpectedly trigger unintentional behavior in a bot, but just a bit ago Dr. Brenton suggested that a third party might be able to hijack a unit. Either event poses a major problem. One that could bring the entire robotics program to a halt." He looked from Chuck to Dice. "Gentlemen, we need to find a way to keep this from happening again, and time is of the essence. We are on the verge of a first-time deployment of our mechanicals. I need you to solve this."

Deployment? Dice glanced at Chuck, who was shaking his head and smiling.

"Ironic, isn't it? All the efforts we've made to allow the human mind to interact with mechanicals, and we didn't foresee having to prevent them from doing it. I don't think the answer is on the human end of the equation, General. The human mind is a delicate instrument—"

"So it has to be at the mechanical end," Dice said, thinking fast and out loud. "We may need to establish a storage protocol. Delink the converter from the servo. That effectively breaks the circuit."

"Yes," said Chuck, seamlessly picking up the thread. "Good

idea. I think we need to design a sleep experiment. See if it's even *possible* to sleepwalk a robot."

Dice watched the two military men weigh what they'd said, barely daring to breathe. He swore he could feel Chuck's gaze on the side of his head. Chuck knew as well as he did that no storage protocol would keep the Forward Kinetics zetas from manipulating the robots. If the Deep Shield zetas were able to manipulate mechanicals directly, Howard would know that delinking the converter and servo interface wouldn't do a damn thing.

Howard only frowned a bit less and nodded. "Yes. A storage protocol. Dr. Kobayashi, I would appreciate it if you would begin working with my staff on such a plan first thing tomorrow. While you, Dr. Brenton, can get to work designing an experiment that will show us if there's a potential for unwitting sabotage by our own operators."

Dice nodded, and Chuck said, "Certainly."

"Would a storage protocol help if it was a clumsy attempt at sabotage?" Reynolds asked. "If it wasn't me dreaming or sleep-walking or whatever?"

"It should," Dice lied. "But how likely is it that it's sabotage? Like the general said, as sabotage goes, it was pretty lame."

"Maybe the saboteur wasn't an expert at manipulating this sort of mechanism. Or maybe they were there for a different purpose. Maybe they were just spying or going for a joyride."

Dice forced his head to move up and down. "Yeah. Yeah, I can see that, I guess. I mean it might be tempting for someone—I dunno, a guard or maintenance guy—to just, you know, try to move one of the bots. If that's what happened, though, they probably scared themselves half to death."

The general's frown deepened again. "We've questioned everyone on duty last night. Perhaps we should do so again—with a slightly different emphasis."

"You said you have a deployment coming up," Chuck said with surprising outer calm. "How much time does that give us?"

The general shot him an inscrutable glance, then said, "The end of the week, gentlemen. You have until the end of the week."

CHUCK AND DICE WERE BOTH silent on the way back out to the less-top-secret confines of the top-secret facility. They found Lanfen in the canteen, holding a cup of tea and looking wary.

Chuck slid into the chair next to hers. "We've been asked to fix a little problem with the bots," he said. "One wandered away from its charging station last night and got everyone in an uproar."

She raised a quizzical eyebrow. "Fix it? Can you?"

"We have to if the program is going to succeed. And we don't have a lot of time. General Howard says they're planning a first deployment soon. I'm thinking at the beginning of next week because he's asked us to solve the hijacking problem by the end of this one."

She stared at him. "A deployment? Of . . . never mind. That's not a lot of time."

"No, it's not. We've got a lot of work to do before then."

She nodded, then rose and bent over to drop a kiss on his hair. Her hand brushed the lapel of his suit coat and patted his chest lightly. "Back to class," she said and left the canteen.

He sat, stunned for a moment by the intimate gesture, then realized she'd slipped something into the breast pocket of his blazer. The jammer. Great, because he was going to need it.

Still, it was a bit hard to concentrate on his way back to Forward Kinetics.

God, she smells good . . .

When Chuck returned to FK, he tracked Matt down. His partner looked up from his laptop and grimaced as Chuck wandered through the door of his office.

"We—"

"Need to talk. Yes, Chuck. You should just have those words embroidered on your lab coat. What are you worried about now?"

Chuck hesitated, deliberately unknitting his brow. "No, it's just . . . Look, has anyone from Deep Shield contacted you about the incident in their labs last night?"

Matt's face testified eloquently to his complete surprise. "What incident?"

"The one where the robot wandered off."

"What?" Matt's fingers froze over his keyboard. "Which robot?"

"One of their training bots. Brian Reynolds's unit, Thorin, went for a stroll, apparently. General Howard said there were several other highly classified bots liberated and some minor damage to lab equipment."

"Let me get this straight: one of their robots went rogue?"

"No, not rogue. Well, not insofar as they can tell. They . . ." How to put it? "They've been less than forthcoming about the sort of changes they've made in their proprietary units. When they say they can't think of any reason for them to go rogue, I have to take them at their word."

"Sabotage?"

Chuck shrugged, trying to ignore the flush of heat he felt creeping up the back of his neck. *Stick to the facts.* "The general thinks not. He said a real saboteur would have done more damage. This almost seemed accidental, a by-product of clumsiness. We've got two theories at this point: one of their trainees was manipulating the bot unintentionally, or someone who's not in the program was playing at being a zeta."

"Is either of those things even possible?"

"That's what I want to talk to you about. They've asked us to come up with some way of keeping the bots from being hijacked. If that's what happened. As I said, we really have no idea what they've been doing to their mechanicals, what sort of features they're giving them." He shrugged again.

"You want to know if I have a clue what they've been experimenting with, is that it?"

"I never did have a good poker face," Chuck said. "Yes, Matt—it would be nice to know, because we might be able to fix it. I'll add that Dice is particularly concerned that they've done something like writing AI code into the interface."

"I can imagine they might," said Matt. "After all, what happens if the operator is injured or killed or disabled in some way? You'd want to be able to retrieve the unit, so maybe they wrote some 'run home to Mama' code for it."

"If they did, they didn't mention it to us. I just want to understand what we've got to contend with. Especially since they're planning some sort of deployment for next week." He watched Matt's face carefully for signs of . . . something.

Matt's brow furrowed. "Deployment? Deployment of what exactly?"

"I don't know. The bots they've been building, presumably. Do you know—?"

He was cut off as Matt's cell phone rang, spraying the office with Thomas Dolby's "One of Our Submarines." The irony was not lost on Chuck.

"Speak of the devil," Matt said, glancing down at it where it sat beside his laptop. "It's Howard."

Chuck took a step backward. "Oh. I'll just head back to my office. Come by when you get a minute, okay?"

He beat a hasty retreat then, reflecting that he'd be surprised if Matt bothered to track him down. He was, therefore, surprised when Matt did precisely that roughly forty minutes later, face neutral, hands shoved deep into his pockets.

Bad sign. Hands in pockets indicated Matt was restraining

himself in some way. The deeper the hands pressed, the stronger the emotion he was suppressing.

Chuck resigned himself to an unpleasant interview and cast a glance at Lorstad's little jammer to make sure it was still on. Mike had "adjusted" the surveillance cameras around Chuck's office, so there was a long blind spot just outside the door in his private lab. Chuck had developed the art of fading into it and turning on the jammer before returning, invisibly, to his office.

He wondered, as he shifted the device farther out of sight, if the mysterious Lorstad was using it to track him. It had never even occurred to him to ask one of the zetas to check that for him. Once again he was reminded that he was not cut out for espionage. His life's work was about revealing things, not hiding them.

And yet, here I go again . . .

"Earth to Chuck," Matt said. He sat down in the chair on the other side of the desk.

Chuck willed his face to relax and met his partner's gaze, trying not to look as if he had anything to hide. "I take it the general filled you in on the excitement last night."

"Yes, he did." Matt was silent for a moment, his eyes never leaving Chuck's face. "He mentioned that Dice is designing what he called a storage protocol to shut the kinetic interface down manually."

"Yes, that was something they wanted us to look into."

Matt's gaze did a circuit of the room, as if he were looking for a hidden message somewhere. "The way Howard described it, it was Dice's suggestion. Did you happen to mention to him that this protocol will only protect his bots from zetas who don't know how to manipulate the mechanics directly?"

Chuck felt heat rise up the back of his neck. "I didn't, figuring that none of his zetas are doing that."

"Why not?"

"We taught them to use the kinetic interface. Just the way our zetas do—did."

"You withheld information from a U.S. government agency. That's what you're telling me."

Chuck licked his suddenly dry lips but decided to turn the conversation. "I'm not certain that's really what they are, Matt."

"What the hell are you talking about?" Any of his composed neutrality was now gone.

"I told you I contacted the Pentagon and the CIA about these guys. I also went to a personal contact in the FBI. My security clearance there goes pretty high because of some work I did for them a couple of years ago. My contact went to his superiors and got back to me. He said he needed to look into it, and I wasn't to discuss it with anyone else."

"Like me, for instance."

"Like you."

"Chuck, you're being paranoid—"

"Of course I am! They're building robot warriors, Matt. Can't you understand that? They're building a robot army. Like—like something out of a Star Wars movie. They're building tech into them that our contract specifically precludes."

Matt's expression was suddenly guarded. "And you know this how?

"You did it, didn't you? You—" Matt broke off and glanced frantically around the room. "Shit, you realize they've been overhearing every word we've—"

"They don't even know we're in here. Don't ask. Just accept it as fact. My office is a bug-free zone. A dead spot."

"You did the break-in last night, didn't you? Somehow you got one of their bots to . . . Sabotage, Chuck? For the love of—"

"No. Not sabotage. Just a little reconnaissance. About *our* company and *our* technology. We needed to know, Matt."

"Building a robot army . . ."

"Yes. There are bots in there with treads, flamethrowers, plasma weapons, EMP generators. Missile launchers! They've got one model that comes with a tank for sarin gas."

Matt's mouth popped open as if to retort, but nothing came out. He closed it and put on the face that said he was thinking rapidly and frenetically—gaze distracted, brow furrowed, mouth pursed.

Chuck waited a beat, then said, "And they're planning a deployment, Matt."

Matt looked up at him. "They are part of the U.S. government. Our military. Whatever it is they're doing, they're entitled to do it. Frankly, you're the reason for all that mealy language in the contract about no offensive uses of the tech. If they're building robots in secret labs where we can't see them or know what's going into them, it's your damn fault."

"*My* fault?"

"I have to tell you, Chuck, General Howard would like nothing better than to get you off the team. He views you as a risk. You're a Pollyanna. Your ideals are unrealistic. You're not a businessman."

"No, I'm a scientist. I've never pretended otherwise."

"In a soft, squishy science. You're a true believer. A crusader."

"And you're an asshole."

Matt didn't even flinch. "Yes—but one who understands that we're going to be in a lot more trouble breaching their security than they are breaching the contract. You need to stay out of the business side of this and let me deal with it. Right now Howard thinks he needs you to work on this bogus protocol. He doesn't suspect you're the one responsible for last night's intrusion, and I think we should do everything we can to keep it that way." Matt paused. "How'd you do it, by the way? Who was the bot driver?"

"I'm not going to tell you that."

"I won't tattle on you, Chuck. Howard doesn't need to know. He'll get his tech and his training, and he'll pay us the money, and the contract will be done. I don't care if he never finds out who penetrated his secret kingdom. It was your girlfriend, wasn't it? That's who you got on the inside."

Chuck suspected he was blushing. He felt as if he was. "My girlfriend . . ."

"Chen." Matt sat back in his chair, a grin unexpectedly creasing his face. "Damn. I would really love to know how you did it— and I don't mean landing a beautiful woman like Chen, although I'm sure there's an interesting story there, too." Matt laughed. "I have to say I didn't think you had it in you. You'd better hope General Howard never suspects you do."

"I hope so, too. But shouldn't our concern also be that he plans to deploy with all that firepower? With sarin gas?"

"No. What's important to me, besides the funds this is giving us to grow our business, is the vindication of this technology." The way Matt said it, with a passion that bordered on zealotry, frightened Chuck, especially as Matt continued. "Lucy died for this, Chuck. Lucy's death is what gave me the formula that made the conversion of thought to kinetic energy possible. This tech must succeed. It must see the light of day."

"And you say *I'm* a crusader? Do you hear yourself? Matt, it would have seen the light of day if we'd pursued the applications we originally talked about—medicine, construction, design, education, emergency services, space exploration. In General Howard's hands, it's only going to be used under cover of darkness. And when he's done with us, I'm not altogether sure we're going to be able to pursue anything related to the work we're doing now. Think for a minute, would you? If we walk out of this Deep Shield business and start pursuing private or public contracts with the same tech, anyone can reverse-engineer it or adapt it or use it. If that happens, Howard's army loses its tactical advantage much sooner than if they shut us down or shut us up."

Matt stared at him for a long moment. Finally, he rose and put his hands on his hips. "You're right on the edge, you know that, don't you? You are pretty damn close to going right off the logic cliff. Nothing you've said makes a damn bit of sense. You're reading everything Howard does in the worst possible light."

"Well, you're being unbelievably thick," Chuck said, also standing, "for some reason accepting Howard's word and ignoring his actions."

They stood there, staring at each other.

"Okay, look," Matt said. "I need you to promise me there will be no more *Spy Kids* shenanigans. You think you're Tony Stark or something, but you're not. This isn't a game, Chuck."

"Funny, I was about to say the same thing to you. I know it's not a game. You're the one who's in denial. I—"

Matt pointed a finger at Chuck's forehead. "Promise me. No more half-assed espionage. I don't think you have any idea how much trouble we all could be in if you get caught doing this crap. Promise."

"You'd accept my word? A promise I won't spy on your hard-assed overlord?"

Matt burst into laughter. "My hard-assed overlord? God Almighty, Chuck. You're cracking my mind. I've never seen you like this. I've never heard you like this." He shook his head. "Yes, I'd accept your word. Because you're such a freaking Boy Scout, I'm pretty sure you wouldn't give it if you meant to break it."

"Fine. No more *Spy Kids*. No more comic-book shenanigans. We're out of the spy business."

"Good. Now, about General Howard's storage protocol. We'll go ahead and have Dice design one. It'll *work,* of course, because

you're not going to take any more of the general's bots for a joyride. He'll be happy; we'll be covered."

"You're not going to suggest direct manipulation to them?"

"Why would I? As you said, they're buying the kinetic interfaces from us. Why would I screw up that deal? You just do what
you do and keep a low profile. I'll handle Howard. Deal?"

Chuck let out a long breath. "Deal."

Matt sketched a salute and sauntered out of Chuck's office, the
very picture of an alpha male who had just counted coup on his
opponent and subjected him to utter humiliation.

"No deal," Chuck murmured to his partner's receding back.

"I quit the Boy Scouts."

MATT WAS FAR LESS SANGUINE about the Deep Shield mess than
he had let Chuck know. He was willing to admit to himself, if not
to his partner, that some of what Chuck had said bothered him.
Still, there was no need to panic. So he didn't. Not even when
General Howard called him at eleven that night and asked if he'd
known that his business partner had called the Pentagon, trying
to get information about Deep Shield.

He told the truth—sort of: that Chuck had told him just that
afternoon about the call.

"You need to keep your partner on a tighter leash, Dr. Streegman. These are matters of national security. We can't have someone on our team who can't keep his head together."

"Chuck just wanted to cover all the bases," Matt told him.
"He's a very cautious soul. Dots all the *i*'s, crosses all the *t*'s. You
know the type."

"My question to you, then, is if we really need him. How big a
problem would his absence be?"

Matt felt a cold shock deep in his gut. The implications of the
question were horrifying at first, but he shook off the feeling of

dread. Howard was only asking if they could fire Chuck—ease him out, not erase him completely.

"You're kidding, right? General, Chuck Brenton is at the heart of everything we do. He and Dice and Eugene are more important to this operation than even the most successful zeta. They're the ones who make zetas happen. Without Chuck you have inventory. You have whatever tech you've already got. Innovation, further development, troubleshooting—you can kiss that good-bye."

"Does it ever bother you," the general asked at the end of the call, "to be so dependent on such a squeamish wimp?"

Matt just laughed and said there was more to Chuck than met the eye. Hell, he'd just discovered that himself.

AT MIDNIGHT CHUCK'S IPHONE UTTERED a sonar ping and lit up on his nightstand. He reached for it, half-groggy with sleep. It was a one-line text message from Matt.

"They know you called P."

Chapter 26

CONTACTS

Dice was the first person Chuck told about Matt's text message. Or, rather, he wordlessly showed him the text. Merely relaying the information recalled that deep, visceral chill he'd felt when he'd read it. He hadn't fallen asleep until close to 5 A.M., when his eyelids had been unable to sustain the weight of their own lashes.

The pallor that swept Dice's tawny face when he saw the message was both a comfort to Chuck (*No, I'm not overreacting*) and the cause of a secondary jolt of fear (*We're in deep shit*).

"How about a house party?" Dice murmured. "Tonight?"

Chuck merely nodded.

"Shall we invite the usual suspects?"

"Sure," Chuck said, forcing his voice to a false lightness. "Mini wants to pick the movie this time. She didn't take to *Transformers* very well."

"Aw," said Dice, "who doesn't like big, beefy battle bots?"

The party plans were completed in a matter of minutes, the information passed from one member of Team Chuck to another.

They couldn't get in touch with Sara's team, all of whom were already bundled off to the Deeps.

Chuck spent the morning ready to crawl or jump out of his skin. At any moment, he imagined, the phone would ring, and he'd be summoned to meet with General Howard, or Smiths would arrive to take him away for interrogation. It wasn't so far-fetched: when the usual driver arrived to pick up his charges, he had a tagalong—a Smith in a black suit who entered the main facility, flashed his ID at the front desk (now manned by his twin), and made his way into the lab area.

Chuck, who was just exiting the conference room after a meeting with their admin, saw the Smith striding up the corridor and felt the bottom drop out of his stomach. He gasped in a breath and held it, feeling an icy sweat spring up between his shoulder blades. The impulse to run was so strong, he nearly bolted, but instead he faced the oncoming agent, clutching his coffee mug in one hand and his laptop in the other.

"Doctor," the man said and nodded . . . then passed him by without breaking stride.

Perhaps a little far-fetched.

Chuck sagged against the wall of the corridor and watched the Smith stop to tap on Matt's office door. He tore his eyes away and returned to his lab, consciously avoiding the blind spot Mike had created for secret egress and turning off the jammer. This was one time he wanted his behavior noted.

Roughly five minutes later, the Smith reappeared with Matt in tow. Chuck saw them through the open doors of his lab as they headed out. Matt glanced at him across the width of the lab, his pale eyes cutting, his thin mouth set in a grim line. Again Chuck felt the impulse to run welling up inside him. Instead he left his office, did a few moments of busywork in the lab, and reentered his private domain through the blind spot, flipping on the jammer as he stepped back into the room.

He then placed a call to a colleague in California and asked him for a very large favor.

THE MOVIE WAS *INDEPENDENCE DAY*—NOT quite the romcom Lanfen had envisioned, but again, the movie wasn't the point. The agenda was, and in Chuck's mind, what they had to discuss was both simple and fraught: he had to get out of the situation he'd gotten himself into when he'd gone into business with Matt Streegman.

With full antisurveillance measures in place, the team gathered around Chuck in their lair. He scanned their faces. They all looked as scared as he was—something that brought him both comfort and unease. Propped on the edge of his desk, he looked each of them in the eye: Eugene, Dice, Lanfen, Mini. Then he spoke.

"Howard knows I've contacted someone at the Pentagon about his operation—I'm not sure he's aware about the CIA and FBI, but I'd have to think he is. Here's the thing. We have knowledge that I'm not sure we can divulge to anyone. I'd call my friend at the FBI—I can trust him, but not the people he works for. And it doesn't really matter anyway."

"What do you mean?" Mini asked.

"The long and short of it is I can't live like this anymore. I've got to get out. As soon as I can make some connections and—"

"By yourself?" asked Lanfen at the same time Eugene said, "Me, too."

Dice was nodding. "I'm in, too. Or out, as the case may be."

Mini just stared straight ahead, her arms wrapped around herself. Her face was eggshell white in the dimly lit room.

Chuck leaned heavily on his desk. "You guys don't have to run. They can't know you're involved with my paranoia—"

"C'mon, Doc," said Euge. "We're in this together. All of us. None of us wants to be involved in whatever sort of war machine they're building. None of us knows who to trust."

"Except each other," said Lanfen. "We know we can trust each other. I agree. I want out, too. What options do we have?"

Chuck thought about the all-white card in his wallet but once more dismissed it. "I have a colleague, a friend, at CalTech. He's a neurologist there, head of his department. He's always been a bit of a subversive when it comes to things military. I called him this morning and—without going into great detail—told him that a technology I'd developed was being manhandled by the military. He said he can help. He's willing to let me hide out someplace he feels is safe. But if all five of us go—"

"Safety in numbers," said Dice. "If we're all in on the planning, there's less chance we'll overlook something important. We need to think of transportation, financial resources, that sort of thing."

"What about the stuff in the labs?" Eugene asked. "We can't just leave all our notes and documentation behind. Dice has gotten the interface down to where it fits in a backpack. Do you think we might get one out of the lab somehow?"

Chuck shrugged his shoulders uncomfortably. "We won't have to. I have one here at the house. I've been . . . practicing. It's best if we don't count on getting anything out of our labs."

"Chuck's right," said Lanfen. "You guys can rebuild the training units as you need to. I mean you are the team that designed and built them in the first place."

That was when it hit Chuck full force: if they disappeared, Howard would move heaven and earth to find them because they were Forward Kinetics. They were the source of the technology he wanted to control.

A tiny noise to his right made Chuck glance over at Mini. She was crying. Huge, silent tears streamed down her cheeks. He and Eugene both moved to put their arms around her at the same moment. He let Eugene beat him.

"Mini, don't be scared."

"I'm not scared," she whispered through clenched teeth, almost shaking his arm off. "I'm mad. Frustrated." She raised her eyes to Chuck's face. "Who are these people? Who do they think they are? We did all this with the best intentions. We wanted to help." She looked around at her peers, who all looked so *helpless*. "We were creating something beautiful. They took our work and turned it around. And now what? We're supposed to run away? They can't be allowed to do this. We can't *let* them do this!"

Chuck stared at her pale, tear-stained face and knew she was right. They couldn't just run and hide. They had to fight. Secret for secret. Intelligence against force.

But first they had to escape—before Howard had a chance to deploy any of his machines.

"Okay, look. Is everybody in? Do you all want to get out?"

There was no hesitation. All four of them nodded.

Chuck felt a flush of raw emotion well up in his breast. He felt exalted. These people trusted him; he trusted them. Whatever they faced, they would at least face it together. He shoved the scientific curiosity aside and let himself savor the moment as a man who had just made a very dire decision.

"All right. Let's try to think of everything we're going to need to do and when we're going to do it."

They made lists; they made plans; they drew up a timeline. The items on the lists would have to be finished by Saturday evening because early Sunday morning, they were leaving Forward Kinetics and Deep Shield far behind.

BY FRIDAY NIGHT THEY HAD backed up their files and sent a great number of them to the cloud—nothing unusual about that. Dice had come up with a storage protocol that would allow the kinetic transceiver to be shut off when the bots were stored and turned back on using a custom kinetic key code that all bot drivers would design for themselves. They also knew they weren't expected to go in to work on Monday morning, ostensibly because it was a federal holiday. None of them believed for a second that was the real reason, but they were grimly pleased by the development. It gave them more time.

On Saturday they worked individually, each to put his or her life in order and pieces into place: acquire money, make travel connections, pack. They had a movie night on Saturday but didn't let it run late. On Sunday morning Mini, Lanfen, Dice, and Eugene met at Chuck's house with backpacks and picnic gear, dressed for a hike. Dice's girlfriend, Brenda, was absent; she'd previously made an appointment to get her mother's minivan serviced.

The weather was mild—sweater weather, Lanfen's mom had called it. They took Chuck's Volvo SUV and drove northwest to Prettyboy Reservoir. It was a serpentine, man-made lake with miles of uneven shoreline, so heavily wooded that the tree canopy was nearly impenetrable in places. They parked at Frog Hollow Cove on the eastern shore and rented a boat to cross to the opposite side of the reservoir, to the banks of a triangular peninsula that angled south. From there they hiked into the thickest part of the woods and headed north.

The whole thing had an air of unreality to it, especially since they hiked in silence, each one wrapped in private thoughts. It was almost, Lanfen thought, as if they figured Howard's bugging devices could hear them even out there. She found herself listening for helicopters or airplanes and frequently glanced up through the tree branches at the patches of sky.

They heard a plane once, and though they took cover swiftly it passed nowhere near their position. The only thing Lanfen heard other than the distant engine was the sound of Eugene's shaky indrawn breaths. She wasn't sure if it was due to the fact that he wasn't exactly the athletic type or if he was nervous as hell even though they hadn't done anything particularly dangerous yet. If Howard's guys tracked them down and intercepted them now, they could still fall back on the pretense that they were just out for a weekend hike and some boating.

So far, so good.

After just under an hour's walk, they came out into a tree-shaded parking lot where Spooks Hill Road came down close to the water and made a loop at the top of a sharp inlet. Pulled up along the verge of the woods, with its passenger side broadside to a dense grove of trees, was a silver Toyota Sienna that had been there since the night before, though it was supposed to be at a Baltimore Big O getting its tires rotated. It was stage two of their escape. And it was so close, they could almost feel it.

The group of hikers approached the van from the thick tree cover. The back passenger door slid open, revealing Brenda Tansy. Wordlessly she slid away from the passenger seat and got back behind the wheel. Lanfen couldn't help but notice that her eyes were underlined with dark circles, and her face was pale.

Silently they arranged themselves in the vehicle, with a heavily camouflaged Dice taking the front passenger seat, Chuck and Lanfen in the middle seats, and Eugene and Mini in the rear of the van.

"Everything go okay?" Bren asked as she started the car and pulled out of the parking lot. She glanced sideways at Dice and smiled wanly. "That's quite a look you've got going."

Dice pulled off the stocking cap he'd been wearing all morning and revealed a spiked shock of blond-streaked hair. With the mirror shades he had on, he looked nothing like their slightly nerdy robotics expert—and by the time they reached their first destination, *none* of them would look like their normal selves. Mini had straightened her hair and put on makeup; Lanfen had cut her hair and brought clothing nothing like what she usually wore; Chuck and Eugene had also changed their appearances.

Chuck's transformation had been the most remarkable, Lanfen thought. It was amazing to her how much dying his hair a darker color, combing it straight back from his forehead, and wearing contact lenses instead of glasses changed him.

I like it.

Theoretically no one would be following them now. Theoretically, if they'd been tailed to the lake, the surveillance crew would be watching Chuck's Volvo, still parked at Frog Hollow. Theoretically they had hours in which to disappear.

Lanfen trusted theories. She tried to relax, to tell herself this was going to work. She must not have been doing a very good job of it, though, because Chuck reached over and put a hand on hers. She only then realized that her fingers had tightened into a fist.

"It's all right," he said, though he had no way of knowing whether it was all right or not. "They'll be waiting for us to come back to the car. If they even bothered to follow us out here. We're going to do this. We're going to be fine."

She forced her fist to flex open. Chuck twined his fingers with hers and squeezed. She squeezed back and began to go mentally through her calming down routine. That made her think of Bilbo, still a prisoner of Deep Shield. He was an inanimate object except when she inhabited him. He was just a machine. Yet somehow, thinking of him surrounded by all those strangers made her intensely sad. It was entirely possible that she would never see him again.

THE NEXT STAGE OF THEIR trip took them to Hagerstown, where they had booked flights from the regional airport to LaGuardia in New York City. Brenda dropped them at Hagerstown's single terminal, and after a tense and tearful parting from Dice, during which he swore this wouldn't be forever, she drove back to Baltimore. From LaGuardia they would fly to Omaha, Nebraska, and from there to Albuquerque. In New Mexico they'd rent a car and drive just far enough to get to a dealership where they could buy transportation.

They did not fly together. They'd planned to reconfigure themselves into different groupings at each airport. So when they flew out of Hagerstown, Dice and Lanfen were a couple of Asian tourists, Mini and Chuck formed a second pairing, and Eugene traveled alone.

At LaGuardia, Mini and Lanfen became two businesswomen on a corporate junket while all three men appeared to be on their own. By the time they set down in Omaha early on Monday morning, Chuck was exhausted, and his nerves were frayed. Still he hoped their absence might not have been noticed until they failed to return to their car by Sunday evening.

Inshallah—that was something one of his Muslim colleagues at Johns Hopkins had often said. If God wills it. He hoped God would will that any security detail Howard might have put on them would become bored enough to resort to Internet card games or playing on their smartphones. He wondered for a second whether God was even aware of Candy Crush. But that was a question for another time. Right now, he had a couple of phone calls to make.

MATT STREEGMAN'S CELL PHONE RANG at six thirty on Monday morning. He was not pleased to see Leighton Howard's office number on the caller ID, but he answered dutifully and with false good humor because the customer is always right to call you whenever they damn well please. At least when the customer was paying as much money as Deep Shield was.

"General Howard, you're up bright and early."

"I usually am. I'd like you to come in this morning, Dr. Streegman. One of our security analysts was just showing me something I think you should see."

Matt tried to call Chuck while he was waiting for the Deep Shield car to pick him up. Chuck didn't answer. Matt only just remembered that his partner and some of the other staff had gone off for a Sunday hike at Prettyboy Reservoir. He was probably sleeping in. Leave it to Chuck to come up with something like that. Movie nights. Dinners. Team-building weekends where they could get away from it all.

Matt's brain cartwheeled over the words, and he had a sudden moment of vertigo. *Get away from it all.* Would Chuck do something that radical—haul his little fan club out into the woods, where the Deeps couldn't monitor them? Make a run for the border? What border? There was nowhere they could run that Howard couldn't find them. Matt was pretty sure of that.

And he realized how much that surety was not pleasant.

He shrugged off the uneasy thoughts. The Deep Shield car had arrived, which meant Howard had sent it before he'd even called. Typical.

At Deep Shield HQ, he was hustled straight to Howard's office, where the general and a tech in an unadorned khaki uniform sat at a small conference table before a large cinema display.

Howard waved Matt to a chair at the table.

"I want you to watch this footage and tell me what's screwy about it," Howard said without preamble.

The video showed a lengthwise view of an empty restroom. The door nearest the camera—which must have been mounted in the corner of the room opposite the row of sinks and stalls—opened, and Mini Mause stepped into the room, holding the door open for Lanfen. Mini complimented the other woman's boots and crossed to open a stall door. There she paused and began rummaging in her oversize purse for her hairbrush, apparently. She moved back toward the center of the room, tilting the purse toward the ceiling lights.

Behind her, Lanfen slipped into the stall Mini had opened, and Mini, giving up on finding the brush, entered the stall next to it and closed the door. He heard her say something about borrowing Lanfen's brush but didn't hear Lanfen's answer. They talked about the movie they'd watched the night before. They talked about boots. Then they came out and moved to the sinks.

Matt felt his brow furrowing. "What was I supposed to notice?"

"Run it again," Howard told the tech. To Matt he said, "Watch the stall door on the left."

Matt watched. Mini dug in her purse. Behind her, Lanfen slid through the half-open stall door, pushing it a bit farther open. Mini went into her stall—Matt fought to keep his eyes on the other door—and . . .

He blinked. The door on the left was half-open; then it was closed and locked. It didn't swing shut or slam shut or shut at all. It simply was open, and then it wasn't.

"What happened?" he asked.

"I don't know," said Howard. "I was wondering if you did."

"Why would I?"

"You know both these women. You know they're both . . . talented."

"You think they messed with the camera for some reason?"

"Not mechanically. All I know is that particular ladies' latrine was the scene of several odd occurrences that same night—the night Lieutenant Reynolds's robot went AWOL. A maintenance man found that the keys to the storage closet in that latrine suddenly wouldn't open it. The next morning, between the time your two colleagues entered the restroom and came out again, someone put a maintenance cone outside in the hall. None of our maintenance people recall having done that."

Matt's brain felt like it was in a hamster ball—running, running, running every which way and hitting into walls. "I assume you're planning on asking them about all this?"

Howard nodded. "First thing tomorrow morning."

"That's probably your best bet, because I honestly have no clue what's going on here. What is it *you* think they've done?"

"I don't know. But I'm wondering if it had something to do with the lab break-in. I'll be frank, Doctor. The timing on your friends' escapade couldn't be worse. I just had to stop the countdown on an important trial deployment."

Matt took a deep breath. "A trial deployment. A trial of what exactly?"

"Of Deep Shield forces in a covert combat situation. That's all you need know."

"What I do know from our contract is that you shouldn't be running missions like that with this technology. It's beyond the scope of our agreement."

"Our agreement? Yes, I wanted to talk to you about that. Depending on the success of the mission, we may wish to discuss changes to the work your group is doing here. Changes that will benefit both of us."

Matt forced his anger down. This was what he worked for. This was where Lucy's last brain waves led him.

"But there will be no mission if they've done something to the bots in those labs," Howard finished.

Matt swallowed hard. "What do you want me to do?"

"What I've always needed you to do: control them. I had thought it was just Dr. Brenton that was the problem. I can see now that it goes further than that. His whole group is infected. I need you to get in with them. Talk to them. Listen to them. Be part of their plans, and make damn sure you know what they're up to, so I know how to counter it."

"Counter it? I don't know what that means. Haven't they been working with your people? Haven't we been fulfilling our end of the bargain?"

"Not if there are extracurricular activities that can harm this project."

You're one to talk. Covert . . .

"And I think that's exactly what's going on," Howard continued, "right under your nose. That's always been the problem with you, Streegman. You're disengaged from your people, your business, from life. You need to reengage, and you need to do it now."

Matt nodded and rose, his brain feeling abnormally sluggish, as if someone had filled it with ice. Something about this whole situation suddenly seemed wrong. Yet Howard was right. Right about Chuck. Right about him.

He found his dutiful guide outside in the corridor, waiting patiently to take him back to the outer layers of the Deep Shield onion. He was standing in the hangar area, waiting for his driver, when his phone rang. He unpocketed and glanced at it. Not a number he recognized. He answered it anyway.

"Streegman."

"Matt, it's me." Chuck's voice was layered atop a background that was almost certainly an airport.

Matt lowered his voice and his head, something that probably made him look guilty as sin. "Chuck? Where're you calling from? I didn't recognize the number."

"It's a burner. Listen, we're gone, okay? I can't tell you where. I can only tell you what I heard from my contact at the FBI this morning: Deep Shield is not on any list of government agencies he's aware of. You know what they're building. And you know they're planning a deployment—"

"Howard just told me he's stopped the countdown—"

"For how long? No, it doesn't matter. These are not rescue robots, Matt. Or medevac units or construction bots or exploration bots or even disaster mitigation forces. They are offensive weaponry. And they are weaponry in the hands of a deeply secret paramilitary organization."

Matt felt as if someone had opened a deep freezer in his gut. "Dammit, Chuck, have you gone completely mad? I told you this comic-book shit—"

"Is *real*. The sooner you get that, the sooner we can figure out what to do. You can help us, Matt, or you can throw in with Howard and try to bring us in. It's up to you. I just wanted you to know. Our contracts don't cover our involvement with the sort of tech Lanfen saw in their labs the other night, and more important, our ethics won't countenance it. If you're not concerned about us or about ethics or about national security or about a supremely powerful paramilitary, then for God's sake think of the copyright infringement."

Copyright infringement? Was that what Chuck thought of him?

And yet . . . why shouldn't he?

He wavered for a moment. Helping Howard would be an act of good faith, possibly enough that the rest of the contracts could be salvaged after this act of insurgence. He could get information, find out details about where the team was hiding. Chuck thought so little of him? So be it. Then he could sum up his feelings for his *ex*-partner in two simple words: fuck Chuck.

On the other hand—*in* the other hand—there was that manila folder Chuck had surprised him with. Matt hadn't opened it on that day or at all during the Forward Kinetics fair. He hadn't touched it for weeks afterward. Then one night, after an endless series of identical nights all spent alone, he wanted to hear what Lucy had to say.

Chuck had written it all out alongside Matt's algorithms. Lucy's brain in a sleep state, a prolonged alpha coma, punctuated by sharp spikes or K complexes—what Chuck had termed *arousal bursts*. Neurologically, he'd noted, this had corresponded with activity in her parietal and temporal lobes—those processing memories, thoughts, and emotions. There had also been exertion in her primary motor cortex; she'd perhaps been trying to open her eyes and lift her arms to hold something. Her brain had been attempting to move a body that wouldn't listen, as if her interface were in need of repair. It had been a partial awakening but not an agitated one. The rhythmic theta runs following these bursts showed calmness, peace.

Matt knew what it meant: she had been aware that he had been there. Lucy had responded to his presence in that hospital room and had tried to reach out and comfort *him*. She had been serene, and she'd wanted to tell him, as she had so many times in their life together, to calm the hell down, stop fighting every-thing, and just accept what he couldn't change because maybe there was a bigger reason for it that didn't fit so neatly into his mathematical formulas. After all this time, Lucy had finally been able to tell him that no matter what was happening to her brain, he was still on her mind.

Chuck had been the one to deliver that message. And no matter what life owed Matt, he knew he owed Chuck something for that.

He took a deep breath, lowered his voice even more, and hunched himself around his phone. "They know something was screwy the other night. Howard just made me sit through a screening of 'What Nerd Girls Talk about in Bathrooms.'"

"What?"

"They have security cams in the bathrooms, Chuck."

"Well, of course they do. We knew that going in."

"Okay, well, you guys missed something. But Howard didn't. And he *will* come after you. Where are you? Maybe I can help."

"Sorry, Matt. I can't tell you that. I just wanted you to know who you're dealing with. I'll try to find a way to contact you later—give you a number you might be able to use if you want to get out. You can reach me through social media if necessary."

"I don't want to get—" Matt started to say, but Chuck had already hung up.

Matt stared at the phone in his hand for a second before deleting the most recent incoming call. God, this was bad. Could it possibly get any worse?

"Sir?"

"Yeah, yeah. I'm ready to leave." He looked up, expecting to see his driver, and found himself confronted by two soldiers and a pair of fu-bots. Since one of the men was Lieutenant Reynolds, he assumed the robot was Thorin. Both men were armed, though their weapons were holstered for the moment.

It had just gotten worse.

"What's the problem, Lieutenant?" he asked Reynolds.

"I need your phone, sir," the young man said with imperturbable courtesy.

The phone. Which was no doubt tapped. Which had the number Chuck had called from somewhere in its memory along with possible clues to their location. He considered dropping it to the floor and crushing it underfoot, but in Matt's moment of inaction the other soldier had already reached out and snatched it from his hand.

Before Matt could object, Reynolds said, almost apologetically, "There's one more thing, sir. You need to come with us."

"I was going to go home."

"No, Dr. Streegman. You have to come back in. There's been a development, sir. Deep Shield is in lockdown."

WHEN SARA ENTERED THE ZETAS' large lab at Deep Shield on Tuesday morning, it felt wrong. Too quiet. Tim was sitting at his instructor's terminal on the left-hand side of the room, moving a couple of scaly dudes in loincloths through wild kickboxing moves. He was getting that 3-D thing down pretty good. She knew it had galled him that an untechy artist like Mini had beaten him to the punch.

On the opposite side of the room, in a rear corner, Mike was seated among his toys—a scattering of construction robots of varying shapes and sizes—drinking his first cup of coffee. The robots were grouped very much as if they were a class huddled around a favorite teacher. The big, mechanical arm—the one Mike called Fezzik—was rocking gently back and forth. Sara wondered if Mike was even aware he was doing that.

Other than her two teammates, the large room was empty except for one security guard, who occupied a tiny office between Tim's workstation and Sara's workspace at the front of the room. She could just see the guard through the Plexiglas window in his office door. He was on the phone.

She hesitated at her console, looking around at the desks that fanned out from hers in a rough arc. Usually members of their classes would already be in the lab, working on projects. Sara set down her tote and moved to the coffeepot on the opposite side of the room.

"Where is everyone?"

"Dunno," said Tim. "Don't particularly care. Just means there's less of a line at the bagel station."

"It doesn't strike you as odd that not one of our eager-beaver recruits is here?"

"Maybe they had a drill."

She glanced at Mike. He looked relaxed, but she realized with sudden certainty that he was far from it. He was watchful in a way that only Mike could be. She moved over to lean against his workbench.

"Talk to me, Mikey. What are you thinking?" she asked him quietly.

"That this isn't a drill."

"I wonder how long we'll have to wait to find out what it is."

"Not long," Mike murmured.

Sara followed his gaze. A pair of MPs had appeared in the hall outside the lab door. Her cell phone, which she'd slipped into her suit coat pocket, buzzed. She took it out and looked at the screen. She saw one sentence in a green message bubble: "They're deploying SOON. CB."

CB . . . Chuck Brenton?

"What?" Mike asked, his eyes on her face.

"I think we've got a situation," she said. "I'm just not sure what kind."

She watched as the MPs conferred with one of the Smiths, then all three entered the lab. The MPs were armed with rifles. A moment later the lab security guy came out of his office. He had his sidearm holstered, but the flap was open. Sara was intensely aware that the three zetas were effectively cornered in the back of the room.

She cleared her throat. "What's going on, Agent? Is there a problem?"

"This facility is in lockdown, Ms. Crowell. There's been a development. Some of your colleagues infiltrated and vandalized a lab and stole proprietary information earlier this week. Now they've disappeared."

Which means we're on our own. "What's that got to do with us?"

"That's what we need to determine."

"I see. How long are we going to be in lockdown?"

"Until we have answers to our questions, ma'am. And until we find your colleagues."

"We have lives, Agent Smith," Sara objected. "I teach a college night class."

"You'll call in sick, ma'am."

"What about my family?" Mike asked mildly. "Am I gonna call in sick at home?"

"We'll take care of that, sir."

"Will you?"

Something in Mike's voice made Sara look down at him. His expression was opaque, his eyes narrowed. When their eyes met, she was pretty certain the moment had come. When Mike stood up, she was sure of it.

"You're right—I am calling in sick," he said. "From *here*. I'm sick of this place. I'm gonna go home."

The two MPs lifted their rifles and moved closer—into Mike's little den of mechanisms. The lab security man also drew his weapon and stepped between Sara's and Tim's workbenches.

Sara glanced over at Tim. The two moved away from their workstations in an instant as Tim threw a flicker of thought at his monitor, which exploded in a shower of sparks and a cloud of smoke. The security guard shouted and doubled over, trying to shield his face from the spray of metal and plastic.

The MPs flicked their rifles up. The one closest to Sara tracked her movement with the muzzle of his gun, shouting, "Don't move!" The other moved swiftly toward Mike, his gun already aimed at the engineer's head.

Tim glanced sharply at Sara's computer monitor; it blew out, showering the MP with debris. Above the man's head, the fluorescent lights shattered, raining bits of plastic, glass, and ceramic down on his head and shoulders. The room dimmed.

The second MP hesitated for only an instant. In that instant Mike made a move so subtle, Sara barely caught it. Fezzik the robot arm ceased its aimless rocking and swung wildly toward the MP. It caught him on the shoulder, knocking him down and ripping the weapon from his hands. He dove to retrieve it but tripped over a power cable that had snaked out of nowhere to whip around his ankles. He fell hard, entangled in cable. Tim laughed, and five more overhead lights blasted apart, forcing the fallen man to throw his hands over his head in defense.

The Smith had been backpedaling toward the doors during all of this. Now he turned and bolted.

"I don't think so," Sara said, and the doors slammed shut in the man's face.

The agent whirled back into the room, drawing his sidearm. Before he could unlatch the safety, an overhead beam fell with such force, it knocked the gun to the floor, almost taking his hand along with it.

"Sorry, pardner," Sara said with a smirk. "Guess you're not the fastest gun in this part of town."

The agent looked up from the fallen beam, raising his eyes to the three zetas.

"What are you people?"

"Right now, Agent Smith, we are the ones in control." Sara looked from Tim to Mike. "Time to shut them down, gentlemen."

Mike smiled very slightly, and all the lights went out, leaving the room in complete darkness.

Chapter 27

SANCTUARY

Chuck and his band of fugitives left Albuquerque International Sunport with Dice behind the wheel of the rental car, headed toward the closest auto mall. Next to him, in the front passenger seat, Chuck compulsively checked all his contact accounts for the third or fourth time since they'd picked up the rental. This time there was a LinkedIn message. From Matt.

"What does it say?" Dice asked.

"'A daring takeover has roiled the deep. They gotta catch some Z's.'"

"Takeover?" Dice repeated.

"Catch some Z's," said Lanfen from the backseat. "Some zetas . . . Do you think he means Sara's team has taken over Deep Shield? Is that possible?"

"Okay, okay, okay." The word was a chant, a prayer for something Chuck couldn't even articulate. He called Matt's number. It went direct to voicemail.

What had the zetas done? *Damn.*

"Damn," said Dice at the same moment Chuck thought it. "Check the rearview, Doc."

Chuck did, glancing up into the mirror. At first he didn't see it. Then Dice veered a bit toward the outer lane, and he did. Weaving out of the traffic two cars behind them—as if to keep their rented station wagon in sight—was a dark blue, late-model Mercedes.

"Are you sure that's . . . anything?" asked Chuck.

Dice signaled and pulled into the leftmost lane. Seconds later the Mercedes joined them. *Funny*, Chuck thought. *In the movies they always drive black SUVs. We got ourselves a tail with some taste.*

"I see it. Looks like we're being followed."

"How?" asked Mini. Her voice was high and tight, partly from fear but mostly exasperation. "How the hell did they find us?"

"I don't know," Dice said, "but I'm willing to bet they're better at this than we are. What do I do?"

Chuck took swift stock of the situation. They were on a four-lane boulevard heading out of town toward a local auto mall, where they had planned to buy a used car with the cash they'd withdrawn from their bank accounts. That plan would have to be scrapped if they couldn't shake the Benz. The area was newly built up; shiny new shopping centers lined both sides of the road. There was a particularly big mall on the left, with popular anchor stores and a parking garage at either end.

"Make a U-turn at the next light, fade into the right lane, and turn into that mall parking lot."

Dice nodded, gripping the wheel so hard his knuckles went white. He pulled the car into the left-turn lane without signaling; the dark Mercedes glided past them.

"Guy in the passenger seat looked right at us," said Eugene. His voice broke. "I'm pretty sure I saw a gun."

Dice tapped his foot on the floorboards, his eyes on the traffic light. "C'mon, c'mon, c'mon."

Chuck watched the Mercedes. It had sped up and was already signaling for a left turn at the next light. Dice's light turned green, and he made a hasty U-turn with a delicate squeal of the tires. Halfway up the block, he turned into the mall parking lot. Straight ahead was the mall's main entrance, with a three-story Nordstrom right behind it.

"Turn right," Chuck said, and Dice turned the car and headed it toward the Target, where the traffic was especially zoolike for a weekday.

"What're you thinking, Doc?" Dice asked, his eyes flicking to the rearview mirror.

"I'm thinking a parking garage might be just the place to get lost."

"Or trapped," said Dice. "What if there's more than one of them? They see us go in, they might be able to trap us as we come out."

Mini leaned forward between the front seats. "Don't go in."

"What do you mean?" Dice asked at the same moment Lanfen said, "I see them. They're coming up the main avenue."

Chuck glanced into the rearview mirror as the Mercedes turned right along the storefronts. It was coming right for them, much too fast for a shopping mall parking lot. He hoped no one would get hurt.

"Oh God," said Eugene.

Dice asked, "What should I do? Tell me what to do."

They were coming up swiftly on the entrance to the parking garage, with the Mercedes gaining on them. *What can the Deeps do?* Chuck wondered. Surely they couldn't whip out their guns and take them by force without witnesses calling 911. Even as he framed the thought, the man in the passenger seat of the Mercedes opened his window and perched a rotating light atop the car's roof.

Don't need to call the cops when they're already here, he thought with grudging admiration.

Mini bounced forward again and laid a hand on Dice's shoulder. "Drive by the garage and turn left at the end of the building."

"But what's—"

"Just do it!"

"Yes, ma'am."

Chuck turned to look out of the back window of the station wagon as Dice sailed by the parking garage's entrance. If anyone had asked him later what he had seen or felt, he couldn't have told them. From inside the car, it seemed as if the vehicle were squeezing out of its own skin, like some large, alien insect. The shed carapace went one way, turning left and disappearing into the dark maw of the parking garage; the real station wagon kept moving toward the corner of the Target store. Chuck couldn't shake the idea that he felt as if the ghostly vehicle passed straight through him.

As they negotiated the left-hand turn at the corner, Chuck saw the Benz sweep unhesitatingly left, following the decoy into the garage. He shifted his gaze to Mini. Her fierce focus evaporated so completely, she slumped against Lanfen's shoulder, panting a little.

"I had to let go of it after the first turn because I couldn't see any farther than that," she said. "But if we're lucky, they'll get lost in there looking for us."

Chuck wanted to laugh. Once more he was glad he had insisted on keeping Mini and her extraordinary gift in the program. He felt a warm rush of relief, which lasted only until he saw several more identical Mercedes-Benzes making their way purposefully toward their end of the mall from several different directions, cop lights rotating silently on their rooftops.

"Dice."

"I see them. Dammit." He swung the wheel hard right and drove up a row of parked cars.

One row over, one of the Deep Shield Mercedes passed them going the opposite direction. It sped up at the end of the aisle and careened around the corner in pursuit. A second joined the chase a moment later.

"Now what?" Dice asked.

"Now this," said Lanfen, her eyes narrowing.

Between their rental and its nearest pursuer, a car backed unexpectedly out into the aisle. The lead Mercedes swerved to avoid it, which put it right in the path of a second car that rolled out from the opposite side. As it squeaked by that obstacle, tires squealing, Lanfen mentally worked the mechanisms of three more cars, plunging them into the aisle: left, right, left. In a matter of moments, the route was completely blocked.

The Deeps driver slammed on his brakes, but it was too late. He collided violently with the rear of an unmoored pickup truck, inside of which a small dog yapped in frenzied outrage. The Mercedes behind it was no more successful; it slammed into the rear of the first car with enough force to set off half a dozen car alarms.

Chuck scanned the lot. They weren't out of it yet—a third Mercedes was barreling the wrong way up the next aisle over, obviously intending to cut them off at the top of their lane.

"There!"

Lanfen turned her head sharply in the direction he pointed. She pulled another quartet of vehicles out into the aisle to block the Mercedes's way. It scraped past them, leaving long scratches in its dark finish, and kept moving until another car pulled into the top of the row and met it head-on. Horns blared; brakes squealed. The Mercedes rocked to a stop, and Lanfen sent one last car careening into it broadside. More car alarms blared.

Dice juked left at the end of the aisle and fled the parking lot into the neighborhood behind the mall. No cars followed.

Lanfen exhaled. "Remind me to thank my dad for teaching me how to drive stick."

After that they drove in silence until they were a half mile from the auto mall, with no suspicious Mercedes-Benzes or other vehicles making appearances. Chuck's heart was still beating too fast.

"My God, that was close," murmured Dice, sweeping a shaking hand across his brow. "That was too close. You ladies are scary."

"Yes, they are," said Chuck, "and what they just did suggests the sort of uses the zeta wave can be put to, the sort of manipulation it allows. Think of General Howard—or any other paramilitary commander—with that sort of force."

"Imagine if our pursuers just now had been zetas."

Apparently no one wanted to imagine it. Dice immediately turned the subject to their next move. The rental car had clearly been identified; they needed to lose it. They avoided the high-traffic center of the auto mall and drove to a neighborhood peppered with smaller car lots. They parked the station wagon, left the keys in it, and walked three zigzag blocks to an independent used car lot that they chose by consensus.

They found a suitable vehicle within minutes—a silver Ford Escape hybrid. Perfect. Small, nondescript color, darkly tinted rear windows. There were thousands of them on the roads. Plus there was that word. *Escape.*

The group nominated Dice as their spokesperson, with Chuck as his second. While the two men tracked down a salesman, Mini stood sentry with Lanfen in the outdoor lot, where they pretended to be browsing for cars while really keeping their eyes on the street. Eugene stood just inside the lot's small showroom, watching the two women watch the roads.

Mini, Chuck noted, did not look like Mini. With the makeup and straightened hair, she actually looked her age or possibly five years older even. She looked like she could be a suburban mom out shopping for a Subaru instead of his friend's daughter.

My friend's daughter.

In their various layovers in airports, he had done some thinking about the friends and families they'd left behind. How long would they be away from them? What if Howard and his foot soldiers showed up on their doorsteps, hoping to pry information out of them?

Or worse.

His eyes sought Lanfen. She was standing near the Escape, wearing dark glasses and a soft hat into which she'd tucked all of her hair. She also slumped, looking nothing like a world-class martial arts expert. She looked lost. Her movements unsure, unfocused, and Chuck wondered how much of that was an act.

Chuck patted the cell phone in his jacket pocket. As soon as they were on the road, he'd call Matt again, try to find out what was going on. Try to get some sense of how bad it really was. Of what they'd unleashed by running and leaving Sara's team behind.

He pulled out of his reverie in time to hear Dice announce to the salesman that the hybrid was just what they were looking for, that its record looked clean, and that they'd be paying cash.

The salesman seemed surprised by this. He glanced from one of them to the other. "Family car?" he asked tentatively.

"Ski team," said Chuck without thinking about it. "We're heading to Oregon for a competition, but our old van broke down. We decided to pool our resources and buy something more trustworthy and newer."

"Skiing. Cool," the guy said, nodding. He indicated they should follow him into his glassed-in cubicle.

Chuck glanced out into the car lot and saw Lanfen jerk suddenly upright. She crossed to Mini's side and spoke urgently in her ear. Chuck felt the bottom drop out of his stomach. He caught Dice's gaze and gestured toward the front of the building.

"You've got this. I'm going to—" Chuck didn't finish the sentence but dashed across the showroom and out the front doors.

Eugene was already halfway across the car lot, heading for the Escape and the two women standing in its lee. Chuck ran the last several yards to join them.

"What's wrong? What is it?"

Lanfen nodded up the street. "Deeps. About a block north. Saw them crossing the intersection. Two cars, lights and all. They're trolling, Chuck. And if they find us, it's going to get very ugly, very quick—I doubt they care about keeping inconspicuous."

"Maybe," Eugene said, "we should all just go back inside the showroom."

Mini uttered a sharp cry and grasped Chuck's sleeve. He turned to find her pointing in the opposite direction down the street. Two more of the Mercedes-Benzes were approaching the intersection, slowing as they reached the corner.

"Don't stare at them, Min," Eugene whispered. He grabbed her arm and started to hustle her into the showroom.

"Too late," said Lanfen. "Too late."

The Deeps were moving, suddenly and with purpose, speeding across the intersection and up the street toward the dealership. There was nothing their quarry could do but stand and wait for the inevitable. There were no further illusions that Mini could use to save them, no machinery with which Lanfen could clog the street. She might block the driveway, but that was unlikely to stop them.

Chuck drew in a breath. It was over.

The two Deep Shield cars barreled up the street and past the entrance to the dealership without even checking their speed. They squealed around the corner to the north and disappeared up the cross street. A heartbeat later three more units sped toward the same intersection from the opposite direction, careened around the corner, and followed their comrades out of sight.

Chuck and company stood staring after them in stunned silence.

"Guys? What're you all looking at?"

Chuck turned. Dice was standing at the rear of the Escape with the keys dangling from his fingers.

"I'll tell you when we're on the road," Chuck said. "Let's go."

They were back on the road in minutes, heading for California. While the others explained the scare they'd had at the car dealership, but couldn't explain why the Deeps sped off, Chuck called Matt again. This time he got through.

"Got your message," was the first thing he said. "What happened?"

"Sara and her boys have taken over the Deep. Shut it down lock, stock, and computer system. And they've exiled the staff. All of them. And me. They've gone down into the core of the operation and are sitting in there like a trio of spiders in a web."

"Did they say why they're doing that?"

"Oh, yes. No doubt about that. Howard and his crew are evil with a capital *E*. They are not to be allowed to unleash their horrors on the world. So the zetas shut 'em down."

"Where are you?"

"Forward Kinetics. Howard's making do, I guess. He's taken over our offices. The zetas let enough vehicles go to transport the staff off the base. So we all loaded in and came here. They grounded all the aircraft, though. By the way, the Deeps were in the middle of a state nature preserve, believe it or not. Under a damn mountain."

"Makes a kind of perverse sense."

"Definitely. So where are you?"

"Sorry. I can't tell you that. We just narrowly escaped an ambush. I don't know how they knew—"

Matt lowered his voice and said, "They took my phone, which of course they'd bugged. They didn't get anything from the number, but they got a shitload from the background sounds in the call. They isolated the flight announcements and figured out which airport you were calling from, then they winnowed through all the booking data until they thought they had you."

"They almost did have us."

"I thought you were the naïve one in all this," Matt said quietly. "Looks like I was. Wherever you end up, do you have room for another defector?"

Chuck realized with leaden certainty that he didn't trust Matt. *Couldn't* trust him. "They're probably listening to this call."

"They can't. They're cut off from all that. It's gone. All their high-tech crap is in their secret hiding place. Hell, they even left my phone."

"And that doesn't seem suspicious?"

"Of course it's suspicious! But considering Sara and her guys have all their toys now, even if my phone is bugged, they aren't in a position to do anything about it now."

Despite what Matt was saying, Chuck couldn't help but hesitate. "Matt, look, it's better for all of us if I don't tell you where I am, better if you stick close to Howard."

There was a moment of silence on Matt's end. "You mean as a mole?"

"Something like that."

Matt exhaled noisily. "There's something you should know, Chuck. Howard has allies in high places. I know he's got someone at the Pentagon who feeds him intel. He also said you'd call. That you wouldn't be able to let go. You'd worry about me and the rest of the team."

"Howard was right. I need you there, Matt. I need to know what's happening with our people." That last part, at least, was the truth.

"I'm not sure what their intentions are. Sara's last message to Howard was cryptic. She gave him a verse of Scripture to look up in the Bible. Something about swords and plowshares."

"'And He shall judge among the nations, and shall rebuke many people: and they shall beat their swords into plowshares and their swords into pruning hooks: nation shall not lift up sword against nation, neither shall they learn war anymore,'" Chuck recited softly.

"Yeah. That one. I should've known you'd have it memorized. Or is it tattooed on your bicep?"

"Forgive me if I fail to find humor in the situation. What's Howard doing?"

"Tearing what's left of his hair out and making top-secret phone calls. I have no idea who to. I think he's trying to raise a covert army to fight the zetas. But how do you covertly attack a national parkland?"

"The same way you dupe a bunch of scientists into building him unstoppable weapons. Do you doubt he'll find a way?"

"No," Matt said. He hesitated before adding, "The thing is, if he can't get Deep Shield back, Chuck, he can't let it go. You realize that. If you're right about the nature of his operation, it would be better if it was wiped off the face of the earth than to let the world know what he was doing there."

They parted on that somber note, and Chuck sat for a moment, staring out the window of their new little SUV. The call had been on speakerphone, so everyone else had heard it, too.

Lanfen glanced over at him from behind the steering wheel. "That goes for us, too, doesn't it? He can't let us go."

"We could go public," said Eugene. "We could—"

"What? The alpha zetas are holding the fort, Euge, but it's a fort that doesn't exist on any map. We have no real proof that anyone would understand. If we're going to call out General Howard, we need to contact Sara. Right now I can't think of any way of making that happen. Not if they're barricaded in the Deep doing God knows what."

"Maybe they'll call him out," said Mini. "Maybe that's the plan."

"Maybe," said Chuck. "But we'll worry about that once we're safe."

"What makes you think we'll ever be safe?" asked Mini, finally putting into words what they surely had all been wondering. "They had us back there. But then they just ran. Why?"

It was a question none of them could answer.

THEY REACHED CALIFORNIA EARLY THE next morning and went directly to the CalTech campus, where they deposited the car in a covered parking structure. The stress was numbing. Every other vehicle was suspect; every pulse of chopper blades made them hold their collective breath. They had kept the radio on, tuned to local news stations, listening for news of something that might have transpired back east. There was nothing. That, too, was nerve rattling.

Now, with the car well hidden and the team spread out within sight of each other between the garage and the campus core, Chuck hoped to be able to make it to his friend's offices in the Beckman Institute. The building was visible from the parking garage—was the closest one to it, in fact. Just shy of entering the institute, Chuck looked back. Dice sat on a bench along the walk. Eugene hunkered cross-legged on the grass a bit farther on, apparently reading. Lanfen was stationed just outside the garage. Mini was with the car in case it needed a quick makeover. Students and faculty moved unwittingly past them, bestowing a glance, maybe a smile. None showed undue interest, though the girls garnered some admiring looks.

Chuck took a deep breath and dove into the interior of the Beckman Institute. Looking extremely nervous, Dr. Douglas Boston appeared from a hallway across the lobby, holding out his hand. He was tall, spare, and had gleaming black dreadlocks. He didn't look as if he'd aged a day since college.

"Dr. Charles." He greeted Chuck using the name they'd agreed on and shook his hand before taking him down the first-floor hallway to his private office. Once inside, he motioned Chuck to a small conference table by a set of floor-to-ceiling bookshelves and sat down across from him, concern in every angle of his face.

"Thanks for this, Doug. For being willing to take us in."

"Good God, Chuck, what's going on?"

"In broad strokes? As I told you earlier, a paramilitary agency I now believe is not part of the U.S. government hired us to do a project for them."

"Relating to your research with brain waves?"

"Yes. We signed a contract that was supposed to limit what kind of work we'd do with them—and what they could do with *it*—but now they want it all. They want *us* all, willing or not, to provide them with training, technology, and material support for purposes I believe will ultimately harm rather than help our country."

"Do you think the government is aware—"

"I don't know, but I think this is a worst-case scenario, Doug. This is an out-of-control group with incredible power."

Doug studied him for a moment, then asked, "What sort of power are we talking about? The last I saw, you had people manipulating software and controlling some simple machines. Has something changed since then?"

Chuck considered what he was about to do. He hadn't shown anyone what he was about to show Doug. Not Dice. Not Eugene. Not even Lanfen.

Next to Doug's bookshelves was an antique orrery made of buffed bronze, with its sun and planets picked out in gleaming brass and silver. Chuck pointed it out for Doug and turned his head toward it, considered the joints, the pivot points, the weight. Then gave it a mental push. The orrery moved slightly, the tiny planets swinging about in their orbits, the central orb rotating on its axis.

"Jesus," said Doug, twisting sideways in his chair to stare at the suddenly kinetic model.

"No. Not Jesus. Just me. Weird old Chuck Brenton. And trust me when I say I am by far the least skilled of anyone on my team who's undergone the training."

"The training? You can *train* people to do this?"

"Yes. It requires working through intermediary agencies at first, but, yes, it's learned. Some people have more trouble getting it than others, but we've yet to have any complete failures."

"How many?"

"Well, that's the thing. I'm not sure. I have two women with me who are adept. Back in Baltimore there are three more members of my team who didn't make it out. And there are the people this organization had us train in various disciplines. Dozens of them."

Doug's eyes went back to the orrery, so Chuck gave it another push. Too hard a push, as it happened; it wobbled on its stand, and the professor had to reach out and stop it from toppling over.

"Sorry," Chuck said. "I haven't quite gotten the hang of it yet."

Doug steadied the orrery, then looked back up at Chuck. "These other people who can do telekinesis—"

"Zetas. We call them zetas because they harness zeta waves."

"These paramilitary zetas are after you?"

Chuck nodded.

"What do you need?"

That was the Doug Boston he remembered from college; any threat to the sanctity of intellectual freedom, and he became the watchdog of creativity.

"We need someplace to lie low for a while. Just until we can figure out what to do."

Doug smiled, his teeth gleaming white in his face. "I've got just the place."

"JUST THE PLACE" WAS A beach house in Marina del Rey. It had belonged to Doug's parents and now served as his bolt hole when he needed to write. It had three bedrooms, all the modern conveniences, and—most important—a garage in which Chuck and his team could stash the SUV. Chuck doubted the Deeps had made the vehicle, but it never hurt to be cautious.

He called Matt once they were settled into the beach house, but couldn't reach him. He fretted and tried again several hours later from a second burner phone he'd purchased. Still no response. He hoped that only meant Matt was with company.

Eugene and Mini went out to round up food and additional clothing. They all made further plans over dinner. Chuck knew the beach house couldn't last. He couldn't do that to Doug. They needed a new start. They needed a complete change of identity. The problem was he had absolutely no idea how to go about that.

And while Dice and Eugene had some ideas—and both were better than competent programmers—neither was a hacker by any stretch of the imagination. Still, it was better than nothing.

At ten on their second night in the house, as the team sat around the living room making lists of assets and resources, Chuck got a message on his LinkedIn account. All it said was "Check the news."

Chilled, Chuck made a mental grab at the TV remote where it sat on the coffee table. It shifted a little then fell to the floor. He took a deep breath. He was really going to have to work on that.

"Chuck," said Eugene quietly. "Is there something you'd like to tell the rest of us?"

They were all staring at him. "Later," he said. "Matt says we should check the news."

Eugene fielded the remote and turned on CNN. There was a chemical leak in Arkansas. "I don't—" he started to say.

"Oh my God, the crawler!" said Lanfen. "Look at the crawler!"

Breaking news: Aircraft from all East Coast air force bases grounded. Pentagon says investigation is under way. Cites possibility of computer malfunction.

The next crawler was equally alarming:

Michaux State Forest and Game Preserve evacuated. Authorities cite potential terrorist threat.

Dice turned to Chuck. "Matt said the Deeps were in a wildlife area, under a mountain. Could that be our zetas?"

"Must be. They screwed with the bases' computer systems so as not to be flushed out from above, and Howard's cordoned off the area to move in with a ground attack."

"D'you think his recruits can get in?"

"Maybe. But only if they can move mountains."

Chapter 28

STALEMATE

Sara looked around General Howard's command center with a sense of satisfaction that she'd never before experienced. They'd restored power to the core of the facility but kept a perimeter of defenses up—steel fire doors and airtight bulkheads. Their bunker was many stories beneath a mountain, they knew, having sampled the surveillance cameras, which they'd also restored to working condition.

Sara reached out through the network of computers and digital connections and savored the feeling of connectedness it gave her. She had tentacles of thought that reached far beyond this massive hole in the ground. She'd used those to good advantage when the air force had scrambled jets to fight a potential terrorist threat in the heart of this wild area. They'd been amazed by how quickly Howard had been able to effect that; he must have been prepared for the contingency of having to get the real military involved and had contacts he could call in. She'd asked Tim to see if he couldn't find evidence of that in his own travels through

354 / PATRICK HEMSTREET

the computer system. It would be useful to know the scope of Howard's network. So far all he'd been able to ascertain was that Leighton Howard was a security consultant to the Pentagon.

But they *had* discovered his first contingency plan in case the Deep was overrun: there were enough explosives planted in the labs to collapse the whole mountain. Mike had disabled most of these mechanisms of destruction along with the gun turrets dotted along the entryway, and Tim had cheerfully deleted any and all computer code that made remote triggering of the devices possible. General Howard (if he was really a general) could punch buttons and send pings until the sky fell, and the mountain would remain intact.

It was amazing how integrated military infrastructure was—and how archaic. Shutting down the air force bases had been easy, and it had made Sara think of that verse in Isaiah. She and Mike and Tim were in a unique position. They could literally force the beating of swords into plowshares. They could bring peace to the world. Or, conversely, they could start wars that would destroy it.

"Howard's trying to reach us again," Tim said. "He wants to talk."

"I'm sure he does," Sara said. "I'll talk to him when we all know how to stop bullets." She hesitated, feeling her way along the pathway they'd used to bring the bases to ground. "Did you know that these digital trails lead to all our international installations? I should have realized . . ."

Tim, sitting at a workstation at the core of the command center, looked up at the huge plasma screens that ran in rows across the curving front of the room. In a moment a map appeared on them, a tracery of lines running from the bright spot that was Deep Shield out to other hubs of activity, and from there . . .

"Hell, you're right. It's amazing. And they—" He broke off,

eyes half-closing, a frown creeping across his face. "They're rounding up jets from Ramstein, and . . . huh, well, that's not good." His gaze flicked back to the map. On the dark bulk of Europe, several of the bright hubs of light dimmed. "That takes care of that. And I wonder what *that* is." He stood and moved toward the big map, pointing to dimmer lines running to dimmer clusters of digital activity.

"Those," said Sara, tracing the lines mentally, "are German facilities that share some connections with the U.S. ones."

Tim glanced back and grinned. "Cool," he said and shut those down, too.

"HAVE YOU SEEN THIS?" DICE asked, shifting the laptop so Chuck could see the screen. "The UN Security Council is in complete meltdown. Just in the last forty-eight hours, military installations have been going dark all over the world. Governments are pointing fingers at each other, accusing one another of hacking and worse. It's nuts."

"Is there any way we can reach them?" Lanfen asked. "The alpha zetas, I mean."

"How?" asked Dice. "We don't have cell phone numbers for them anymore. We tried messages on social media. If we're going to talk to them, they're going to have to find a way to reach us."

"In the meantime, though, we have to decide what *we're* going to do," Eugene said. "We obviously can't squat here forever."

"We need to find a place to set up shop," Chuck said, "and a way to contact Sara and get real evidence against Howard. Our only hope is to expose him. If we go about it the wrong way, we'll end up in prison, and he'll be free to deploy his army. Whatever the alphas are doing, they're at least keeping that from happening. But you're right—we can't just sit here. We have to move soon."

The house phone rang. Mini answered it and handed the receiver to Chuck. "It's your friend Doug."

"Hi, Doug, what's—"

Doug cut him off. "Someone's looking for you, Chuck. Someone left an anonymous message saying you're going to have visitors, then some guy claiming to be from the CIA called to ask if I'd been in contact with you. Naturally I lied and said I hadn't seen you since the neuroscience convention a few years back and hadn't talked to you since last summer. Both of which were true until this week. They left me a number. Asked me to contact them if I heard from you. When I seemed hesitant, they told me it was a matter of national security."

"It is," Chuck told him. As he set the receiver back in the cradle, he realized he'd made a decision—some shadows were simply darker than others. He pulled Lorstad's card out of his pocket and dialed the number on his burner phone.

"What's happened, Chuck?" Lanfen asked, watching his face.

"We have to get out. Now."

"How?"

"I don't know. But I hope I know someone who does."

The call connected immediately. "Lorstad," said the man on the other end.

"Mr. Lorstad, this is Chuck Brenton.

"I need your help."

Chapter 29

LOCKDOWN

Matt had a new laptop. He'd paid cash. It was compact enough to fit into a small shoulder bag, and he never let it out of his sight. He'd backed up every bit of important data to an external hard drive and no longer stored anything critical to his private work in the cloud, on the theory that someone might hack his account. He knew the Deeps couldn't do anything at that point; they were completely cut off from their base of operations and all their slick tech. They had only human surveillance at their disposal, but they were working very hard to reestablish themselves.

The news stories bleated about a "terrorist action" that resulted in some sort of environmental disaster at Michaux State Preserve. Clearly Howard had gotten some cover story into circulation, but he seemed to have nothing to do with the government's reaction. Matt suspected that Howard's contact at the Pentagon was at a fairly low level. He even thought he might know who it was: the guy he'd originally contacted about Forward Kinetics—Schell or Snell or something like that.

The Deeps had let all but the technical staff go and kept Brenda's robotics team working ten- and twelve-hour days to build new units. Matt was less a working member of the team than a hostage, but after the first week of watching him with an eagle eye, Howard mostly ignored him. He was a tool of limited use as far as the general was concerned. In fact, his only real duty was to set up as many Brewster-Brentons as they had on hand so Reynolds and the other class leaders could use them to train more troops.

That was problematic. Whatever Howard had been doing to recruit potential adepts was not providing him with huge numbers of them. He had a small standing army or militia, which Matt was beginning to suspect was actually a group of mercenaries, but one of the best-kept secrets about Howard's operation, he had discovered, was that it had far less manpower than it first appeared. Thus the charm of an army of robots: it was clear Howard had intended his drivers to eventually control multiple bots deployed as teams.

So while Howard scrambled to acquire new resources, the zetas were wreaking havoc on all things military. They had shut down anything that flew—including on international bases—and seemed immediately aware of any attempt to pry them out from under their mountain. Howard had pulled out all the stops and, in his legitimate capacity as a consultant, had somehow managed to sell the Pentagon on the idea that there really was some terrorist organization at work beneath Michaux's tree-covered slopes.

One thing Matt was sure of—Howard had come to the same conclusion he had about the alpha zetas: only other zetas could combat them. Howard had also quickly tumbled to the fact that without their robots, his handpicked, combat-ready telekinetics could do very little against those who had trained them. That gave him two options, as far as Matt could see. One: he could try to get his zetas close enough to the Deep to gain access to their robots and try to assault Sara's team from the inside. Two: he could locate and capture Chuck and his team.

The latter seemed like a long shot to Matt. He was in touch with the escapees and had no idea where they were. That Howard did seemed unlikely . . . until Brenda passed Matt a terse note: "Deeps deploying agents to Pasadena, CA."

He was in her lab to calibrate a Brewster-Brenton unit to the robot interface at the time. The six-word scribble, wedged between the Brewster-Brenton and its frame, had sent his mind scrambling. Of course. Chuck had earned his first degree from CalTech. Had spoken about a friend there—a college colleague whose name Matt couldn't quite recall.

"When?" he mouthed to Bren.

She held up three fingers and mouthed, "Hours."

He finished up his work on the unit and took himself and his laptop off to a local bistro for lunch, his "security" sitting not so discreetly by the door. A brief surf of the Web, and he had it: Dr. Douglas Boston. Chuck had said he was a character. He looked more like a reggae musician than a college professor.

Cloaked in the ambient noise of the restaurant, Matt used his shiny new burner phone to call the neuroscientist's office. The professor was in class, so he left a message: "Tell our mutual friend he's going to have scary visitors." He didn't leave his name.

Then he sat back to think. Only zetas could even hope to corral other zetas. Even with Mini and Lanfen, though, Matt wondered if Chuck had enough coercive power to stop the Deeps from whatever they were ultimately planning to do. They might be all "swords into plowshares" now, but if they were threatened, or their loved ones were threatened . . .

He suddenly thought of Mike's wife and kids. *What has happened to them?*

There was one solution to this escalating situation, and it was Chuck Brenton. Matt was certain the zetas trusted Chuck and his team. He knew they'd been passing intel back and forth in the last days before Team Chuck's great escape. If this was going to end without serious disruption of world communication at best and carnage at worst, someone had to find Chuck. That someone, Matt decided, had better be him. If Howard found him first . . . Well, it didn't bear thinking about.

This left Matt with a dilemma. He couldn't leave Maryland without being followed, and no matter the semblance of freedom afforded him, he knew he was under constant surveillance. If he succeeded in finding Chuck and his team, it was a safe bet that Howard would be right there to scoop them all up.

"Dr. Streegman."

Matt looked up. Brian Reynolds, dressed casually in civvies, stood looking down at him. Behind him, lounging in the door-way of the café, was a female officer Matt had seen around Deep Shield HQ. She, too, was dressed in civilian garb.

"Doctor," Reynolds told him, "I need you to come with me. We've found the missing group. We may need you to help bring them in."

Matt said the first thing that came into his head:

"Hell, no."

"I really don't think you have a choice, sir."

Matt wanted to hit him. "Fine. Then I have no choice. So much for this being a free country."

"You signed a contract, sir, which your partner is in breach of. Consider this part of your contractual obligation."

"Contracts? You're talking about contracts?" Matt laughed out loud. "You can't kidnap someone for breaching a contract—you sue them. If you want to go see a judge, let's go."

Reynolds was impassive. "Dr. Streegman, I'm not going to ask you again."

"Screw you," Matt muttered under his breath. Then he gathered up his gear and followed Reynolds and his companion from the café.

MIKE WATCHED THE ADVANCING TROOPS with a bizarre mixture of dread and anger. His family was safe, that much he knew; his wife had messaged him through the number Tim had given her. But that they'd had to flee to his parents' in Canada, that they'd had to flee the home he'd built for them—the home they had been renovating since his work at Forward Kinetics had drastically increased his income—that was galling and terrifying. This sort of thing shouldn't happen in America. It was so wrong on so many levels, Mike couldn't begin to articulate it. Anyway he was done articulating. He'd let his actions do the talking.

The man who had caused the uprooting of his family was now sending troops after them. That they thought they could sneak up on the mountain fortress Howard had built was incredible. Mike could only imagine they assumed that the zetas would not know how to make use of the Deep Shield surveillance systems.

He smiled grimly. They did know and were prepared to prove it.

"How close are we gonna let them get?" Tim asked. He was rocked back in his chair at the console he had adopted as his own. His gaze, like Mike's, was on the red dots that represented the two hundred or so soldiers working their way up the mountain. The red dot soldiers blipped through the trees and down the long, broad tunnel that provided egress and regress for the Deeps' vehicles.

Sara stood at the center of the large, half-moon chamber, her eyes roving from one huge plasma display to another, tracking the invaders. Several of the screens showed live, real-time images of the advancing troops sent from stationary cameras and drones that Tim had sent out to snoop.

"They've reached the secondary perimeter," she said. "It's time to stop them."

"Cool," Tim said, grinning.

He turned to watch Sara for a few moments, though the real show was occurring outside. As she concentrated, things began to happen. Bad things—at least for General Howard's troops.

On the mountain slopes, barrier fences sprang up from the ground, blocking the way for the advancing army. As they halted in momentary confusion, Tim took over.

On the view screen, the game programmer revealed a talent that Mike and Sara had no idea he possessed. Instead of just mentally operating the double gun turret nearest the video drone— which was outfitted with a machine gun and flamethrower—he reconfigured its mechanisms and changed it into the shape of a scaly, metallic dragon. It spat out bullets, blocking and containing some of the oncoming troops, and then used the flamethrower portion to belch out balls of fire, setting the forest ablaze. The scene erupted into chaos. Camouflaged bodies fell, flew, and caught on fire. Bright splashes and smears of red jarred against the colors of earth and tree trunk. It was like a number of video games he had designed, only more lifelike; Mike could almost smell the charred human flesh on-screen. He twisted to squint at the tactical display. Had some of the red dots winked out?

He returned to the real-time views from Tim's drones and saw men withdrawing, burnt and bloodied. He saw one booted foot emerging from a pile of leaves and bark. He saw abandoned weapons strewn on the forest floor.

"Tim . . ."

"Watch this!"

Another double-turret-turned-dragon appeared some yards away, loosing its bullets and fiery barrage. On one screen soldiers ran and tumbled and shouted and screamed; on the other more red dots disappeared.

Tim laughed. "Tremble before the great and terrible Smaug!"

The majority of the troops were now in full retreat, dragging their wounded away.

"Okay, Tim. They're going," Mike said. "You can stop."

He didn't stop. Rounds of bullets and flaming breaths roared from the dragon's mouth. Hell had been unleashed on the mountainside. And Tim's fury would not end until the ammo ran out.

Mike found himself laboring for breath. In a horrific way, Tim reminded him of his son, Anton—a child playing with toy soldiers. Only this was not a game, and those were not some plastic pieces fleeing down the mountain. Mike said nothing more, though; they had a more immediate problem: the attackers on the surface had been repelled, but those who had made it into the tunnel were still advancing. They came cautiously along the road, several Humvees in their rear guard, weapons at the ready. Where they met each of the huge shield doors that Sara had closed to keep them out, they employed manual override codes and kept on coming.

Tim was covered in sweat. His metallic dragons had morphed back into now-empty turrets, and he was no longer smiling. "I got nothin' left, Sara," he told her. "The doors are the big thing in the tunnel, and they've got the hardware codes for those."

"Shooting blanks, Timmy? I guess it's time for a woman to take charge."

She studied the structure of the shield doors, her gray eyes hard and narrowed until she hit upon the solution: the soldiers couldn't override a system that was broken.

Sara moved to stand directly before the view screen that displayed the troops advancing toward the next shield door. After that, she knew, there was only one more. The manual controls for each door were to its left, behind a thick metal panel. She knew what was in there; she'd studied not only the architecture but the interior workings. As the leader of the troops approached the barrier, Sara—arms crossed and eyes closed—simply reached into the door mechanism and twisted. When the soldiers opened the control compartment, they found warped scrap metal. While they digested that reality, Sara blew the hydraulic lift mechanism along the top of the door apart bolt by bolt.

Mike exhaled sharply. Surely they would turn back now.

But they didn't. The leader of the Deep Shield troops ordered a shoulder-mounted rocket launcher to the fore.

"What are they doing?" Mike murmured. "They shouldn't do that."

"It won't work," Sara said. "I've studied the schematics of this place. That door is too thick. They'd need something far more powerful than that rocket launcher."

"They're not aiming at the door, dammit," Mike said.

They fired the portable rocket launcher—once, twice, three times—at the top of the shield door—right at the spot where one of the huge bolts bored into the weakened rock. The third time, the rock above it began to crumble, loosening a patter of stones, some as big as baseballs. Soldiers shouted and began to retreat. Too late. The rock of the tunnel's ceiling groaned, and the patter became a hail of stones the size of men's heads.

Above the soldiers a cleft opened in the roof of the tunnel. The rocky hail became an avalanche. There was a roar like the passing of a freight train, and dust and debris blinded the camera's eye. When the dust began to clear, the shield door was still intact, but the zetas could see that at least half of the recruits had gone down under the rocks. Blood ran in tiny rivers and pooled on the tunnel floor.

They got a good look at the carnage before the lights in the tunnel flickered and went out. Troops screamed and called for help in the dark.

Mike glanced at Sara and saw her gazing back, her face resolute, her eyes glittering. His lips felt numb. His whole body felt numb. "What do we do? Sara, what do we do?"

She shunted the view to a different set of cameras to see if they could make out anything. "Nothing. They'll have to count on their own people—whoever's left—to get them out. I just hope they've learned their lesson."

"But they're injured."

Sara turned on him. "Mike, think. What are our options? The shield door is wrecked. Even if I could raise it, what purpose would that serve? We're not doctors. We can't help them, and we'd only end up losing control of this place."

"I think some of us have lost control already."

Sara's glare was expected. What surprised him was Tim's laughter. "You think I lost control, buddy? You're wrong. I've never had so much control in my life. You'll see. You realize what's next after the doors, right?"

Mike was all too aware of what came next. His insides quaking, he knew he didn't want to do what Tim and Sara had just done. He also knew he had no choice.

"There!" Sara was staring into the security monitor. In the tunnel, barely lit by a backup generator, she could make out images of soldiers scurrying forward. She wasn't sure just how many were left. But she was sure of one thing. "Mike, you've got to stop them. Now."

FROM A SAFE DISTANCE DOWN the mountain, General Howard watched the shaky footage of the video feed. Reynolds and the surviving soldiers were making their way through the tunnel. In minutes they would be at the last remaining door—the one barrier left before the inner sanctum.

Reynolds was in front, the camera mounted to his helmet, sending back black-and-white images like some low-budget attempt at an indie horror film. Except the horror was real.

Surefooted and stealthy, he was advancing like a ninja after having climbed up the avalanched rocks, atop the bodies of his fallen comrades, and over the previous shield door. Reynolds knew the Deep Shield compound by heart. Knew it almost as well as Howard did. Even in the darkness.

But then there was a brilliant flash, and the tunnel wasn't dark anymore.

IN THE CONTROL ROOM, MIKE was leaning on his workstation for support. His palms were pressed hard against the desktop, and his arms were locked tight. Shoulders stiff, he hunched forward to peer at the monitor's grainy images: the camouflaged backs of a few remaining soldiers as they beat a hasty retreat back down the tunnel.

"Not a bad hit, but I don't feel like your heart was truly in it, Mikey." Tim swiveled his chair to give Mike his full attention and a grin that only a mother could love—if she were Mrs. Manson. "This next one's the money shot, baby. Make it count. Keep your mind on your missile and your missile on your mind."

"Tim, cut the commentary." Sara was regarding Mike out of the corner of her eye. He'd always been the calm one, like her. Under control. But now he looked about ready to snap. And when he did, she knew, it could go either way.

"Mikey, how you holding up?"

"How am I holding up, Sara?" He turned his full face toward her. She could see the veins protruding just above his temples. It reminded her half of her father, half of Frankenstein's monster. Or was that redundant? "I just shot a missile into a group of adolescents pretending to be soldiers."

"They aren't adolescents, Mike."

"No? I'm willing to bet that half of them have less body hair than our friend Tim here."

"Hey, I can't help it that I'm naturally smooth. And the rest I manscape. Wanna see, Sara?" She shot him a look. "It's like the gardens of Versailles in my shorts."

"Okay, that's enough." Sara slammed her fists down on the console. "Mike, why don't you peel your crying eyes away from the soap opera on that screen and take a look over here?"

She was standing in front of a display showing the air force bases they had recently disabled. Some of the blips had come back to life.

"See those red lights there? CFB North Bay is back up and running. Goose Bay, too. Both house U.S. aircraft. CFB North Bay is in Ontario." Sara turned to face him. "Your family's in Ontario, aren't they, Mike?" She turned her attention back to the screen. "Look at Russia. A few of their bases are also operational now."

Mike wasn't looking at the display. His eyes were closed. His head hung down.

Sara went on. "You saw the same newsfeeds I did about different governments blaming each other for shutting down their military installations. You heard what Russia said about attacking any target thought to be a threat."

Mike slowly lifted his head. As he did, a large missile launcher breached the ground in the tunnel below, rising up out of the earth like a colossus standing before the final door and shedding dirt and rocks off its drab metal skin.

Mike's eyes were still squeezed shut, as if that would stop Sara's words from entering his brain. "The sooner we end this thing with Howard, the quicker we can set things right out in the real world," she continued unceasingly. "No military strikes. No bombs. No collateral damage. No civilians killed in places like . . . let's say, for instance, Ontario, Canada."

Mike opened his eyes; they looked harder than before, dilated, as if all the color had been drained out. At the same time, the missile launcher's hatch slid open, and it stared like a Cyclops, unblinking, focused only on its target straight ahead.

Mike's gaze was fixed on the security monitor in front of him. But before Tim and Sara could make out what he was seeing, they felt it underneath their feet. The ground rumbled as an upgraded Hawk missile ripped through the air below, hitting its mark while the soldiers backtracked through the tunnel, hoping to reach safety outside its mouth. They never made it. Not even close.

The blast tore limbs from bodies, tore down the last shield door used for defense, and turned out every light in the entire compound.

Mike's security monitor went blank. Howard's video feed died. And all of Deep Shield was oddly dark and still for a few seconds. Until the silence was broken by the slow, steady sound of Tim's clapping.

Chapter 30

THOSE WHO TRESPASS AGAINST US

Matt stood on the sun-drenched street next to one of the Deeps' vehicles. His eyes were trained on the ridgepole of a beach house that sat just below the roadway in Marina del Rey. A Deep Shield officer, armed and deceptively casual, stood next to him. They both wore flak jackets under windbreakers. Why, he had no idea. The thought of Chuck Brenton posing a danger to anyone was ludicrous.

"Car's still in the garage." The crackly voice came from his guard's walkie-talkie.

Matt tensed. They hadn't gotten his message. They hadn't run. They were still inside. He wasn't sure whether to be relieved or terrified.

He heard a commanding voice shout out, "Government agents! Open up!"

Then nothing.

He heard the door go down.

There was more shouting: "Government agents! Show yourselves!"

More nothing.

His guard's walkie-talkie said, "There's no one here."

Matt all but collapsed against the side of the vehicle. Chuck and his little team of unlikely runaways had gone rogue again. But how? And where?

SARA STOOD IN THE MIDDLE of the command center. She hadn't moved since the lights went out. The darkness made her aware of something she hadn't experienced in a long time: a feeling of vulnerability.

"We have to do something about this."

"If the generators are fried, there's nothing we can do," Tim said. "We won't have anything to work with."

"I don't care," she snapped, her voice getting louder, sharper. "We need some damn lights in here!"

And suddenly there they were: two red lights about six feet off the ground, coming toward them. Followed by another pair of glowing red orbs. And another.

"Shit," Tim said. "Some of them must have gotten in."

The three robots were advancing steadily through the darkness, aided by their infrared vision. Sara cursed under her breath. Her team's body heat was giving them away. In this arena the mere fact of being human—of actually being alive—was a weakness. Or could the robots smell their fear?

The lights of the monitors flickered on behind them. "I found one," Mike said. "One backup wasn't damaged." These were the first words he'd spoken since wiping out most of General Howard's troops.

Sara wished he hadn't said them. Wished he hadn't found a working generator. Because even in the half-light, she was better off not seeing what was in front of her.

Two of the bots were sturdy and muscular, though the muscle, of course, was all man-made. They reminded her of those old muscle cars, Chevelles and Chargers, all beefed-up metal and chrome with mean-looking grilles and who knew how much power under their hoods. She almost expected to hear them revving their engines. The softly insistent whirring was somehow worse.

One bot had its right arm raised, ending in something that looked like a cavalry saber—one long, sharp, perfect piece of metal that could slice through the human body like it was no more than deli meat. The other held its left arm out, showing a hand that resembled a Stryker crossbow. Both were perfect weapons for maximal short-range attacks with minimum collateral damage to the control center. Sara realized that if there was anything good about this scenario, it was that General Howard was in charge. It was obvious he still cared about saving as much of his investments in Deep Shield as he possibly could—physical, financial, emotional, and otherwise. *Human weakness,* she thought with a smirk.

The third, taller droid was more like Lanfen's Bilbo—agile rather than angular, sleek instead of squat. A fu-bot without any weapons . . . except for its entire body.

The most remarkable thing about any of the robots, of course, was that there wasn't an operator in sight.

The zetas were stock-still for a moment, like the subjects in some ancient frieze depicting a civilization that had been snuffed out long ago. Then in a flash, they came to life and did the first thing that teams of people tend to do.

They split up.

Tim ducked behind the console station, the bow-bot in pursuit. Sara sprinted to the far end of the control room; it was darker there, yes, but she wanted to put as much distance between her and the fu-bot as possible. Mike, counterintuitively, ran toward his attacker, sidestepping the saber-wielding droid like it was a defensive tackle and then heading out the door.

"Coward," Tim called after him before turning to face his own assailant full-on. From his place behind the monitors, he had barely enough light to see the robot raise its arm, aiming the weapon straight at his head. And he had barely enough time to . . .

No. He had no time left at all.

The bolt shot from the crossbow, traveling a short distance before piercing the skull and entering the brain. Tim fell to his knees, motionless.

For a few moments, nothing stirred in the near darkness.

Then Tim raised his arms in triumph. "Fucktards!" he shouted. "I know the workings of a crossbow with my eyes closed. I reached level eighty in World of Warcraft using that same weapon. Didn't they realize how easy it would be for me to make it shoot backward?"

He looked at the robot standing above him. The bolt was still lodged in the control center in its head. Delivered from a few feet away, the shot would have been easily deflected by the armor casing, but at such short range it was fatal, causing the system to short-circuit.

Sara was too busy to take part in Tim's victory celebration. She was facing the fu-bot fifty feet away from her, doing her best stare-down, like a fighter at a weigh-in who knows she's outclassed. The robot's eyes dipped for a moment to waist height before straightening up again; it had bowed to its opponent. She wasn't sure of the significance of this gesture but figured it was similar to saying grace before devouring a meal.

The robot charged, and Sara swallowed hard. From a full sprint, it suddenly started sailing through the air, ready to deliver one fatal flying kick to her chest. It had perfect form and precise aim as it homed in on its target. But there was one thing it hadn't counted on.

"Watch out for that wall."

From her corner of the control room, Sara caused one of the steel panels to disconnect from its girder and enfold her in a partial cocoon. In fewer than two seconds, a wall stood where there once had been none—just as easily as when she was building virtual houses—and the fu-bot connected full-on, fracturing its foot. The impact caused half its leg to snap off, and Sara practically winced; the sound was so much like breaking bones. The limb lay on the floor like discarded scrap metal, the foot damaged beyond repair, the rest of it unscathed up until the severed knee joint. The fu-bot had landed several inches away, prone and unmoving; its head was twisted to one side at an awkward angle, and the lights of its eyes had gone out.

Sara stepped from her hiding place and walked up to the body. She bent over to examine the metallic spine and cable tendons at the base of its skull, where some multicolored wires had come loose.

"I guess the great Daisuke Kobayashi's designs aren't as great as we tho—"

The fu-bot's eyes flicked on. Its head locked into place, and its right arm shot up, catching Sara by the throat. She could feel the pressure on her windpipe as its hand closed as tightly as a pincer.

Sara stared into the robot's lifeless red orbs. She stared until she felt herself starting to black out. Then she closed her eyes and concentrated.

The severed leg flew into the air then came down hard on the fu-bot's neck, sticking straight up like a spear. The jagged knee joint had cut through the cable tendons, causing partial decapitation. The red orbs were extinguished.

Sara ripped its claw from around her throat and breathed in deeply before delivering a kick that made its head fly off.

"Goooooooaaaaaaaaaalll!" Tim called from the center of the room, where Sara soon joined him.

With the light of the monitors, they could see Mike's challenger standing by the door, frozen. It was still holding its sword, which had a slightly wet, pinkish sheen.

"I wonder what happened to Mike," Sara said as they moved closer.

"Forget him. I wonder what happened to this robot."

It was in pristine condition, at least on the surface. The same could not be said for Mike when he reentered the room.

"Nothing happened to the robot. I just . . . shut it down."

The other two zetas said nothing. They stared at his face, beaten to a pulp. At his knuckles, bloodied and bruised. At his side, where his white shirt was turning red.

He noticed their looking down to where he was holding his torso. "That damn droid nicked me on my way out."

"You call that a nick? I get nicks from a shave, not a saber. I'd say that's more like a gaping wound," Tim offered.

"Who you kidding?" Mike said, walking past him. "You don't shave."

Sara was still standing by the doorway, shaken by Mike's appearance, most of all his eyes. They looked dead. Inhuman. Almost robotic.

"How did you shut down that droid?" she asked, almost not wanting to hear the answer.

"I figured if our students were the ones controlling them,

they'd have to be close by. Even with practicing behind our backs, their powers without an interface couldn't be too strong yet."

"So you . . ."

"Went to the source."

"What does that mean?" Sara pressed.

"It means he went animal on their asses," Tim said with some respect.

Mike slumped down at the monitor station, still clutching his side. "Sara, no," he warned when he noticed her walking toward the hallway. "Trust me . . . you don't want to go out there."

"Are they all . . . ?"

He struggled to sit upright. "They told me just before . . . before I . . . They told me that Reynolds is here, too, somewhere. I didn't see him. But he's the only one who can still cause a problem for us."

Sara hesitated a moment before turning again toward the doorway.

"No!"

"I don't care what kind of mess you made, Mikey. You did what you had to. We all did. But what I have to do now is go out there and find some first aid for you. I'll be damned if I let you bleed out all over my console."

TIM WAS ON THE FLOOR near the control station, his face gray in the dull light flickering from the screens. He seemed at home there, in his element, as he sat cross-legged, busying himself with the defeated bots he had dragged over.

"Hey, Mike, remember *Robocop*? I introduce you now to Robocorpse."

Mike didn't respond. He had actually passed out more than twenty minutes before, a fact that didn't seem to concern Tim in the slightest.

"You know, you're a lousy conversationalist, Mike. That's why all the zeta chicks want me. I swear I caught Sara trying to unzip my fly with her mind." He grunted as he pulled the crossbow bolt out of the robot's head and continued with his work. "Ah, Sara," he said, hearing her enter the doorway. "You must have known we were talking about you. Actually I'm glad you're back. I tried getting Mike's opinion on my new outfit, but the man knows nothing about style."

He stood to show her his new suit of armor, fashioned from several metal plates removed from the robocorpses. He was wearing the fu-bot's arm coatings for flexibility; besides, they were the only parts of the droid still in one piece. He had on a helmet—the hollowed-out headpiece of his vanquished opponent, which he wore like a war trophy despite the hole in its forehead—and some breast and shoulder plates, also taken from the squat bots for better fit. Overall he looked like the unfortunate result of a storm trooper and a hockey goalie having a baby.

"So, Sara, what do you think?" Those were going to be the next words out of his mouth. What came out instead was, "Whoa."

Whatever was standing before him most definitely *wasn't* Sara.

Chapter 31

BOSS FIGHT

Reynolds felt like he was trapped inside a six-foot coffin. He couldn't stretch to full height, and there was barely any space for movement. Luckily his practice had paid off; he'd be using his mind more than manning control switches.

His headset squawked. It was General Howard. Though his voice was filled with static, the message was clear: "Those people are using our base against us. Both need to be destroyed."

THE CREATURE WAS EASILY TEN feet tall. Eleven maybe. Tim didn't have a tape measure. It had tank treads for feet and slashing propellers at the ends of its arms to slice through groups of men. There was a siege cannon where its stomach should have been. Its heart was a howitzer.

It was the perfect doomsday weapon—though Tim noted a few imperfections. Its fish-scale armor was incomplete, and the flamethrowers on its shoulders weren't attached to fuel lines.

It had no eyes in its tyrannosaurus-shaped head, but it didn't need them. From the pings it emitted, Tim could tell it was using active sonar. And from the way it was advancing, he could tell it had already zeroed in on him.

Tim ran to the far end of the control room, to where Sara had bent the panel back, and slipped through the gap to the lab next door. The *T. rex* robot followed behind, steamrolling over the bodies of its fallen brethren. It shot the howitzer once, tearing a sizable hole in the wall, before Tim reached in and disabled the breech screw. It tried the siege cannon next, but the plunger spring had already been straightened.

Tim crouched in the dark behind a workstation. He couldn't see a thing, but he knew the sound of the propellers as they cut through the brushed-steel wall as easily as opening a tin can. The sound stopped once he disabled the governor drive. But by then the robot was already in the room.

Tim heard the sonar pings coming closer along with the whir of tank treads about thirty feet away. Then the lab went quiet. The only sound left was Tim's heartbeat, which had been the loudest of all.

At once the room was bathed in light so bright, Tim had to divert his eyes. The robot was emitting a searchlight. Its tank treads folded up and tucked inside its body; a clang echoed as massive anchoring mechanisms dropped to the floor. The robo-boss was standing its ground.

Tim looked to the right, through the lab window. He thought he saw movement in the hallway. "Reynolds, you worthless bitch! You . . . you yes-man! Why don't you show yourself?"

"Yes, sir. I'm right in front of you."

The voice was coming from inside the creature. Tim blinked in disbelief.

The behemoth robot was not yet outfitted or tested to be accessed remotely. Reynolds could not control the robot from without like he'd done with Thorin. But he could control it from within. He proceeded to do so from the circuit-laden and mildly cramped cockpit of the massive metallic beast.

"And now I'm going to show you something else . . . sir."

A hatch opened in the robot's torso, and a pair of conducting rails started to extend. Looking at the length of them, fifteen feet in all, Tim suddenly got the feeling he was standing on the tracks, staring at a speeding train.

"What in the hell is that?" he asked aloud.

"A rail gun." Sara had stepped in from the hallway unnoticed. She was standing by the door, holding a medical kit and a portable light in one hand and a six-pack of Dr Pepper in the other.

Tim glanced at her before returning his gaze to the weapon. "How in the hell does it work?"

"I don't know," she said. "I saw a video of a navy test launch. Once it's deployed it takes about a minute for the projectile to shoot out and reach hypersonic speeds."

"It's already been almost twenty seconds. Tell me how to disable it!"

"Quickly."

Tim's mind was blank. He couldn't reach into the mechanism if he didn't know what it looked like. So he did the next-best thing. He reached onto a lab worktable in front of him and grabbed one of the spherical brain cases the Deeps had been working on. Tucking it under his arm, he charged toward Reynolds's robot, jammed it deep inside the gun nozzle, then ran into the hallway and dove on top of Sara.

The implosion was instant.

The pieces of shrapnel lodged in the lab walls were all that was left of the doomsday droid. The blood on the walls belonged to Reynolds alone.

Sara stood up shakily, dusted herself off, turned on the light, and went to survey the scene through the blown-out window. Neither she nor Tim had a single cut from a sliver of glass. His half-assed armor had saved them.

As she studied the remains of Howard's army smeared across the lab, her reaction surprised even Tim. Sara started to laugh. It was sharp and grating and reminded him of the sound of propellers against steel.

"Let's give the good general a call," she said. "It's time for him to accept once and for all that the power has changed hands."

Chapter 32

BENEFACTORS

On approach, Lorstad's facility had looked like a stunning, modern home of native stone and glass perched on the edge of a hill. Once they'd entered and moved through the structure, it became clear the house was just the tip of a very much bigger iceberg. It reminded Chuck a bit of Forward Kinetics' headquarters that way, only the effect was much more pronounced.

"We call it simply the Center," said their guide. "It is the center of our . . . community."

Chuck turned his gaze from the stunning view of canyon walls and forested mountains beyond and gave Kristian Lorstad his entire attention. "What community is that exactly?"

"We don't really have a name. We're not an organized group in the usual application of the word. Our purpose, though, is to aid mankind in its next steps of evolution. You, Doctor, are well aware that for millennia, mankind has been controlling—or at least affecting—its own evolution. Unwittingly, for the most part. We prefer it to be more conscious and directed . . . and benign.

Men like General Howard pose a threat to that evolution. Men and women like you," he added, "can help speed it up and determine its course."

Chuck grimaced; the impact of their work on human evolution was exactly what kept him up at night. "Why us in particular?"

In answer, Lorstad turned and made a gentle gesture at a bronze statuette. It rose from the floor, turned a delicate pirouette in the air, and lowered itself back to its pedestal.

A widening of the eyes was all the reaction Chuck and his teammates showed.

"We have been using external stimuli to produce the desired results. We used it earlier when the Deeps, as you call them, had you surrounded in the car dealership."

"That was you?" Chuck asked.

"Yes. We were there. But don't imagine that our abilities are always that strong. Because the impulse is external, the adept's abilities do not grow once he or she has achieved a certain level. The treatment, if I may call it that, must also be repeated to retain the effects. You, however, have managed to train adepts to produce and harness zeta waves, thus allowing them to explore and enhance their abilities—to diversify their skills by applying what they've learned to new situations. While our abilities are, in a sense, artificial, yours are organic and natural—in a word, evolutionary. It's remarkable. And it's something we would like to learn from you. We would also like to help you solve this problem that General Howard has created, hopefully in a peaceful manner."

Before Chuck could respond, a door slid open where there had not been a door. It appeared to be an elevator, its walls softly lit from within. There was a young woman standing in it.

Lorstad smiled as if he were sincerely glad to see her. "This is my colleague, Alexis. She'll be helping you settle in here at the Center."

The woman—a tall, willowy blonde—stepped from the elevator, which remained open behind her. "Hello, Doctors, Ms. Mause, Ms. Chen."

"Settle in?" said Chuck. "Settle in to do what? I know you've said you can keep us safe here, that there's no way for Howard to track us, but what do you intend for us to do?"

"To work, of course, Doctor. In fact that's why Alexis has come up to help me show you our operation. Shall we?" He gestured toward the elevator.

They entered and were whisked downward so swiftly and to such a depth that Chuck's ears popped twice. At bottom, the elevator doors slid open on a vista that made Deep Shield look like a steampunk nightmare. The ceiling was far away, gently radiant and curving. The vast, open area was gleaming, sleek, pristine, and possessed none of the Spartan rough edges that seemed an affectation of the military—as if comfort of any kind somehow went against their belief system.

People were at work in the sprawling space, seated at computer terminals or standing at large plasma screens that were embedded in the walls. Some of them turned to observe the newcomers and smiled at them before returning to whatever work they did. It was a human gesture, natural, meant to be comforting. So why did Chuck find it unnerving?

Lorstad led them down the center of the cavernous room toward its nether end. "This is the shop floor. We prefer working in an open space. Walls in this environment only cause compartmentalization and difficulty in communication. Your new lab is a separate facility modeled on what you built at Forward Kinetics but larger. We think you'll find it an improvement."

"Our new lab?" repeated Dice. "What kind of lab?"

"One outfitted with everything you need to do your work. Everything."

"Wait," said Eugene. "We've just gotten here, but you already have a lab outfitted for us?"

"Yes. We've been anticipating your visit for some time. Would you like to see it?"

He led them to a featureless set of sliding doors at the far end of the main room. Before they had quite reached them, the doors slid open, allowing them to see a portion of what lay within.

Lorstad gestured at the room. "Go on in, please. It's all yours."

"Wow," murmured Dice. He glanced at Chuck, then went through the doors.

Everyone else paused on the threshold, but Chuck knew only why *he* hesitated. He knew entering that room would be a crossing over, an acceptance that what Lorstad had told them on the plane was true: that he and his mysterious benefactors were the only chance Chuck and his team had to remain free, their only chance of reestablishing contact with the other zetas. Stepping through that door would be an acknowledgment that his old life was gone forever—that all of their old lives were gone, and they had only this unknown ahead of them.

He turned to Lanfen. "What do you think?"

In answer she took his hand and faced the laboratory doors. "Really, Doc, what choice do we have?"

He looked to Eugene and Mini. They both nodded.

They stepped through the doors together—out of their old lives and into an uncertain and frightening future. One that they'd helped to create.

ACKNOWLEDGMENTS

My agent Emma Parry.

Read on for a sneak preview of

The God Peak,

the explosive sequel to

The God Wave

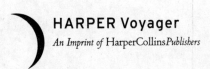

HARPER Voyager
An Imprint of HarperCollins*Publishers*

UNDER MOUNT OLYMPUS

Mike Yenotov watched the blood pressure cuff inflate, grunting when it hit its max and began to deflate. The LED screen of the little machine ticked off the numbers in time with a soft, repetitive beep. Blood pressure looked good. So did his wound. It was scabbing over cleanly with no sign of infection.

He tried not to think about how he'd sustained it.

Mike pulled off the cuff and returned it to the basket below the blood pressure monitor. The machine rolled away from him to stand against the wall like a silent sentinel. He looked around the infirmary with its pristine surfaces and wondered how long it would stay clean. Even down here there was dust, and he wasn't sure his kinetic abilities ran to vacuuming.

Stupid. Thoughts like that were stupid, irrelevant. Dust was the least of his worries—their worries. He shared this domain beneath the mountain with Sara and Tim. *Sorry—Troll.* Regardless of what he called Tim, those two were his only companions at the moment. They were—or rather had been—his colleagues. He couldn't think of either of them as friends. Not now, at any rate. Now they were . . . he wasn't sure what.

Partners in crime, maybe.

Dust might not be an issue, but other things were. Take those full spectrum lightbulbs that Deep Shield had everywhere. They allowed the staff to live underground for extended periods of time without the medical problems that came from long-term lack of exposure to sunlight. He assumed that there were replacement bulbs and other supplies somewhere down here, but they hadn't found them yet. Of course, he was the only one who'd even thought of looking for anything beyond food, water, and a way to wash bodies and clothing. Sara and Tim were focused on the outside world—specifically, on ways to control it. Mike, trying to think ahead, had constructed an observation deck on the eastern slope of their mountain home—just in case.

He slid off the exam table, wincing a little at the pain in his rib cage, and considered raiding the canteen for something to eat. Or maybe do another inspection tour. He knew what he was doing. He was putting off going back down to "Ops." If he went back, he'd have to deal with Sara and Tim's outrage. It wasn't that he was bothered by anger—he'd worked with too many foremen to worry about being yelled at. But a Zeta's outrage . . . that could be toxic. He wondered if they weren't poisoning each other, creating a sort of feedback loop that just fed and fed on itself. They were furious at General Leighton Howard for his assault on their position. Furious at the military establishment he represented. Furious at whatever politicos knew of and sanctioned Deep Shield's operations.

Mike was pissed off, too, but not so much at that stuff as at the hijacking of his life—of all their lives. As he saw it, the whole damn mess was a cascade of what-the-hell-did-you-expect? What the hell had Howard expected when he'd essentially made them prisoners in his secret mountain military base? What the hell had the Zetas expected when they'd exiled the general and all his crew to the outside? Of course they were going to try to get back in. Of course there were fail-safes and self-destruct plans and booby traps. Of course, the general was going to try to limit their access to the outside world.

As per usual, thinking about their current situation gave Mike a headache. He wandered into the dispensary where medicines and other medical supplies were kept in a locked cage. The door to the cage lay on the floor where he'd flung it the first time he'd accessed the dispensary's stores. He started to reach for the dial at the top of the ibuprofen dispenser—a device that reminded him of a gumball machine—but the bandages over his wound pulled. So he reached for the dial kinetically; it was second nature at this point. He just visualized a hand turning it, and two tablets dropped into the little plastic tray on the front of the machine.

He tossed back the pills, and followed it with a swig of water from a water dispenser. (How soon before we run out of water?) A crackling sound came from his shirt pocket. He gave a thought, switching the walkie-talkie on.

"Yeah?"

"You get lost, Micky?" Tim asked.

"Changing my bandages."

"Sara wants you back down here. She's getting ready to call Howard. Figures you oughta be in on the conversation."

Conversation. That was one word for it. More like ransom demands. Sara had, just that morning, crashed a small regional banking system in the Midwest as a sort of demo—a moderately destructive reminder that, though he'd clipped their wings somewhat by restricting their access to cell towers, there were still things she could do beyond the halls of Deep Shield's ex-HQ. Howard would have to be an idiot to think she wouldn't employ every resource she could to achieve her goals. It must totally burn him that the communications and computer network he'd worked so hard and so secretly to build was now being used against him.

Whatever they want to call this next phase in discussions, I definitely need to be there.

"Yeah. I'm on my way," Mike said.

He shut off the walkie-talkie and took a deep breath, reminding himself that Sara's goals were his goals. He just wasn't sure about her means of achieving them. He shook himself mentally for that. Everything they'd done had been defensive, he told himself. Everything. They just wanted a better world. A world where men like General Leighton Howard and organizations like Deep Shield were not allowed to exist.

He remembered pictures in the Bible story books he'd read as a boy. Lions and lambs playing nice. Tanks rusting in junkyards. Orchards full of fruit being harvested by smiling families dressed like they were on holiday. He didn't take those images literally as he had when he was a kid, but he still wanted that world in which lions and lambs just got along.

Problem was, he didn't feel so much like a lamb anymore.

He retrieved a couple more ibuprofen and popped them into his shirt pocket. Well, not his shirt, really. The shirt pocket belonged to whoever's uniform he'd borrowed a piece of. He wondered if it had been one of the soldiers who'd died in the assault on the mountain. Odds were pretty good.

Mike shook off the image that conjured and headed down to the operations theater. On the way, he passed by a series of long, narrow rooms in which Deep Shield had stored row upon row of robots built expressly for remote manipulation. He had tried to count them manually at one point, only to give up when he reached 500. There might have been many times that number in this warren. He had no idea. What he did know was that they would never rust. Steel and titanium and aluminum didn't. He wondered how long it would be, though, before their wiring harnesses desiccated in the dry air. It almost didn't matter. The Deep Shield guys had built them with servo mechanisms and a rudimentary AI because their Zetas hadn't known how to manipulate the bots directly. He and Sara and Tim did. The wires could all disintegrate and they'd still be able to make use of the robot army.

Except that they wouldn't. That would be his personal part of their endgame, he decided—destroying every last one of those war machines. Well, maybe he'd have to let Tim take down a couple hundred. The thought almost made him smile.

He entered Ops quietly and slid into a chair at a console near the back of the room, angling a glance at the faraway ceiling. The place had a state-of-the-art fire suppression system. In this room alone, there were enough nozzles to flood the place. He wondered what effect all that water and fire retardant would have on General Howard's metal army.

"Where the hell's Mike?"

Mike jerked his head up and peered at Tim through the muted light in the room. The overhead lighting was dimmed in favor of bright, full-spectrum LEDs that lit the workstations the Zetas had appropriated. The kid was sitting in a pool of light about four feet in front of him at another console with his Converse-clad feet propped up on it, his face bathed in a rainbow of radiance from the lights on his control panel. Sara was pacing back and forth beneath the wall of tactical and real-time displays at the head of the room. Mike glided his chair forward on silent casters and tapped Tim on the shoulder.

The younger man yelped, twisting so violently he pitched himself out of the chair and onto the concrete floor.

"Son of a bitch, Mike! What the hell'd you do that for?"

Mike shrugged. "Just letting you know I was there. Thought you heard me come in." He thought nothing of the kind, but wasn't about to admit it. Tim had always rubbed him the wrong way. He'd come to view him with a sort of annoyed fondness, but under their present circumstances, there was less fondness and a lot more annoyance.

"Bastard," mumbled Tim.

Mike raised his head to see Sara regarding both of them with impatience. "I'm here, boss lady. What's the plan?"

"The plan is, we're going to issue some demands to General Howard. Demands that he will disregard at his peril."

"Okay. What demands?"

"First of all, that they stop trying to pry us out of this mountain. Second, we hear from your wife and kids that they're okay; that they're not being harassed in any way—"

Mike felt as if someone had poured ice water over his head. "My family is in Canada."

"Yes, and if I were Howard, I'd be looking for a way to extract them."

"The Canadian government isn't going to just give them up. My wife's got dual citizenship."

Sara crossed her arms over her breasts and gave him a look that was almost pitying. "Mike, Howard has no real authority in the American government or the military. His extraction would not go through diplomatic channels. He'll probably just send one of his black ops teams . . . if he has any left."

Mike stood slowly. "The hell he will! That son of a bitch touches my family and I will end him."

"And that is something that I want to impress upon our dear general. You need to communicate with your family and your family needs to remain free."

"Canaries in a coal mine," Mike murmured.

"What?"

"My family. You're saying they're like canaries in a coal mine. If they get locked down or fall silent, you'll know Howard's plotting something."

Sara stared at him for a long moment, then said, "I suppose it would have that advantage, Mike. But I care that your family is an obvious point of leverage. We need to do what's necessary to keep them safely out of harm's way. I'm sure you agree."

"Sure I agree."

"Then we're in accord. I also want Howard to get the real U.S. government involved. He's a traitor. He has no authority to be speaking on behalf of the government or the people of America."

"Howard is scum." Tim had climbed back into his seat and resumed his casual pose.

Sara ignored him. "I'm sure you'll agree we need access to the real power, Mike."

Tim snorted. The sound echoed harshly in the cavernous room. "I'm pretty sure that'd be the heads of multinational corporations, who are just as scummy as Howard, in my book. Man, but I'd like to take those jerks down."

Sara cut him a swift glance, a Mona Lisa smile on her face. "You'll get your chance. I did some snooping in Howard's private files. He's beholden to a number of multinationals who have interests that his little robot army were intended to serve. They'll no doubt be asking him embarrassing questions about how that's going."

"So," said Mike, "what are you going to demand?"

"Access to the Oval Office and the Pentagon."

Mike laughed. "Like that's gonna happen. Like you said, he doesn't have that access to give."

Sara's smile became a grin. "We'll see." She opened a channel to the Deep Shield camp at the foot of the mountain. "This is Sara Crowell," she told the tech who answered. "I want to talk to General Howard. Immediately."

Tim snickered, then cupped his hands over his mouth and called out in a high, singsong voice: "Paging Leighton Howard. Will Leighton Howard please report to the principal's office?"

Howard was there so fast, Mike imagined he must have been standing right next to the communications console.

"Howard here," he identified himself.

Sara got right to the point. "By now you will have ascertained that none of your attack forces survived the attempt to kill us and that you are unable to detonate the charges you intended to destroy this mountain. And you will have gone to Mike Yenotov's house and found it empty."

There was a moment of silence, then Howard said, "Yes to all three. But you should be warned that we know where Yenotov's family is. We traced them to Ontario."

Mike tensed.

"And you should be warned," Sara said, "that if we do not hear from Mike's wife in twenty-four hours and continue to hear from her on a daily basis that she and the kids are still in Ontario and free—well, let's just say you really wouldn't like the consequences."

When Howard didn't answer, Sara continued. "Now, I think we're clear that you're not getting back in here by force and that you are not going to be able to trigger your explosives. Are we, indeed, clear on that, General?"

"Yes." Howard ground the word out between his teeth. Mike was convinced he could literally hear the man's molars chipping.

"Wonderful. So, here's what I want. I want to talk to President Ellis. In fact, I want a direct line of communication with her."

"That's—that's impossible."

"Why? Because she still has no idea that the little snafu in Pennsylvania had nothing to do with hackers or cyberterrorism? Because she still doesn't know it was connected to military bases going dark all over the world? Tsk, tsk, General Howard. You're withholding information from your own commander in chief."

Silence again. Mike exhaled sharply. He admired the way Sara could peg this guy, but it infuriated him that this traitorous jackass would try to maintain his authority in the face of what the Alpha-Zetas had already proven they could do.

"Maybe," he said aloud, "he needs a reminder of what the stakes are, Sara."

Sara glanced back at him over her shoulder, then turned to Tim. "Tim, pick a corporation. A corporation that's monkeyed with people's lives—maybe they've gobbled up little independent companies, stolen their tech, and then fired all their employees. Or maybe they've polluted the natural resources of the people living downstream from their facilities. Or maybe they've sold defective equipment to the military— the real military. Think about what you'd like to do to that company's resources." She hesitated, smiled and said, "Then do it."

"Hot damn!"

Tim swung his feet down from his console and rotated his shoulders as if to loosen them. Then he looked up at the set of displays that covered the front wall. On the central one, a map of the United States appeared, but a map that showed, not highways or state boundaries, but the unbounded filaments of the national telecommunications system. Grinning from ear to ear, the programmer lit up several hubs on the map in lurid red. A second later, traceries of equally bright green began to flash and pulse like lightning.

"Very Christmas-y, Tim," Sara said. "Can you describe what you're doing for the general?"

"I'm moving financial resources, General. Some of them are going into my personal coffers—think of it as a commission. But a lot of it is going to where I think it would be better spent."

"Going from where?" Howard demanded. "What company or companies are you attacking?"

"Oh, I'm sure you'll hear about it in the news, dude. And given the twenty-four-hour news cycle, I bet you'll hear about it pretty quick. Hey, you can blame the same cyberterrorists that you blamed for the 'Battle for Olympus.' Did you tell Madame President that you'd taken care of that?"

"Oh, no, Timmy," said Sara, her voice cool and sweet. "He hasn't told Madame President a damn thing. But he needs to. Don't you, General Howard?"

"I don't think you understand, Ms. Crowell—"

"I don't think you understand, General Howard. If you don't put us in touch with the POTUS, we're going to continue to pull things apart. And we're going to figure out how to get in contact with her ourselves."

The man laughed. He actually laughed. "I'm sure you and your friends are clever enough to figure out how to contact the president, but I doubt you'll be able to convince her that you're not just some wing nut who's not even living in the real world. Remember, all this stuff you do is completely unknown in the White House."

"Well, it won't be for long, now will it?" Sara broke the connection kinetically, drawing a finger across her throat in a gesture that graphically relayed her contempt for the man she had cut off. She swung around and glared at Tim. "If he tries to reestablish communications, just ignore him. He clearly needs to stew for a while. Mike, how long is your mental reach?"

"How long do you need it to be?"

"Can you reach D.C.?"

Mike considered that. "If I have line of sight, yeah."

She moved to the console he was seated at and perched on the edge of it. "Okay, so let's say I can isolate surveillance cameras in target areas—show you what I'd like you to manipulate."

"If I can see it, I can work it."

"You seem pretty sure of yourself, Micky," Tim said, pivoting in his chair.

"I am, *Timmy*. What's the target?" he asked Sara.

"Let me find one for you," she said and turned to look at their windows on the world. "And Timmy, I'd like you to start thinking of some interesting viruses."

* * *

Matt Streegman stared at the man sitting across from him in his office at Forward Kinetics with a riot of thoughts having a melee in his head. What finally came out of his mouth was "Why didn't you ask me this before?"

General Howard's graying brows lowered in obvious displeasure. Which was saying a lot as they had been set in a perpetual scowl since Chuck and his team had bolted. Matt was surprised the man hadn't keeled over of a heart attack by now and was sure his stomach lining must have been eaten through.

"I'm asking now," the officer said. "Help me understand these—these people. How do I communicate with them? How do I control what they do?"

"They're not controllable. No, wait. Let me be very specific: you can't control them because they will never give you the opportunity. They don't trust you. They no longer need to trust you. The time for trying to understand them was back before you tried to force them to do your bidding. You treated them as if they were machines that you just had to understand well enough to make use of. Or even as soldiers that could be ordered about and wouldn't question your authority. Either way, they were never human beings to you."

"Were they human beings to you, Streegman? Weren't they just a product?"

Matt had to acknowledge that there was some truth to that. "Touché. Although, to be fair to myself, I'd have to say I thought of them as . . . students or—"

"*Specimens?*"

"*Proofs of concept.* They were never intended to be the product, General. I wasn't selling them. I was selling potential. I was using them only to show you what your own people could achieve. You're the one who changed the game."

"No, your lame-brained partner did that when he took his crew and bolted."

Matt shook his head and sat back in his office chair. "Look, Leighton, you can argue all day about causality. But in the real world, you'd lose that argument. I understand why you took some of the security precautions you did, but you went to lengths you didn't have to and, more to the point, shouldn't have gone to. Replacing our grounds crew with agents? Firing our administrative staff? Bugging our offices, our homes? Putting tracers on our vehicles? You started treating us like we were . . . dangerous."

Howard's broad face reddened. "Damn it, Streegman, they *are* dangerous. You made them that."

"No, General. *You* did. You cut them off from the real world and tried to intimidate them. When that failed, you tried to destroy them. If I'd had any idea what sort of outfit Deep Shield really was going in, I'd never have gotten into bed with you in the first place. But I was drunk on my own sense of accomplishment. And I was greedy and stupid. Chuck was right to do what he did. It was the only thing he could have done."

"This debate," Howard said, rising from the side chair across from Matt's desk, "is getting us nowhere. We need to get those people out of that facility and we need to do it immediately. Do you know what Sara Crowell just demanded of me?"

Matt shrugged.

"She demanded that I get her in touch with President Ellis."

Matt chuckled. "She demanded that you out yourself, you mean.

That you humiliate yourself and probably get yourself arrested. I'm willing to bet that Sara finds your behavior treasonous and she's thinking the POTUS just might agree with her about that."

"I can't 'out' myself, as you put it."

"You mean you won't. How highly you must think of yourself, Leighton, to imagine that your reputation, even your life, is more important than the lives already lost through your . . . patent evil. More important than the lives that potentially could be lost. More important than a full-throated revolt that devastates this nation's economy and infrastructure."

Howard's lip curled. "I never took you for a bleeding heart liberal."

"Oh, cut the crap, Leighton. I never took you for a coward. But that's what you are—a greedy, self-absorbed coward. Hiding behind your soldiers and your well-funded 'programs' and the people who are bankrolling them. Do you think those people are going to continue to support you when you show up on the evening news?"

"Where the hell do you get off calling me—"

Matt stood, slamming his hands down on the top of his desk. "I can call you a greedy, self-absorbed coward because it takes one to know one. Now, if you really want my advice about how to handle the Zetas, do what they want. Go to the president and explain to her what's happened. You can blame me, if you want. I'll be your mad scientist—or mad mathematician—whatever. Just do it before more people get hurt."

Howard didn't reply. He fixed Matt with a look that would have been lethal if Howard himself were a Zeta, and strode out of Matt's office. Mere minutes later, Matt heard the chopper lift off from the parking lot and collapsed back into his chair. He was like Howard in other ways, too, he mused. He was every bit as hoist by his own petard.

★ ★ ★

"I have the perfect target." Sara sat down next to Mike at the console he'd adopted as his station in the ops theater and at which he had been trying to figure out how to run a trace on his family. That wasn't really his forte—working with electronic signals and networks—but he hadn't wanted to ask Tim or Sara to do it. They were both occupied elsewhere.

The central display at the head of the room switched from its view of the Deep Shield installation at the foot of the mountain to a vastly different and very familiar scene. The Washington Monument, dominating its end of the National Mall. The morning sun illuminated the construction equipment and scaffolding that surrounded it. Two huge cranes stood like twin sentinels on either side of the obelisk. There was a crowd gathering on the grass and paths around the structure, and news trucks had congregated along the closest curbsides.

"What's going on there?" Mike asked.

"The upper stories of the monument have gotten a fresh cladding of white marble and the capstone is being replaced with one covered in gold, if you can believe it." Sara gestured with one hand and the view moved closer to the base of the building. "See? That's it there in that heavy-duty sling. Today at noon, it's supposed to be lifted to the top of the structure by one of those cranes and nudged lovingly into place, while officials sing George Washington's praises and mouth the wrong words to 'The Star-Spangled Banner.'"

Mike sat up straighter. "What do you want me to do?"

"I want you to start the festivities a little early."

"But . . . all those people. If I screw up, somebody could get hurt."

Sara rested a hand on his shoulder. "Mike, you worry too much. I'll call Howard, tell him to keep an eye on the proceedings at the monument. He'll move people out fast, I'll bet."

"How? You keep saying he's got no authority—"

"But he *does* have connections. Trust me, Mike."

He was getting tired of people saying that to him. His trust had gotten him locked inside this mountain with these two. Yet he took a deep breath and said once more, "Okay. What do you want me to do?"

"Work the capstone's crane. Give that archaic status symbol a nice little crown."

Mike frowned at the crane, let it fill his vision, then his thoughts. He felt its gears, drivers and mechanisms. He tasted the vinyl air in the cab and smelled the steel and lubricant. "Okay. Sure. I can do that."

"Great." Sara stood and the communications channel to Deep Shield crackled to life. "I need to talk to Howard," she told whoever was minding the store.

"He's on his way in."

"Put me through to his cell phone. I know you can," she added when the guy started to protest. "Don't stall me, soldier."

"Just a moment."

In mere seconds, Howard's voice came across the connection. Mike imagined he heard relief in it. He was sure that wasn't going to last.

"Ms. Crowell. I have a proposal to make."

"Really? Does it involve me talking to the president?"

"It involves you getting to keep the mountain. Or leave it if you'd rather. You may go wherever you like in the world. Anywhere. We won't follow you. We won't approach you. We won't attack you. Just go wherever you would like to go and do whatever you would like to do."

"What we would like to do, General, is put an end to war. That means putting an end to your asinine plotting and manipulations of people's lives. So, here's my counterproposal. You get me in touch with President Ellis and you confess your part in this and the parts played by any associates or aiders and abettors you have in Washington, and then you disappear. We won't follow you. We won't approach you. We won't attack you. Same deal you offered us."

"That's unacceptable."

Sara glanced from Mike to Tim who had taken a break from whatever he was doing to monitor the interaction. "How did I know you were going to say that? General Howard, as you may be aware, there is a special ceremony taking place at the Washington Monument today. I recommend that, when you get back to your base, you grab a TV or surveillance feed of the area around the monument. I'll supply one if you can't get it."

There was silence on the other end of the line. "What are you planning? What do you think you can do—?"

"Pretty much whatever we want. Whenever *we* want."

"I'm arriving at the base now. Let me— I don't—" He cut off from his end. "Wow," said Tim, winding a lock of his riotously curly hair around one finger. "You really rattled the guy. I think he's about to implode."

"We'll see."

"How long are you going to wait?" Mike asked.

Sara made a face. "He just got there. Give him five to assess the situation. Another five to contact someone in Washington. Maybe ten to actually get something to happen."

"Get what to happen?" asked Tim.

"We'll know it when we see it," Sara said. "If we see it."

Roughly fifteen minutes later, something changed in the feed they were watching. Police cars appeared at the periphery of the camera's eye, and officers began to move into the crowd, directing people away from the base of the monument. Then the view leapt to what was apparently a television feed. A reporter, microphone in hand, waved her crew back, glancing over her shoulder at the monument and its attendant cranes.

"I don't know," she mouthed. She said more, but it was lost on Mike.

Sara made a frustrated sound and audio kicked in.

The reporter tapped her earpiece. "They're just telling us to fall back to the truck. Maybe a terrorist threat? I don't know. Back up. Back up. But keep filming."

"Now, Mike," said Sara softly.

Mike already had the feel of the crane. He'd worked one like it before. Knew it. It fit like a glove. He willed the engine to life. The operator—who could be seen in the TV camera's view standing on the crane's treads—reacted by climbing into the cab. Mike ignored him. There was nothing the man could do. Ultimately, even turning off the engine wouldn't stop Mike; it could only slow him down a little. He worked the controls with ease, lifting turning. He grunted as he felt some push back. It was the operator, trying to stop the crane. The guy gave up after several tries and left the cab. He scrambled down from the huge tank treads and ran toward the camera, joined by a group of his fellows who had been on or near the scaffolding.

By the time Mike had lifted the capstone clear off the ground, the area around the base of the monument had cleared. Mike watched the progress of the capstone in its sling, rising toward the apex of the structure it was designed to top. Sunlight flashed like fire from the gold overlay. It was like a phoenix, Mike thought. It was a symbol of American greatness and it would help them wrest power out of the shadows and restore it to the democratically elected leaders—and to the electorate, itself. To people like him, like his family. Folks who gain a skill, get a job, and contribute. People who have but one ambition: to create and maintain a home for their family. The people who are always pawns on the chess board and invariably hurt when people like Howard meet and plan in dark smoky rooms.

No more.

Mike had gotten the capstone within twenty feet of its resting place when Sara bent and spoke into his ear. "Break the damn thing."

What broke was Mike's attention. He let go of the crane and the slow rise of the capstone stopped. The sudden change caused it to swing and tremble at the end of its thick cables.

"Break—what?"

"The damned obelisk. Break it. Bash it in with the capstone." Sara's eyes were bright with zeal, and there was a fine dew of perspiration on her lip and forehead.

"You go, girl!" whooped Tim.

Mike ignored him. "Sara, do you realize what you're asking me to do? This thing has been standing since the nineteenth century. It's a symbol of this country's founding and first president. You're an architect, for God's sake. How can you—"

She grasped his shoulder. Hard. "It's become a symbol of power, Mike. The power of the privileged over the disenfranchised. Of the strong over the weak. Of male dominance over everyone else. We need to break it. Don't you see? We need to force Howard's hand. If we make this public a display, there's no way he can keep his damned secrets."

Mike glanced at the screen.

No more.

No more secrets.

He saw that, since the crane had stopped moving, the construction workers and some police officers were making their way across the grass back toward the monument. He gritted his teeth, put his mind back to the task and pivoted the crane to the left so that the capstone swung out over the approaching men and women.

Several of the ancillary displays in the operations room had come online now. They showed a close-up on the driverless cab of the crane, the empty scaffolding behind it, and stunning footage of the gleaming capstone swinging at the end of its tether.

Like a priest's censer during mass, Mike thought. A prayer sprang to his thoughts: *Please, God, let no one be hurt.*

Mike reversed the movement of the crane's long arm, the capstone following on its trailing arc. The crane's arm cleared the naked top of the monument, but the capstone, dangling tens of feet below, crashed into the marble sheathing like some bizarrely shaped wrecking ball. Marble shattered, crumbled, and fell, larger chunks tearing away pieces of the scaffolding and carrying it along on their plunge to the ground. Mike could hear the sound of people shouting and screaming now, their voices bleeding through the open TV audio feeds, overlaid with the excited commentary of the reporters on-site.

"Again," Sara said.

Mike swung the crane back, realizing that a new sound had entered the mix—the sound of helicopter rotors.

"Holy shit!" cackled Tim. "It's a gunship! It's a damned gunship! An Apache Longbow. I've digitized those babies. That is one badass machine. With Hydras or Hellfires, I bet—missiles to you noobs. That'd be ironic, wouldn't it, if they start shooting at shit and bring the whole thing down into the reflecting pool?"

"I seriously doubt if it would reach the reflecting pools," said Sara blandly.

Mike ignored all of it—the copter, the crowd sounds, Tim's exclamations of amusement—and swung the crane back toward the monument a second time. Tim got his wish—the gunship opened fire on the empty crane cab, though only with machine guns. As might be expected, the bullets merely ricocheted from the metal surfaces and sent those closest to the crane into full retreat.

At the same time the bullets slammed into the crane, the capstone struck the northern face of the monument a second time, ripping away more scaffolding and bringing down an avalanche of stone. The topmost part of the tower seemed to shift slightly.

"That's it," murmured Sara.

The helicopter gunship had not given up, though. It circled the crane, angling south and changing its orientation, looking for a clear shot. Even Mike suspected the thing carried Hellfire missiles, but it was hard to imagine the pilot might be persuaded to use them. What could he possibly do that would not cause even more damage that Mike could?

A shot of adrenaline coursed down Mike's spine. What if the idiot pilot did fire a missile at the crane from that oblique angle? What would happen to the people clustered around the firetrucks and police cruisers on the avenue just to the east?

Mike did the only thing he could think of: he reversed the crane and cranked it into as swift a 360 as he could. The capstone, beginning to slip from its damaged sling, flew around, centrifugal force pulling it away from the center of the spin. At the end of its pivot, the crane's long arm collided with the second crane in a scream of metal on metal. Its flight interrupted, the capstone tumbled erratically at the end of its cables.

Now, finally, it slipped from the sling and hurtled toward the monument's southern flank. The cables and sling, freed of the capstone's weight, backlashed like a flail and clipped the hovering copter.

The capstone smashed into the monument, crushing the scaffolding on its northern side and loosing another cascade of stone. The copter slewed wildly, its missile systems belching flame as it attempted one last Hail Mary against the rogue cranes.

It didn't have a prayer.

The Hellfire missile instead glanced off the roof of the crane's cab, striking the monument roughly thirty feet above the base and exploded. The cranes were enveloped in a cloud of debris and smoke amid the cacophonous sounds of shredding metal and shattering stone. The top of the obelisk shuddered and settled and then, like a great tree felled by Paul Bunyon's axe, it began to topple . . . toward the road behind it.

Mike reflexively reached out with his increasingly developed sense of the atoms that made up the world and applied as much force as he could to check the fall. He exceeded beyond his wildest expectations. As if a giant's hand had slapped it aside, the towering structure shuddered again and swayed back away from the crowds and the emergency vehicles and the media crews. It even missed the helicopter as it fell due west.

"It's pointing right at the Lincoln Memorial!" crowed Tim. "Damn it, but you're good, Micky! Man, you can plan my castle assault anytime." The programmer jumped out of his chair and did a celebratory jig. Mike put his head down on his console and tried not to notice that when Tim danced, something in the shadows danced with him.

ABOUT THE AUTHOR

Patrick Hemstreet is a novelist, neuroengineer, entrepreneur, patent-pending inventor, special-warfare-trained Navy medic, stand-up comic, and actor. He lives in Houston, Texas, with his wife and sons. *The God Wave* is his first novel.